The Ghost of
Carmen Miranda

The Ghost of
Carmen Miranda

And Other Spooky Gay and Lesbian Tales

Edited by
Julie K. Trevelyan and Scott Brassart

alyson
books

LOS ANGELES • NEW YORK

© 1998 BY ALYSON PUBLICATIONS INC. AUTHORS RETAIN RIGHTS TO THEIR INDIVIDUAL WORK.
ALL RIGHTS RESERVED.

MANUFACTURED IN THE UNITED STATES OF AMERICA.

THIS TRADE PAPERBACK ORIGINAL IS PUBLISHED BY ALYSON PUBLICATIONS INC.,
P.O. BOX 4371, LOS ANGELES, CALIFORNIA 90078-4371.
DISTRIBUTION IN THE UNITED KINGDOM BY TURNAROUND PUBLISHER SERVICES LTD.,
UNIT 3 OLYMPIA TRADING ESTATE, COBURG ROAD, WOOD GREEN, LONDON N22 6TZ, ENGLAND.

FIRST EDITION: OCTOBER 1998

02 01 00 99 98   10 9 8 7 6 5 4 3 2 1

ISBN 1-55583-488-4

LIBRARY OF CONGRESS CATALOGING-IN-PUBLICATION DATA

THE GHOST OF CARMEN MIRANDA : AND OTHER SPOOKY GAY AND LESBIAN TALES /
EDITED BY JULIE K. TREVELYAN AND SCOTT BRASSART.—1ST ED.
ISBN 1-55583-488-4
1. GHOST STORIES, AMERICAN. 2. GAYS' WRITINGS, AMERICAN. 3. LESBIANS—FICTION.
4. GAY MEN—FICTION. I. TREVELYAN, JULIE K. II. BRASSART, SCOTT.
PS648.G48G46 1998
813'.0873308920664—DC21   98-8393 CIP

CREDITS

"ECHOES" AND "MATCHES" BY M. CHRISTIAN FROM *GRAVE PASSIONS: TALES OF THE GAY SU-
PERNATURAL*, EDITED BY WILLIAM J. MANN. BADBOY BOOKS, NEW YORK, 1997.
"THE GHOST OF CARMEN MIRANDA" BY DON SAKERS FROM *CARMEN MIRANDA'S GHOST IS
HAUNTING SPACE STATION THREE*, EDITED BY DON SAKERS. BAEN BOOKS, NEW YORK, 1989.
"OLD AS A ROSE IN BLOOM" BY LAWRENCE SCHIMEL FROM *PHANTOMS OF THE NIGHT*, EDITED
BY RICHARD GILLIAM AND MARTIN H. GREENBERG. DAW BOOKS, NEW YORK, 1996.
"MY POSSESSION" BY SIMON SHEPPARD FROM *GRAVE PASSIONS: TALES OF THE GAY SUPERNAT-
URAL*, EDITED BY WILLIAM J. MANN. BADBOY BOOKS, NEW YORK, 1997.

COVER AND TEXT DESIGN BY B. ZINDA.

☙ CONTENTS ☙

≈ Introduction ≈

Ghosts. Spooks. Haunts. Phantoms. All tinged with a decidedly lesbian and gay spirit. This concept enthralled writers from the moment we put out the call for submissions. When the stories began trickling, then pouring, then wildly flooding in, we were told again and again what a fun idea this was and how quickly the tales materialized from thought to paper. We had an enjoyable time reading each one, and the decisions were difficult. We want to thank everyone who answered the call, and we wish we had the space to include more of this ghostly fare.

We were struck by the humorous tone of some, including the drag queen drama of the title story by Don Sakers, Andrew Berac's tongue-in-cheek "Closer," and the briny "Scents and Sinsemilla Tea" by R.E. Neu. The peanut butter-loving ghost in "Taking Care of Faith" by A.J. Potter and the vampish wraith in "The Case of the Sapphic Succubus" by Abbe Ireland also left us chuckling.

Several tales wove erotic elements into their spectral doings, including two disturbingly twisted tales, "Echoes" and "Matches," by M. Christian, the S/M-tinged "My Possession" by Simon Sheppard, and the dreamy, sensual "A Midsummer's Haunt" by Susan C.

Coleman.

Ted Cornwell's "Sounds on a Summer Night" and "There With Bells On" by Julia Willis explore more writerly fare, while "Retrieval" by Carol Guess mixes bison and the ghost of a dead veterinarian on the high plains with literary flair.

Jessica Kirkwood's "Paisley" and d. g. k. goldberg's "The Course of True Love" bring up the possibilities of love lasting throughout the centuries, while Michael Price Nelson's poignant "The Haunting of Room 110" and Anne Seale's "Waiting for Hannah" muse on lovers who await their beloveds even after death. "Simon Says" by Marshall Moore explores the inseparable bond between two lovers as well as the consequences of having one's phone number be known to ghosts.

"Old as a Rose in Bloom" by Lawrence Schimel is a sweet foray examining the strength of a mother's love. Clumsy magic brings about some basement-dwelling entities in "Moving Into A New Place" by Regan McClure. "Through the Eyes of the Artist" by Barbara J. Webb throws a wrench into the stories—it is told from the viewpoint of the ghost.

Then there are the truly chilling stories, the ones that give "haunted" its skin-crawling meaning. Hall Owen Calwaugh's "amat67.jpg" presents a look at a computer with a sly, calculating ghost that won't ever let go. "The Thing at the Bottom of the Bed" by J.M. Beazer preys on fear of the unspeakable things that live under the bed and in dark corners of the night. And "Eyes" by E.J. Galusha will freeze your blood—it did ours—and produce a horror-filled shudder at its grisly conclusion.

Spectral chills, spooky laughter, and simple nostalgia await within these pages. We dare you to peek inside.

Julie K. Trevelyan
Scott Brassart
Los Angeles, October 1998

⋇ The Ghost of Carmen Miranda ⋇

by Don Sakers

"**H**appy birthday to me, happy birthday to me, happy birthday dear Tarawa…"

He trailed off, unable to continue, and took another sip of rum. The bottle was almost empty.

"Seventy isn't so bad," he said aloud. His voice was thin in the narrow confines of the utility closet that Tarawa called his dressing room. "Seventy isn't bad at all," he repeated, just to see what it sounded like.

It sounded terrible.

Seventy years old. "Oh, dah-ling," he said to his reflection, "I tell you, it's a tragedy. An honest-to-God tragedy." He looked around the room, and for a moment his tired eyes rested on the mementos of a career: a few yellowed placards, a couple of plaques so tarnished that he couldn't even begin to read them, a plastic-encased red rose from the one time he'd appeared on stage at Radio City. A few movie stills and some old issues of *TV Guide* were stacked on a shelf. Above his mirror, a 30-year-old movie poster proclaimed: "See *NYLON*: Starring the incomparable Tarawa Beachhead!"

1

Someone knocked at his door and shouted, "You're on in 15 minutes." He swallowed the last of the rum and belched. At least no one else in the station knew it was his birthday. He couldn't bear it if they found out, simply could not bear it.

Seventy years of life—and what did he have to show for it? He hadn't dared to step on a scale for years; the 270 pounds it showed then had probably increased. His movie career was long gone, his money lost by a broker who had since vanished to South America. At a stage in life when other men were enjoying their retirement, Tarawa was reduced to doing dinner shows on the space station circuit. What a disgraceful fate for a self-respecting drag queen.

He sighed and threw on his wig with a practiced flip of the wrist. Five shows a week, and the crew here on Space Station Three gave him food and lodging as well as his own dressing room. In just 13 minutes he would step on stage, sing a couple of songs, do Talullah and Bette and Liza and Joan, make a few jokes, then exit stage right. Same old songs, same old jokes. Same old show.

Same old life.

And 70 years, thought Tarawa Beachhead, was far too much.

"You are peetying yourself again, no?"

Tarawa looked into the mirror and saw *her* standing behind him. She was but a phantom, the bulkhead easily visible through her ghostly contours—but there was no mistaking those gaudy skirts, those twinkling green-flecked brown eyes, and that absurd fruit-filled hat.

"I am pitying myself, yes," he answered. He wasn't the only person in Space Station Three to have seen Carmen Miranda's ghost; but he thought he had a special rapport with her. "We are sisters under the skin," he'd told Cooky, his drinking buddy and the source of the best homemade rum in the Clarke Belt. "We speak the language of the stage, and that is why she is drawn to me."

"Here," she said, "Have tangerine. Bring color to the cheeks, warm the heart."

"Carmen, honey, *nothing* could bring color back to these ancient

The Ghost of Carmen Miranda

cheeks." Just the same, he accepted the tangerine: it was cool and quite firm in his hand, and when he set it down on his dressing table it rolled uncertainly under the influence of the Station's spin. "Thanks for thinking of me."

"You are too lonely, fat man." She tweaked his cheek, a feather-touch just on the borders of sensation. "You should get out more. Dance the samba with your friends. Enjoy life!"

"Look at me, I'm listening to advice about life from a ghost." Privately, Tarawa knew he was in bad shape. It was bad enough when you started talking to ghosts—but when they started *answering*—well, Mary, it was time to take a trip to the funny farm and say hello to the rough trade in the white coats. Or, better yet, time to take the decent girl's way out and pop a couple dozen of those pills you've been carrying in your makeup kit for lo these many years.

"You should leesten to me. Ghosts know many theengs. We see many theengs, and we learn about life."

"Thank you, dear, but right now your auntie is developing a killer migraine, and she's got to go onstage in a moment to titillate the tourists. Thank you for the fruit. Come again when you can stay longer."

She faded like the Cheshire Cat: first her arms and legs, then her torso and turban, until she was nothing more than a grin and two eyes floating in midair. "You will see, fat man. I am right." She winked, and then she was gone.

Tarawa heaved himself to his feet, adjusted his brassiere, then threw open the door. "Honey," he whispered to himself, "it's show time!"

He noticed the little girl at the first table right away. It wasn't often that children were seen on Space Station Three, and still more infrequently were they present at the evening show.

She couldn't have been more than six. Her black hair was in pigtails; her eyes were wide and brown and her skin the color of deep, rich chocolate. A handsome young man and a beautiful woman sat with her, but it was the girl who captured Tarawa's attention as he pranced onstage, put his hands on his hips, and proclaimed, "What a dump!"

3

Who did the parents think they were, to bring a child to his show? Not that there was anything unsuitable in his impersonations and jokes—especially not these days. It was just...damn it, he *hated* children. She threw him off his stride, made him lose a step in his first dance number, and her compulsive giggle grated on his poor abused nerves.

By damn, Tarawa told himself, *I am a performer and I will get through this somehow*. And one way or another, he *did* get through it: another hour, another show, only three more left until the week was over and he could look forward to the overwhelming thrill of another paycheck.

He stumbled back into his dressing room gratefully; the ordeal was over. But he should have known better. After a moment there was a knock on the door, and he opened it to reveal the little girl and her father.

"I hope you don't mind," the man said. "I'm Darnel Washington and this is my daughter Mandisa. She loved your show and she wanted to meet you in person."

Tarawa shook Darnel's hand, then crouched down next to Mandisa with a sigh. The sacrifices he made in the name of professionalism! The girl retreated to her father's legs, then took a brave step forward.

"Hello, Mandisa. That's a pretty name. I'm Tarawa."

"Is that your real name?" the father asked.

"Honey," Tarawa replied, "if I ever had another name, it's lost in the dim distant mists of history."

Mandisa put her hands on her hips. "That's not your *real* hair," she said indignantly.

"No, it's a wig."

"Let me see."

Reluctantly, Tarawa flipped off his wig, revealing a bald pate. He felt naked without the wig—even worse, he felt *silly*. "See, I'm just an old man with makeup and a wig." He knelt next to her.

She fingered the wig and Tarawa looked up at her father. "Are

4

you folks just passing through, or have you come to stay?" Space Station Three was a popular transfer spot for ships plying the Lunar and L5 routes, but occasionally (*very* occasionally, Tarawa thought) some poor demented tourists would come to enjoy whatever native ambiance Three possessed.

"Oh, we're coming back from two weeks on the Moon. We decided to lay over here for a few days so Mandisa could see what a space station is like."

"Well, dear, I hate to tell you, but Three isn't quite the champagne-and-caviar of space stations. More like cheap red wine and… Hey!"

The girl snatched Tarawa's wig from his hands and then set off down the gangway, leaving behind only the echo of her giggle.

"Come back here, you little brat!" Tarawa started after her at a dead run, then quickly fell back to a kind of swift, lumbering walk.

Her father stood, put his hands on his hips, and loudly said, "Mandisa Winnie Washington, I'm going to count to three."

And then what are you going to do? Tarawa wondered, *Count some more?* He didn't have to worry; by the time the father reached "Two" the girl reappeared, wig in hand and head hung low.

"Now give the nice man back his wig. And tell him you're sorry."

"Yes, Daddy." She looked up at Tarawa, her eyes as wide as the full moon in naked space. "I'm sorry."

Her father nodded. "You're forgiven. Just don't do it again."

"I won't. I promise."

"Now come here. We have to get back to your mommy." The father turned to Tarawa. "Thank you for letting us take up your time."

"Think nothing of it. Look me up if you pass this way again."

They strode off in the direction of the main lounge, and Tarawa let himself back into his dressing room. If he changed fast enough, he might still be able to catch Cooky in the kitchen. After *that* performance, he needed a drink.

Cooky was a small man with thinning black hair and vaguely oriental features. His kitchen was a rabbit warren composed of ovens, freezers, lockers, sinks, and strange utensils attached to every surface. Tarawa squeezed in the narrow door and shouted, "Alice, I've arrived!"

Cooky appeared from an anonymous passage, holding a chopping knife in one hand and a dangling piece of something pink in the other. "Alice? Who is Alice?"

"You are, honey, and this place is certainly Wonderland. Put down that chicken and get me a drink. I am literally *dying* of thirst."

"Ha ha, you are funny." Cooky threw his burdens aside and gestured for Tarawa to follow him. "It is late and I have been hard at work all station day. Many tourists to feed. Perhaps I find us a drink or two somewhere."

Tarawa followed, bending low to avoid a rack of hanging pans and inhaling mightily to fit between a bulkhead and some nasty-looking pipes. "Don't," he grunted, "try...to fool...your maiden auntie...with that 'somewhere' talk. Save it for Garcia." The Portmaster took a dim view of Cooky's rum-brewing business—but so far he had been unable to find Cooky's still in the uncharted nether regions of the kitchen. "Jesus H. Christ, Cooky, you've got to clear some more *room* in here. It's not natural to be cramped in the middle of outer space."

"Sit, have some rum."

The passage opened up into a room about six meters wide—Cooky's own little speakeasy, complete with two small tables, a few chairs and a viewport in the floor that showed dark space and the endless wheeling stars. Tarawa made a hard landing in one of the chairs and gratefully took a mug from Cooky. He drank deeply and then sighed as the rum warmed him from within. "Ah, that's better."

For a small man, Cooky could put away truly stupendous amounts of rum. Tarawa kept up with him, mug for mug, and watched the viewport as Earth tumbled past once every 54 seconds. Cooky talked, droning on about administrative maneuvering and office politics among the station's staff; Tarawa nodded in the right places, made encouraging grunts now and again, and otherwise paid no attention to what Cooky was saying. The man loved the sound of his own voice and loved to grumble about his lot in life; and Tarawa was used to being a sounding board for others.

Finally Cooky said, "But how are *you*, my friend? You do not look happy."

Tarawa waved his hand in drunken dismissal. "Mother of God, don't ask. Worse than ever. Don't ever get old, Cooky."

"The alternative is worse."

"I'm not so sure of that anymore."

With difficulty, Cooky focused bloodshot eyes on Tarawa. "Maybe you should talk to Dr. Khalid, my friend. He can help if you are down on a dump."

"No, darling, I just don't think so. He's a wee bit too butch for the likes of me." In fact, Tarawa *had* spoken with Rayhan Khalid, Three's staff psychologist, not once but many times over the last year. Dr. Khalid nodded, made notes on his lapboard terminal, and drank cup after cup of the most noxious brew Tarawa had ever smelled. Now and again he asked what he obviously thought was a penetrating question—but Khalid was only a kid, fresh out of school. What did he know of the problems of an aging drag queen?

"Honey," Tarawa had told him, "I grew up in the gritty world, where a man like me took what work he could get on the stage, any stage, or became a florist. And I have allergies you would *not* believe. Get me near a geranium or a chrysanthemum, and I suffer the agonies of the *damned*. So you see, I didn't really ever have any choice about my life. I was a ship who sailed where the winds blew...and mercy, did they ever blow!" Khalid had made more notes. "All I'm saying is that you modern lads have no *idea* what your mothers went through in the Bad Old Days."

"You seem to enjoy talking about the 'Bad Old Days.'"

Tarawa had forced himself to laugh, when inside he felt like crying. "Goodness me, Greta, but when you get to be my age—and don't you *dare* ask what age that is—all you have left are memories."

Khalid had nodded and sipped from his cup.

"Cooky, be a dear and fill up my mug, will you? I've gone dry."

Cooky, swaying as he stood, filled the mug. No matter how drunk he got, he never wasted a drop of rum. He sat back down heavily.

"Thank you, you're a good friend. The only friend I have left."

"Don' you have any other friends?"

Tarawa sighed. "I did, once. The nicest man you'll ever meet."

"Wha' happened to 'im?"

"Gone to meet his maker, I'm afraid, years before you were a gleam in your daddy's eye." Tarawa lifted his mug. "He made me a star, and I had the poor grace to outlive him." He was surprised to find his eyes filling with tears. "*C'est la vie*. That's what happens when you get old, Cooky. They all go away. Everybody you ever loved…" His voice caught, and he couldn't continue.

"Frien', I–"

Tarawa held up his hand. He took a breath, threw back his shoulders and said in his best Bette Davis voice, "But enough about me, darling. Let's talk about *you* for a while."

The gentle chime of the public address system interrupted Cooky's answer. "Attention, staff and visitors. This is Portmaster Garcia. We've just received a severe solar storm warning from Earthspace Traffic Control. Radiation levels are climbing outside and are expected to reach dangerous values soon. For the duration, I must caution all personnel to remain within the Station's shielding. Flight 78 outbound to Luna will be delayed until the storm is over. All delicate equipment is to be brought aboard at once. Station airlocks will be sealed in exactly one hour. That is all."

Cooky struggled to his feet. "Damn. More mouths t' feed. Tourists gonna stay 'til storm's over. Flight crews. Gotta cook twice as much f'r next shif'." He stood in place, swaying slightly as if searching for a sense of balance that eluded him. Then all the color drained out of his face. He raised a trembling arm, pointed at something directly behind Tarawa and screamed.

"What?"

"*Her* again!" Cooky made a strangled noise, then passed out and dropped gently to the floor.

Tarawa turned slowly, knowing what he would see. Phantasmal green-speckled brown eyes twinkled at him from beneath an improbable turban whose major feature was a great red pompom. Huge silver earrings, a massive gold necklace and high white puffed sleeves framed her pixie smile. Her white dress flashed brilliant red underskirts when she moved.

"Hello, Meester fat man," she said with a giggle.

"Love your dress, darling, but I think you've frightened Cooky to death."

"Nonsense." She bent to peer under the table at Cooky's prone form, then straightened and wagged a finger at him. "He has just had too much of the rum. He will sleep some, yes?" She did a quick samba around the kitchen, passing through walls and food lockers without apparent effort, and ended up near a bare counter. "I bring him present." From nowhere, she produced a huge basket heaped with tangerines, grapefruits, bananas and two or three enormous pineapples. It landed on the counter with a solid "thump" and a few errant grapes rolled free. "There, Meester Cook, now you will make beeg fruit salad and feed all your extra guests, no?"

Tarawa poured himself another mug of rum, but said nothing.

Carmen Miranda put her elbows on the table and propped her chin up in her hands. Her face was only centimeters from Tarawa's. "You should not be dreenking so much. Is bad for the figure." With that, she rotated her hips in a manner that Tarawa would kill for.

"It's a little late to worry about that now, I think." He drained his mug, reached for the bottle, then thought better of it. "You're right. It's time I *did* something, instead of moping around being unhappy."

She sprang upright and clicked her castanets. "That is the spirit! Let us dance until the evening is gone, no?"

"No." He shook his head. "Not tonight." It was quite an effort to stand, but Tarawa forced himself. "I hope I can find my way out of here," he muttered, squeezing through the narrow passage.

The station's corridors were darkened; a glance at a clock told him that it was the middle of the night. He'd been drinking longer than he thought. Funny, though, he didn't feel tired.

Carmen Miranda followed him, a pale shadow just visible out the corner of his eyes. He ignored her and climbed purposefully upward, weight dropping as he went, toward Airlock Six. His pressure suit was right where he'd left it after the last abandon-ship drill three months ago. The suit was specially tailored to fit his girth, but still he hated cramming himself into it. He shrugged and started pulling it on.

"Meester Beachhead, what *are* you doing?" She pointed to the airlock display, which flashed red letters: "All airlocks will be sealed in 38 minutes."

"I'm going outside."

"But why? I do not understand. Ees nasty outside. Much…how you say…radiation." She shivered. "Not good for people. Put suit away now."

Tarawa hiccuped. "Listen, ducks, why don't you just get off my case? There comes a time in every woman's life when there's nothing better to do than take a bow. And that time's long past for me." He pulled on his helmet and dogged the seals. "After a long and unhappy life, Auntie Tarawa is finally going to turn her teacup over. Ta, love. It's been *très, très* real." Carmen Miranda was gone, faded again into whatever limbo she emerged from. No matter. For this final show, better that a girl didn't have an audience.

He slapped the palmplate, and the airlock's inner door slid open. A step forward, another slap, and the door closed.

Now only a few feet of shielded metal separated him from the immense blackness of space. "Now's the time to chicken out, Bessie, if you're going to," he told himself. He glanced down at the suit's emergency switch, which at a touch would activate a radio beacon and scream for help on the space operations band. Then, with a single, sharp movement, he smashed the switch against a bulkhead, leaving it broken and nonfunctional. No use giving himself an out.

Odd, with all the rum he'd put down, he didn't feel particularly drunk. Nor frightened. In fact, what he felt most was a kind of welcome peace.

"Let's do it, then." With a deliberate forefinger, he punched in the access code, and the outer door ponderously slid aside. Departing wisps of air tugged at him, but his magnetic soles held tight to the deck.

Slowly, Tarawa moved forward. He was near the hub of the Station, so gravity wasn't too much of a bother. Three wrapped around him, an enormous, ragged wheel of silver-gray and brilliant mirrors. The stars cascaded about the wheel like ten thousand peering eyes. His faceplate automatically blanked out the sun's disk, but he could tell where it was by the shadows that raced across deckplates.

I wonder, Tarawa thought, *how long it will take to die?*

The hard radiation of a solar storm was nothing to take lightly. A severe storm could strike a man dead in minutes. No pressure suit could be made thick enough to stop all radiation—in fact, a pressure suit made things even worse because radiation impacting on the suit's fabric gave rise to all manner of "secondary particles" that were even more deadly than the radiation itself.

Funny how the early training tapes were all coming back to him now.

Tarawa shook his head and moved away from the airlock. He was sweating, and his suit smelled like a month's worth of old socks. How long would he have to put up with this misery? He didn't care how long it took—he just wanted to die.

A thin crescent of blue and white shone against blackness just a handful of degrees away from the sun. In Indonesia, directly below, it was near midnight. Did the people down there know about him? Had they seen his movies? Would any of them care that an old fat man was now dying 35,000 kilometers above their heads?

"Damn it, I never knew that dying could take so long."

There were quicker ways. Pills. Razor blades. Probably a dozen methods in his own cabin, any of which would allow him to make a dignified exit much more quickly. He shrugged. Now that he was out here, he might as well see it through.

He strode around the deck, away from Earth and sun, and gazed into star-flecked blackness. The sky pinwheeled, the Milky Way turning drunken circles—but there was no feeling of motion. It was the sky that turned, not him.

Little by little, as his eyes grew accustomed to the dimness, he began to see indistinct swirls of pastel colors. At first he didn't think they were really there, then he watched more closely and actually caught them. What could they be? Ghostly apparitions, more pale than Carmen Miranda herself, ribbons and sheets of color, yellows and pinks that whirled against blackness and then vanished, almost like the flash of aurorae against the nighttime surface of the Earth…

That was it, he realized. Aurorae. What with all the spaceship arrivals and departures at Space Station Three, several a day during busy times, there had to be a fair concentration of exhaust gases in nearby space. Not enough to make a real atmosphere, to be sure—but enough to fluoresce under strong enough ionizing radiation. The light show ought to grow even more impressive as the solar storm intensified.

He grinned weakly. At least he would be going out with a show. Bright lights for the performer until the very last!

His suit intercom crackled, making him jump. A tiny voice said, "Hello, is anybody out here?"

Tarawa tried to ignore it. Some technician, rushing out to get a forgotten piece of equipment. He glanced at his chronometer, red numbers displayed on the sleeve of his pressure suit. Only a few minutes until the airlocks were sealed. Then he'd be alone again. Then the storm's full rage would hit, and he could find peace at last.

"Hello there. You're Mr. Beachhead, aren't you?" Static squawked in his speaker.

The figure that appeared from the vicinity of the airlock was very short, dressed in the brilliant reflective white of a tourist's pressure suit. Tarawa couldn't see into its helmet, yet his breath caught anyway. Lord, don't let it be… "Who are you?"

"Mandisa Washington. You remember, I tried to take your wig. I hope you aren't still mad at me."

"What in hell are you doing out here?"

"I wanted to see. Daddy and Mommy are asleep, I snuck away. I know how to put my suit on all by myself."

"Child, whatever possessed you to come out here? Now, of all times?"

She crept closer. "There's going to be pretty lights. The nice lady in the fruity hat told me."

"Sweet Mother of God, now she's talking to the children. We've got to get you inside, honey. Trust a kid to ruin this woman's farewell scene. Turn around and march, little girl, right back to that airlock." He reached for his emergency beacon, then swore under his breath. Fool, he was a fool.

Mandisa crossed her arms over her chest as best she could in the over-inflated pressure suit. "No."

"Jesus, Mary, and Fred!" Was it just his imagination, or were the pastel wisps of ionization a little more distinct? That meant the radiation was growing stronger. "Kid, you have ten seconds to start moving, or I'm coming over there. One, two, three…"

"Betcha can't catch me." She started in the opposite direction, moving as if through deep mud.

"I will have a nervous breakdown *later*," Tarawa said. "Right now I am going to *kill that child*." He took a deep breath. "Mandisa, listen to me. Are you listening?"

She stopped, a small figure 20 meters away. "Yes."

"Good. It is very dangerous for you to be out here. Do you know what that means?"

"I–"

He kept his voice level. "It means that you *must* come back to me right now, or you may get hurt very badly. Do you understand?"

"I…" A sob broke through. "You're *scaring* me. I want my mommy," she wailed. "Mommy!" As he watched, she tripped and slid another 15 meters down the hull, pulled by ever-increasing centrifugal force. She landed hard against a radiator fin, bounced, then stopped, blubbering, at the base of a structural beam.

"God help us all and Oscar Wilde," Tarawa said quickly. "Can you move?"

She continued crying. "I can't." Her voice was almost lost in the growing static of the storm.

"All right. Stay there, honey, and I'll come get you."

It was slow going. She was too far down, and weight had a grip on her. She huddled against the hull, holding onto a metal strut and crying her lungs out. He moved as fast as he dared, and soon had her by the hand. He reached for her emergency switch.

Somehow, in the fall, her primary controls had been smashed. The switch was gone.

"No time to waste." He pulled her along like a captive balloon and made his way to the airlock. But a glance at the telltales confirmed what his chronometer had told him long minutes ago: the airlocks were already sealed.

"This was a bad idea." Why couldn't he have taken pills like every other respectable drag queen? For a moment he hammered at the airlock, then stopped. Nobody would hear him.

He turned, and although the sun was still blacked out by his faceplate polarizers, he imagined he could feel its blazing heat right through his suit. Who knew, maybe he *could*. Was that what radiation was supposed to feel like? "Come with me," he said to the girl.

"You're hurting me," she cried.

Shielding. Where could he find some shielding? Near the shuttle dock, probably—but it was clear on the other side of the hub, across some very nasty antennas and high-power lines. Besides, he'd never reach it in time.

You wanted to die, Alice May. So here's your chance. But how could he keep from taking the girl with him?

The station's dark side offered no protection. The aurora was just as bright, and the sunburnlike feel of radiation was just as intense. But he found a narrow corner between two shielded equipment housings, and thrust the girl in between. She was all cried out, but her breath was still harsh in his ears.

He had nothing left to shield her with. Nothing except his own body.

Was a meter of water and fat, encased in a pressure suit, enough to protect a little girl from radiation?

He had to believe it was.

"You just lay there, Mandisa, you hear me? Lay there and don't move." Sooner or later the storm would be over—she would be missed—someone would come get her. With Sweet Agnes God's help and a lot of luck, she would still be alive.

Tarawa backed into the niche and faced the stars. The sky was alive now with multicolor strands and whorls of living energy, and he felt the heat in his bones. Gingerly, he switched off his intercom. The sudden cessation of static left his ears ringing.

"I'm sorry," he said aloud. "I'm sorry for everything. I've been a big baby, I've been a very selfish woman." His faceplate misted with tears. "God, I know it now…I don't want to die. I never did. I just wanted…someone…to care."

Light eddied around him, almost hiding the stars completely. "I've been feeling sorry for myself instead of doing anything." He needed to blow his nose. "Now it's over, and I wish it wasn't. *I don't want to die.*"

Red, yellow, green. The colors spun, twisted, and took the form of a small, slim woman in a gaudy striped skirt and an absurd basket hat filled with fruit…

"Johnny? Johnny, I'm coming to see you now. I've always loved you, you know that? Always…"

She reached out a slender hand to him, then she swam away and everything went black.

Tarawa opened his eyes on Dr. Khalid's face, and he yelped. The doctor drew back sharply.

"Where am I?" He recognized his surroundings at once: he was in bed in the Station's small infirmary, covered with brightly-colored sheets. An intravenous tube was stuck in his right arm, and an electronic display was winking at his feet. Dr. Khalid stood over him, and Cooky was sitting at his bedside. A basket of fruit sat on the nightstand next to him.

"You are okay," the psychologist said, lifting a mug from the nightstand. "You've been unconscious for two weeks. You were in very bad shape when they brought you in, my friend. Another ten minutes and we wouldn't have been able to save you."

"I'm *thin*."

"You have lost about 80 kilograms."

"The girl?" He tried to sit up, but was too weak.

Khalid nodded. "She lived. She has returned to Earth with her family. You were very lucky. The Portmaster found you and brought you inside just before the storm hit its greatest intensity." He tapped a note on his lapboard, drained his cup and then smiled. "I must go, but I will be back to talk with you later. Take care."

As soon as he was gone, Tarawa turned to a smiling Cooky. "All right, what *really* happened?"

"He tells the truth, my friend. Portmaster Garcia rescued you."

"How did he know I was—we were—out there?"

Cooky's grin broadened. "*She* told him. Carmen Miranda. You have your own guardian angel. She left this behind for you." He gestured to the fruit basket.

"You're telling me that I was saved by a *ghost*? Pardon me, Mary, but I don't believe it for one…" He stopped, and Cooky looked at him in alarm.

"What is it?"

"Why would she have told the Portmaster where we were? She's the one who sent the girl out there to begin with."

"Carmen Miranda? I cannot believe she would do such a thing."

"Neither can I. Unless…"

Unless it was the only way she could think of to help a silly old drag queen regain his interest in life. But she wouldn't have taken such a chance, suppose he *hadn't* changed his mind?

Or did she know him that well, to be certain he would?

Over his bed, just at the threshold of vision, Carmen Miranda appeared and, with a wink and a smile, nodded.

"Well," Tarawa said, "All's well that ends well, don't you think? I'm alive, and that's what counts." He winked back at Carmen Miranda. With a wave, she faded from view.

"What do you think, Cooky? *I* think my old act is getting a little stale. It's time I had a new one." He looked down at his newly-thin body, wrapped in the gaudy sheets. Some new heels, earrings, and maracas. That would do it.

He smiled and pointed to the nightstand. "Hand me that basket hat, will you?"

⇒ Taking Care of Faith ⇐

by A.J. Potter

The peanut butter was my first clue that something was wrong. I like peanut butter, but I do tend to remember when I eat it. And I don't leave it sitting on my shelf, with the cap off. I couldn't imagine anyone breaking in to eat my peanut butter, but there it was.

One night, I could believe I might have forgotten to put it away. Two nights in a row was downright strange. The third time I wandered into my kitchen and saw the familiar aqua Skippy label staring at me from my shelf where it had *not* been exactly one hour earlier, was enough to seriously freak me out. I stopped dead and stared at the peanut butter jar with a crawling feeling in the pit of my stomach. I walked over to it slowly, as if it might gather itself and spring at me, though what I expected a jar of peanut butter to do to me is anyone's guess.

Without giving myself time to think about it, I opened the silverware drawer, dragged out my serrated knife, and prowled the apartment, turning on every light, throwing back the shower curtain, and swinging open closet doors with a pounding heart. The empty apartment laughed at me at every turn. Heading back to the kitchen, feeling like a complete moron, I can honestly say I wasn't all that surprised to see the peanut butter jar levitating toward me through the arched doorway from the kitchen to the living room.

I screamed anyway, but I wasn't all that surprised.

"Enough already. Hold it down, you'll have the neighbors calling the cops, and then how are you going to explain me? Hmm?"

I stared in the direction of the disembodied voice, which allowed me to keep my eyes on the floating peanut butter jar since they came from the same relative area. I brandished the knife and chose not to answer, mostly because I couldn't think of anything to say.

"Please. Like that would touch me. Get a grip. And why do you buy lowfat? It's peanut butter, for chrissakes. If you're going to *eat* peanut butter, eat the real thing." The hand—for it was now definitely a hand holding the Skippy, even though the arm was still mostly insubstantial—gestured with the jar; the voice sounded disgusted. Momentarily, a sneer on an otherwise see-through face solidified, confirming my guess at my visitor's attitude. Dark hair coalesced around the pale face, falling over the forehead, in need of a cut.

"Every little bit helps," I croaked, wondering even as I said it why I was defending my dietary preferences to a ghost.

"Put that down." The ghost came toward me suddenly, ambling quite naturally now that his legs were fully visible. He actually looked damn solid at this point, and I yelped and leaped back as he reached out and took the knife from me, his hand brushing mine and leaving a cold sensation in its wake.

"What do you want?" I squeaked, backing away.

He stared at me for a long moment, then smiled and waved at the closest chair with the knife. "Why don't you have a seat…?" He paused, waiting for me to fill in my name. I found it a bit insulting that he hadn't even bothered to learn my name before haunting me. He'd been eating my peanut butter for three nights and he didn't even know who I was?

"Victor," I managed.

He nodded. "Victor. I'm Brandon. I'd shake your hand but…" He lifted the jar and the knife and grinned. He walked back into the kitchen, calling over his shoulder, "So, what do ghosts always want?"

I sat, and pondered that for a moment while I tried to get my legs to stop trembling. Revenge? I shuddered. But I hadn't killed him. What did I have to worry about. "I don't know," I finally offered in a small voice. "What *do* ghosts always want?"

He reentered the room sans knife and peanut butter, which was an improvement. I may not have been able to do anything to him with the knife, but I was pretty sure he could do something to me with it, if he chose. His grip on the jar had looked pretty steady. He flashed me a crooked smile, and I suddenly realized my ghost was damn goodlooking.

"I want you to help me, of course."

"So let me get this straight. You want me to find this Evan, and bring him to see you. Here." The steadiness of my voice impressed me.

"That's about the size of it."

"Why can't you just find him yourself?"

"I'm a ghost. I have my limitations."

"You found me."

He sighed and rubbed the bridge of his nose. It was a nose that looked like it had been broken a couple of times. It certainly would have been a large enough target in a fight. "Victor. No insult intended, but I didn't find you. You could have been anyone. I found this *place*." He paused and looked around wistfully. "I died here."

I sat bolt upright. "Oh, fuck. Does that mean you're stuck here? They never said anything about a tenant dying here!"

Brandon gave me a look that told me his estimation of my intelligence had just plummeted drastically. "It's usually such a good way to get new tenants."

I flushed. "OK, point taken. Uh, how long ago…"

"Couple years." He shifted his bony frame restlessly in his chair. He'd been doing that most of the night, and it had nothing to do with the fact that parts of him still wavered in and out of sight occasionally. Even when he was fully visible there was an impatient quality to his fidgeting. He seemed like one of those people who just didn't sit still well, which I thought was odd for a ghost. Except for the fact that I could see the chair directly through him now and again, it wasn't much different from having a cocky, sarcastic, *live* man sitting in my living room. I hadn't decided yet if I would be dropping down to the local psychiatric facility the next morning or not, but I was figuring it was likely.

"So you can only appear here?"

"I didn't say that."

I sighed. My ghost had an attitude and it was getting on my nerves. It was also making it harder to be scared, though, so I wasn't complaining. "You didn't say much of anything except you want me to find this Evan. Where and who is he?"

"If I knew where he was I wouldn't be sitting here with you, Vic."

"Victor."

My ghost rolled his eyes. *"Victor.* Anyway, Ev is my ex."

"Your ex?"

"Mmm hmm. I'm the ex-tenant's ex-lover."

"Ex-tenant? Evan used to live here? I thought you did."

He gave me that "just exactly how stupid are you" look again, and spoke precisely. "We lived here together, then I killed myself, then he lived here alone until he moved. Then you moved in."

"Oh." I licked my lips and crossed my legs, then uncrossed them. This was the first he had mentioned that he'd killed himself. It seemed impolite to ask why, so I cleared my throat and went back to the subject of Evan, deciding I was definitely going to be stopping by the psych hospital; when you start worrying about being polite to the bitchy ghost in your living room, it's time for a mental health checkup. "So you don't know to where Evan moved. Do you even know if he's still in the area?"

"I'm sure he is. Evan wouldn't leave Brattleboro, or the immediate area." He gave me a smug look, a knowing smile curling his lips.

"Where does he work? Or where did he work…last?" I couldn't bring myself to say "when you were alive."

My ghost cleared his throat and glanced off to one side. "Evan doesn't exactly work."

"He doesn't work?" *Is he broken?* my mind immediately supplied, but I managed to not say it. Brandon didn't offer any further information on Evan's lack of employment, so finally I spoke again. "How am I supposed to find him?"

"Your problem. This is a small town. Just find him and bring him here."

"Whoa. That's the second problem. Bring him here? What am I supposed to *tell* him?"

"That I'm here and I want to see him."

Oh, sure. No problem. Easy. I gave him one of the looks he'd been tossing at me all night.

His eyes narrowed. "You're having trouble believing this, aren't you?"

I sucked in a deep breath. "You're asking me to go tell a guy I've never met that the ghost of his dead lover is in my apartment. Hello? Does this not sound a little strange to you?"

"Considering I'm the ghost, no, it doesn't. But listen, I do understand your hesitation. Really. I'm telling you though, find Evan. You won't think you're crazy once you talk to Evan. And don't worry, he won't think you're crazy either. He'll believe you. Trust me."

Famous last words. Never trust a man who says "trust me." I tried again, "How the hell do I find him?"

"How should I know? I'm a ghost, remember?" He flashed me a smile that I would have called sexy if he hadn't been dead. Oh, hell…it was sexy even though he *was* dead. Then he was gone.

Finding Evan turned out to be the least of my problems.

Brattleboro *is* a small town. I stopped by my landlord's office and got a forwarding address. It was that easy. I couldn't quite believe it myself. I thought of telling Brandon he should have just dropped in on the landlord, but I was secretly pleased that I had gotten the information so fast. Apparently, somewhere in the course of chatting with my handsome young ghost, I had subconsciously decided I wanted to impress him. I found I didn't want to examine that thought too closely.

So I drove down Main Street to the new address, instead of out to Route 30 for that psychiatric evaluation. I sat in my car and stared up at the apartment building for a long time. This guy was going to toss me out on my ear. I was probably going to get arrested for harassment. If his ex-lover really *had* killed himself in my apartment, how would he react to my...news?

I couldn't do this. I turned on the ignition. An image of the open peanut butter jar sitting on my shelf three nights in a row filtered up through my brain. I hadn't imagined that. And Brandon had been so confident Evan wouldn't think I was crazy. *You're listening to a ghost, you idiot. What does he know?* But I shut the car off and got out before I could change my mind.

I climbed two flights to the apartment, knocked on the door, and waited. And waited. I knocked again. The door swung inward so suddenly I stepped back, startled. A young blond man stood with one hand on the door, staring up at me serenely. His hair was pulled back in some kind of clip, strands of it falling forward into a nondescript face dominated by blue eyes. He was wearing battered jeans and a baggy, red-plaid flannel shirt that did horrible things for his coloring. The clothes hung as if they had been made for someone else, or perhaps he had lost weight and not gotten around to updating his wardrobe. He tilted his head to one side and opened his mouth. I don't know what I expected, but the soft Southern drawl that emerged definitely wasn't it.

"Yes? What can I do for you?"

When anyone else said that, it was a standard-issue greeting, as meaningless as, "How are you?" When this boy said it, my spine tingled. From him, it sounded sincere; something in his voice offered the tangible help the words always hinted at but seldom delivered, as if he *really* wanted to do whatever he could, and nothing would be too much to ask. I coughed and managed, "Evan?" even though I already knew I'd found the man my ghost was looking for. I don't know how I knew, but I knew.

"Yes. I'm Evan. Would you like to come in?" He stepped back and waved me into the apartment with a shy smile. I blinked. This was not how you greeted strangers at your door.

"Thank you. I'm Victor." I walked past him.

"Victor." He sounded like he was trying it out. I turned to face him, and found him watching me with those same serene eyes. He nodded once, as if deciding the name suited me, and then closed the door. "How are you, Victor?"

Again I had the feeling that he actually *meant* what he said, as opposed to just tossing off the expected platitudes everyone mouthed. I had the distinct sensation he would be genuinely interested in hearing how I was. It should have had a warm, positive effect, I suppose, but I only felt uncomfortable. "Fine," I mumbled, still trying to figure out how I was going to say what I had come to say. I glanced away from those eyes. The first thing I noticed was the peanut butter. The open jar of Skippy smooth sat on a small end table beside his couch, next to an open bag of Pizza Goldfish crackers. The second thing I noticed was the pictures.

I caught my breath. That was my ghost all right. In living, breathing, full-Fuji color. I walked further into the small apartment, my eyes jumping from one photo to the next. They were everywhere—some hanging on the wall, others propped on the back of the kitchen stove or on top of the VCR. The dishes in the sink and the dust kitties in the corners said Evan was an indifferent housekeeper at best, but the pictures were all meticulously dust free and the glass of the framed shots gleamed.

And it was him, over and over again—my ghost. The bony

arrogant face, the black hair that looked like it needed a cut in every single picture, the skinny restless body. And that *nose*. One of the shots was in profile, and I almost laughed out loud as I realized why nearly all the other shots were face on. In profile the nose dominated the shot almost comically. I could just hear that caustic voice of his condemning the photographer for catching his bad side; but then anything from the side would be his bad side. The boiling, surly energy I had sensed in my house screamed out of every picture. He had a dangerous air that was intoxicating even in two dimensions.

I realized I was holding one of the framed photos, staring at it. I jumped as I noticed Evan was right beside me, looking over my shoulder. The picture was of him and Brandon, leaning into each other. Evan was grinning. Brandon wasn't. He had an arm around Evan's neck—protective or proprietary it was hard to say—and wore the expression of casual arrogance I'd gotten used to in just one night of his company. I put the frame back down, stammering, "I'm sorry...I didn't...I didn't mean..."

"That's all right. Handsome devil, isn't he?" Evan picked up the picture. That honey-drawl still sounded vaguely out of place. I watched him touch Brandon's face lightly in the picture, smiling down at it.

"Evan?"

"Yes." He looked up at me with wide, guileless eyes. I found myself wanting to go out and buy a dead bolt for his door, and to explain to him he shouldn't just invite people into his apartment. I swallowed hard.

"The man in these pictures..."

"Brandon." His voice was sweetly melancholy. "He's dead now."

A pause hung in the air. I couldn't catch my breath. "I've seen his ghost," I blurted, then clapped my hand over my mouth, as if that would somehow help. I could almost hear Brandon's sneering voice in my head, *"Smooth, Vic, very smooth."*

Evan simply blinked at me, and then sighed. "Oh, dear. Well, then. You'd better sit down."

"You don't seem surprised."

"I'm not."

I had watched Evan's face as we sat on his sofa and I described my visit with his incorporeal ex-lover. Guilty pleasure and excitement warred with flashes of disappointment and uncertainty, but surprise had no part of it. You'd have thought I was telling him that I'd run into a common acquaintance at the supermarket, who had told me to look him up. I suddenly had a sneaky suspicion. "Evan, when did Brandon die?"

"One year and seven months ago."

The way he reeled it off, I could almost hear him adding the days designation in his head. I cleared my throat. "And when did you last...talk to him?"

Without blinking an eye, he quoted immediately, "Ten months. Give or take."

Again, I knew he knew exactly how many days the "give or take" involved. But the months was all I needed; he had confirmed my hypothesis. "So he's appeared to you before."

Evan sighed and looked at his feet. "It was my own fault. But I didn't mean to." His slow voice picked up an agitated edge. "I didn't do it on purpose, I swear I didn't." He looked at me as if I was going to accuse him of doing "it" maliciously.

"You didn't do what on purpose?"

Evan's huge eyes widened impossibly. I found myself wondering for about the eighth time what the two of them had been doing together. They didn't seem like a match, somehow. "You mean...he didn't tell you about me?" Evan asked.

The trepidation in his voice was enough to shiver my spine. "Tell me what?" I flushed as my voice cracked nervously.

He tilted his head to the left and stared at me. Then he shrugged and stared down at his hands. "I'm a faith healer."

His soft voice was so low I almost missed it. When I reviewed the words in my head, I was sure I *had* missed it. "Huh?" I said intelligently.

He lifted his eyes to mine, and they were so solemn they made my heart squeeze. "I'm a faith healer. I...I can heal people. And animals too. Sometimes. Depends." He lifted one hand and looked at it as if it had a mind of its own, then waved it at me. "Hands-on healing. You know?" I knew my mouth was hanging open because I could feel my tongue drying out, but I couldn't seem to close it. "That's what we figure did it. This time I healed a ghost. By accident. My gift, whatever it is that lets me heal people...well, it was working when I brought him up out of the ground. But I *swear* I didn't mean to do it. I didn't mean to get him stuck here."

I got my mouth closed with an effort and cleared my throat, stuttering awkwardly. "I-I'm sure you didn't." I knew I should have gone out to that psych hospital. Well, maybe I could still go. And take him with me. I rubbed my forehead and tried to think. "So, uh, he started appearing to you? His ghost I mean?"

His eyes shone, a winsome smile blossoming. "Every night. We used to sit up in the cemetery together. Just talk and sit and listen to the wind. But he came to the apartment once too. Until he asked me to...let him go." The smile faded, and his brows drew together, forehead wrinkling in consternation. He gnawed on his lower lip. "He shouldn't be here now," he fretted. "I thought I healed him good this time."

"I—I'm sure you healed him just...fine," I soothed. His eyes met mine and a small smile wandered across his face.

"You don't believe in me do you." It wasn't a question.

"Umm...well, that is..."

"That's OK." His voice was matter-of-fact, peaceful. "Neither did Brandon. Let's go to your place, hmm?"

I bounced to my feet as he stood. "My place?"

"Brandon wants to see me, doesn't he?"

"Well, yes, actually he—"

"And he's at your place, isn't he?"

"Well, yes, actually he—"

A beatific grin spread across Evan's face. "Then let's go to your place."

We went to my place.

Evan walked straight through my house, touching this or that lightly, murmuring under his breath, his gaze sweeping the apartment. I would have felt invaded if I didn't have the distinct impression that he wasn't even looking at the apartment. He knew exactly what he was after, and it wasn't here. He finally turned back to me with a heart-breaking puzzled look. "Where is he?"

"I...I don't know. He was here."

"I believe you. Did he say he'd be back at a special time?"

"No. I—I'm sorry, I should have asked."

Evan smiled and shrugged, then whispered as if imparting a secret, "You probably weren't used to talking with ghosts."

I found myself smiling back at him. I dropped my own voice conspiratorially, "No. No, I wasn't."

Evan closed his eyes, then sighed heavily. "He's not here. I don't think he's coming. He'd be here by now."

"But he said..."

"He'd be here by now," Evan repeated dejectedly, shaking his head and dislodging more wisps of wayward hair. "Believe me, I'd know. All those nights sitting at the cemetery with him..." He snapped his fingers. "Cemetery. That's it." He swung to me with excited eyes. "Will you take me to the cemetery?"

I opened my mouth, but found I couldn't even begin to come up with a way to say no. We were driving to Dummerston before I could even fully wonder why. As I drove, I tried to think of casual conversation. Evan seemed happy enough to sit and hum. "So, were you raised down south?"

"No."

"No?" I did a double take before I could stop myself, and had to jerk to steady the wheel.

"No." He glanced at me. "Oh! You mean the accent." He laughed. "No, I was born and raised right here in Vermont. I just like to give people what they expect, is all."

I pondered that, and still couldn't make heads or tails of it. "I didn't expect it," I finally offered.

"Would you have expected it if Brandon had told you I was a faith healer?" he asked mildly. Unbidden, images conjured up by the words "faith healer" popped into my head. Men in suits on television shows, smacking people on the forehead and asking for donations. *Southern* men in suits. I smiled in spite of myself, and he nodded knowingly, watching me with that calm smile.

I cleared my throat and fiddled with the radio, then tried again. "So, you're pretty…religious?" I swallowed hard. I'm about as nonreligious as they come. An atheist masquerading as a pagan on my good days.

"No."

"No?"

Evan grinned over at me. "Why do you keep saying that?"

"You keep saying things I don't expect."

"You don't have to be religious to be a faith healer," he said seriously, as if he'd had plenty of debate on the issue.

"But…isn't that the point? Faith healing? Faith."

"Oh, it is faith. I believe I can do it. I believe I can heal. I've got faith in my ability." He nodded as if that solved everything. "Faith healing. No gods. Just faith. The real thing—believing in something you can't see, when there is no proof and no good reason why it should be. It just is. That's faith." He stopped talking as abruptly as he'd started, and again silence descended. I lasted for about forty seconds.

"So, tell me more about Brandon." Jackpot. He was talking before the sentence had fully left my lips, and he didn't stop for the entire remaining 20-minute ride to Dummerston. He lit up like he'd been plugged in, and practically bounced in his seat. It was somewhere on that drive up Route 5 north that I realized Evan didn't still *love* Brandon. He was still *in love with* Brandon. Actively.

I could see why. If the pictures and my own meeting with his spectral ex-lover hadn't been enough for me, Evan's impassioned testimonial would have done it. I was uncomfortably aware that I was developing a bit of a crush on a man almost two years dead. I tried to ignore that niggling awareness as we drove up the winding hill of the cemetery.

He directed me to the very top, and we parked. Walking in through the break in the stone wall, I followed him to the right until we stopped at a square, four-person plot. There were no headstones, just a rectangular sea of flowers covering one complete end of the plot. On the grave next to the one covered in flowers, a plain wooden cross stood in place of a headstone.

Evan pointed to the cross. "My brother," he said softly. Then he pointed to the flowers. "My Brandon."

As I watched, he dropped down onto his knees slowly. The cross was weathered gray wood, and had a well-tended yellow mum planted around the bottom. I glanced from it to the spread of color in the next space. Evan was carefully removing dead blooms from flowers I couldn't begin to name, all fading with the onset of fall.

"My mother takes care of my brother," he said simply as he worked gently at the flowers.

"Does your mother mind?"

"Mind what?"

That you talk with a fake Southern accent, you odd little man. Where's your Yankee pride? I kicked the thought out of my head. "Uh...this," I waved my hand at the unequal distribution of flowers.

Evan grinned. "No. Why should she? She understands me."

I swallowed the words that bubbled up—*It's a good thing somebody does.* Evan was settling back onto his heels, looking around with an air of contentment.

"I love it here. But, Victor, he's not here either."

"You're sure?"

"Do you feel him?"

I paused and thought for a moment about how charged the air had felt in my apartment when Brandon sat across from me. The cool wind circled me, but the Dummerston air just felt empty. I shook my head.

Evan sighed and pushed to his feet. "Let's walk down to the bottom of the hill and back to make sure. He and I used to do that. We walked this whole place more times than I can count."

I followed him wordlessly, down over the sloping hill of the cemetery, weaving in and out of lines of headstones, watching with reluctant interest as the stones got older and older, thinning to angular pieces of slate with notched corners, leaning at odd angles. The uneven ground tripped me up three times before I actually fell, reaching out to grip one of the headstones reflexively as I tumbled headlong. I yelped as the edge of stone laid open my palm, then I was on my knees, cradling my left hand in my right, watching the blood well and drip to the ground. "Shit!"

Evan turned back at my outburst, and sank beside me without a word, reaching out instinctively and taking my hand in both of his. His left hand folded over my palm and his fingers brushed over the ragged cut and pressed. A well of heat exploded in my palm. If I weren't already on my knees, I would have been. As it was I sagged forward, gasping at the sizzle of sensation. My breath stopped. The warmth tingled out through my entire body like a steady flush, my groin tightened, my toes curled in my boots. My lungs flexed and dragged in air, and the warmth faded slowly, settling to a background thrum that was uncomfortably like arousal.

Evan looked up at me sharply, an odd expression on his face, then sighed softly. "Chemistry."

I felt the blush start at my ears and flood my face. "What?" I squeaked, embarrassing myself further.

He grinned at me. "No, not that kind. Although," his left hand still clamped over mine, his right fingers lifted, brushing my cheek, "there might be some of that too." His gentle fingers at my face called forth an echo of the sizzle. He smiled that serene smile again. "But no. I meant healing chemistry." His bloody fingers lifted from my palm, and I wrenched away from his eyes. Looking down, I almost fell over again. My palm was marred with a jagged red line— of totally sealed skin.

"What the—"

"That mark will fade. Like a scar, really." He got to his feet, wiping his bloody fingers on his jeans without concern. "Sorry about that." He looked embarrassed himself suddenly. "I usually ask. But it was just kind of…umm…involuntary." For the first time he looked like he was avoiding my eyes. "It's like that with some people," he mumbled. Then, in a more matter-of-fact voice, he added, "Besides, it's never a good idea to bleed in a graveyard." He turned and climbed back up the hill. "We should go home, I guess. He's not here."

I was sitting in my rocking chair, staring at my palm, when I heard my cupboard door creak. "Where were you?" I asked.

He wandered into the living room, solidifying as he moved, then sprawling in the other chair. "Sorry." He lifted the peanut butter jar and inhaled. "Man, I miss this stuff."

"He…he actually did it. He healed me." I didn't know why I was saying it, I only knew I had to say it to someone. And this ghost was likely the only person that would believe me.

Brandon chuckled. "You guys got chemistry?"

I blinked. "That's what he said."

"Sure." Brandon grinned wickedly and put on an exaggerated Southern drawl. "He can only heal people when the chemistry is right. Between him and the…healee, I think he calls it. So," he dropped the drawl and gave me a shrewd look, "feel good, did it?"

"Ex*cuse* me?" my voice peaked. I wasn't sure how he was going to react; he struck me as the jealous type.

He laughed. "Thought so. I always thought it felt *great*. Used to hurt myself on purpose occasionally just so he'd do it. Only one time it didn't feel good, and that was after I was dead. Bringing me up outta the ground like he did. That felt like…well, you know when you get really cold and numb, and then start to warm up? It felt like when the feeling starts to come back. Like when your foot has fallen asleep, and starts to wake up." He shook his head absently. "Prickly. Almost hurt."

"You didn't believe in him."

"Huh?"

"He said you didn't believe in him."

"Oh." He shrugged. "He's right. I didn't. I had to learn how." He looked away, his voice hardening just a touch. "In the long run, it didn't exactly help. But Evan's a good teacher."

"Why didn't you tell me about this…thing he has?"

"Would you have believed it if you hadn't seen it?" He had his nose in the peanut butter jar again.

I paused, knowing the answer. I still wasn't sure I believed it, and I *had* seen it. "Why didn't you show up?"

"Had a bit of trouble. You'll have to bring him back."

"I know where he is now. Why don't you go to him?"

Brandon shook his head. "Told you, I have my limitations."

"I thought you said you weren't limited to appearing just here?" My voice was agitated. I wasn't sure I wanted to see Evan again.

"I never said that. Not in so many words."

I huffed out an irritated breath and stood up, pacing. "Fine. I'll fucking bring him here again." I stopped and turned to him, suddenly hesitant. But I had to ask. "Brandon. Is Evan…all right?"

Brandon's head snapped up, annoyance settling over his features. "He's better than all right," he ground out, like a challenge.

I lifted both hands. "Hey, no offense. He just seems a little…well…"

"Slow?" Brandon's voice was caustic. "Not quite right in the head?"

I cringed at the sharp edge. "Look, I'm not trying to be mean, I just wondered. He seems a little…off."

"He's more *on* than you are," Brandon snapped, shoving out of his chair.

I lifted my hands again reflexively. "*Okay.* I'm sorry."

He sighed and sat back down. "No, I'm sorry. I just… Everybody always treated Evan like some kind of village idiot. They didn't get it. At all." He got up and stalked into the kitchen, tossing my peanut butter into my sink with a *thunk*. "I thought you might. Whatever.

Seven o'clock. Tomorrow night. Get him back here."

Seven o'clock rolled around. And then 8. And 9. No ghost. Evan and I sat in my apartment. When we exhausted the topic of Brandon, I asked Evan about himself. Somehow though, we always ended up talking about me.

Talking to Evan was like talking to no one else I'd ever met. He didn't think linearly, and the conversation bounced unpredictably. He watched me with those halcyon eyes, twisted his hair around his fingers, and *listened*. The way he went about it made me wonder if anyone had ever really listened to me in my life. Then he would ask something completely out of left field and tilt his head to one side and wait for an answer again. His drawl was growing on me. His laugh was infectious. Occasionally he would stop in the middle of a sentence, look up and around hopefully, and then suddenly settle back, disconsolate. I wanted to scream for Brandon to show the fuck up. I hated to see that look on Evan's face.

At 11 o'clock he finally shook his head, eyes gleaming suspiciously. "He's not here. He's not coming." I drove him home, and was back in my apartment at 11:30. At 11:50, Brandon materialized in my bedroom.

"Sorry I'm late." Can a ghost sound breathless? Where was he racing from? Had a haunting run overtime?

"Where. Were. You?"

"Trouble again. This isn't as easy as it looks, you know." He looked around expectantly, then sighed in disappointment. "Damn. I was hoping he'd wait."

"He did wait," I said coldly. "For four hours." If Brandon noticed my attitude, he didn't comment.

"Same time tomorrow. I'm *really* sorry, Vic."

"*Victor*," I snapped at the thin air as he disappeared.

Seven o'clock. Eight o'clock. Nine o'clock. I took Evan out for a late dinner when I found out he hadn't eaten most of the day. He resisted, I insisted. He sat on the other side of the table and pushed his food around on his plate.

"What if he shows up while we're gone?"

"Then he can bloody well wait for us this time." I drained my beer, set the glass down with a thump, and signaled for another. "Evan. Don't you ever get angry at him?"

"Angry?" The blond head lifted. That soft voice wrapped around me. "Why?"

"He *killed* himself, Evan. That's an incredibly selfish thing to do. And right in front of you?" Over the course of the two nights I'd heard the full details of my ghost's demise. I was still shuddering.

"He wasn't rational at the time," Evan defended stolidly.

I sighed. Yes, I'd heard about the severe clinical depression too, even though Evan hadn't called it by that name. What he had described couldn't be labeled anything but, though. I rubbed at my tired eyes. "But do you ever get angry?" I insisted.

"I—angry?" The big blue eyes stared at me, painfully confused.

My heart twisted. Every once in a while I got a forcible reminder that Evan was not like everyone else. I spoke softly, reaching out and covering his hand with mine before I even realized what I was doing. "It's OK. Forget it. Do you want dessert?"

I definitely wasn't scared anymore. I was pissed. And I was doubly annoyed that I was attracted to the dead bastard. When he showed up two days later, a full hour and a half after Evan had given up and gone home yet again, I lit into him without a second thought. "Why are you doing this? Why aren't you showing up for Evan? You *asked* me to get him here."

"I'm having trouble...manifesting."

"No, you are *not*. You are lying through your fucking transparent teeth. You're not even *here* when he is."

He looked at me sharply. "How do you know?"

I glared at him hotly. "I...don't know. You just aren't. I don't feel you. Like I feel you now."

His expression became interested. "Are you Sensitive?"

"What?"

"You know. Sensitive. With a capital S." He grinned. "You know, I never believed this bullshit until Evan. But he's...the convincing sort. Wouldn't you say?"

All I could *say* was that his lackadaisical attitude was really starting to burn me. "Shall I call Evan? Get him back here? Now?"

"You can. I may not be here when he gets here. I don't know how long I can maintain myself. It'd probably be better if he got some sleep and we tried again. Maybe we could try the cemetery. I used to have good luck there."

My lips curled back off my teeth and I realized I was yelling, but I didn't bother to stop. "Are you playing some kind of sick game? Because Evan is *hurting* here."

Dark brows rose, and the insolent look he shot me made me want to slap him. "So?"

My hands pulled into fists. "You're kind of an asshole, aren't you, Brandon?"

He shrugged, and gave me that familiar, sarcastic smirk. "I'm dead. What do you want from me, Vic?"

"Victor," I ground out. "Vic*tor*."

He rolled his eyes. "Oh, Christ. You're not one of those fags who always has to use the fuuuull version of his name, are you?"

"Oh, like you're not, *Brandon?*" I snapped.

He shrugged again. "You come up with a good short form for Brandon, and I'll take it. I tried all my life. Not that it was a very long life, but I did try." He grinned suddenly, sadly. "Only one I ever liked was Evan's. He called me Brandy. Or Brandiwine."

The tone of his voice, the look on his face, stopped me dead. It was the sound of Evan's pain, and the corresponding love I'd begun to question was reflected with such clarity I caught my breath. "What are you doing?" I whispered tiredly. "You do love him. That's obvious. Why aren't you showing up?"

He looked at me for a long moment, then reached out and stroked my face, just as Evan had at the cemetery. Cool shivers traced outward in an icy mimicry of the spreading heat I still remembered from that previous afternoon. "I told you," his voice was husky. "I'm having trouble manifesting. Tomorrow night. OK?" His hand cupped my face. I nodded as he faded.

When Evan showed up the next day, for once he wasn't wearing the red plaid shirt that I'd since found out had been Brandon's. It had probably looked great on Brandon, but I was glad to see Evan in dark blue.

Evan walked over to the rocking chair and sat down, his face solemn but calm. He looked up at me and spoke in that funny, matter-of-fact way he sometimes pulled out of his hat. "I don't think Brandon is going to come, Victor. I don't think he'll be late, I just don't think he's coming. At all."

I wanted to curl up around him and swear that I could make it all better. I knew I couldn't, I knew I shouldn't even try, but the words started to come anyway. "But Evan, he said—"

"I know what he said. I believe what you've told me. I do. I just… He's not coming, Victor. He can't, or he won't. I think," he paused, swallowed hard, then stood up resolutely. "I think maybe I should buy *you* dinner tonight." My mouth dropped open, and I stood there staring at him like an idiot. He looked suddenly uncomfortable. "Unless," he muttered hurriedly, "you'd rather not, I mean I understand—I—oh dear."

"No!" I leaped forward, closing the gap between us, needing to wipe that horrible uncertainty off his face. Especially when it shouldn't be there; not considering the way I felt. Now I was grinning like an idiot, but I didn't seem to be able to stop. "No, Evan, no. I'd *love* to. Really." I spoke as honestly as I could. I knew, Evan being Evan, he'd hear it.

He did. An answering grin brightened his face instantly, striking that internal glow I'd come to associate only with the times he was talking about Brandon. "Oh. Good." His hands lifted and slid over my jaw, reaching up to stroke through my hair. His lips lifted to mine in a shy kiss. My arms closed around him and drew him in tight, deepening the kiss instinctively.

At first I thought the tingling electricity that raised the hair on my arms was a reaction to kissing a boy who heals with his bare hands, but then I recognized the feel. Without breaking the kiss my eyes flew open suspiciously. The misty, coalescing figure behind Evan confirmed my fear. I almost choked, my concern about him being the jealous type resurfacing. But the silencing finger Brandon had pressed to his lips as he materialized stopped me. I broke the kiss and lifted my head reflexively. Oblivious, Evan nestled against my throat, arms wrapping around me with a happy sigh.

Brandon shot me that dangerous grin, and winked. "Take care of him," he mouthed distinctly, and faded as quickly as he'd appeared.

But why do I get the feeling he's going to be taking care of me?

→ The Thing at the Bottom of the Bed ←

by J.M. Beazer

It started the night of her father's funeral. Haley came back to her apartment alone late at night, trying not to think. The feelings were too conflicting; her relationship with her father had not been good. In later years, after he'd become a relatively harmless old man, they'd achieved a superficial harmony, but she'd never been able to forgive the abusiveness—the sadistic contempt, the flarings of blind rage, the beatings—of her childhood and adolescence. She'd never confronted her father; she'd just ignored the memories and acted as if she'd forgotten them.

She dreaded going to sleep that first night. She was afraid she'd have nightmares. She'd only recently become used to sleeping alone in her bed, and she felt it was high time she'd done so: Nearly two years had passed since Beth had left her. She didn't wish she was still living with Beth—she'd come to realize the relationship had been doing her more harm than good. Nor did she wish she'd found a new live-in lover, or at least she wasn't sure. She'd just started seeing Allison a few weeks before, and even though she liked Allison and held high hopes for the relationship, it was still difficult to imagine ever feeling close enough to actually live with her. She wasn't sure she would ever feel that close to anyone again. But she wished she had a roommate. Just another, friendly presence in the house.

She stayed up reading a 19th century "comfort novel" while eating a bowl of hot rice cereal—baby food. She could eat in bed now that Beth was no longer around to raise objections. Before she'd even finished her cereal, her eyelids started drooping no matter how hard she tried to keep them open. She put the cereal bowl on her nightstand, turned out the light, and pulled the covers up high under her chin.

A little while later, she realized her eyes were wide open and her thoughts were spinning around the day's events. She saw the oversized gray hearse, the coffin in front of the altar, the curling brown leaves crackling under her feet on the pathways of the cemetery. She was a half orphan now, and who knew how much longer her mother would last? Her mother's hair had turned almost completely gray in the past year or two; like her father, her mother had started to look elderly.

With a soft heavy *whump,* something jumped onto the foot of the bed. Her heart caught for a second before she remembered it was only Gulliver. She really had to put him on a stricter diet. Even though she'd switched him to the food for "inactive" cats, Gulliver was fatter than ever. She could tell even from the weight that settled down and leaned heavily against her lower leg. And lately it would sometimes take him two attempts to make the leap from the floor to the bed or coffee table. Pathetic. She hoped he wouldn't discover the cereal bowl on the night table; he wasn't well-trained enough not to lick it clean, and he certainly didn't need the extra calories.

She must've drifted off soon after that. The next thing she knew—and whether it was three minutes or three hours later she hadn't a clue—Gulliver was meowing at the door. Pain-in-the-neck cat, always wanting in and out. It was his territorial instinct, of course; he needed to constantly rub himself against the furnishings to keep the apartment safely marked—as if any rival cats were likely to show up. If she were entirely rational, she'd recognize this fact and sleep with her bedroom door open, so he could roam the apartment at will. But she couldn't sleep with the bedroom door open; it gave her the willies. Since early childhood, she'd always had to sleep with the door shut, and later, when she got her own apartment with locks on all the doors, she needed to lock it as well. It wasn't burglars she feared. She lived in a doorman building, in a safe neighborhood, on the 23rd floor. Open doors just made her feel too exposed. For the same reason she could never sleep without wearing pajamas and underwear, and without at least a sheet to cover her body, a sheet pulled high under her chin. She did this even on the hottest nights in summer, even without air conditioning. She did this even with a lover sleeping next to her. After making love, she always got up and climbed into pajamas.

She thought she'd ignore Gulliver's cries until he gave up, but after a short pause the meowing continued, and then came a scratching at the bottom corner of the door. Something was wrong. Gulliver scratched at the door like that only when he wanted to come *into* the room. It was part of his attempt to push the door open with his paw and head. Dumb cat: He never seemed to learn the door would always be locked this time of night. Then she realized she still felt a heavy lump leaning against her lower leg. If Gulliver was meowing at the door, then what was that lump lying against her leg?

Perhaps it was only because it was late at night, but she sat up in a panic, snatching her legs away. She flailed to find the lamp on the nightstand, desperate for the reassurance of light. Her fingers found the switch and turned it. But the bulb burst with a short flash and an unvoiced "ping" that made her fingers dart away. God, of all the times for a bulb to blow out!

Already she'd leapt out of bed. She stumbled across the room for the spring-tension work lamp over the computer desk. She felt her way over the top of the lamp, praying this bulb wouldn't also blow, her entire body rigid against any touch or impact. She found the switch and turned it on.

This time the bulb bathed the room in light. She stood holding the lamp with both hands, hardly daring to look over her shoulder. But the room was empty. Her eye passed along her bureaus, the bookcase under the window, the bed. Her heart pounded. Was that an indentation in the comforter at the foot of the bed? It was hard to tell when she'd left it so rumpled. No, everything seemed to be in place.

In the hall outside her bedroom a sconce was located directly across from the bedroom door. She didn't like the idea of opening the door, but she couldn't stand the idea of remaining alone in her room. And where was Gulliver? She forced herself to the door, and with trembling fingers tried to turn the knob. It was locked, as it should have been. She turned the bolt and gingerly opened the door. She stepped across the hall and flipped on the light.

The hall was empty. She walked down it to the living room, where she turned on the light on the end table. She proceeded into the dining room, turning on every light she passed. She found Gulliver huddled at the front door, his nose pressed against the crack between the door and the jamb. His tail had puffed up to the size of a raccoon's. The fur along his spine stood straight up. He hissed when she bent to reach for him. The only time he ever hissed was at the vet. She could see the fur along his rib cage beating furiously with the pounding of his small heart. What had frightened him to such an extent?

She stood back up, confusion jamming her brain. The bedroom door had been locked, and here was Gulliver, definitely on the outside. Then what was that lump at the bottom of the bed?

The next night, Haley came home late from work. She opened the front door and flipped on the front hall light. It blew out.

A chill ran down her neck. She stood stock-still in the hallway outside her apartment, her eyes peering into the darkness. Was she imagining it or was the air cool and fetid just inside the door? Was there a patch of blacker blackness hovering in front of her? And that smell, much stronger than the night before. What was it? A mixture of skunk and boiled cabbage?

Her nose wrinkled with disgust; without intending it she turned her head to the side. She thought she felt the clamminess slide past her neck and shoulder. When she looked inside the apartment again, the darker patch was gone.

She was being ridiculous. Lightbulbs blew out all the time. She walked into the kitchen and turned on the light. It didn't blow out—of course. Why would it? She grabbed a fresh bulb off the shelf above the stove and replaced the bulb in the hall. She went through the house turning on lights. They all switched on without incident.

She found Gulliver way at the back of the apartment, puffed up and shivering behind the sink in the bathroom. He growled when she offered him her fingers to sniff, but after a few minutes he let her touch him. She stroked his fur until she'd smoothed it all down again.

"You look exhausted," Allison said.

Haley looked up from cutting her mesclun salad. "I haven't been sleeping well," she said. "I guess my father..."

"Oh, of course," Allison said. "I'm sorry."

"It's okay. I'm sure it'll pass with time."

Don't think about it, just do it. That was Haley's motto. It had gotten her through her work as a lawyer, her daily run and weight-training routine, difficult phone calls and meetings, even thank-you notes. It would get her through the process of mourning her father.

She was also trying to apply it to that strange incident with the lump at the bottom of the bed. She had decided she must've imagined the lump after she woke up. Perhaps the comforter had become bunched up against her legs, so that it felt like a heavy weight. As for the "cat" jumping up on the bed earlier, perhaps it had been Gulliver then. Perhaps she'd woken up at some point earlier than the time when she panicked; perhaps she'd let him out and locked the door behind him, then forgotten she'd done so. There had to be a rational explanation for it, and now that she'd come up with a couple of plausible alternatives, she shouldn't trouble herself with it anymore.

It was just that her motto didn't work that well late at night. It was useless in any attempt to fall asleep, for example. The more she refused to think about troubling thoughts, the more rigid and tense she became. She couldn't force herself to fall asleep; it had to come naturally. Some nights she wanted to hit herself on the head with her cast-iron skillet, just to knock herself out. Just to stop from thinking.

And so once again she found herself lying awake in the middle of the night. She had turned out the light only once her eyelids had become heavy, but a few moments later, she'd heard a small clicking sound. It came from the direction of the bureau, where she kept a pair of wicker baskets, and the clicking resembled the sound of the wicker settling against itself. That was probably all it was. Or perhaps it was an insect crawling around inside the basket. She hated to think she had cockroaches, but it was nothing to keep her awake at night, either. It shouldn't have left her eyes wide and bright and her heart thumping. It shouldn't have caused her to lie there listening—and there it came again. Like a shifting inside the wicker basket. Or wasn't it more like something leaning against the top of it?

Something—what? Her father's ghost? A demon?

No. Utter nonsense. She'd buy some roach traps in the morning. Maybe it wasn't even a roach, but something less disgusting, like a spider or a beetle. Her adrenaline surge was a completely irrational—and hence contemptible—reaction.

Still, there was no arguing with her bodily state. Especially when the air had that same dank, stagnant quality against her cheeks, and she could again detect the faint odor of skunk and boiled cabbage. No, she'd have to pull out her book again and read until the adrenaline worked its way through her system. She rolled over, stretched for the lamp on the nightstand, and turned the switch. It blew out.

Her stomach fell inside her. She had replaced that bulb not one week ago! The last time— She jumped out of bed and hopped over to the lamp on the computer desk. But that bulb blew out too.

She ran to the door. The room rolled and lurched. Something soft and spongy grazed the back of her neck; she let out a short scream. She had to have light. The door was locked, but she fumbled it open. She grabbed for the sconce in the hall, but when she flicked the switch, that bulb also blew. Was she losing her mind? She ran to the living room, but the lamp on the end table blew as well. She tried the sconce over the dining room table last. When it too blew out, a wave of nausea left her reeling. She ran to the front door, where she nearly tripped over Gulliver. He hissed and spat. She unlocked the door and unhooked the chain. Gulliver slipped out into the hall just ahead of her. She slammed the door behind her, then stood staring at the closed door and heaving breaths, her only comfort the pale light of the hallway around her and her cat.

She'd locked herself out, but she didn't care. She was wearing pajamas, but she didn't care. She couldn't bear the thought of returning to the apartment, not while it was still dark out. Gulliver had skittered to the far side of the hall, beyond the elevators. After she calmed him down, she picked him up and took him with her into the stairwell. She sat down on the step and held Gulliver in her lap. There she waited until the sky lightened through the window over the landing. She called security and told them she'd accidentally locked herself out.

By the time security came to let her in, she felt like a fool. She'd fled her apartment, lost an entire night's sleep, and subjected herself to the embarrassment of having the security guard see her in her pajamas just because a few lightbulbs had blown.

Yes, it was unusual that five bulbs would blow out at the same time, especially when she'd replaced one recently. But she could see how over time one's lightbulbs might become synchronized, so they would all burn out at about the same time. She could recall occasions when she'd failed to replace a bulb for a few days because she'd run out of fresh bulbs and the usual craziness at work made her keep forgetting to buy new ones. Say she'd delayed for a week, and by the time she'd gotten around to replacing the first bulb another one was ready to go. As for the recently changed bulb in the lamp on the nightstand—well, that one could've been defective. Or perhaps a power surge had destroyed all the filaments at once.

And now thanks to her silliness, she'd be dragging herself through work all day. She'd have to cancel with Allison that night; she'd be way too exhausted to handle a date.

Once she was back inside her apartment, she tested all the lights that had blown out the night before. She flicked each switch two or three times, but the bulbs all remained dark. She also checked the circuit breakers: None had been tripped. So she hadn't imagined it at least. That was something.

Nevertheless, she decided to call her former therapist to make an ad hoc appointment or two. It seemed obvious she was experiencing some kind of disturbance on an unconscious level. It was probably the shock of her father's death; it must be affecting her more than she'd realized.

That afternoon, she found herself nodding at work. She shut her office door and put her head down on her desk. Just for a few minutes. Then she'd get right back to it.

"Look at me," a voice rasped.

She started awake. The voice had been clear and distinct, as if it had been whispered by her ear. She looked around, but of course she was alone in her office.

It was one of those mild aural hallucinations that sometimes occurred just as one was falling asleep, that was all. Just the beginning of a dream. She'd experienced this sort of thing before on rare occasions, and she was pretty sure she'd read about it too, although she couldn't recall where. She'd read it was normal to experience such half-dreaming aural hallucinations from time to time. One time she thought she'd heard her mother calling her down to dinner. That sound had also been sharp and well defined, just as if she'd heard it said out loud, not the grayed-out, inside-the-head copy the imagination would've produced. It was distinctly her mother's voice she'd heard, not her own mimicking it, and it had called her with just the same cadence and pitch her mother had always used. It was the same thing with this rasping voice.

Fortunately, the voice had banished her sleepiness. She returned to her work.

In the middle of the night, Haley awoke from a deep sleep. She sensed something was wrong, but she couldn't tell what it was. Then she realized one corner of the mattress, down by her feet, was sloping toward the floor, as if pressed under the burden of a heavy weight.

"Look at me," a voice rasped. "Let me touch you."

She tried to sit up and reach for the lamp, but she couldn't raise her head. Her arms and legs refused to respond to her efforts to lift them. It felt as if her entire body were being pulled down into the bed. She tried to scream, but no sound came out. Her mind pitched and swayed. The force pulling her down into the bed was also pulling her back into sleep; she was powerless to stop it.

In the morning, she told herself she'd had a nightmare.

The next night, Haley's friend Margot called from California. Haley had known Margot since grade school, and they'd been through a lot together. In particular, Haley's family had helped Margot through a crisis. Margot's stepfather had started sexually abusing Margot and her younger sister when they were 13 and 11. The stepfather had alternately threatened and cajoled the girls into silence, but when Margot was 15 and came down with chlamydia, she told Haley about the abuse. Haley didn't know what to do, but she managed to serve as a sounding board for Margot while Margot slowly decided to take action. Margot told her mother, and when her mother refused to believe her, she told her English teacher. During the uproar that followed, Margot and her sister moved in with Haley's family for several months, until Margot's mother came to acknowledge the abuse and threw the stepfather out. Both Margot and her sister had been in therapy ever since. Margot had overcome the trauma sufficiently to have married; the wedding took place about a year ago. She had called Haley to tell her she was pregnant with her first child.

After Haley got off the phone with Margot, she suddenly recalled that she had seen the lump once before. It all came back in a rush: It was when she was 15, when Margot and her sister were staying at her family's house. A patch of blacker black in the darkness. A lump that would leap onto the foot of her bed and then sit there heavily, creating a downward slope in the mattress. A smell like the mixture of skunk and boiled cabbage. And a voice that would rasp out, "Look at me," in ever more insistent whispers, a voice just like the one she'd heard in her office. How could she have forgotten that? And what did it say about her mind that she could've done so?

Then she recalled something else: How she had eventually made the lump go away. She'd said she would look at it after her father died.

With her therapist a few years back, Haley had explored the possibility that, like her friend Margot, she had been sexually abused, but that in her case, the abuse had occurred at so young an age that she'd retained no memories of it. At one time or another, Haley had exhibited almost all the symptoms associated with so-called post-traumatic stress disorder, ranging from extreme modesty about her body to a near total lack of interest in sex to a general difficulty with intimacy and trusting other people. She even had some of the uncommon symptoms, like a penchant for setting fires. For as long as she could remember, she'd had disturbing nightmares and flashes of images that could be interpreted as echoes of sexual abuse. And in her strained relationship with her father, she arguably could have found echoes of sexual abuse at his hands: Her need to maintain a distance of at least four feet between him and her whenever she had visited her parents. Her disgust when he would play "pocket pool" in his pants pockets or stand behind one of the ladderback chairs in the dining room, rhythmically pressing his pelvis against the chair's slats. Her inability to look him in the eye.

But as she worked through the issue with her therapist, she'd come to decide it was pointless to try to recover such putative memories. Even if she came to "remember" something at that late date, how would she know the "memory" wasn't the artifact of therapeutic suggestion? Or societal suggestion: Perhaps she'd merely become caught up in the media frenzy over the "recovered memory" movement in recent years. Either way, she had to acknowledge any such "recovered memories" would've been wholly unreliable. As a lawyer, she knew such "memories" couldn't fairly be introduced as evidence in a case against an alleged abuser, and as a person who considered herself fair-minded and rational, she felt that even outside the context of a courtroom she couldn't in good conscience base any action—or even any feeling—on such a "memory." To be sure, it was too bad and a shame. It meant some instances of child abuse would forever go unpunished. But Haley was familiar enough with the legal system (not to mention the ways of the world) to know many wrongs have to be left unrighted.

And she did have an alternate explanation for her symptoms and echoes. It was entirely possible they were attributable only to the emotional and physical abuse she remembered all too well. Those "vigorous debates" to which her father had subjected her as a child, and which he would cut off with a contemptuous dismissal as soon as he'd reduced her to tears ("If you're nothing but a cry-baby, then this discussion is over"). The times her father had flown into a rage and beaten her. And the enemas her parents had given her when she went through a period of constipation at age five. She remembered screaming and crying at the humiliation when her parents bent her naked over the side of the tub; she remembered the nasty orange-rubber squeeze ball they'd filled with the warm, soapy water. The only thing she failed to recall was any physical pain, a fact her therapist found noteworthy.

But Dr. Worth believed it ultimately didn't matter whether Haley had been sexually abused. What mattered was the symptoms that were troubling her in the present, and it was the effort to heal those symptoms that should be the focus of their therapeutic work.

Haley agreed, and she put aside the effort to uncover repressed "memories." But after she did so, therapy didn't seem all that worthwhile anymore. Yes, she had symptoms, but she was able to function at a pretty high level despite them, at least at work and with friends. Leaving work at 6 P.M. two times a week for her appointments added a great deal of stress to her life, as 6 P.M. was practically considered lunchtime at her firm. And by that time she was no longer quite as distraught over Beth's departure. Soon afterward she had terminated her treatment.

But the strange tricks her mind had been playing had brought her back. She told Dr. Worth everything that had happened, including how she had encountered the lump before, when she was 15. She offered all the rational explanations she'd already made to herself. Dr. Worth agreed the recent death of Haley's father must lie at the root of the disturbance. But she also asked whether Haley was still working those long hours at the firm. When Haley acknowledged she was, and that she hadn't even taken any bereavement leave to attend her father's funeral, Dr. Worth urged her to take a vacation. Yes, she understood vacations were frowned upon at Haley's firm, that they were seen as evidence that an attorney lacked a full "commitment to practice," but it was obvious Haley was starting to show serious signs of wear and tear. It was better to bend than to break. And at least a vacation would allow her to catch up on her sleep.

By the end of the session, Haley came to agree a vacation was in order. She didn't tell Dr. Worth, however, that one small, secret part of her brain was thinking if she left her apartment, she might escape the lump. And then she could move to another apartment. To be sure, the lump might follow her no matter where she went, and it did give her pause to recall she'd heard that voice in her ear at her office. But it was possible the voice in her office might not have been a supernatural manifestation like the other incidents; it might well have been an aural hallucination attendant to the beginning of a dream. Her instincts told her otherwise, but what were instincts but the label we put on our illogical reactions? An excuse to close one's mind to other, more sensible points of view? Escaping the apartment was certainly worth a try.

Allison was disappointed to hear Haley was taking a vacation without her.

"It's because I had to do it at such short notice," Haley told her. Inside she felt she really didn't know Allison well enough yet to contemplate spending an entire week alone with her. "And for some of the time I'll be helping my mom with—with straightening out her finances. It's really not a pleasure trip. Just a time to catch up on my sleep."

"I know," Allison said. "It's just that a whole week...I'll miss you, that's all."

"And I'll miss you. But that's good, isn't it? That's how it should be, right?"

For her vacation, Haley rented a house at the beach, easy enough to do off-season. She drove out with Gulliver on a Saturday morning, feeling better than she had in weeks.

She tried not to think about the lump, but she found her mind kept returning to it. She wanted to understand what it was, and that one small, credulous part of her mind was willing to entertain supernatural explanations. But even allowing for the supernatural, she still couldn't figure it out. For one, even though the timing suggested the lump was her father's ghost, how could that be when the lump had visited itself upon her when she was 15, at a time when her father was still very much alive? If her father had in fact abused her when she was a small child, could the lump have been an emanation of that part of him, later repressed, that had committed the abuse? Perhaps. But perhaps it was just the energy of her own repressed memories, begging her to "look at" them. Which raised the key question as far as she was concerned: Had the lump come for evil or for good?

And why, if it wanted her to look at it, did it keep blowing out all the lights? Was it something she could view best in the darkness? Had Gulliver—who could see in the dark, after all—seen more than she, and did that explain his abject terror?

The house was a small cottage on the bay. While unpacking she let Gulliver out, and he explored the back yard with dainty, careful steps, tail high while he sniffed the lavender that grew wild just above the high-water mark on the shore.

She took a long bike ride down to the ocean and back, drove to the supermarket for groceries, and fixed herself and Gulliver some dinner. She rented a video, and then went out on the porch to read another one of her comfort novels. The air was fragrant with the scents of early fall: wood smoke, mud, and fallen leaves. Her shoulders dropped an inch, and she let out a long, full breath. She couldn't imagine the lump having followed her out here. Maybe she could just move out to the country and commute to work. Maybe that would be enough to get rid of the problem. But as a precaution, she took the flashlight out of the glove compartment of her car and brought it with her to bed. She also locked the bedroom door, trying not to think about how little that had helped her before.

But the long bike ride had left her pleasantly tired, and she fell asleep almost at once. What awakened her some hours later was the sound of Gulliver growling. It started low in his throat and rose to a high, hysterical pitch before breaking off.

She sat bolt upright. Gulliver leapt off the foot of the bed and skittered across the floor to a corner of the room. He avoided the door, and then she knew why. In front of it, something heavy was shuffling and dragging itself across the floor. It made an off-balance slithering noise, followed at irregular intervals by a small, sudden thump: *Shhhr-chunk, shhrr-chunk, shhhhhhrr-chunk*. It was making its way toward her, and it blocked her escape route through the door. A scream died in her throat. She couldn't remember where the light was in this room, and that gave her time to think the lightbulb would probably blow out.

She remembered the flashlight. She reached under her pillows for it, but she knocked it off the bed. It rolled across the floor and hit the wall under the dresser.

The slithering stopped in front of her, at the foot of the bed. Knees drawn up to her chest, she pressed back as far as she could against the wall behind her. She peered into the darkness, but all she could make out was a patch of deeper blackness, a large, irregular space where the moonlight and shadows that fell across the desk were blotted out. The blackness leapt, and with the same heavy *whump* she recalled from the first night, it landed on the foot of the bed. It seemed to crouch there, ready to spring.

She forced herself to speak. "What are you?" It came out in a quavering croak.

"Look at me," a voice rasped.

Again she forced out the words. "I am looking. All I see—"

"Look with your mind, not your eyes. Open your mind to me."

"No." She said it without thinking.

The weight shifted forward on the bed, and the blackness reached out to her. With heavy, doughlike fingers it pressed itself firmly against her chest, on the bare skin right between the lapels of her pajamas. A shriek tore itself from her lungs.

She jumped out of bed and ran to the door. The door was locked with a hook-and-eye latch, and she floundered to get it unhooked. She felt a cold, clammy exhalation on the back of her neck, and then came the moist fingers fumbling at her neck and shoulders. They were crumbling and pulpy, like a piece of foam rubber soaked with a corrosive chemical, and their touch made her own flesh seem to crumble and fall away. With a strangled scream, she unhooked the latch and wrenched the door open.

She ran through the house in the moonlight, pausing only to scoop up the car keys out of the basket by the front door. She ran outside to the garage and raised the sliding door on its runners. She ran to the car door on the driver's side, but there she hesitated, remembering Gulliver. How could she leave him alone with that thing? Except—it was useless to deny it any longer—it seemed the lump would always follow *her*. If anything, Gulliver would be safer if she left him alone. Or gave him away to someone else.

A soft *shhhhr-chunk* came at the garage door behind her. She turned. A patch of blackness obscured the moonlit gravel on the driveway. *Shhhr-chunk, shhhhhr-chunk:* The blackness bobbed and swayed as it approached her. It had her cornered.

She opened the car door and jumped inside. But before she could shut the door, the blackness reached out to her. She turned her head away in disgust. It reached for her eyelids; it tried to push them open, but she kept them squeezed shut.

"Look at me," it repeated. "Turn and remember." The stench was overpowering.

"I won't look," she said, still squeezing her eyes. "Not till my mother dies."

"No. Now."

She took a breath, steeled herself. "Will you leave if I look?"

"And not before. Gaze upon my features."

"I don't need to. I know exactly what you are." It was the energy of her repressed memories; she knew that. And she knew, in a rough and general way, what she would see if she looked into the blackness.

But the lump stood there waiting, implacable. She summoned all her courage and turned to face it. She opened her eyes and searched into the blackness. It swirled and deepened, like a vortex turning before her, drawing her in. At its center she caught a glimpse of the outlines of a tormented face, its eyes running and the corners of its mouth twisted downward in an expression of abject terror and pain. Her face.

There was more, much more, swirling just behind the face, but she couldn't stand it anymore. It was too repulsive. She wrenched her eyes away.

"That's not enough," the lump said. "Look at all of it. Acknowledge the enormity."

"No!" she screamed. "I'd rather die."

She slammed the car door, bracing herself for the abomination of the lump's amputated hand dropping into her lap. But nothing came, and she turned the ignition and put the car in reverse. She screeched out of the garage, half hoping she would run the thing over. As she backed out onto the road, she glanced through the side window. From the black square of the open doorway she saw something misshapen and lumbering drag itself into view, something that eclipsed the neat white clapboard of the garage siding. Even over the roar of the motor she could hear its slow, inexorable steps. *Shhhr-chunk, shhhr-chunk, shhhhhhrr-chunk.*

She had decided. She would never again look at the lump. She'd rather live with it.

She'd learn to sleep with the lights on. She'd get used to the heaviness at the foot of her bed, or at least she'd get used to not getting used to it. She'd carry around a flashlight to keep it at bay. She'd find a less stressful job, one she could perform on less than a full night's sleep. And she'd break things off with Allison; she'd have to. How could she explain her strange nocturnal habits to a lover? But she'd never look again. She wouldn't think about it, she'd just do it.

She sat at the foot of the bed, her head lolling a little to one side. She felt the crumbling embrace of the blackness around her.

⇒ Echoes ⇐

by M. Christian

This guy had blond hair. Red's had been black as ink: a late night mop of unkempt curls. Same with the mustache—Red's had been a silent film villain's handlebar that, if he was going out tricking, he might or might not actually twirl into ridiculous spirals. So like Red, so very like him: head a blenderized mess, mustache prissily maintained.

The guy Chev had on his living room sofa now, though, had a perfectly maintained surfer coif. Looking at this guy you could tell he spent way too long in front of the mirror, spraying down his perfect honey blond locks minute after minute, making everyone late.

Red used to say, "You don't kiss with your hair. You kiss with your mustache."

This other guy, Chev wished he could remember his name, said, "Gotta bait the hook with something," when Chev said he liked his hair.

Red had liked to fuck to Japanese drums and the *1812 Overture*. This guy, this mystery of Friday night tricking, had been dancing to Frankie Goes to Hollywood and fuckin' Abba like he'd been stricken with queer palsy: jerking and bouncing to his deep, spiritual connection to disco.

Still, Chev had to maintain, running his long, thin fingers over the blond God's chest, *he really knows how to kiss.*

Red had been a tough trick. Chev had pursued and hunted and chased the man 'til he gave up that night after Alex's birthday party. This guy (name? name?) had been too easy: An early Friday drop by the Big Ear, a Tequila Sunrise for strength, an ogle at the guy jerking to *Go West,* small talk, small talk, small talk, "I live up the block," then the couch and finding out the guy was pretty good at kissing.

Red had been good at kissing too. He'd had what he liked to call a "learned tongue, professorial lips, and a doctored mouth."

Red had liked to test your lips when he kissed: gentle little touches and scrapes with that smooth mustache, feeling your lips for softness and that subtle hint of opening. Red hadn't been a wet lamprey fastening to your mouth with suction and gallons of cold spit. He had been a strong and supple kisser, with a strong, darting tongue that was just where you wanted it. He'd had a very unique range of acrobatics with his tongue: touching tip to tip, following with tongue tantra every move you made until you *were* your tongue, dancing tip to tip with his. He'd liked to follow that narrow groove in your tongue as he kissed, feeling its texture and smoothness (or so he said). Chev had been with lots of guys. Bad. Good. Indifferent. Forgettable. Memorable. Only one, though, that kissed exactly like Red—and that was Red himself.

Except, Chev suddenly realized with cold, clammy shock, for this blond, empty-headed surfer clone on his sofa.

In the woods up near Mount Tam, hidden in a corner no one visited—beneath a stunted mesquite bush, marked by nothing but a particular bluish stone, after six months Red's body was as cold as the high mountain.

The man on Chev's couch kissed exactly like Red—who was dead, from a single bullet, and buried.

Headaches can come on suddenly, he explained, shaking and stroking the guy's strong leg. Blinding migraines. Sudden pain for which the cure was a couple of extra-strength meds and sleeping in the dark. Sorry, sorry, sorry.

When the blond left with maybe a slight irritation at having wasted an hour of precious Friday night tricking time, Chev didn't take anything except a hefty shot of Black Death vodka.

Red wasn't anywhere around anymore. His books were sold or given to friends. He hadn't come with any furniture, and what few clothes he had brought ended up at Community Thrift.

Looking around his apartment, Chev couldn't see Red at all. There was nothing to show that they had lived together for six months, had fucked and kissed and talked long into the night. There was nothing to show the eventual friction, the fights, and the strange tension that had come between them. The gun had been Red's as well, a heavy revolver, probably an antique, that he had said was for protection. Chev had dropped it into the Bay on the way back from burying Red's body.

Everything of Red was gone. Not a trace.

No. Everything of Red *should* have been gone.

His name was Raul. And he was quite a Raul—a beautiful son of the Aztec's with a strong nose, high forehead, and skin the color of stained wood. Strong, too. Chev had been talking and sipping Black Russians with Jack and Alex when Raul had been introduced as an ex of an ex. "Worth sleeping with that bastard just to get an intro to this beautiful man," Alex said, ruffling Raul's thick black locks.

He and Chev hit it off, and soon they were making the two-story trek up to Chev's flat. Raul had a few more in him, and was frisky and clutching. As Chev fumbled with his front door lock, the giant Hispanic had grabbed him around the waist and lifted him right off his feet.

Red had never lifted him like that.

Raul must have studied with Houdini. Not seeming to mind that Chev wasn't in the mood to kiss, he had Chev's belt and jeans down in seconds. Never, never, never one to protest a boy's enthusiasm, Chev just smiled as he watched Raul's excited eyes dance over his strong legs, furry crotch, and straining cock—eager for Raul.

Raul got right down to it.

And Chev screamed.

Their first time was right after Alex's birthday party. More than slightly drunk, they had stumbled back to Chev's place—mutually agreeing, silently, that they were going to go fuck.

Oh, they did, all right. They did, indeed. Once inside Chev's place they fell into a hot clench. Hot mouth to hot mouth, bodies strong against each other. No prelude: just tongues dancing the fandango in each other's mouth, hands on very hard cocks beneath Chev's jeans and Red's cotton drawstrings.

Red had been a big guy, a smart guy: like some kind of strange hybrid of an 18th century professor of philosophy and a lumber-jack. That first night, after a long and luscious clench in the hall, Red had simply picked up the slight Chev, threw him neatly over his shoulder in a fireman's carry and bumped around Chev's apart-ment 'til Chev finally stopped laughing and said, "Second door on the left."

Throwing him down—Chev instantly glad he hadn't purchased that futon he had been eyeing when he first moved in—Red make quick work of his jeans. Chev remembered it like it had just hap-pened: Red yanking off his pants, tearing down his boxers and whistling as he eyed Chev's long, strong cock pointing just about straight up. Chev remembered Red's eyes as he measured Chev's cock: taking it all in, measuring and panting as he thought about… well, taking it all in. Chev remembered clearly, cleanly, how Red had gotten down on the small bed and kissed Chev's cockhead, tasting the tiny glimmering spot of precome that had slowly formed there.

"Just the thing. I'm feeling a mite peckish," Red had said, licking from the base of Chev's balls to his bobbing, throbbing head.

He remembered it too well. Raul, six months later, had said exactly the same thing, and had licked and tried to suck him—exactly, precisely, *identically,* the same.

But there was a difference. Maybe it took a little time for whatever Red was now to get through completely. Maybe the soil he was buried in had some special quality. Whatever the cause, as Raul got down to it, the sensations, the techniques, the performance was all dearly-departed, dead, Red. It was Red sucking on Chev's cock—with all of his little tricks of tongue and lips and teeth and mouth. But, but, but something added. Red, after all, was dead and buried, rotting on Mount Tamalpais. So it was: Red was sucking on Chev's cock, a Red eaten by insects, covered in mold, bursting with putrefaction and disintegration. Raul's mouth wasn't just an echo—Raul's was the mouth of a man dead for many months.

Insects and their children squirmed around Chev's cock. A tooth, loosened by decay, rattled and abraded against his shaft. The tissues of Raul's tongue seemed to stretch and tear and fall, loose and much too wet around his balls.

Till Chev screamed and he stopped.

Alex was an art nut. His place was little larger than Chev's, but it was so crammed with the graying, 50-plus, ex-architect's collection of sculptures, paintings, mobiles, books, and photographs that it seemed like a museum's closet.

Chev sipped Earl Grey, feeling the warmth of the Picasso mug through his cold and shivering hands.

He imagined Alex saying it just before he actually said it: "You've been under a lot of stress lately. That could be it."

Chev nodded, staring down at his warping reflection in his hot tea. "I don't want him back, Alex." He tried to keep the growing panic out of his voice, hoping dear, sweet Alex would just take it for sadness.

"There's probably a part of you that does. But you made your decision, didn't you? It just has to settle a bit, that's all."

"It's too real."

"It was a very hard decision, wasn't it? Give yourself some credit for how hard it was, Chev."

Alex and Chev's relationship had been a good one, but not all that memorable. Chev liked fire in his men—Alex was more like warm smoke. While a very good, and very kind man, Alex seemed to be always somewhere else. Even in bed there was a part of Alex that always seemed to be in the next room listening to 20s jazz, looking at Post Impressionists, or feeling up a Moore sculpture. Still, Alex was kind and caring and supportive—though from across the room.

Harder than I hope you'll ever know, Alex. The body was heavy and I had to dig down very deep.

Alex knew a lot about what had gone on between Red and Chev, but not all of it. He knew about that night after his birthday party— how Big Red seemed to be just the thing for long and lanky Chev. He knew about the heat, the passion. He knew about the looks they used to give each other and how those looks changed after a point. Alex had helped Chev try to get in touch with what was going on between Red and him, and had even let Chev bunk on his couch when things got too much for him.

But Alex didn't know about that night. The gun. The mountain. He thought that Red had just left.

"He asked you and you couldn't do it," Alex said, sitting next to Chev on the sofa and putting a slightly wrinkled hand on Chev's shaking knee. "It wasn't what you wanted, but you still loved him, right? Think of it this way: if he really loved you he would still be here."

He does love me. He still is here.

"It's natural," Alex said, stroking his leg. "You're having second thoughts. Part of you wants him back and part of you is frightened of having him back—so part of him *is* back."

From Mount Tam and soft soil. "But I don't want him back, Alex."

62

"Sorry." Alex sipped his own tea. "I wish I could make it better. You know, sometimes you just have to go through it to come out the other side. You should just try and let go of the fear, the pain. Tolerate it so you'll know that he's not here, not with you, that he's really gone."

Chev could only nod.

"Remember, I'm here for you"

"I know that, Alex." *So is Red.*

Red hadn't really been a racist, he simply wasn't turned on by black men. It was something they used to laugh over—back when they could laugh together—cruising the crowds coming and going from the Castro: "He's for you," Red would say when a gorgeous black man walked by.

His name was John. He seemed a nice enough guy.

John had been folding sheets down at the Spindizzie Laundromat. Even if Chev wasn't looking for something to take his mind off Red he probably still would have approached John; tall and thin, but with a broad chest and a face composed of soft features pressed on a hard skull. He didn't look like a baby, more like someone without much of life stamped on him.

He was as black as powdered chocolate. Chev hoped, strongly, that he really, truly wasn't Red's type.

John may not have been experienced, but he was certainly enthusiastic. The thin hook Chev laid for him was that Chev had a rare copy of a Billie Holiday album (he didn't, but Alex did). The hook might have been thin, but John tagged right along.

Inside Chev's little place, things got tense. Between John's shyness and Chev's mounting panic over what might happen, all they did for almost an hour was hunt for the mythical record. Finally, after splitting a spit-soaked roach over their failure to locate Ms. Holiday's record, they found themselves dry-humping in the kitchen. There was something powerful about the shy black man, something that, for a moment, was like a wave crashing into and through Chev: he felt John's excitement like a kind of surge in himself, and, despite a tiny voice screaming panic in his ear, soon Chev's cock was screaming for the touch of a hand, a mouth, an asshole—anything!

They stumbled into the bedroom, John whispering a mantra of "beautiful, beautiful, beautiful…" as Chev slipped off his shirt, yanked off his shoes, and dropped his pants.

As John leapt for his cock, Chev pushed him carefully away. "Let me," he said, trying to cling to some kind of control. He had a plan—or hoped he would after John pulled down his pure white boxers and showed off his own lovely, straining cock—no more Mr. Passive. He had been that with Red, he had always been on the receiving end of everything: his ridiculous rules, his demands on his precious time, everything. Maybe if he could turn the other way…break the pattern…escape.

Gently, he pushed John back on the bed and set to work on his cock. John tasted of salty precome, with a gentle background of healthy sweat and a hint of old soap in his course, black, curly pubic hairs. His cock was large and had a beautiful (Chev couldn't help saying it, making John smile) shape to it—a gentle tapering to a smooth, almost pointed, uncircumcised head.

Chev kissed it, licked it's length, tasted the salt again.

Then he put John's cock in his mouth.

It wasn't John's cock anymore

In a flash of heated seconds (ringing of the near-madness of total panic), Chev wasn't tasting thick black skin and salty sweat. He was tasting rot, the foul bitterness of decomposition, and the sickly-sweet smell of corruption. He was sucking on a bloated, dirty-choked worm of a cock, a wrinkled finger oozing puss and insect larva.

He didn't scream. He almost made it to the toilet before throwing up on the chilled tile floors.

At least John was nice. He soothed and calmed the quaking and crying Chev 'til almost dawn—then he had to go to work.

This time the tea tasted like blood. That, or maybe he had bit his mouth or tongue the night before.

Morning. John was a fading memory, and Alex actually looked— ruffled. He made Chev tea and toast with a kind of waking somnambulism that Chev had never seen before. But then he'd never gotten the gray-haired ex-architect up at 6 in the morning before.

"How are you doing?" Alex said, sitting next to him, leaning against him.

"Better." Normally Chev didn't like to be reminded of the more physical past of their relationship. Normally he liked to consider Alex "Just A Friend." Normally he felt a good portion of guilt and self-hatred over his coolness toward his old ex-lover. But, that morning, Alex was something warm, caring, and familiar.

"You need help," Alex said, stifling a yawn and sipping his tea.

"No shit," Chev said, full of grim uselessness and sarcasm.

"You know he's gone."

"Also, no shit." *Can't get more gone than a bullet.*

"Did you see him recently? Maybe that's it?"

Chev shook his head. "He's long gone."

"Do you feel guilty about him leaving?"

I killed him, Alex. I shot him. I put his body in my car and drove him up to the mountains and buried him. "I guess so."

"You have to get over it."

"Don't you think I want to?"

Alex sighed, put his cup down on the floor and put his head on Chev's shoulder. The older man's breath was a warm patch on Chev's chest. "I think you'd like to. I don't know if you can." Absently, Alex started to play with the buttons on Chev's shirt.

It had always been that way between them—the cruel kind of game that ex-lovers play when they need each other too much but have grown apart. Alex pursued and Chev ignored. This time, Chev was simply too tired, too scared. Alex was there, as Alex had been before, would be again and again, to take care of him and try to make things right. This time Chev might just let him.

M. Christian

Chev didn't protest as Alex managed to get his shirt buttons undone. It was like coming home. It was like being a teenager again and necking on the rec-room couch.

"What more do you want?" Red had said when they had shared a couch, too. "Aren't I enough for you?"

"If this upsets you," Alex was saying, as he undid the last button, "please, just say 'no.'"

Lost in the familiarity and the comfort of Alex, Chev did nothing but nod softly, letting his old friend Alex rub is smooth hands up and down Chev's faintly haired chest and over his hardening nipples.

"He's gone, Chev. You just have to face that."

"You're home is here, with me now," Red said with simple words and soft tones. "Don't you want me to be here with you? I thought we might make a home together. Wouldn't you like that?"

"You made your decision. You didn't want him around anymore." Alex deftly undid Chev's belt and slipped his soft cotton pants to the floor. Chev's BVD's were tented with his hard cock—hard from the comfort in Alex's words.

"You don't own me," Chev had said, gripped with panic, confused and feeling trapped, seeing nothing but Red, and ready to chew off his own foot to escape. But he had also wanted no one but Red. But he had also been scared of not being free, of being trapped with the man. No, with any man.

"Relax and just be here with me, now," Alex said, pulling Chev's underwear down and softly stroking his hard, smooth cock.

"I don't want to own you. I love you. I want to be with you—forever, if I could," Red had said.

"It's just me, now. Just old Alex. You know I wouldn't hurt you, Chev." Alex's soft lips bathed his cock in satin skin. Alex's mouth was wet and hot—like a tiny sauna over his straining cock. It felt good. It felt like home. Safe.

"I want to be with you. Why is that so scary? Why are you so angry because I love you? Damm it, Chev, I want to be with you. I want to live with

you, play with you, and grow old with you. Why are you so scared?"

Red used to do exactly the same thing. The same hot mouth. The same bath of steaming saliva and—there—the same scrapes of teeth across Chev's cockhead.

The gun had been heavy in Chev's hand, so solid and firm—not like his thoughts, stabbing at his mind and his body. His gut had ached, his legs had felt cramped. He wanted, he wanted, he wanted—he wanted Red, he wanted out, he wanted to be in love with him always, he wanted to be free. He wanted to stop hurting. He wanted to stop being so panicked and confused.

The one thing he didn't want to do was pull the trigger.

"You have to live with what happened," Alex said, stopping his cock sucking to stare up at Chev with kind eyes. "You didn't want to settle down. He did. He left. You stayed. It's your decision and you have to accept it."

The gun was a small caliber. The shot was perfect. It was late at night and the street was quiet. He was lucky. Down the stairs and into his battered old car and up into the hills. He told anyone who asked that they had fought and Red had left.

Alex licked and sucked his cock again. Tasting the saltiness of his excitement and the strength of him. Red had done exactly the same thing…

"He's gone, Chev. Be here, with me."

…exactly. But then it wasn't exactly the same. It was still Red working his cock, but it was Red under the dirt on top of the mountain. Worms. Dirt. Dust and bones. The same nips and washes of Red's tongue. The same caresses with his cheeks and the gentle pressure of the back of his throat on the head of Chev's cock. Corroding flesh peeling and breaking over his softening cock, maggots wriggling and nibbling at his thin skin, the slick liquid of pus washing down and over him.

Crying and screaming, Chev reached down and pushed and pulled at the sensations, at the unceasing cocksucking of dead and rotting Red.

Somewhere, Alex was saying, "Just relax. It's for your own good."

Chev panicked and pushed and heaved and bucked and tried to get Alex to stop. Chev's scream burned his chest and ripped his throat apart. His panic was hot metal in his arms and his legs. His hands were flying everywhere, trying to get Alex to stop.

Then Alex did stop. Breathing, too. He rolled heavy and empty onto the floor. His eyes were still and quiet. His chest didn't move. His lips were slack and faintly gray.

Chev could still feel his hands around Alex's throat, trying to push Red away—trying to push the all-encompassing love of Red away.

Robot, Chev got up, adjusted himself, and walked out the door.

Luckily, he had enough in his bank account for a ticket. Luckily, he had his passport up to date. Luckily, Chev knew, good picture framers could find work almost anywhere.

Chev lost himself in his panic and the run. In his more lucid moments—half asleep on the trans-Pacific plane, waiting to pass through customs, watching strange television in his first hotel—he allowed himself to actually think. But when his thoughts turned to Alex slowly cooling on the floor, or the feeling of Red, he tried not to do it anymore. *Just doing what I've always done,* he actually thought once—just once—*I'm running away from it all.*

Back home, he knew, things would go on without him. Like he had never really happened. A few rough spots, maybe—like his disappearance, like Alex's death—but he knew it would be like nothing had ever happened before too long. The police never cared. They would chalk it up to what it was: a strangulation accident. Sure, some of his friends would think of him with suspicion or hate. But then others would get the same look. People left suddenly all the time: Thailand, France, New York, and yes, even Australia. Alex was sweet, lovable, Alex—warm and reassuring, kind and gentle, popular and giving. You can't interrogate or blame everyone who'd ever sat on Alex's couch and sipped tea, or anyone who traveled quickly, impulsively.

It was many months before Chev went to a club. First he found work in a place all too similar to his old job. Then he found a room, and then a small apartment. It was many months before he was comfortable going outside and feeling anything like free. Many months before he could be touched without looking for something of dead and decaying Red in it.

Finally, he did it. Finally, he got drunk enough to get picked up by a burly guy named Nick. Nick seemed bound and determined to prove that Aussies could give and get as good as someone from the mecca of San Francisco. Chev actually laughed at his humor and his sparkling smile. He felt light as Nick hauled Chev off to his tiny room, poured a whole tin of Fosters down him, and set to work on what he called "the Australian Crawl"—his one-of-a-kind cock and balls treat.

For a minute, Chev was there in the room with the bawdy Australian. He was there laughing and feeling good again after so much death and the echoes of same. He was free and easy and, while things were hazy with the passing of Alex, he knew that it would all be okay. The Australian was fun, and his cock sucking was nothing, nothing, nothing like Red. Not at all.

The sensations of Nick's one-of-a-kind cock suck filtered through Chev: the tongue work, the teeth touches, the washes of tongue. Nothing like Red.

But perfectly, *exactly*, like poor, dead, Alex.

❧ The Case of the Sapphic Succubus ☙

by Abbe Ireland

It sat on the end of a rocky ledge, an eerie white dot in the distance, briefly visible through pine boughs as Frances Drake veered around a switchback, climbing higher, leaving the desert below. Her four-cylinder rental churned hard to handle the incline to reach that dot—her destination—more recognizable long minutes and several switchbacks later as The Red Rock Inn, a thick-walled, hacienda-style adobe, stark white in pale moonlight. Normally, such slow, labored driving would annoy her. A lot. Frances liked speed. She especially liked driving fast listening to a musical soundtrack dictated by her mood and whatever feelings an environment inspired: a Bach fugue, Delta blues, classic rock, country, whatever. Since she'd hit open desert outside Phoenix, it had been Carlos Nakai—haunting, Native American flute music that matched the splendor of desert formations she'd raced toward earlier in the day, towering rock columns and sheer cliffs glowing fiery red in the last hot rays of summer sun.

Listening to haunting music in broad daylight had been fine, Frances decided, but now, in the dark…Well, considering where she was headed—another Dr. Dekker job—it was starting to have a different, unwelcome effect.

She flicked off the tape and wished her flight had arrived earlier. Starting a job in daylight always made it easier to get a feel for a place before any weirdness started. Weird being the potential of every Dr. Dekker job. Especially *this* Dr. Dekker job.

All Frances's assignments for The Breckenridge Institute—a privately-funded research facility housed in an elegant Colorado mountain manor—were strange, but this one definitely took the prize. Just thinking the words, "sapphic succubus," gave her a peculiar chill. Did such things exist? Succubi like men, historically speaking. So if the old Spanish inn—recently reopened as a women's resort—*was* being disrupted by a female entity that liked women a little too much, this definitely would be the weirdest assignment she'd ever had as a private investigator. *And* as a human being no doubt. Setting herself up as a guinea pig for a demonic dyke, an insatiable lesbian sexpot that hadn't gotten enough in her earthly life…Yup, this would be the strangest experience of her personal as well as professional life. *If* it was true. *If* it wasn't a publicity gimmick contrived by the owner, or a revenge attempt by some disgruntled lover or other enemy. Based on Frances's report, Dr. Dekker would decide if the Inn was worth investigating, worth shipping the Institute's high-tech equipment and research associates to the location to study its paranormal phenomenon.

Working for the Institute wasn't the only work Frances did as sole operator of New World Investigations, but it certainly paid the best. Way best. So well, in fact, that she hadn't worried about finding other jobs since a mutual friend introduced her to Dr. Dekker over two years ago. Except it felt like a scam sometimes. Most claims she checked out proved false. Meaning she got paid for nothing. Yet she did what her client wanted: she acted as a paranormal pointman and got paid for it.

Usually, it didn't bother her—checking out apparitions, peculiar energy disruptions, cold spots, odd smells, inexplicable sounds—if she dove in fast, not thinking much, and got familiar with a place before anything happened. Again, such orientation went better in daylight, which could've happened this time if she'd requested different travel arrangements. Only she'd have had to admit to nerves, and no way was Frances admitting nervousness to Dr. Dekker. Not with the relationship they had.

"This assignment is perfect for you," the doctor had declared the night before, handing Frances a complete travel packet plus two hundred dollars expense money. "Help you get over that she-twit you've been mourning—what—two years now? Or is it longer than that?"

The she-twit Dr. Dekker referred to in her typically cool voice was the fabulous femme, Jill Morrisey, who unfortunately had also proven fabulously unfaithful yet phenomenally difficult to abandon—even after she'd abandoned Frances for a beer heiress.

"I'm not mourning," Frances had countered peevishly, annoyed the subject had come up.

"Well—pouting then."

"Not pouting either."

How in the world, she thought, scowling as the tiny car downshifted again, could anyone pout over legs up-to-here, a thick mane of silky blond hair, luscious, dark brown Bambi eyes—not the innocent fawn kind, the Miss July kind—and a perfectly curved ass that had made Frances's clit hum and grow six inches longer just staring at it. Frances couldn't relate losing all that to the wimpy emotion of pouting.

"Maybe it'll bring you back to the living," the doctor had continued, staring at the clutter covering her massive mahogany desk, shifting paper, growing uncomfortable it seemed. "Just think…a supernatural fuck." She finally raised her eyes to meet Frances's. "If it works we'll have discovered the ultimate in self-help recovery for lovelorn dykes."

Such benign digging happened more and more often whenever Frances and Dr. Dekker met. Otherwise, Andreas Dekker was exactly the kind of woman Frances would be instantly attracted to: tall, smart, sophisticated, European-educated, with a dry, caustic wit. The kind of woman with a crisp, competent, assertive shell masking intense sexual heat. The kind, too, that looked stunning in the simplest attire: white tailored shirts—cuffs rolled, collar open—tucked inside faded blue jeans. By the time Frances woke up enough to notice, however, a wary distance and false coolness had been established.

"You're not saying I *have* to sleep with this...thing. Whatever it is? It's not part of the job, is it?" Frances retaliated, annoyed by the doctor's airy taunting.

The doctor gave her a chilly stare. "No. Of course not. I was being—attempting, I should say—to be facetious. No, it is not part of the job."

A hint of something...anger?...annoyance?...impatience? hung in the air. Frances tried guessing which exactly while vaguely imagining vaulting over the huge desk between them and flat out tackling the damningly inaccessible doctor. Instantly she felt embarrassed by the thought, then annoyed and frustrated knowing she would never do it.

Truth be told, the doctor had, in fact, succeeded in being facetious with her supernatural fuck crack. If Frances hadn't been so prickly. Any comment related to the she-twit could make a conversation go bad quickly. Frances didn't need any reminding about what a long-term horse's ass she'd been. Especially from Andreas Dekker.

"Well, I guess it's time to go try what the doctor ordered," she'd quipped as a parting shot while heading for the office door, thinking possibly she heard a crisp "You do that" before the elegantly carved door closed. Only she wasn't sure, a typical feeling when it came to Dr. Dekker.

Long minutes later, Frances finally reached the gated turnoff to the Inn, where she bumped slowly along a gravel drive bordered on the right by an unscalable cliff wall, and on the left by a spectacular view of tiered rock terraces sparsely dotted with tall green pines and pointy pin oaks. The cliff dropped away to a stunning expanse of desert plain and all was illuminated by an enormous moon, cool white and blue-veined in an ink-black sky.

Parking the car beside three others, Frances stepped outside into still hot, but pleasant, desert air and inhaled deeply the tangy fragrance of juniper. Stretching from the drive and trying to find an end to the cliff wall, she tilted her head way back before finally seeing star-studded night sky. The incredible height made Frances feel very small and somewhat safer. Nothing but lizards or birds could launch an attack from that direction. Not that Frances needed to worry about outside invaders. Unless, of course, the "entity" was being launched from the outside.

The sudden takeoff of a large night bird startled Frances as she leaned into the car trunk to grab her bulging overnight bag. No, outside invaders were not her biggest worry; nerves were.

Pushing open a heavy, antique, wooden door in an arched, white stucco wall, she walked across a charming courtyard. Inside, both the architecture and decor were classic Southwest with viga beams, an earth-toned tiled floor, exposed wood lintels over rounded doors and windows, and a black-slabbed hearth in front of an inviting fireplace that dominated the living room. Frances recognized the slatted wood, mission-style furniture from books she'd studied during her flight. She also recognized pottery decorating the appealing room as Mimbres; the rugs, Navajo; paintings by Georgia O'Keefe; and hammered copper kettles that were…hammered copper kettles.

Since starting to work for Dr. Dekker, Frances had begun studying the history, art, culture, and native plants and animals of wherever she was sent on a job. A defensive, catch-up habit at first—she could admit that now—she'd grown to enjoy the process for its own sake, for the simple pleasure of learning new things, rather than trying to impress someone.

Frances checked in quickly, not wanting information from the owner in case she was involved. Besides, Frances had been briefed by the doctor the night before.

"The entity, if there is one," Dr. Dekker had explained, "appears late at night, rather fetchingly dressed, I'm told. Then proceeds with suggestive and inappropriate behavior. Touching. Fondling. Generally wreaking havoc since it's couples that have rented the room so far."

"What does she, it, look like?"

"That's a source of contention. Everyone has her own description. It's caused some fierce arguments, serious accusations, the like. Not exactly the best reputation for a place trying to establish itself as a romantic getaway. Which means the owner probably isn't responsible. I understand at least one couple broke up for good over the whole thing."

"What happens with a single occupant?"

"Don't know. Nobody wants to volunteer. You'll be the first."

"Is it violent?"

"Not so far. But maybe you can piss her off. Who knows." Dr. Dekker had almost smiled outright delivering that crack.

Yeah, right. Funny. "Very funny," grumbled Frances as she unlocked the door to the last room down a long narrow corridor.

She liked the room the instant she flicked on the light. Soft rays through a leaded shade cast an amber glow throughout a large room with an enormous bed set inside a thick-walled alcove to the right of the door. Beyond that was a charming beehive fireplace with fat, vanilla candles in wrought-iron holders on its mantel, a cozy sitting area and minilibrary, a picture window, and glass doors opening to a patio and private walled-in garden. No wonder it was the most expensive room in the place.

Tossing her purple nylon bag on the bed, she kicked off her sandals, strolled across the cool tile floor, opened the glass doors and entered the tiny garden, lovely in full moonlight with a large mesquite tree in a far corner shading a stuccoed wall seat. The garden consisted of cactus and other desert bushes housed in various sizes and colors of pots, all pleasantly arranged within the textured walls.

Before settling in for the night, Frances conducted a cursory room search looking for odd mirrors, cameras, microphones, unexplained cables or wires. She didn't expect to find anything, but felt more comfortable checking before showering away the sticky feel of travel.

After showering, she slipped into a faded blue, oversized workshirt, pleasantly cool on her wet, runner's body, then brushed her hair back and enjoyed the cold water dripping down her neck. Too bad it wouldn't take long for her short, wavy mop to air-dry. Thick, dark brown strands would then fall over her blue eyes, requiring a head toss, a tuck behind an ear, or a finger sweep—annoying habits, but unavoidable unless she wore a hat, and hats gave her hat hair, an even more annoying glamour death.

Refreshed, she opened a bottle of good Chardonnay, perfectly iced in a thermos-style carrying case she'd had specially made. The case contained two bottles and two wine goblets, one of which she liberally filled with the clean, clear, golden liquid before heading outside, carrying the bottle with her.

By midnight—two hours later—she was relaxed enough, even a little tiddly, to start talking to herself. Out loud. Around 1 o'clock she started pacing, no longer transfixed by the starkly beautiful night view, impatient for something to happen. After opening the second bottle somewhere past 2 A.M., she began singing quietly to herself, waltzing in and out of the garden, sipping demurely from the glass in one hand or slugging from the bottle, whichever hand felt stronger and more inclined to work at the moment. Soon after, she ended up stretched across the bed, leaning on cream-colored pillows piled against a polished mesquite headboard, speaking out loud in a normal, slightly slurred voice.

"OK, you sapphic surge of nocturnal naughtiness. I'm waiting."
Followed by...

"Come on, you ectoplasmic lump of lesbian lust. Come get me, you sapphic sexpot."

Minutes later…

"Hey. You. Demon dyke. Front 'n center."

Ending with…

"All right you cunnilingual craver. Where the hell are ya?"

At which point she slithered down under a delightfully cool, natural cotton sheet, chuckling to herself while watching a ceiling fan spin slowly round and round… and round… and round until she fell pleasantly asleep.

She woke with a start sometime later, amber lamp still glowing, ceiling fan turning, moonlight streaming in bright, radiant shafts through patio doors left open across the room, white lace curtains rippling gently in the softest of late night breezes.

But there were no lace curtains on the doors. There were no curtains anywhere. Still, there was a bare foot stepping from the lacy-white shadows, attached to a long lovely leg that curved around a nude hip and pelvis easing gradually into view, just enough to reveal a silky triangular patch of beckoning black hair.

Instinctively, Frances's body stiffened; her breathing and pulse quickened rapidly as she jerked onto her elbows, mind suddenly clear and racing as the form approached, seductive as hell in moonlight revealing more of a gorgeous nude body inside gently undulating lace: stomach; navel; bare torso; round tits with erect, pink, succubus, suck-you-these nipples below an elegant neck and delicately defined collarbones.

Suddenly, Frances couldn't tell if the adrenaline racing through her body was caused by fear or excitement. It wasn't at all what she'd expected. Even before the fabulously unfaithful Jill, and certainly after, she hadn't been attracted to anyone for a long, long time. Except Dr. Dekker. She'd thought for sure she'd be totally immune to the real or unreal charms of any nighttime spook. She'd thought, too, that if the entity did appear, there'd be something repulsive about it. A chill. An emptiness. An unnatural gleam in the eyes.

But no. The stunning, lace-clad creature that stood at the end of the bed was exactly her type. She even looked vaguely familiar with long, thick black hair, dark, intense eyes, pretty, symmetrical features, and an incredibly sexy body. Definitely familiar. Definitely Frances's type. Definitely attractive. A wave of intense desire coursed through her entire body, ending with an almost-forgotten ache between her legs. The lonesome hole. A humming clit. Firing up, ready to go.

"Goddamn," Frances swore under her breath, swallowing hard over the nervous lump rising in her throat.

One side of the entity's mouth smiled slightly as she began slowly unbuttoning the filmy gown, gently sliding the sheer fabric back until one tit was fully exposed for delicate caressing by long fingertips, circling around and under and around toward the bulls-eye center—an engorged nipple she squeezed and tickled between thumb and forefinger.

Frances stared, entranced, mouth open, dazzled, agog, growing more and more excited, ready to explode, the need to touch and be touched rising exponentially with her body temperature and pulse.

Completing her sexy play with one breast, the entity stopped to glance at Frances, who gasped out loud. For one startling second, the woman looked exactly like Dr. Dekker.

Frances jerked back in bed before realizing what a silly thought that was, then watched gauzy material fold down off the second tit. Both breasts now exposed, the entity let the gown slide off its stunning shoulders as well.

Smiling at Frances, she cupped her breasts, one in each hand, and massaged them lightly, then more firmly, circling harder, palms centered over both nipples until her eyes half-closed and her lips parted. Again, she glanced up to check Frances's reaction. And again, she looked exactly like Andreas Dekker—for a second—causing a shiver to race down Frances's back.

"Like what you see?"

Frances nodded, unable to speak, pleased that the voice didn't sound unnatural. In fact, the voice sounded incredibly like Dr. Dekker as well. At least the way Frances imagined she'd sound if she were being sexy and seductive rather than terminally professional and so enigmatically reserved.

"Good. I'm glad," the entity continued in a whisper, gliding around the bed, moving towards her. "Are you afraid?"

"No," Frances replied in a barely audible whisper.

"Interested?"

"Very."

"Excited?"

"Extremely."

As the woman came closer, Frances saw Andreas Dekker—no doubt about it this time—and almost stopped breathing. It was the most awesome, heart-pounding, breathtaking, clit-throbbing sight she'd ever seen; the most alive and excited she'd felt in forever. Even the she-twit hadn't induced this kind of feeling.

"Don't take that off." Frances blurted suddenly as the woman began unbuttoning more of the lace gown. "I want to touch you through the fabric."

"Touch away," the Dr. Dekker lookalike said.

One last time, Frances was afraid there would be something chilling or repulsive about the woman's body that would ruin the spell. But no. Her skin was warm, smooth, and voluptuous to touch. Frances slid her hands up both thighs, thumbs gliding along leg creases, over hips, curving in at the waist, sliding the lace back over the entity's breasts so she could feel hard nipples pressing through the delicate fabric into the palms of her hands.

And the kiss—nothing strange there either—hot, gentle at first, lips only, growing more intense, mouths opening, breathing faster, tongues searching tongues, gums, teeth, generating more heat until Frances pulled the Andreas lookalike onto the bed and rolled on top of her, still liplocked, turned on beyond reason, feeling an intense urge to lick and suck every bit of body through the lace—

a desire she satisfied until they both moaned with pleasure, and the subtle barrier of fabric gave way to final full naked contact, skin to skin, tits to tits, thighs to mounds, tongues to hot salty necks, nipples, navels, and netherland wonder glands—swollen, juicy, greedy, needy, throbbing—producing explosive convulsions that left Frances soaked and exhausted with a stupid, goofy grin plastered on her pungently-scented, angular face as she fell fast asleep.

Frances woke late next morning, at noon almost. Hot sunshine hitting the shuttered window filtered through cracks and around edges. She had a slight headache and a dull ache in her chest. She was, of course, alone. But still smiling, thinking, *Damn. What an amazing night.* Yet feeling strange, too. A little sad? Confused? Guilty maybe? No. More like embarrassed, she decided, padding barefoot and bare assed to the shower.

Yeah. Definitely embarrassed, she concluded minutes later, pulling on clean shorts, running bra, and sleeveless T-shirt. How the hell was she going to write this report? Even worse, how the hell could she look Andreas Dekker in the face next time they met?

Frances checked out quickly, telling the owner she definitely had something unusual in Room 8 and suggesting she not rent it until Dr. Dekker contacted her. During the drive back to Phoenix she worked out her report in her head, then wrote it on her flight to Colorado. By the time she landed, she'd created a masterpiece of vague nothingness. But it would have to do, no matter the consequences—which came quickly.

"Not much of a report," Dr. Dekker said. "Why is that?"

Frances felt herself bristle. As much time as she'd had to come up with an answer to this exact question, she hadn't thought of a thing. She'd considered trying to continue the joke about supernatural fuck therapy, but decided she probably couldn't pull it off. Not without looking Dr. Dekker in the face, which she had trouble doing. Already she noticed her eyes darting everywhere around the room: at tall panes of sun-drenched windows that formed the far wall; at the huge stone fireplace; at rows and rows of books; at the doctor's two Georgia O'Keefe originals; everywhere except at the frowning woman in front of her.

"There's enough," she replied, heading toward the fireplace, sticking one hand in her jeans pocket and running the fingertips of the other along the mantel edge.

"Enough what? There isn't a single detail in this whole mess. It's pure verbiage. Classic Faulkner. Sound and fury signifying nothing. What the hell happened?"

As if Frances could possibly tell her.

"Something," Frances hedged. "Something worth checking. That's what you wanted to know. That's what I found out."

"You didn't answer my question. What happened down there?"

"She—it—appeared. I saw her."

"And?"

"And what?"

"And what?" Dr. Dekker's voice grew louder with frustration. "What do you think what? What did she look like? What did she do? Details. I want details. I expect details. Like you don't know. Like every other report you've ever written hasn't contained who, what, when, where, why, and how. Maybe you'd like to try again on this one?"

She picked up the report and tossed it onto the desk, glaring at it, then glaring at Frances, who managed a furtive glance before feeling her chest tighten as it always did when someone got angry at her.

"No," she muttered. "That's it. That's my report. You know all you need to know. There's something there."

"I know diddly-squat. Exactly," the doctor practically roared. "That's what I know. What's wrong with you anyway?"

"Nothing."

"Nothing, huh. Right."

A long, uncomfortable silence filled the room. Dr. Dekker stared at Frances who intently examined the toe of her shoe as it traced tiny patterns in the parquet floor.

Suddenly, Frances had a brainstorm, a way out. "Why don't you check it out yourself? Alone. No cameras. No crew."

Dr. Dekker looked puzzled. "I pay you to do that."

"Just go see."

"See what? Why don't you just tell me?"

"Go."

"Oh, for chrissakes. Stop playing games, will you? Tell me."

"No."

"No? Why? What's the big secret anyway? You slept with it? Is that it? Don't tell me you..." The doctor cut her harangue short, leaning back suddenly in her chair, eyes widening, fingertips tapping together. "You did, didn't you?"

Frances didn't answer. Besides the tightness in her chest, she felt a lump rising in her throat.

"My god. You could probably make *The Guinness Book of Records* with that one. If you could prove it."

This was exactly the conversation Frances dreaded. She tried hard not to blush, but felt her face redden as another uncomfortable silence grew longer. Fortunately, Dr. Dekker swiveled sideways and stared at the tall windows overlooking the manor's well-tended backyard. Frances couldn't imagine what she was thinking.

"Well... I guess you took my crack about supernatural therapy seriously," she said finally.

Frances didn't respond. She wished she could bolt. On the other hand, as usual, she didn't want to leave.

"So how was it?" Dr. Dekker snapped, swiveling back around, trying to look calm and amused, in direct contrast to an obvious bite in her voice.

"I told you. See for yourself."

Another staring standoff occurred with Frances quitting first, unable to look at Dr. Dekker without thinking about the night before, without feeling suddenly, alarmingly turned on, plus frustrated, pissed, and embarrassed all at once.

"Fine. Maybe I will."

"Fine. You do that."

"Fine. You still could've written a better report. Been scientific instead of childish. It would've saved us both time."

Frances felt her entire body responding to the rebuke. Anger canceled her embarrassment.

"Fine," she replied tersely, clenching her teeth, tapping fingers on the mantel, glaring at Andreas Dekker glaring at her. "I'll do that next time."

"Good. We have an understanding then."

By the time Frances hit the door, anger had totally overwhelmed her common sense. She couldn't resist a last shot. "Scientific sex. I should've guessed," she sneered, not turning around, slamming the heavy door as best she could to punctuate a comment she instantly regretted.

Three miserable weeks passed before Frances received a call from The Institute. She felt an instant wave of relief, although the secretary calling instead of Dr. Dekker didn't pass unnoticed. Obviously, all was not right, a fact that registered as a queasy knot in the pit of Frances's stomach.

The knot grew larger when she received her briefing in heavily accented English from Maxim Bogdanov, a research transplant from Russia. All was definitely not right between Frances and the doctor.

Heading to her car, Frances's queasy feeling grew to annoyance—their argument hadn't been *that* serious—then upgraded to anger. She spun around and headed back, ready to track down the doctor and confront her, but halfway there her nerves returned. She again headed to her car. This time she got in and fired the Mustang's engine before turning it off and storming back inside.

She tried the office first. No Dr. Dekker there or anywhere else in the research part of the estate. That meant she was hiding in her private apartment on the top floor of the manor's left wing. Damn. Never having been there, Frances wasn't about to burst in uninvited. After all, Dr. Dekker could have company. Or she could be sick.

The more inaccessible her thoughts made Dr. Dekker seem, the more pissed Frances got. She decided to sit in the doctor's office and wait. For as long as it took. Just then, however, she caught a glimpse of the doctor's pretty profile through a window, heading for her car in the parking lot. Frances hurried to a side door to "accidentally" meet her.

It worked perfectly. As the doctor walked through a showy bower of white and purple lilacs, Frances descended onto the same gravel path. Obviously surprised, Dr. Dekker froze.

"Hello," she said crisply, shifting her briefcase to her other hand, seeming flustered.

"Hi."

Frances's intention to demand an explanation, launch an attack— no one was going to treat *her* this way—evaporated.

Dr. Dekker finally broke the impasse. "Look, I have to go." She ducked her head as she passed Frances.

Frances couldn't believe that was it. She spun around, glared daggers at the doctor's retreating back, and shouted, "What's going on? What is this?"

"Nothing," Dr. Dekker replied, not bothering to turn around.

"Bullshit," Frances said, hurrying after her. "Since when do I get passed off to someone else for briefing?"

"Since I was busy."

"Yeah, right," Frances muttered under her breath, stopping on the passenger's side of a shiny black, Mercedes convertible while the doctor fumbled with her key at the driver's door. Trying to make the conversation last, Frances thought to ask, "So, what happened? Did you go down there?"

"We investigated." The key didn't seem to be fitting the hole very easily. "She, it, didn't show."

"Not at all?"

"Not for the cameras."

"So they're renting the room again?"

"No. Look, I'm late for an appointment. I have to go."

It was hard to tell with Dr. Dekker wearing sunglasses, but Frances got the feeling suddenly she wasn't looking at her directly. Strange. No way Frances's stupid comment over three weeks ago had caused a reaction like that. Very strange. So was the uncharacteristic fumbling with the key.

"Why not?" she asked.

"Why not what?"

"Why aren't they renting the room? If nothing—"

"I suggested they use it for another purpose, OK? I really must leave now."

Door finally unlocked, Dr. Dekker slipped quickly inside and started the engine. Frances deliberately walked behind the car so the doctor couldn't leave. Because of summer heat, the doctor had to open her window before the air conditioner cranked high enough.

"Hey. I didn't think our argument was *this* bad," Frances finally blurted, unable to avoid the subject anymore.

"Don't be silly. I told you. I was busy, that's all."

"Then why are you acting so funny?"

"I'm not. I'm late. You're making me later."

"Bullshit. You're avoiding me. Why?"

"You're paranoid. Get a grip."

"Did you go?"

"Where?"

"The Inn?"

"I already told you."

"Off-camera. No crew. You, by yourself?"

The doctor gripped the steering wheel and eased the Mercedes, and Frances, backward.

"I have an appointment. I'm leaving."

"Yes or no. It's a simple question."

"Some other time, Frances."

It was all too weird. And Frances had a feeling if she stopped now, it would get weirder, harder.

"So what's the big secret?" she asked, mimicking the doctor's earlier question to her.

Finally with enough space, the normally ultracontrolled Andreas Dekker kicked it into drive and peeled rubber taking off. Then, just as suddenly, the Mercedes squealed to a stop and roared back.

The doctor glared up at Frances through the open window. "You know, I'm surprised you haven't moved in down there. Taken up permanent residence."

"What do you mean?" Frances asked, totally puzzled.

"Oh, come on. You and the she-twit. Hell, you could screw her every night. From now to eternity. The closest thing to it anyway."

"What? You mean the succubus?"

"Who turns into whatever piece of ass the heart desires. Just another teeny, tiny detail you neglected to tell me."

"*That's* what you're pissed about?"

"No. Having to play juvenile games. Going all the way there to find out something you could've easily told me is what pisses me off. You wasted my time and the Institute's money."

"Hey. I found something. Something you obviously saw yourself. If the damn thing didn't perform for your equipment, that's not my fault."

"No, but I still don't like playing stupid games."

Frances couldn't figure it out. None of the doctor's explanations fit so much anger. It might be annoying to move equipment and have nothing happen, but anger? And so much of it? What the hell happened to Miss Cool, Competent Researcher? Or maybe—it suddenly dawned on Frances—*who* the hell happened to the doctor? An old flame she didn't want resurrected? Or…

On impulse, Frances reached inside the window for the doctor's sunglasses.

"What're you doing?" the doctor demanded, grabbing Frances's hand before she could pull the glasses off.

It was the first contact they'd had since an introductory hand-shake over two years ago. The instant heat and shot of tingling energy that surged up Frances's arm was electrifying. She left her hand where it was, hoping Andreas wouldn't let go.

"Who did you see?" Frances asked, lowering her voice.

"None of your goddamn business." The doctor stared straight ahead, jaw locked.

Frances smiled, adrenaline starting to pump. "I'll tell you my story, if you tell me yours."

"I already know yours. Now let go of my glasses so I can leave."

Frances leaned closer and said firmly, "No, you don't know. You don't know at all."

A sudden turn of the doctor's head left the sunglasses in Frances's hand and uncovered the doctor's stunning dark eyes—staring directly into Frances's.

"What? What did you say?"

Frances grinned as she gazed deeply into the obsidian heat of a simmering volcano. "I said, you show me your succubus. I'll show you mine."

Dr. Dekker leaned hard into her seat and smiled. "Oh, shit," she exclaimed softly, glancing down at their still touching hands hov-ering near her left tit, a situation that made both Frances and the doctor grin—from ear to ear.

❧ Sounds on a Summer Night ❧

by Ted Cornwell

The wind billowed up Lexington Avenue the way it does on the coldest days of winter, thrashing my coat and scarf. I was hurrying toward the entrance to the Chrysler building when a woman passed, equally flummoxed by the wind, walking an aged miniature schnauzer that seemed the spitting image of McDuff, a dog our family had owned while I was growing up. The dog looked up at me as we passed, and, as if in actual recognition, struggled ferociously against its leash to reach me. The woman yanked it back and they disappeared around a corner of the building, the dog still looking back toward me. But dogs will be dogs, and I suppose that dog probably does the same thing to any potential source of affection.

I swirled through the revolving doors into the mercifully warm lobby of the Chrysler building, which I'd never visited. I waited in front of the art deco elevator doors for a lift to the 66th floor, where a $200-a-ticket fund-raiser was being held by a new and little known group in the panoply of organizations formed to fight AIDS, probably an ideological splinter from one of the older groups. I'd received a flyer in the mail and decided to go, largely because it might be my only chance to see the newly refurbished Orion Club, which after many years of dormancy recently had been reopened in the black tie, big band tradition. I also figured it was a chance to meet some new people.

That's the thing I love most about New York—the city's endless capacity to startle you with new faces, new dreams, new possibilities. Perhaps it's why so many of us live alone, single, with our scrapbooks of photos and mementos of old lovers, and our endless recitals of flings that lasted half a summer or so. Why settle down with a man who may be Mr. Right when Mr. Perfect could be lurking just around the next bend in time, waiting to take you in his arms?

At the coat check I had the good fortune to run into Ernie Boyer, an old friend and the manager of one of the largest public pension funds in New York. It was only in the past year or so that I'd reached an income level allowing me to attend events of this nature, and I felt a cozy comfort in being able to finally maneuver, if only once in a while and at the fringes, in the social circles Ernie had moved in for years. I had come to rely upon him as my guide or even chaperon, if you will, from time to time.

I tapped him on the shoulder.

"Ernie, it's so good to see you. I was afraid I wouldn't know anyone here."

"Well, that premonition may be more real than you think. I'm actually on my way out. There's an opening at the Helen Schwartz Gallery that I have to catch."

"No, already? It's only 9 o'clock. Things must just be getting under way here."

"Well, true enough, John. This event still is in its gestation. In fact," he whispered to me, "just poke your head inside. This gala gives new meaning to the phrase 'a thin crowd.' Why don't you join me and come to the opening?"

"Oh, I couldn't just skip this. I've never even been here before.

I have to stay a while. Maybe I'll catch up with you later."

"Very well. All I can say is enjoy the view, because the company isn't much to speak of."

"It'll pick up. It's still early."

"I should hope so, but it doesn't look promising. Anyway, cheerio. I trust I'll see you at my holiday soiree next weekend."

"Yes, of course. You know it's my favorite party of the year."

In what seemed one continuous gesture he buttoned his wool coat and tied the belt with a flourish and kissed me on the cheek and strode to the elevator with the haste of a man perpetually trying to squeeze too many events into one evening. As the elevator door closed, he gave me a sly, comic smile and a wistful wave, as if seeing me off on an ill-advised cruise.

True enough, I entered the ballroom and found a light crowd. A handful of men milling about the open bar, a few men and women surveying the hors d'oeuvres or taking in the view by the window.

Before I went into business, I spent several years as a cub reporter on a small newspaper, and I retained some of the unfortunate cultural habits from that occupational field. Though I'd long ago given up wearing frayed pants and shirts I'd owned since college, I still couldn't resist the sight of free food. I soon held a small plate overflowing with shrimp, dainty crackers topped with brie, a brownie, and several celery sticks to assuage my guilt at eating so much of the stuff that's bad for your heart. As soon as my mouth was full, I realized there was no point in trying to mingle for the moment, and I drifted over to one of the arched windows to take in a spectacular view of Midtown at night, my back to the crowd so that nobody would have to witness my messy eating habits. After all, without Ernie to keep me in line, I was sure to be a little more uncouth than generally acceptable.

When I had finished my first helping I turned and drifted over to one of the candlelit tables to discard my plate. That's when I noticed Anthony Goldman. Wearing a navy blue suit and a thin, burgundy tie that seemed not out of place but strangely daring amid the tuxedos in the room, stood Mr. Goldman, an up and coming novelist. His dark brown, curly hair, longer than I'd remembered it, set off his handsome face. He wore thin, possibly antique, gold frames on his eyeglasses. Though we'd only met once, at a reading he did after his first novel came out, I'd always felt a certain kinship toward him. We'd both grown up in western Pennsylvania, in suburbs of Pittsburgh, and were only three years apart in age. And we'd both gone to the University of Pennsylvania. He was a senior when I was a freshman, some dozen years ago. I had imagined, reading that lyrical and gothic first novel of his, that I'd passed him on campus, or served him fries and soft drinks while working at the campus canteen, or perhaps even seen him in the shower after an intramural soccer game, though of course I had no idea who he was at the time and have no recollection of such an encounter.

But there he was, warming the room with his gaze as he stood with his elbow on the bar. I was ready for a drink myself. Mercifully, the space to the left of him was open. I ordered a vodka tonic.

"You're Tony Goldman, right?" I asked.

"Yes."

"My name is John Fleming. I met you several years ago at the reading you did at the old Books & Company store. I enjoyed your novel a great deal."

"Well, thank you. I do remember you. You're from Pittsburgh. And you're a poet, if I recall?"

"Well, yes, of a sort I am. You've a good memory." It's true, avocationally I'm a poet with a handful of publication credits in the most obscure literary journals in the country. Though I couldn't recall mentioning my interest in poetry, I was flattered he remembered such a thing.

Tony began telling me about a recent trip he'd taken to Eastern Europe, just sort of reeling into the story as if he'd been talking to himself and, now that he had an audience, was happy to share his thoughts about Warsaw, Berlin, and Budapest. I made a mental note to ask about his next book. I'd read in one of the papers, some time ago, that he was working on a second novel, "Sounds on a Summer Night," a title taken from a contemporary painting he admired by an artist whose name escapes me. Next to Tony a thin, tall man, perhaps German or Swiss, turned toward us to join the conversation, though he didn't introduce himself to me. I soon gathered that he'd been on the trip with Tony, because he occasionally corrected or added small details, but said little else. After Tony had recounted most of his itinerary he just stopped talking in the middle of his assessment of Prague, as if thinking something over. I had finished my drink. Another man edged closer to the Swiss or German chap, confiding something in his ear privately. It gave me a chance to whisk Mr. Goldman away from his rather dour companions.

"Would you like to check out the food?" I asked.

"Sure, let's."

He put his hand on my shoulder as if to tell me to lead the way, and we walked over to the buffet, where hot foods recently had been wheeled in, far in excess of the needs of our sparse crowd. We walked along the line, observing the pastas, the carving station with its bulks of ham and turkey, the rolls and salads, and smelling the clam chowder in its cauldron at the end of the line. He said he'd already had dinner and wasn't hungry. The idea of crumbs and chowder dripping onto my tie in his presence stifled my appetite as well.

I led him to a window that offered a spectacular view of Midtown and the great shadow that is Central Park at night. The Empire State Building seemed to preside over the city, aglow with green and red holiday lights. Again, he put his arm on my shoulder, but this time he left it there. I was preparing to ask when his new novel would be published, but the warmth of his arm lulled me into a silent reverie. I couldn't bring myself to say anything. He slid his arm down and gently scratched my back, then he let his arm drop to his side and clasped my hand in his. I turned to scan the room, nobody new had arrived. Those few that were there, including his friends at the bar, paid no attention to us. I squeezed his hand; he squeezed back.

He let go of my hand and raised both of his to my face, caressing my cheeks for a moment, and then running his hands through my hair. He pulled me close and kissed me, gently. Then he embraced me and we kissed again. Our spectacles clanked together. He reached up and removed mine, carefully folding them and setting them down on the window sill. He did the same with his own. There was no longer any use in trying to see if our courtship had attracted any attention.

He slid his arms beneath my unbuttoned tuxedo jacket so that his hands were rubbing my starched shirt. Soon I had put my hands under his jacket, and I could feel his ribs and the swell and shrink of his breathing. He pulled up my shirt—thank God Ernie wasn't there to witness this—and began stroking the bare skin of my back, all the while pushing me back until I leaned against one of the tables. The next thing I knew he practically had me pinned down on the table, I might have screamed out for the pain in my back, but the glorious feel of his body pressed tight against mine and his lips kissing my mouth and then my ears and neck outweighed any sense of hardship. I tingled with the glee of a lottery winner. It seemed the most beautifully erotic moment of my life, save for the heat of the candle centerpiece grazing my neck as he pushed me further down. I feared my hair would catch fire. I pulled my mouth free of his.

"The candle, I'm afraid the candle's going to tip over."

"Oh, my goodness, I didn't even notice. I'm sorry."

He stood back and pulled me up to face him. We stood there holding hands and looking into each others' eyes.

"I can't tell you how much I enjoyed that. What a gift it was," I blurted.

He smiled. "You don't have to thank me."

We stepped back toward the window, holding hands.

"What made you come here tonight?" I asked, immediately sensing it was the wrong question. He just stared out the window for a long while before speaking.

"You go through life, and there are so many things you want to do. And by the time your life is half over, you've only done a quarter of what you wanted. But you always think there's enough time and that you'll do the rest. And you go on."

It seemed an odd bit of musing. He'd already established himself as a young literary star. Granted, that's a quiet, small part of the world's stage, little noticed in the din of celebrity revolving around sports, politics, and show business, but to me he felt like a giant of my generation.

The thin friend of his approached and whispered something in Tony's ear. When he left, Tony turned back to me and held my hand again. "I have to go. I promised some friends I'd go with them to another party."

"I'd love it if we could get together again, for dinner or something," I said, reaching into my wallet for a card, which I handed to him. He didn't say anything at first. He just looked at the card and smiled at me as he put it into his shirt pocket. "I know you're busy, but if you have time. Maybe lunch or dinner sometime?"

He reached up to touch my lips, as if to quiet me. "Someday I want to tell a story to you, my story, though I'm afraid it's long winded and confusing. But then all good stories are."

It puzzled me, but perhaps it meant he really would call. We started to walk back toward the bar.

I hate introductions, and it seems especially ridiculous to be introduced to people on their way out the door, so I stopped before we reached his friends to bid farewell. We kissed gently, and I refrained from begging him to call me. As we hugged, he whispered something to me, perhaps in answer to my earlier question.

"I came here tonight for you. Thank you for sharing this moment with me."

It left me feeling cold and bleak. It seemed an opaque statement, and to auger against the likelihood that he would call. From the exhilaration of making out with him I felt suddenly fallen. My hopes dimmed. It would be a while before I could appreciate our little adventure for just that, and be content with it.

After they—Tony, the thin German, and the third man—had left, I did not stay long myself. My appetite had wilted, and I felt sure that people were discussing our little display of overzealous affection, though the entire crowd consisted of only three small groups of people clustered about tables in that airy ballroom and one woman, an older lady, who stood alone smoking in a corner by herself. Oddly, she waved at me as I was leaving, perhaps in a mocking way, perhaps as a friendly gesture. I couldn't tell which, so I bet on the latter and waved back on my way out.

Outside, the wind accelerated the bitter cold weather again. Strangely, I thought I caught a glimpse of that woman with the schnauzer again, a block ahead of me. They turned a corner, and I didn't get a good view of them. I hurried to catch up, but by the time I got to the corner they had disappeared. Perhaps she lived on the block.

Tony didn't call, not the following day or the next. By the time of Ernie Boyer's party, I'd pretty much given up hope that I'd hear from him. But I was anxious to relate my experiences to Ernie, who is as well connected as anyone I know, and might have something of an inside scoop on Tony Goldman, or at least know someone who did.

Ernie and his lover lived in a brownstone in the west 80s, a beautiful prewar building. They had the top two floors, and had done a fabulous job of taking out walls and rearranging rooms to transform a maze of Victorian cubbyholes into a flowing apartment with peach-colored walls on the lower floor, and a deep blue motif dominating the upper. They had a pleasant street view from the front windows, but the Ernie considered the gem to be the river view from the deck off their bedroom. I had waded through the entire apartment chatting with acquaintances along the way before

I ran into Ernie, on the deck with a handful of guests leaning over the guardrail to appreciate the full spectrum of their view of the Hudson, which in truth could *only* be seen well by leaning over the railing. I joined them.

"In the summer," Ernie explained, "the sun sets and the whole river seems to blaze in oranges and reds. It's a gorgeous sight. We'd like to extend the deck, but I doubt we could get permission."

Ernie's audience was not bearing the cold well, and quickly retreated indoors. I had a moment alone with him. "You'll not believe who I ran into at the Orion Club last Saturday."

"Possibly not, but do tell."

"An author I've always admired. One I've had a secret crush on."

"Who?"

"Anthony Goldman, you know of him, don't you?"

"Yes, I do, and you're right. I don't believe you."

"But it's true. He was there."

"John, Anthony Goldman died last summer. It wasn't him."

I was stunned. It made no sense. Ernie's information is always good, but I felt sure he was confusing Tony with someone else.

"That can't be right, Ernie. He was there. I even spoke with him."

"Well, if you spoke with Anthony Goldman, then the fund-raiser was an even spookier gala than I thought. I know Anthony Goldman's editor at Farrar, Straus and Giroux. He died in Prague last summer. He was traveling and he became sick, probably nothing that couldn't have been dealt with if he'd had the right medical care. But they didn't know what to get him. My understanding is that when he first got sick, his friends tried to talk him into going home, but he wouldn't leave. And then it got worse and he went into some primitive Czech hospital and two days later he was dead. It never would have happened that way here. Anyhow, you were speaking with an imposter."

"But Ernie, you must be thinking of someone else. I know exactly what he looks like. It was him. And anyway, I would think I'd have heard about his death. I read all the papers and—"

"You were in Chicago all of July, as I recall. It happened then. If I'd have known it was of interest, I would have sent you a news clip or something. My understanding is that FSG is trying to work something out with the manuscript for his second novel. But the editor makes it sound like a real risk to even put it out. It's over 700 pages, much of it in draft form, some of it redundant, some of it a stream of consciousness. I'm not sure what they'll do with it."

True, I was in Chicago over much of the summer, overwhelmed by business dealings.

"But he even had friends at the party. I heard one of them call him Tony. It had to be him."

"John, I hope this isn't a joke of some kind. There was nobody at the gala when I left. Only caterers, waiters, and untouched food, and one poor woman who might have been the hostess. I couldn't even bare to go over and try to console her. I know how dreadful it is when you host an event like that and nobody shows up."

"Well there weren't many people, but there were a handful. But I think Tony Goldman came in after I did because I didn't see him at first…"

"John, literally nobody. When I left there was nobody but staff people there and one older woman. And you arrived just as I left."

"You're exaggerating. Perhaps you didn't look around, because there were a half dozen or more people…"

"John, I'm not exaggerating. There was nobody there. Have you been taking something?"

"No, nothing. It really happened. I even, I mean we, Tony Goldman and I, well, I thought it was him. Maybe I was dreaming or something."

Ernie was speechless for just a moment. You could almost hear the gears clicking in his head. If there is one thing I must always credit Ernie with, it's that he always offers wholly practical, clean advice.

"John, I'd suggest you not tell anyone else about the fund-raiser last weekend."

As it happened, Ernie's story checked out. I looked up the news clips electronically. It was covered in most of the gay papers and a few major dailies, but not the Chicago ones, strangely. Without John's knowledge, I've called FSG and talked with the editor. I simply identified myself as an acquaintance of Anthony Goldman, naturally exaggerating the extent of our friendship, and said I'd be interested in helping him try to make sense of Anthony Goldman's intentions on the manuscript. He seemed inclined to take me up on the offer, especially if I could help decipher some of the handwritten margin notes. He promised to call me in a week or two, when he has time to turn his attention to that book again. When he does, I may finally get a glimpse into the long story Tony said he wanted to share with me.

❧ The Course of True Love ❧

by d. g. k. goldberg

Maureen plastered her fish with tartar sauce and anointed her fries with salt. This was to have been their trip to England, Sandy's and hers. She couldn't believe they were no longer together. The thin woman blinked back tears and concentrated on her dinner. Six o'clock in the U.K., Sandy was in her office in Atlanta. Tuesday night. *Does Sandy still play bridge on Tuesdays? Who does she play with?* Maureen sighed. A vacation alone. It seemed that vacations alone weren't all that unusual in the U.K., though. Both of the bed-and-breakfasts she'd stayed at had rooms with single beds. She shook the salt shaker violently to blot out images of a queen-size bed with Sandy in it.

"You must really fancy salt," the young woman with auburn hair said. She was sitting at the table next to Maureen, an open book and a glass of cider before her. She had a lilting, melodic, English voice.

"Excuse me?" Maureen answered, her American accent obvious.

"Oh, you just seemed lost, sitting there drowning your food in salt. I often do things like that when I'm lost in thought. Or is it jet lag?" The English woman had clear green eyes in a round freckled face. A thick barrette enslaved her unruly auburn hair. A bulky cable knit sweater obscured her body.

"Might be jet lag. I don't know," Maureen said. Then, thinking she sounded rather abrupt, she glanced at the woman and added, "Lincoln is beautiful. Do you live here?"

"Actually, I'm only here temporarily. I'm an actress with the Lincoln Shakespeare Company this season; I live just round the corner. I'm on my own just now… I used to have a roommate… but…she moved on… I'm meeting some friends for dinner about nine, but I'm not terribly keen on sitting home alone until then." The woman paused to take a sip of her cider. "Are you on holiday then? On your own?"

"Yes, this is my vacation. I had a friend who was going to come with me but she changed her plans." Maureen stared at her food. She had been half of a couple for years. She didn't know how to interpret the woman's friendliness. Where was all the British reserve she'd heard so much about?

The young woman made a face. "I really resent it when people do that to me. Oh, I nearly forgot, I'm Elspeth, an as-yet-unrecognized dramatic genius." She scrunched her face into a self-mocking, childish smile.

Maureen smiled. "I'm Maureen. English teacher and admirer of theater. We're complementary. You're an actress and I love being an audience." *What am I doing? Am I flirting with her?*

"Hear, hear!" Elspeth said, raising her glass. "The world needs more audience members. So, what's your take on *The Merchant of Venice*?"

The floodgates opened. Sandy, who worked for a high-powered accounting firm, had absolutely hated it when Maureen took off on literature. "It makes me furious when people call that play anti-Semitic. Shakespeare was not anti-Semitic, look at the lines he gave Shylock, *Doth not a Jew bleed*? You know, I have always wondered why so many of Shakespeare's works were set in Italy. There's quite of bit of his life when his whereabouts are unaccounted for. But, anyway, did you ever notice that the dynamics in *Merchant* rest on the two women?"

"Yes!" exclaimed Elspeth. "I would kill to play Portia. Now, that's a woman. Shakespeare was way ahead of his time. But he had Queen Elizabeth on the throne. That had to have enormous impact on his view of women."

Somehow Maureen had devoured most of her dinner. She hadn't had much of an appetite since Sandy and she broke up.

"I'm getting another cider, would you care for one?" Elspeth asked.

Maureen looked regretfully at her watch. "No, I'd better be leaving. I'm planning to take the 'Lincoln Ghost Walking Tour' in a few minutes."

Elspeth looked disappointed. "Well, it was super meeting you. Perhaps we'll meet again. There's nothing I like better than a good chat. Cheers."

"I'd like that." Maureen flushed. "Well…bye." Gathering her things, Maureen moved towards the Tourist Information Office where the tour met. *Stupid! Elspeth was a really interesting woman. Probably straight, probably dates 45 men a week. Stupid. But it was great to just talk to someone. Stupid Ghost Walk. Whoooo! Had to run away, didn't you?*

A small crowd clustered outside the half-timbered building near Lincoln Castle. A trio of women compared notes about other ghost walks they had taken. Evidently it was something they did together regularly. A pudgy woman put her hands into a skinny man's pockets while complaining of the cold. A group of students made plans for where they'd go drinking after the walk. Maureen felt the odd vulnerability of the recently uncoupled.

A pale young man with shoulder-length midnight-black hair walked assertively across the cobblestone square, swinging a gilded cane. His boot heels echoed in the chill night. On his head perched a top hat. He wore a billowing black cloak over his dark vest and trousers. His face seemed as white as his high-necked shirt. A few members of the crowd giggled nervously as he materialized. When they fell silent, he introduced himself.

"I am Ian, I will be your guide on tonight's walking tour of haunted Lincoln. Please be aware that on this particular ghost tour, we do not have the hired help jumping out at you and shrieking or dropping cloths from upstairs windows as do some of our colleagues in other locales. That would be tacky." He daintily mopped his forehead with a handkerchief. "We would like you to be aware that strange things have happened on some of our walks. Should you be sensitive to psychic phenomena, I must caution you: You are standing in the haunted center of England's most haunted town."

With a graceful movement he passed his hat to the crowd for payment and deposited the pounds in his pouch. Then, with a swirl of his cape, he led the eager tourists to the gates of Lincoln Castle. He relayed the story of a horseman foolishly diverted from delivering a pardon that would have prevented the execution of an innocent man. He described sightings of the ghostly horseman as he had appeared through the years, the hooves of his horse click-clattering loudly on the stones. One of the students snickered, "It'd be more likely the poor bastard they hung would come back." Ian quelled the scoffer with a vampiric glance. Next he shepherded them down Steep Hill to reveal the tale of the girlish apparition that disturbed diners in Brown's Pie Shop. "More likely the prices bother them," the pimply student said. Undaunted, Ian directed the group into a back alley where he captivated the crowd with the story of an evasive serial murderer whose footsteps were said to echo through the alley. Before the student could pipe up again, Ian supplied some particularly gruesome details. No heckling this time.

The crowd stopped for a drink at the Lion, and Maureen was surprised to find herself really enjoying the outing. For the first time since Sandy had left, she felt the pall of gloom lift. Carrying a cider from the bar, she approached the three women who seemed to be together and asked if she could join them.

"Why, certainly," said the oldest of the group. "I'm Megan, my mates here are Liz and Corey. Always room for another. Have you done a ghost walk before?"

"No, this is my first," answered Maureen.

One of the tourists was asking Ian questions about the granny-ghost rumored to haunt the Lion. Ian explained that he only mentioned ghosts when he knew stories about them, a simple reported sighting didn't warrant inclusion on his tour.

"We must have done 20 in the past three years," Megan said. "We love them. This bloke's much better than the guys we've seen in York."

Maureen leaned forward to hear over the clatter of glasses and the pong of the Sega machines.

"Near as good as that girlie in Edinburgh," chimed Liz.

"She was brilliant," Megan enthused. "But I have more of a sense here, a sense like…maybe there really is something."

"Oh, you," Corey said, cuffing Megan affectionately, "the American will think we're all nutters."

As Maureen laughed companionably, Ian gathered the group to venture out into the night. "All fortified?" he asked. "Very well then. Onward." Using his cane as a pointer he directed them down the street to the Roman arch.

"The way they're driving though the arch those cars are probably responsible for a whole group of ghosts," the student said.

"I've not lost a tourist yet," Ian said, "but should you perish in the traffic, I would be delighted to encounter you on future tours." The crowd laughed.

At the arch Ian regaled them with a series of sagas about ghosts whose origins were lost in antiquity. The group then moved back up the street, stopping in front of The White Hart Hotel for a mysterious tale of haunting by a highwayman. Finally they reached the front of Lincoln Cathedral.

Ian paused for a moment, looking up appreciatively at the remarkable stone edifice. "Ladies and gentlemen, we are almost at the end of our tour. Almost at the scene of my favorite story—the one I, myself, most fervently hope is in some way true. Before we go any further, though, let's take a second to look at Lincoln

Cathedral, the most glorious gothic structure in England—beacon
to returning fighter pilots during the second World War, and scene
of tragedy, murder, betrayal, and romance." The illuminated spires
piercing the night awed even the rowdy students. Although Maureen had toured the Cathedral during the day, it seemed larger at
night, more magnificent in the stillness. Under the floodlights the
stones seemed to glow golden. A low wind swept a few leaves
around.

*"Oh, bother! John, 'tis that fool and his following again," said a voice
that no one on the tour heard.*

*"Edmund, my beloved…don't fash yourself…he doesn't signify,"
answered John. No one in the crowd heard him either.*

*John and Edmund shimmered in the moonlight. John was a tall,
broad-shouldered man with characteristic Celtic coloring. Edmund was
a slender youth with the fey look of a poet. He had luminous gray eyes
and a Norman nose. Something in Edmund's posture suggested an aris-
tocratic heritage; it had once been common for younger sons to be con-
signed to the church with the same lack of regard for their feelings as
unwilling noble brides experienced.*

*" I just wish someone would get the story right. We're masqued in the
grave as we were hidden in life," Edmund sulked.*

*"Come here, love…give us a kiss…think of other matters," crooned
John.*

*Edmund gave John a quick kiss on the lips, then scampered away from
his lover. "I want to hear the story," he said.*

*John followed. He didn't much care to hear Ian tell the surviving ver-
sion of their tale, he simply followed Edmund. John would always follow
Edmund, for forever and a day.*

The crowd gathered on stone steps at a side entrance to the
magnificent building. Ian motioned for the people to draw closer.
Maureen felt a tremor pass through her body. Suddenly she experienced a remarkable visual acuity. She was aware of each portion
of the lacy carving, saw all the details of design with remarkable
clarity. Her skin surface seemed unusually alive, tingling as each

infinitesimal shift in the wind ruffled the faint hair on her forearms. Her hearing was incredibly sharp; she could discern the laughter of a group on the far side of the street, and she heard the beating of each heart around her. She was energized, somehow more alive than ever before. Her body was electric, all of it glad; it seemed the soles of her feet inside her boots rejoiced in the pressure of the damp stone beneath.

Ian waited imperiously for the tour group to cease coughing and shuffling. He stood on the top step looking down at the crowd.

"God's wounds!" exclaimed Edmund impatiently. "Get on with it."

Ian tightened his grip on his walking stick, a barely perceptible motion. Maureen noticed his knuckles whitening.

"Be patient, my pet," John soothed.

"The original structure of Lincoln Cathedral was completed in 1092. It has been the scene of much divine worship. Yet there is another, darker side to the history of this sacred place. Within these walls there has been murder, insurrection, greed, and revenge. Foul deeds have been as much a part of the history of this Cathedral as the pure, refined, spiritual emotions we equate with such holy places."

Edmund moved close to Ian.

Ian stepped to the side, as if avoiding a chilly draft. "Direct your attention to this sculpture," he said. It was a lovely Madonna and child. The face of the medieval Mary was radiant, all-loving. The arms that cradled the infant seemed archetypal maternal arms; the statue was evocative of eternal peace. "Look on the face of pure love," he said dramatically.

"God's nightgown!" spat Edmund. "What does he know of love?" Edmund had developed an irrational dislike of Ian.

"Not as much as you and I do, sweetling," John said. "Still, my love, methinks there is a reason for our presence this eve."

Edmund brushed through the solid students to lean his head on John's shoulder. John wrapped his arms around Edmund's waist. The curve of his arm was as loving as the stone arms of the statue.

"You are my reason, my love," Edmund sighed. *"You are my reason for being."*

Maureen stared intently at the statue; she was overwhelmed with a need for an answer to a question she could not articulate. She shook her head slightly at the mother and child. The answer was not there.

Ian cleared his throat and began a grim recital. "In the 12th century a sub-Dean named Bromfield was murdered by one of the vicars. On St. John's Day in 1392, one of the Dean's servants killed a man attached to the Treasury; the murder occurred during Vespers. On New Year's Day 1393, again during Vespers, a bell-ringer was killed. Vespers was apparently a dangerous time in centuries past." A few of the students laughed. Ian smiled slightly before continuing. "When Stephen fought his cousin Matilda for the throne, he commandeered the Cathedral as a base to lay siege to Lincoln Castle. The saints took their revenge, for Stephen lost the battle and very nearly his life. But we are not here to talk of war," he said. "I wish to tell you the sad story of a man and a maid."

A cold wind blew around Ian, blasting beneath his cloak.

Undaunted, Ian continued. "The Cloisters are frequented by ghost monks. They drift around in silent procession as they did in life. There are other shades in the eternal ether that remain caught in the passions of this world. The Cathedral was home to a convent of sisters as well as monks. *("Never," said Edmund. But no one heard him.)* In fact, early church history is full of scandalous tales of bishops with bastards, priests with wives. But, I am not here to speak of licentious clergy and loose-moraled nuns. I'll leave that to the tabloid press."

The students snickered; they were on Ian's side now.

"I am here to talk of a love of remarkable purity. Around 1235, when the cloisters were full of devout brothers and the hallways crowded with saintly sisters, a nameless monk cast his eyes across the way and was blinded by the beauty of an unknown sister."

"Bollocks!" fumed Edmund. "Sister?" He stomped his foot.

"Shah, love. Look there, the thin woman standing alone, the one with brown hair." Excitement tinged John's voice.

"Her?" Edmund glanced at Maureen.

"Yes, I think so," John said.

Maureen felt an odd prickling in her legs.

"Daily at prayers the monk would search the crowd for his beloved. Should she glance his way, his heart soared. Should the lady not, he was cast into deep despair."

"That part's true enough," John said.

Edmund giggled boyishly.

Maureen felt something brush her cheek.

"And so it continued—stolen glances, longing, sighs—neither of them willing to profane their love with a word or a touch." Ian paused to let the crowd consider the romance of it all, and to catch his breath. A mist surrounded the crowd. A few people shivered in their anoraks, but Maureen was suffused with warmth. She felt wonderful.

"Profane?" shrieked Edmund. *"If I were alive I'd call him out. Is that how he sees it? Profane? What a vile minstrel he is."*

"Shah, love." said John. *"She's receptive. Oh, sweetling, she'll let us in."*

"She's alone," Edmund whined.

"Courage, dear one."

Icy drizzle began.

"Bishop Grosseteste held the Episcopal Seat at the Cathedral at that time. He was a bitter, self-righteous man. He continually berated his fellow clergy for their lack of spirituality. He was relentless in his quest to purge his community of the taint of any sin." Ian studied the crowd as if he could ferret out the sinners in their midst. All of them save Maureen shivered in the damp.

"Righteous, my buttocks," said John. *"He wanted you for himself."*

"I have always been yours," Edmund whispered.

"And I, yours," murmured John, kissing his sweetheart softly.

"This crusading prig of a Bishop cast his eyes on the lovelorn monk and the fair nun. In his own evil thoughts he manufactured an unholy alliance between the two innocents. Without benefit of ecclesiastical court, he had the monk flayed alive. The good brother would not confess to a sin he had not committed. The Bishop thought women did not have souls. He did not press the maid for her confession. The sister was dragged from the convent in the dead of night and placed in a pit beneath the very stones on which we stand. She was placed in a stone tomb with the battered body of the brother. She died in the darkness. No light. No food. No water. A lingering death."

The crowd gasped.

Edmund quivered; part of the story was true.

Maureen had the briefest illusion of a tear on the Madonna's cheek.

"The story does not end there. For through the centuries, the lovers have been seen on these steps. They reveal themselves only to those who have been injured by false love and are near to finding true love. Look carefully among the shadows as you leave this place. Should you be blessed by a visit from the ghostly lovers, it means your true love is around the corner." Ian bowed slightly as the crowd applauded. Maureen wanted to ask him something; she didn't know what. As the crowd dispersed, Maureen stood alone on the steps. She felt as if the story was not quite finished.

"She'll do nicely," John said.

Edmund nodded. A smile softened his sharp features.

Maureen walked towards Pottersgate. She was only a few minutes from her bed and breakfast. She turned back toward the cathedral to look at it one last time.

"Well, hello!" A cultured voice shook Maureen from her reverie. It was Elspeth.

"Hi," said Maureen, feeling the anxious attraction of a school girl crush. But beneath her nervous energy there was something deeper, something calm.

"There, see, she's not alone anymore," said John.

"Ahhh," sighed Edmund, "how fair they are, how the rain bejewels

their hair, how glorious they look each beside the other." Edmund embraced his lover. *"They are near as fair as we were."*

"Imp," chided John.

"Did you hear something?" both women said simultaneously. Then they giggled nervously.

"Perhaps the wind," Elspeth said. There was an ironic tone to her voice, as if she spoke in inverted commas. "Although, you've been on a ghost walk, any haunts about?"

"No, just you and I." Transfixed, Maureen looked into Elspeth's eyes. The two women stood motionless. Maureen finally said, "Did you meet your friends?"

"Actually, no. I rang them up and canceled…then I sort of followed the walking tour…I just felt compelled to find you…as if I had to see you again." Elspeth looked at Maureen, waiting to see what would happen.

"I am so glad you did," Maureen said. "Have you ever had the sense that something was meant to be?"

"Not before this evening," Elspeth answered.

As the two women walked arm in arm toward Elspeth's house they passed two young men in medieval costumes. The men huddled close, their arms around each other; they walked in unison, as couples do who have been together a very long time. When the pairs passed in the narrow street they exchanged the smiles that happy lovers bestow upon the world. With American impulsiveness, Maureen grinned and said, "Hello."

"Hail and fare-thee-well," Edmund said, as he and John faded into the mist.

So absorbed were they in each other, the women didn't notice that the two men they had passed simply vanished.

✙ The Haunting of Room 110 ✙

by Michael Price Nelson

During the scorching summer of 1993, there had never been so many deaths in the house. Thirty-three. It was a record, that's for sure, and for most of us who worked there, it was an experience we weren't anxious to repeat. We were used to four or five deaths in a month, and to my memory seven was the most number of residents we had ever lost in a single month. But 33 in three months? It weighed heavily on all of us, like an unseen hand pressing down on our hearts, and we wondered if the dying would ever relent. Would we ever be free from this onslaught? Free from death by AIDS? Such was the burden of working at Chris Brownlie Hospice.

The copywriters who wrote our brochures used to wax poetic about our locale. It was "nestled," they liked to say, in verdant Elysian Park, just north of downtown Los Angeles. But I always felt "cradled" was the better word. It reflected more accurately what our staff of 40 did for those who came to spend their last days with us. We cradled them with nursing care, cradled them with attention, and, in a good many instances, cradled them with love.

In the seven years our doors were open, we had become a

national model for residential AIDS hospice care. Eleven hundred people died under our roof, and the place was rife with stories of residents (we never called them patients) who saw mysterious, invisible strangers standing by their beds or in a corner of a room, only to succumb hours later. At staff meetings, our speculation on these experiences ranged from near-death hallucination to angelic visitation. As I recall, we were pretty divided on exactly *what* they were. But if you raised the subject of ghosts, as some did on occasion, almost everyone was willing to concede that, yes, spirits walked among us. After all, there had been multiple deaths in every room, so there had to be specters roaming the hallways, they reasoned.

I was the lone holdout on this point. As assistant director of the facility, I came in close daily contact with residents and their families. I assisted with admittance, maintained daily operation of the office, and closed far too many medical charts with certificates of death. I had never seen any evidence of ghosts under the piles of paper I pushed and wasn't eager to give such tales credence, lest I be put on forced administrative leave for stress. Besides, I had seen too many friends die of AIDS, and none of them had ever come back, hard as I may have wished. In my cold, hard world of file drawers and paper clips, the idea of ghosts was wishful thinking.

However, all of that changed in the summer of 1993, when even I couldn't explain away the unexplainable.

It began with the admittance of Daniel Monihan. Daniel was a 33-year-old white gay male, pretty typical of the AIDS population in those days. The doctors had noted in his chart that he was "unremarkable," but of course they were only speaking medically. He suffered with toxoplasmosis, CMV, wasting syndrome, neuropathy, thrush, and a panoply of other diseases that made you wonder how he got this far. In better, healthier days, Daniel had been a struggling artist who had just begun to find success in the Los Angeles art world when CMV cruelly intervened to rob him of his vision. In recent months, he had been cared for at home by his lover of 15 years, Patrick Moreno, until they decided together that the time had come for hospice care.

Daniel was admitted the first day of June, and despite the oppressive 90-degree heat, he refused a wheelchair and walked in with Patrick's help. I was the first to greet him, and he shook my hand warmly. Although he was wasting quickly, you could tell from his lanky frame and deep, seductive voice that he had been a gorgeous hunk of man. His sunken brown eyes still had a warm, sexy twinkle, and his gaunt smile flashed blinding white when he smiled at me. In our first conversation, I realized he would be one of those residents the staff quickly fell in love with because of his winning sense of humor and singular sense of purpose. He told me he knew why he had come to Chris Brownlie, and was there to do it as cheerfully and peacefully as possible. This said, I led him to room 110, which was to be his home until the end arrived.

Patrick, in contrast, was the picture of health. Tall with rugged features, dark stubble, piercing blue eyes, and a muscular frame highlighted by a tight white T-shirt, his devotion to Daniel was evident from that first day. In the coming weeks, with Patrick always lovingly by his side, Daniel settled into a regimen of care that offered a sense of independence and normalcy to his daily life. Unlike hospitals, hospice allowed him to go to dinner with friends, to a movie with Patrick, or even on a shopping spree.

Once, having just returned from a department store, he insisted on proudly modeling a new silk bathrobe for me. Patrick dutifully helped him into it, and Daniel walked an imaginary runway past my desk. When I asked where he'd purchased it, he flashed his blazing smile and paraphrased a popular store slogan. "I do all my shopping at Shroud's!" I winced at his gallows humor, which only made him laugh all the louder. Like I said, he knew what he was there for.

During those warm, fleeting June days, Daniel finalized his will, put his business affairs in order, sold a few last paintings, then invited a stream of friends and family into room 110 to say his good-byes. He did it with such aplomb that the entire staff marveled at him. But we could also tell the toll it was taking on Patrick, and our social service staff did what they could to give him emotional support throughout the process.

In his fifth and final week with us, I realized I hadn't seen either of them for several days, and when I inquired after Daniel in "morning report," I was told he was now completely bedridden. The nurses were doing all they could to keep him comfortable until the inevitable happened.

One of my duties, aside from paperwork, was to assist residents with their finances. This included storing valuables in our safe, so it wasn't unusual that that afternoon Daniel should ring my desk and ask me to come to his room. Patrick had gone home to get some well-deserved rest.

As I entered, I recognized all too well "the look." His skin was ashen, the weary eyes had sunk deep in their sockets, and his furrowed brow was etched with lines of worry. A sheet covered his near-skeletal frame. A bony foot protruded, and I pulled the sheet over it. He managed a faint smile.

"Thanks, Michael, " he whispered. "Sit down. I want to tell you something." I moved to pull up a chair. "No, here. By me. Please."

I gingerly sat on the edge of the bed so I wouldn't jostle him. Experience had taught me that at this delicate stage, even a handshake could cause a resident to wince with pain.

"Do you have your book with you?"

He was referring to my "bank book," a binder that listed each resident's belongings. "Yes. Right here." I read off the belongings he had stored in our safe: a hundred dollars cash, a watch, a wallet with credit cards, six postage stamps, a single key.

When I came to the key, he cut in. "That's it. The key. It's to a storage locker. There's a painting there I want the hospice to have. It will look wonderful in the living room."

I smiled. *What is it about gay men,* I thought. *Here he is dying and he's still decorating.*

"Tell Patrick," he continued. "He'll bring it to you."

"That's very generous of you, Daniel." I held his hand. It was cold as ice.

"Do you see those flames in the corner?"

Up till now, he had never shown signs of dementia, nor had I noticed any mention of it in his medical chart. But in his condition, it would not be uncommon for him to imagine things. "No, Daniel. There's no fire. I think your eyes are playing tricks on you, that's all."

"I love Patrick, you know. I'm going to wait. I hope you won't mind."

"Do you want me to call him for you?"

Without answering, he closed his eyes and in moments was asleep. I sat silently by him for a few minutes, trying to imagine what he must have looked like when he was healthier. AIDS has a way of transfiguring a person's face beyond all recognition. But in my experience with the terminally ill, I had learned that disease seldom ravages the spirit. Instead, the true inner essence of a person is magnified. And Daniel was no exception. To me, he was beautiful.

Suddenly, I noticed a shift in his breathing. It had become shallower, more rhythmic. "Daniel? Daniel?" No response. I pushed the call light to summon a nurse.

Carmen, a cheerful nursing assistant, entered. "Hi, Michael. What's up?"

I indicated Daniel with a nod of my head. She checked his vital signs. "Poor baby. It's starting." That was hospice-speak for "it's ending." Daniel had begun the process of what we called "active dying," which usually began with shallow breathing. The breath would gradually slow, and the extremities would grow colder and colder till the body finally gave up. It could take hours, even days. The medical staff called it "chain stoking."

I drove home that night knowing that Daniel was finally on his way. He was doing what he had come to do. I hoped it would go quickly for him.

Returning the next morning, I found a census report waiting on my desk. My eye caught the words, "Daniel Monihan. Expired at 0400." *So it is over at last,* I thought. I'd miss him.

"Michael?"

I looked up to see Patrick. He had waited for me to collect Daniel's things. I said all the comforting things that could be said, but of course, Patrick was exhausted and I don't think he really heard them. We sat down in the conference room where I removed Daniel's belonging from the safe and ticked them off out of my "bank book" for Patrick.

As Patrick signed a receipt, I remembered my last conversation with Daniel. "I'm not sure what you want to do about this," I began, "but Daniel mentioned that he had something in a locker that he wanted to donate to the hospice."

"Yeah, he told me. I'll take care of it." His mood was testy. And why not—he had just lost his life-partner.

"Whatever you want to do is fine with us. Take your time."

Not long after we said our good-bye, Virginia, the charge nurse, appeared at my cubicle with Daniel's chart. It was my job to archive medical records for the deceased. I flipped to see that all the proper forms had been included. Notification of Death, Permission for Removal of Body, Final Doctor's Note. They were all there. But something caught my eye in the last nursing entry: "Resident regained consciousness at 1:25 A.M. Saw flames in corner, but nothing there. Patrick and friends by his side. Time of death, 4 A.M."

Poor Daniel, I thought. *He hallucinated to the end.* I filed the chart and thought no more of this last entry until two weeks later, when I began to suspect the haunting of room 110.

It began innocently enough the very next month—July—as Arthur Pomeroy, the charge nurse on the night shift, made his midnight rounds. I must first explain that a hospice differs from a hospital in that there is no limitation to visiting hours. Families or friends may come at any time of the day or night. At least that's the way we ran things at Chris Brownlie Hospice. And because we were in Los Angeles where security is always a concern, the doors were always locked at midnight.

On this particular July evening, two of our newer residents had died, which meant an unusually busy night for the nursing staff. Nurse Pomeroy had just locked the doors for the night and was running back upstairs to the nurses' station when he caught a glimpse of something in the first floor hallway. It was outside room 110.

"It was definitely a dark figure. A shadow," he later told me, "right outside the door. I saw it out of the corner of my eye, but when I turned to look directly at it, it disappeared. I froze for a moment, and then went toward room 110 to look around. There was no one there."

But following a "gut feeling," he decided to check on the resident inside, who had occupied the room since Daniel's death. Her name was Monica, a Latina transsexual. She was a fast-talking, colorful character who had brought a lot of life to the hospice. Monica loved to dress for dinner and had an endless array of evening gowns from which to choose. She ate a hearty evening meal, flirted with every man in sight, then returned to her room around 8 P.M. to watch a *Dynasty* rerun. (She said she loved the clothes.) But when Nurse Pomeroy entered room 110 at midnight, after seeing the "dark figure," he found Monica unconscious on the floor. She died later that night.

When I heard the story of the "shadow" outside room 110, I chalked it up to the twin demons of overwork and an overactive imagination. After all, there had been three deaths that night, and two more just days before. But at week's end, when Monica's chart was sent to me, I noticed the following in the last nurse's entry: "Resident regained consciousness briefly at 2:30 P.M. Said she saw flames in the corner. Nothing there."

Flames in the corner—just like Daniel! My mind reeled. To my knowledge, Monica hadn't known Daniel or any of his friends, and I had never mentioned his seeing flames to anyone on staff, let alone a resident. Quietly, I began to have conversations with the nursing staff. I questioned them about the flames, asking if anyone else had ever reported a similar phenomenon.

"Funny you should mention that," said Ginny Knight, a nursing assistant on the 3:30 to midnight shift. "Remember that guy who was in room 110 just before Daniel Monihan was admitted? Dale something or other. Ericson, that's it. Well, the day he died, he talked about a fire in the corner too. I figured it was his dementia. I made a note of it in his chart."

I flew to my computer, looked up Dale Ericson's medical number, and went immediately to the file where I stored medical charts. Sure enough, on the night he died Ginny noted his comment about "fire in the corner" in his medical chart. Now I had documentation of three separate residents who had seen the phantom flames in room 110. And it also indicated that the haunting, if that's what it was, had begun long before Daniel died. I studied Dale's chart, but found no other hints of unusual occurrences, nor any hint as to why he, or any of the others, might see flames as they lay dying. It was curious that in all three instances, the flames appeared as death approached. What could it mean?

After that, I decided to keep an ear open for any mention of flames from the next resident who was admitted to room 110. The sad fact of the matter was our beds were never empty for long, and within hours, Jimmy Gleason, a good-looking African-American, was admitted into Monica and Daniel's former room.

Jimmy, 23, had hoped to attend law school until illness struck and derailed his plans, as well as his life. After an initial bout of depression, he came to terms with his fate and eventually settled into hospice life. Friends visited, and occasionally he went out to dinner or a movie, courtesy of one of our volunteers. He made every effort to enjoy whatever time he had left.

One summer morning, he stopped by my desk in the front office to make a complaint. "Michael, you got to do something about that guy. He keeps sitting in my room at night."

I had no idea what he was talking about. "What guy?"

"The white dude. Says his name is Daniel. Twice I woke up this week and he was just sitting in the chair staring at me."

I checked the resident room roster. There was no one named Daniel, so it couldn't have been a resident who wandered into his room.

"I'll tell you what. Next time you see him, put on your call light. When a nurse comes, I'm sure they'll be glad to ask him to leave."

I could tell he wasn't particularly satisfied with this, but it was the best I could offer. He padded out of the office, and I thought little more about it—till the next morning.

Nurse Pomeroy had left a note on my desk: "Michael, please call me at home. Arthur." I picked up the phone and dialed. He answered sleepily.

"You won't believe this. I had the weirdest experience," he began. "I was going around at midnight locking the outside doors the way I usually do. I thought all the visitors were out of the building when I noticed this guy sitting with Jimmy in room 110. Jimmy was sound asleep. Anyway, I went upstairs and told the med nurse that I had thought all the visitors were gone and had been startled by this guy with Jimmy. But the med nurse said she'd just been in there and that Jimmy was alone. I hightailed it back down there and Jimmy was all alone. The guy was gone!"

"Maybe he just left," I suggested.

"How? I double-locked all the exits. I'm the only one with the key. He'd need me to let him out."

"What did he look like?"

"You won't like this…"

"Arthur!"

"Well, of course, I never saw him when he was well, but he looked a lot like…Daniel Monihan. Not sick, though. Healthy looking, with weight on him and everything."

I thanked him and hung up. Daniel's last words came back to me.

"I'm going to wait. I hope you won't mind."

Was Daniel waiting now, even in death? And if so, for what?

I shrugged off these thoughts. There had to be a logical explanation. Jimmy's mysterious visitor must have left the building some other way that Arthur didn't know about. I filled out an incident report and filed it away in my desk. So much for that.

Life went on. So did death. Throughout the summer, we lost a phenomenal number of residents, among them Jimmy. He died peacefully in his sleep, in the same bed as Daniel and Monica before him. He never again mentioned the man sitting in his room, nor did he report flames in the corner. Once again, room 110 sat empty, awaiting its next guest.

I closed the room for painting and repairs. In those days, before the miracle of protease inhibitors, we didn't like losing a bed when the demand was so high. But maintenance was important if we were to keep the place livable and attractive for future residents. It was a never-ending task. And I must confess that secretly, I harbored a hope that a coat of fresh paint and new furniture might exorcise whatever entity had made this room its home.

Within a few days time, the room looked better than new. I ordered new window treatments and commandeered a new lamp and bedside table from the thrift store that supported the hospice. Finally, I received a phone call from Cesar, our admissions officer. A new resident was on the way.

Cesar explained that although the newcomer had had his choice of several rooms (with so much death that summer, we had lots of beds to choose from) he had specifically requested room 110. When I received our new arrival's paperwork over the fax, I understood why. The name on the face sheet was Patrick Moreno.

According to Cesar, Patrick was seriously ill, and rather than a prolonged fight, he had chosen hospice care. He wanted to be in room 110 to feel closer to Daniel.

It was an emotional moment for the entire staff when Patrick arrived by ambulance on a sweltering August afternoon. Several of the nurses wiped tears from their eyes when they saw his disease-wracked body. Daniel's loss had seriously impacted his health. He had dropped 40 pounds from his burly frame, and the purple lesions of Kaposi's sarcoma spotted his neck, chest, and arms. He smiled feebly as the paramedics wheeled him to room 110.

In the two weeks he was with us, I can honestly say Patrick received as much love and attention as we ever lavished on anybody. We remembered how faithful and caring he had been to Daniel, and it inspired us in kind. He declined quickly, however, and it was difficult to watch.

At the end of his first week, I received a phone call at home in the middle of the night. That rarely happened except in emergencies. It was the charge nurse.

"What's wrong, Ila?" I asked.

"I'm sorry to bother you, but I just heard something funny. I...I can't explain it."

"What was it?"

A pause. Then she said, "A horse."

"You mean, like, with hooves and the whole bit?"

"No, just a whinny. I was leaving room 110 when I heard it in the living room. At first I thought it was the TV, but the set was off."

"Maybe it was a TV in one of the other rooms?"

"I checked. They were all off. Everyone was asleep."

"Anyone else hear it?"

"No."

Obviously, I needed to talk to her about vacation. "It was probably just the wind, Ila. Don't worry about it."

"Well, I just wanted you to know."

On my desk the next morning, I found a note from Ila apologizing for waking me. I put the incident out of my mind till a few days later when Mrs. Cummings, the mother of a resident in room 114, stopped by my desk.

"I hate to bother you with this," she began. "But the funniest thing happened last night. I was in the kitchenette off the living room pouring myself a cup of coffee. It must have been 3 A.M. or so. Anyway, I heard—this is so silly—I heard—"

"A horse?"

"How did you know?"

"A lucky guess. Actually, one of the nurses reported the same thing to me a few nights ago. It gets windy on top of this hill. I'm sure that's all it is, but thanks for telling me."

Contented with this explanation, she thanked me and returned to her son's room. Flames, shadows, and now horses. *What's going on here?* I wondered. But there were no answers. No easy ones. Not yet, anyway.

Patrick Moreno died that same afternoon. Although his death was not unexpected, it was sudden. One of the nurses was changing his sheets, and he simply laid back, gave a last breath, and died. It was very peaceful.

I watched silently from an office window as Patrick's body was removed by the mortuary several hours later. The black body bag was lifted from a gurney and slipped unobtrusively into a white, unmarked van which drove quietly down the driveway and out of sight.

"I love Patrick, you know. I'm going to wait. I hope you won't mind."

So that's what Daniel was waiting for, I thought. *For Patrick, to join him.*

Two days later a pickup pulled into the parking lot, and two dark, muscular men with earrings and tattoos bounded into my office.

"You Michael?" one of them asked. When I answered in the affirmative, they smiled and offered firm handshakes. "We're Tim and Howard, friends of Patrick and Daniel's. We've been breaking up their apartment and have something for the hospice. It's from a storage locker. Patrick left instructions to deliver to you after he was gone. Mind if we bring it in?"

In short order, they hauled in an object covered with a canvas tarp. It was at least four feet wide by six feet long. The picture Daniel had mentioned to me at the beginning of the summer! I had forgotten all about it.

Carrying it to the living room, they moved to the north wall. "I think this is the wall Daniel had in mind," said the hunkier one as they sat the long frame on the floor.

"You'll love it. The colors are perfect for this room."

With that, they pulled back the canvas and unveiled a beautiful painting in mellow tones of gray, earthy reds, and rich purples. A magnificent stallion moved across the canvas in various stages of full gallop, nostrils flaring, tail flying, intense black eyes staring forward, ever forward. It was a striking testimony to Daniel's exquisite artistry with a paintbrush. Everyone said so, and it was, as Daniel predicted, perfect for the room.

But it brought to my mind the ghostly whinnies that had been reported to me earlier in the week. Were they, in the final analysis, a harbinger of Patrick's sudden passing? Were they a sign from Daniel that his last wish was about to be fulfilled? Had Death arrived on a magnificent steed such as this and swept Patrick away to be with his beloved Daniel?

As the searing heat of August gave way to an unseasonable September cooling trend, the dying at the hospice mercifully slowed. For three blessed weeks, there was not a single death, and it was as refreshing to us as a cool spring rain. After a dry summer of unrelenting death, we finally had the chance to catch our collective breath.

To the best of my knowledge, after Daniel's painting was hung in the living room, the eerie occurrences in room 110 came to an end. At least no more were reported to me, and I always felt in my bones that the ending to Daniel and Patrick's story had a lot to do with that. They were together again and at peace.

"I love Patrick, you know…"

In my years at the hospice, I learned much about the nature of life and death. How we live and love surely affects the quality of our dying, and, conversely, how we die affects the quality of our living and loving. In ignorance, we may dismiss mystical encounters as commonplace occurrences, but we should not dismiss as commonplace our encounters with the mystical. For me, room 110 at the hospice will always represent one of those encounters, for it was there that Daniel waited for Patrick with a love that transcended death.

❧ Through the Eyes of the Artist ❧

by Barbara J. Webb

My heart skipped a beat as I saw his face through the Technicolor smoke of the bar. Understand I use that only as an expression. It's amazing, really, how many expressions don't carry over well, how many day-to-day phrases become pale and meaningless when you move from one world to the next.

My beautiful Nathan. I should have known when I ended up in this bar that he would be here. Tonight he hardly looked different than any other night, sitting hunched over the bar, seeming somehow set apart from the smothering closeness of the twisting mass of people. Black hair—obviously redyed since last time—framed a too-thin face and dark soulful eyes that seemed to absorb all the pains of the world. Pale, eloquent fingers gripped a glass of beer as though it were the only thing anchoring his ethereal form to this earth. This evening, a ragged black T-shirt and jeans at least two sizes too large tented over his wiry frame—very much in style, I know, but they only accentuated his delicacy, his fragility.

To me, he seemed to glow—one ray of sweet purity in the hungry shadows of the bar.

For a while I was content to sit and watch him. He hadn't noticed me quite yet—his entire attention was focused on the way the dark beer sitting before him swallowed the pulsing green light of the bar. At this moment, I only wanted to savor the night, the anticipation. There was no hurry; he would not leave this place without me. For now, I teased myself with thoughts of my Nathan and what the evening would bring.

I don't know if he ever left with anyone else on those nights when I wasn't here, if jealous eyes watched me from the recesses of the throbbing room. Perhaps he went to a different bar, a different part of the city, to the arms of a different man. Or maybe he stayed home, desperately alone, pouring his agonized vision into the paintings by which he made his living. Even now, all I know is that whenever we met, it was in this tight, smoky room in the dark basement of the city. Whenever he needed me, I was here to greet him. Such was my nature, and thus was the way of things.

Growing tired of this game, I slid from my bar stool and walked slowly over to him, moving easily through the pressing bodies to stand right behind his shoulder. Gently, I reached out to touch his hair, running a lock of it through my fingers. "No more blond?"

He started, jerking his head away. Then, as he saw me, he relaxed, pulling a bit of hair away from his cheek to look at it. "I got tired of having my roots show through so badly." His face broke into a shy smile, making him look very young and very vulnerable in the murky gloom of this place. "Hi, Evan."

"You shouldn't drink by yourself." Our ritual. It was the way I had opened the conversation that first night when I'd seen him sitting all alone. Every night since, our dialogue began the same way; the difference came in the path it chose to travel from that point.

"Maybe I like being by myself." His pattern response. I hadn't believed the words then and I certainly didn't believe them now. The first time we'd gone through this I argued with him, talking him down from his ledge of solitude. Now I only leaned in and kissed him.

His response was hesitant, reserved. He saved his true fire for more private moments. Here he doled it out carefully, like a precious but limited resource, but I knew the truth to be otherwise. Later, behind closed doors, his passion would flood over me until I was drowning. For now, only the slight tremor of his lips against mine betrayed the deep river of feeling that lay hidden beneath his cool exterior.

"Come home with me, Evan." Tonight, there was no preamble to the plea whispered against my cheek, no pretense that we would not end up locked closely together against the power dawn held to separate us. Tonight, it seemed, Nathan needed me more than ever.

He was silent on the brief subway ride to his cramped apartment. Something had happened today—someone had hurt him. It seemed inconceivable that anyone could want to bring pain to my lovely one, but I could almost see the fresh scar on his soul.

The door was barely locked behind us when Nathan turned to me, running his hands under my shirt, locking his mouth over mine. I let him ravish me with desperate kisses, eager to give whatever he needed.

We made it into his bedroom and collapsed as one tangled entity onto the paint-stained bedspread. Everything he asked, demanded, I provided until finally we lay wrapped together, sweaty and sated.

Now he seemed inclined to talk, as I adjusted his head to a more comfortable place on my shoulder. "The gallery closed my show two weeks early." His voice was soft, full of shame and despair as he buried his face against my chest. I ran gentle, massaging fingers down his spine, trying to soothe away the sadness. "They said it wasn't enough of a draw to warrant its continuation."

"I'm so sorry. I know how much that show meant to you." Yes, I could remember the last night we had spent together, nearly three weeks ago, when he had spoken triumphantly of how this art show would mark the beginning of his life. He had spoken for hours of his dreams and ambitions, his words painting an image of a bright and glorious future. And now, it seemed, those dreams were shattered. "Surely there's another gallery you can go to—someplace where they'll recognize your art for what it is."

Angrily, he shook his head, striking my chest with a tightly clenched fist. "No, they were right! My work lacks something. Somehow, it needs more. I can feel it, but I just can't translate—I can't quite see. I can't put it on the canvas."

I had always found Nathan's art as compelling as Nathan himself, ephemeral, beautiful. If only the rest of the world—if only Nathan himself—could perceive it as I did, he would never lack an audience. If only they could all observe Nathan and his work through my eyes. "What are you going to do?"

A deep sigh traveled through the entire length of his body as it lay against mine. "I don't know. Tonight, I don't even want to think about it."

Cradling his shoulders in my arms, I rocked him gently to sleep. He clung to me as he slumbered, his fingers curled around my arm, his head pillowed on my chest. I held him like that all night, until the first red aura of dawn began to brighten the room. And then, slowly, I dematerialized into the light.

I don't know why some of us come back as we do—why death is unable to pull us completely into her country. In my time, I have never met more than a few others of my kind. We are never able to talk to each other for long, but the stories are always the same: although we still walk among the living, we are no longer of them. We are shadows, shaped by people's needs, mirrors of their deepest desires, images created by their fantasies. We are only real because they perceive us to be, only alive because they believe us to be.

But from sundown to sunup, we are real. I have shape and substance, can still feel pain and pleasure. A juicy rare steak still tastes heavenly, and too many bourbons still make me talk too loudly and stumble over bar stools. The only difference now is that I never have to worry about gaining weight or waking up with a hangover; I never have bruised shins or baggy eyes. No doubt for some, an ideal existence.

I can't remember much of Before. I think I may have been a computer programmer or something similar—occasional flashes of sterile rooms filled with gray cubicles and people dressed in drab identical suits are the best I can do when trying to recall my life. Not that I try very often. I do remember dying: a screech of tires, the horrible impact of the car I had not looked for, the bitter smells of blood and oil as my life drained away onto the pavement. I suspect I was dead before the ambulance arrived.

Then, for a while, nothingness—until I woke up lounging at a table in a small, sleazy nightclub. A man was sitting across from me, talking, and I could sense his loneliness, his desperate need of someone to be near him that night. We had spent hours talking, then later I had been powerless to resist his invitation, to come home with him—not that I had at all wanted to. In the morning, at first light, I had felt my body slipping back into nothingness until the sun set once more and I found myself in a different bar with a different man.

Every night, it went on like that. As soon as I awoke, I knew who I was there for—who needed me. Every evening a new face, a new life I touched, a new soul I helped to heal just a little bit. Most were hurting; all were lonely. I suspect more than a few have been close to suicide. But I brought them a moment of hope, of warmth, hopefully reminding them of the good that still existed in the world. I never saw the same man twice—not until Nathan.

He had seemed different from the very first. Always before, they had been actively seeking company, responding eagerly to me. And why not, when I was little more than a phantasm called and remade by the strength of their desire? But Nathan had tried to shut me out, insisted he needed no one's company, turned me away. That first night it had taken hours to break through his barriers to the point that he could admit he was lonely. Once removed, however, the walls had released a flood of sharing that had lasted nearly till dawn. I had never been more loathe to see the sun slip over the horizon as when I had felt myself leaving the warm circle of his arms.

I had tried, unsuccessfully, to put him from my mind. Surely, I told myself, there would be others I would meet along the way who would touch me as Nathan had. It was something I was just going to have to get used to.

But that didn't make it any easier.

Not ten days later, I was back in the same bar, looking once again at Nathan's angelic face. He had seemed as surprised as I at my presence, but it hadn't taken nearly so long to convince him to take me home. Again, we talked nearly till dawn, his warm breath tickling the hair that fell down over my neck. And again, in the morning, I was gone.

Nights filled with strangers came and went, but miraculously fate kept bringing me back to Nathan. I'm not sure what made him so unique—if his need was just that much greater, or if there was some other, deeper connections between us. I only knew that I grew to need his presence as much as he seemed to need mine.

Neither of us ever asked what the other did in our time apart. He never asked for my phone number or questioned the fact that I was never there when he awoke. I never asked if the faces I saw scattered around his apartment, captured in oils and canvas, were friends, family, other lovers. The time we spent together seemed magical somehow, as though time outside our meetings didn't exist. He told me of his paintings, his childhood. We spoke of current events, of movies, of books I could barely remember reading. Our topics ranged from the profound to the playful, from the morality of truth to whether Mel Gibson or David Duchovny would be a better Batman. In all honesty, for the most part he talked and I listened. But he never discussed his life in the present outside his work, and I never asked.

I couldn't imagine that anyone would find his art lacking in passion; Nathan was certainly not lacking in that area. The few evenings I had the opportunity to watch him paint, he put everything into his work; I could almost see the life pouring onto the canvas. Most of the images he worked from were all in his head—I had never seen a live model—and while the question remained unspoken, I still wondered who they were.

But he was frustrated too. Sometimes, a painting I thought was going very well would be angrily thrown in a corner or painted over in black. They were never what he claimed he saw in his mind, never quite good enough, never exactly matching his vision.

In my opinion, both the images and Nathan himself were full of as much passion as I could ever ask for. I told him so when, four nights later, we were sitting together on his small balcony overlooking the street.

"You inspire me, Evan." He was sitting on the floor in front of me, my legs draped over his shoulders like a life vest, his cheek against my thigh.

"I don't know why." My fingers were whispering through his thick hair—still black halfway down, but now he'd dyed the ends a vibrant purple.

His head tilted back, looking up at me. "You're different, somehow. Special. Beautiful." His eyes lit and he jumped suddenly to his feet, nearly knocking me backwards. "Let me paint you."

I hesitated, weighing my own fears against the burning intensity of his eyes. It was an idea that scared me in ways I couldn't explain. What if he would then want me to pose for him during the day, or even every night? I had no control over when I appeared to him, and how could I tell him that simple truth? On top of that, I had absolutely no idea what he would be painting.

I had figured out that I appeared differently to different people. Little clues—compliments on my hair and eyes, comparisons—I had put together that no two people ever saw me quite the same way.

Mirrors were no help. My reflection was as elusive at night as my body was by day. I was certain that they saw my reflection—at least no one had ever commented on me having that sort of bad special effect—but I had no idea how I looked to anyone.

And now Nathan wanted to shatter that mystique, wanted to show me my face, wanted to make me real. But it would be his vision I was seeing, and looking in his eyes, I couldn't say no.

His eyes clouded over at my hesitation. "What's wrong, Evan? Don't you want me to paint you?"

I reached up to touch his face. "More than life," I whispered. "Paint me, Nathan. Make me immortal."

He slid into my lap, melting against me, kissing me so hard I couldn't breathe. My arms wrapped tightly around him; his fingers dug almost painfully into my sides.

We made love on the balcony, in full view of anyone walking on the street five stories below. I was swept away, excited, completely enraptured by Nathan's spell on me.

That night he began the painting. As I sat posed on a stool, his eyes bore into me, measuring me inch by inch. They seemed never to leave me as his brush moved fitfully between canvas and palette. I was bound in place by the force in that intense gaze.

I coaxed him into bed as dawn approached. He pulled a cloth over the portrait, for the first time refusing to let me see the work in progress. He did not ask when he would see me again, and I could not bear to bring up the subject. Instead, I lay beside him the scant hour we had before the sun rose, tasting his warmth and feeling his closeness. I never wanted to let go.

I was surprised when, the next evening, I was standing in front of Nathan's door. As it swung open, he grabbed my arm and dragged me inside. "Hi." His lips found my ear. "So glad to see you."

I let him press me against the wall, burrowing my hands under the bulky shirt that covered his thin frame. "So glad to be here."

"I ordered pizza and Chinese food. Hope you're hungry." He led me into the kitchen where, sure enough, a pizza box sat on the table surrounded by nearly a dozen boxes that held as-yet unidentifiable Chinese takeout.

"How did you know I would be here?" I reached carefully into one of the white unmarked cardboard towers and pulled out an egg roll.

Nathan shrugged, as though the answer was obvious. "I just knew. You had to come, because I'm painting you."

He sat in my lap as we ate, one arm draped around my shoulder as we talked and laughed. But there was an air of anticipation—we knew we were only going through the motions of socializing. The real event for the night was Nathan's art.

I gave myself over to Nathan, became both model and muse. I soothed his tension with words and kisses when he became frustrated, watched him for hours without moving when he became lost in his work. I don't know how many nights were spent in this fashion—only that every single night I would wake up with Nathan there beside me. Slowly, a fire grew in his eyes and he would spend more and more time painting. No longer would he throw the brushes down in frustration. The painting itself became his inspiration. Less and less time was spent gazing at me; his entire focus was on his masterpiece.

And then, one night, he stepped back, his eyes catching mine with a burning radiance from which I could not turn. "Come see, Evan."

I was afraid. What would I see? What did Nathan see? My face created by Nathan, translated through Nathan's eyes and his passion to the canvas before him. Nathan smiled encouragingly at me. "Please come look."

How could I deny him anything? Walking to the other side of the easel was more difficult than anything I could ever remember doing, and a threshold of change that seemed greater than death itself. He reached out to take my hand at the end, helping me across, and I *saw*.

Nathan had finally found what was missing. Every bit of feeling that he possessed was expressed in this glorious work. I was beautifully radiant, seeming to glow with an inner light that lit the canvas around me. I wondered, for a moment, if this was how I really appeared, and then I realized it didn't matter. This was how I appeared to Nathan, and that was the only reality I cared for. The only reality that truly existed for me.

"What do you think?" I was speechless. What could I say to communicate what this painting was? The angels themselves would not be able to find words of enough beauty.

"Oh, Nathan. This is everything I am."

"Everything we are," he corrected gently.

I shook my head. "It's all you. Every bit of it. I only sat and waited."

"Evan, my Evan, you made this possible. Before you I could taste the passion, but I couldn't make others see it. You taught me how—showed me how—inspired me with your presence. Everything this piece is, it owes to you." And then he was touching me, caressing me, thanking me in all the ways words could not express. I fell back with him onto the bed, careful not to kick the canvas in our moment of passion.

"I love you." He did not seem surprised by my words, only kissed me deeper, pressing his body against mine as though trying to make us one. "Always, I love you."

That night was perfect. I can still remember every touch, every breath, every sound. Nathan had created me and I had created Nathan and together we attained a perfection that I don't believe was ever intended for this world. Never before had I felt the way I did that night, and never again will I.

I never saw Nathan again after the sun rose that final morning. I'm not sure if there was anything I would have said differently if I'd known it would be the last time, or done differently. Not that it matters, but it's those deep regrets that keep us real.

From time to time I see a painting of his hanging in one person's house or another. I can always recognize them before I ever get close enough to see the signature. His spark, his vision is expressed so clearly in every one that I think they would burn through even the darkness of a blind man. I hear people speak of him in fleeting conversations. They say he's going to be great, perhaps the most important artist of the decade. Instantly famous, destined for immortality. I'm happy for him, and wonder if he ever thinks of me, remembers his muse. Even more, I miss him.

But the sun rises and sets to a different face each night. Perhaps someday I will meet another Nathan and perhaps not. I cannot escape my fate, my calling, so I try not to think about all that I might have otherwise. I can sleep though, secure in the knowledge that if he ever needs me again, I will be there.

For I still have one gift from him, one way in which he changed me that remains with me always, keeping him fresh in my memory. My face. Every time I look in the mirror, I see Nathan's vision looking back at me.

And I miss him.

→ Waiting for Hannah ←

by Anne Seale

It was a dream come true, a two-bedroom home on a quarter-acre wooded lot within 20 minutes of work—at a price I could afford if I made do with my old furniture, a few apartment-sized pieces that would be lost in the comparatively spacious Cape Cod.

Another plus, then, was that the house was being sold partially furnished. In the kitchen there was a worn but sturdy maple table, four captain's chairs, and a matching hutch you'd have to take out a wall to remove. (Was the house built around it?) And in the smaller of the two rooms at the top of the stairs a handmade bed frame nestled under the eaves, flanked by bookshelves and a built-in three-drawered dresser.

The Realtor had been honest. She'd told me the place was haunted, but I just smiled and signed the contract. I figured moldering castles and appreciative bed-and-breakfasts might attract ghosts, but not a cheerful '50-something Cape. Anyway, if there were ghosts around, you'd think I'd have run into one in my years of living in one ancient apartment building after another.

I moved in on a sunny 30th of September. By noon, the movers had placed the last box, pocketed their cashier's check, and departed. Later, while sweeping tracked-in leaves from the entryway, I noticed someone watching from a window across the street. Thinking I might receive a welcome-to-the-neighborhood visit, I went to put fresh coffee on, but the watcher was gone by the time I returned, and nobody came to share the pot.

At about four, a Budget Bedding truck pulled up with my one indulgence, a new mattress and box spring. I'd decided to sleep in the room with the built-in bed and use the larger bedroom as my studio. What a treat not to have my easel in the middle of the living room. After a couple of pay raises, I intended to put a skylight in the studio.

The noises started right away but I chalked them up to a settling house. Why a house would settle every morning at 2:32, I didn't wonder. I also didn't let myself wonder why the settling would sound like someone running up the stairs.

It did unnerve me, though, when I realized that things were moving while I was at work—one thing anyway, the brass hand mirror on my dresser. It didn't move far, but enough for me to notice. I'd lived alone enough years to become a creature of habit. I knew where I kept my mirror.

Thinking I might be the victim of a neighborhood prank, I called in sick one morning, then carefully sprinkled bath powder on the mirror and on the dresser around it. Donning painting clothes, I crossed to my studio, leaving both doors open. All morning as I applied oil to canvas, I kept an ear cocked for sounds but there were none. At 11:30, on my way to the kitchen for a sandwich, I couldn't stand it any longer—I stopped in the bedroom. The mirror had shifted. There was more than an inch of unpowdered wood showing at the right of it, and the mirror's handle was pointing in a slightly different direction than before. Shaking, I showered and dressed and unexpectedly showed up at the office, explaining that my headache had suddenly gone away. In truth, I now had one.

After work I wiped up the powder and put the mirror in the top drawer. I considered sleeping on the sofa that night, then remembered it was a foot shorter than I was, and lumpy. Instead, I stayed up as late as I could watching Jay Leno and a Bette Davis movie on AMC before dragging myself upstairs, where I instantly fell asleep.

When the now-familiar footsteps on the stairs half-awakened me, I was dreaming, or thought I was. A lover's arm was around my waist. I nestled into it, regretting that with full consciousness, it would be gone. In the background, I heard Elvis Presley singing "Heartbreak Hotel." I smiled about having Elvis in my dream, when something caressed my hair, brushed my ear. A voice, a young woman's or girl's, whispered, "Hannah, come to me. I love you."

Something dropped on my cheek, something warm. I opened my eyes and raised my hand, touching the wetness with my fingertip. The arm around me tightened. "Hannah," I heard again. "Come to me."

This was no dream.

I moaned in terror and sat up, bumping my forehead smartly on the slanting ceiling. The music stopped, and the arm vanished. I jumped up, switched on the light, and looked fearfully at the pillow. Empty. There was no wetness on my cheek or finger. Who had been holding me? Who was Hannah?

After four hours and three pots of coffee, I called and woke up my Aunt Joan. She's the family "loony," obsessed with things like horoscopes, mediums, and UFOs. Her biggest disappointment was that she has never been abducted, but she still had great hopes. She was delighted to hear about my problem and promised to phone back soon. Instead, after an hour and a half, there was a knock on the door. When I opened it, Aunt Joan swept in followed by a woman who groaned, placed her hand on her left breast, and plopped on the nearest chair.

After a hug, Aunt Joan told me the groaning woman was Gloria Barney, a "sensitive." "If anybody can get rid of your dear spirit, Gloria can," she said, "and she only charges $10 an hour."

"That's fine," I said. I'd sell my soul—well, my car at least—to get rid of whatever was in this house.

Gloria wore a white and dark green gingham smock over white polyester slacks. She looked more a waitress than a sensitive, whatever that was. Her long blondish hair was held back by two green plastic barrettes. She stared at me intimately, as if she'd known me for years. "Hannah," she muttered. My skin crawled. "Hannah, come to me. I love you."

"I'm not Hannah!" I shrieked. Aunt Joan scowled at me—this was obviously her ball game. She crossed to Gloria and bent over her.

"Who's Hannah?" she whispered.

Gloria's chest was heaving mightily. "I'm waiting, Hannah," she said. "Come to me, Hannah, I'm waiting." Suddenly she stood up, nearly knocking Aunt Joan over, and crossed to the stairway. She climbed quickly, and I recognized the cadence of the early morning footsteps. At the top, she turned toward my bedroom and entered, with Aunt Joan and me right behind her. Lying on my bed, she stuck her arms out, palms up. Her head rolled back and forth a few times, then she looked directly into my eyes and said, "I'll wait for you, Hannah. Forever." At that, Gloria closed her eyes and fell asleep, snoring loudly.

Aunt Joan started for the doorway, motioning for me to follow. My knees were buckling, so I had to go slowly and hang on to the handrail as we descended. "What have you got to eat?" she asked when I finally reached the bottom. "Gloria's always ravenous when she comes to."

We made tuna salad and I asked Aunt Joan what was going on, but she put her finger to her lips and looked at the ceiling. I took this to mean we had to wait for Gloria, so we sat drinking coffee, bringing each other up to date on various relatives as if she had dropped in for a friendly chat, except I was paying $10 an hour for it. After a while I heard plodding footsteps on the stairs, nothing like the light ones Gloria had used when going up. She came in the kitchen and sat heavily. Aunt Joan quickly put a cup of coffee and a sandwich in front of her. Gloria ate half of it before saying to me, "What's your name again, honey?"

"Lois," I said.

"Boyoboy, Lois. You have one big problem here." She bit into the other half of the sandwich.

I was speechless, so Aunt Joan took over. "The spirit, Gloria. Who is that poor spirit?"

Gloria swallowed, drank some coffee, and proceeded to tell us the tragic story of my house. It went like this—in the late '50s, a high-schooler named Betty lived here with her parents. She and a classmate, Hannah, were secret lovers. They took turns staying at each other's houses where they made love far into the night.

I looked sharply at Gloria when she said this, and then at Aunt Joan, but neither of them showed any evidence of being scandalized by this behavior. I, on the other hand, was in an emotional tizzy. I had wanted to make love far into the night with more than one woman in my lifetime, and though fear and confusion had kept me from ever acting on my desires, I felt my face turn crimson. Luckily, neither woman was looking at me.

One night, it seems, Betty and Hannah were upstairs in Betty's bed. Betty woke Hannah at 2 A.M. with urgent kisses and they began making love, confident Betty's parents would be sleeping. Betty's mother, however, was having a wakeful night and rose to fetch a sleeping pill from the bathroom. Passing Betty's bedroom, she heard low music and other sounds. She opened the door to find the girls naked, their bodies tangled in the moonlight. She screamed, waking the father, who ran in, wrested Hannah from the arms of the sobbing Betty and ordered her to leave their house and never return. Hannah threw on her clothes and left, but never made it home. She was hit by a car and killed on the way.

Betty was inconsolable. One day while her parents were working she ingested a bottle of her mother's sleeping pills, but she was found in time. After that, a neighbor was hired to keep an eye on her while her parents were away, but she soon managed to fatally carve her wrists. It is Betty who haunts my house now, waiting in vain for Hannah to return.

When Gloria told us this, I blurted, "Tell her Hannah won't come back. Tell her to go away."

Gloria turned and looked at me squarely. "She won't listen to me. You're the one she's formed an attachment to. You have to tell her."

"Me? How?"

"She's back in her own time, the '50s," Gloria said. "You'll have to go there."

"What?"

"You'll have to go there," she repeated calmly. "It's easy, I'll send you." She took my hand and led me to the living room sofa. I sat and she plopped next to me, asking, "Have you ever been hypnotized?"

"No," I said, and raised my frantic eyes to Aunt Joan standing nearby. She was all smiles and reassurances. "I couldn't," I said.

"Of course you could," Gloria said, taking a device from her pocket that looked like a toy I once owned. When you spun the toy, it made a spiral pattern and gave off sparks. Hers didn't give off sparks, but once the spiral started swirling, I couldn't look away. I felt my head drop, heard Gloria droning, pronouncing words I couldn't make out.

I raised my head to tell her so, and found myself looking at a sad-eyed girl in a navy pleated skirt and pink short-sleeved sweater. She was sitting where Gloria had sat a moment before, except now the sofa was gold and fuzzy instead of brown plaid. I glanced about wildly. The walls were papered with big flowers, and on a television screen in the corner, in black and white, a man turned his back on a sobbing woman while organ music swelled. Suddenly, though I seldom drank anything but wine, I felt a deep craving for something stronger.

"I'm going to lie down for a while and read, Ruth," the girl said to me. "I feel tired." In a flash, it came to me. She was Betty, and I was the neighbor hired to make sure she didn't try to take her life again. I found myself knowing all about Ruth, her sad life in the house across the street with an abusive husband, her bouts with alcohol.

"All right," I said, surprised by the raspiness in my voice. I turned off the TV and followed Betty upstairs, recognizing the pattern of her nightly footsteps. I watched as she sat on the edge of her bed—my bed—scanning the titles on the bookshelves. I forced my eyes to the top of the dresser where I saw a pink, tortoise shell hand mirror lying just where I expected.

"Darn," she said. "I think I left my book on the kitchen table. Will you get it for me, Ruth?"

"Sure, "I said, and went back downstairs, secure in the knowledge that there was nothing in the house with which she could hurt herself. All drugs had been thrown away; the knives and scissors were locked in a kitchen drawer; even Betty's father's razor blades were beyond reach. I hurried to the kitchen. *As soon as I get back upstairs,* the Lois part of me thought, *I'll have a talk with her, convince her that it would be better to stay alive.*

There was no book on the kitchen table. I found myself crossing to the maple hutch, reaching for a big black handbag. Taking a pack of Camels and a half-full pint of whiskey from it, I pulled out one of the captain's chairs. "No," I said to the half of me that was Ruth. "Don't do this. There isn't much time." My body paid no attention. I sat down, lit the cigarette, and lifted the bottle to my lips.

I was on my second cigarette and the bottle was close to empty when I heard the distant sound of glass breaking. I stood and immediately lost my balance, knocking the bottle on its side. I cursed as the last of the precious liquid ran out. Finally I made it to the stairs, scrambling up on hands and knees.

Betty was on the bed, head to one side, arms splayed, blood pouring from deep gashes in her wrists, reminding me of the crucified Christ on Ruth's childhood rosary. The hand mirror lay on the floor by the bed in pieces, one of the pointed shards covered in blood.

Sobered a bit by shock, I ran to her parents' room to phone for an ambulance, then grabbed a sheet from the bed, tearing it into strips on the way back. I tied them around her arms, tourniquet-style, then applied pressure directly to the wounds with my hands. But the blood kept flowing. She steadily got paler.

"Hannah," she whispered. "Come to me. I love you."

I let go of her arms and slid my arm under her shoulders, lifting them. "Don't die, Betty! Please don't die!"

She paid no attention. Her eyes were looking off into space. "I'm waiting, Hannah. Come back to me. I'm here, waiting."

"Betty, listen to me," I raised my voice. "Hannah's gone. You'll have to find her. Go find her." She looked at me, blinking. I shouted, "Go find Hannah, Betty. Don't stay in this house. Promise me you won't stay in this house."

"Hannah…" Her lips formed the word, but no sound came out.

"Go to her!" I screamed as she fell against me. "Go to Hannah, Betty! Go!"

"Shhhh," said Aunt Joan, sitting beside me on my bed, taking me in her arms. "It's all right, Lois, it's all right."

"It's over, honey." I looked up to see Gloria smiling, nodding. "You did it! Betty's gone."

I broke into wrenching sobs.

That was almost three years ago. Betty has never been back. For a long time I grieved as if I had lost someone dear. I even painted her—Betty's sad sweet face hangs above my fireplace.

I finally met Ruth, white-haired now, and blessedly a widow. She still lives in the house across the street. I visit her now and then, and she tells me stories about Betty, whom she knew from birth. Sometimes she speaks of Betty's dying, and I can see in her eyes that she carries a tremendous amount of guilt. She tells me that after that day she never took another swallow of liquor. I listen and console, but I'll never let her know that I was there.

Ruth refuses to enter my home even though I've assured her it's no longer haunted. It's just as well. I can't imagine her reaction to

Betty's portrait.

At some point in my grieving, it occurred to me I was in grave danger of never finding my own Hannah, never having her to love for however short a time. This fear has led me to look for her. I've come out now, and have been dating women for several months. Though none has turned out to be the right one, like Aunt Joan and her alien abduction, I still have great hopes.

✢ Old as a Rose in Bloom ✢

by Lawrence Schimel

My fingers trembled as they skimmed across the scroll of roses engraved along the box's sides. I had not touched it in years, and I could barely detect the shadow of my reflection beneath the large curving script on its tarnished silver lid. MFG. Marilyn Francine Gardiner. My mother.

She gave the box to me before she died. Inside, a pair of silver moons slept on a velvet bed beside a matching strand of stars. I had held my breath as I stared at them sparkling under the hospital lights from the box on my lap, like the glitter of sunlight on water.

"My mother gave me these on the day of my prom," she told me, her eyes misty with recollection. "I felt so proud as I wore them, old as a rose in bloom, and as beautiful." She took my hand in hers and made me look into her eyes. "I want you to wear them to your prom. Think of me when you put them on, so I can be with you. In spirit, if not in person." She ran a hand through my hair as if she were combing it for me before the prom, and I nearly spilled the box and its moons and stars to the floor in a flood of silver as I turned to embrace her, crying.

I blinked back my tears again and set the box on the bureau, still not ready to open it.

Downstairs, I could hear dad and his boyfriend saying good-bye. Ed worked as a drag singer at a bar in town. At work everyone called him Natasha. Dad had been seeing him for eight months now, and Ed had basically moved in with us, but every night when Ed left for work they still spent five minutes hugging and whispering as they kissed each other good-bye. Dad was often asleep when Ed got back from work in the middle of the night, since he woke up at six to be in at the office on time. But I knew that sometimes he stayed up, worrying, or just waiting for Ed to come home.

For a moment I worried what my date would think if he showed up at the door and saw them through the window as he was about to ring the bell. It didn't matter, I realized as I began putting on my make up. Dad was happy for the first time in years, and I was happy for him. If I could only find the right lipstick to match my dress perhaps I could be happy for myself as well. I was the only freshman girl going to the prom and I wanted to be stunning.

Dad began calling out to me as he climbed the stairs, "Erica? Erica?" He knocked hesitantly at my open doorway, suddenly shy or perhaps trying to give me some privacy. Whichever, my chest tightened in response to that tiny gesture, and I felt in that moment how much I loved him. He poked his head through the door and in a softer, excited voice declared, "He's here."

I turned to him and smiled, shyly.

"You look stunning," he said, coming towards me. He held me at arm's length for a moment, then kissed my cheek. I felt on the verge of tears, I was so happy. "How long should I keep him busy? Your mother kept me waiting for 45 minutes. I sat wedged between her father and her older brother the entire time, too afraid to move a muscle, almost too afraid to breathe."

"I shouldn't be much longer," I said. "I just can't find the right lipstick."

"Twenty minutes, then," he said as he walked toward the door. He laughed, and I knew he was just teasing me. "I'll make sure he's occupied. Don't you dare come down sooner than ten, y'hear?"

"Thanks," I whispered, watching in the mirror as he went back downstairs. I was left staring at my reflection. I really was almost ready, except for the lipstick. I couldn't find the right shade, everything I had was too dark or too light or the wrong color completely. I looked at Mom's box again and realized I couldn't put it off any longer. I held it in my lap for a long moment; the metal felt cool even through my dress. I traced the large, curving letters, remembering her, missing her. My fingers wandered along the stems of roses around the sides. Finally, I opened the box. I'd promised her, and even more, I wanted her to be a part of this special moment with me.

The jewelry lay on its dark velvet bed and sparkled as brightly as that first time I had seen them, still untarnished even after all these years. I lifted the twin moons and held them before me, trying to imagine Mom as a girl wearing them. I put them on and stared at myself in the mirror. *I look just like her,* I thought, as I recalled the picture from her high school yearbook. I lifted the necklace—strands of tiny silver stars twisted gently, almost like a braid—and let the cool metal lie against my neck. I was amazed as I fastened the clasp how much I looked like Mom. She was so beautiful then, and now was again, in me.

I closed the box and placed it on the bureau. Something nagged me out of the corner of my eye, something I couldn't quite see. I looked at myself in the mirror again and realized that my reflection had not moved at all! My heart began to pound within my chest. *Could it really be her?* I wondered. It was almost too much to hope for. I turned and stared at the young version of my mother who sat in the chair I had just vacated. No wonder I looked so much like her when I put her jewelry on; I had been seeing her!

I was scared, I must admit, even though it was my mother. And sad, as well. She opened her mouth to say something, but no sound came forth, and I could not read her lips. What had been so important to bring her back from the dead? I was elated to see her again, but felt guilty that I had disturbed her eternal rest, somehow. The ghost stood and spread her arms to hug me but passed through me with a cold chill that froze my tears and made me catch my breath. Mom did not stop, however, but continued past me, and out the door into the hallway. I hurried after her, unwilling to lose sight of her when I didn't know if I would ever see her again. She had walked (or floated, I realized later, since she glided from place to place) to the end of the hall and waited in front of Dad's bedroom. She was pointing at the closed door, and when she saw me following her she ghosted through it.

I hurried down the hall and stood in front of Dad's closed door. As I put my hand on the knob, I couldn't help thinking about how he knocked at my open door earlier that evening, honoring my privacy. But I turned the handle nonetheless, and entered his room. It was dark, but I was afraid to turn on the lights. He was still downstairs, entertaining my boyfriend. What if he came upstairs again to see what was taking me so long and saw the door to his room ajar?

I looked around the room in the light from the hallway, wondering what had disturbed Mom's rest. It looked like there was more of Ed's stuff in there than Dad's. Suddenly it hit me—was Ed the reason Mom had come back from the dead? Was she upset that Dad was sleeping with a man now that she was dead? I looked to Mom for confirmation, and sure enough she was pointing at Ed's stuff on the bed. I felt sorry for Dad—he really liked Ed, and I sort of liked him too. Most importantly, Dad was happy again. He'd been so lost after Mom had died, and bitter, as if he felt she had abandoned him. But if Mom was so upset by his boyfriend that her ghost came back to tell me so, I guess I couldn't keep thinking things were good. I didn't know what she wanted me to do, however, and I looked at her again for another clue. She was still pointing at the bed.

She began to wail in frustration when I didn't understand. It was the first time she had made a sound, and I swear, it was loud enough to wake the dead. But maybe that was what she wanted.

Dad didn't hear a thing, or if he did, he never said anything about it. I moved closer to the bed, to see what she was so upset about, try and figure it out and stop her cries. Ed's drag stuff was all over the bed still, wigs and dresses and makeup kits, all the stuff he had been using when he got ready for work a little while ago. Mom kept pointing at one cosmetics bag, and at last I picked it up and held it out for her, wondering what she wanted me to do with it. She shook her head and kept pointing at it. Finally I realized she wanted me to open it. I felt nervous about going through my dad's boyfriend's stuff. I had no idea what was inside. Drugs? Money? Condoms? At least they used them. Dad had sat down with me and had a long talk about it, since he knew I might be concerned about him being at risk for AIDS and all that. Or did Mom mean them for me? Dad had given me some a year or two ago, but Mom wouldn't have known that. How embarrassing! My mother came back from the dead to explain the birds and the bees to me on my prom night!

I opened the bag. It was full of makeup: rouge, eyeliners, lipsticks. There was even a shade of lipstick that looked like it would match my dress. I didn't think Ed would mind if I borrowed it, so I pulled it out. I glanced up at Mom, wondering what it was she wanted to show me in there, but she merely smiled at me and faded away.

I wanted to laugh with relief, or cry. She hadn't been upset with Dad's boyfriend at all! I put Ed's bag back down on the bed, and walked to the mirror. The lipstick *was* the perfect shade; at last, I was ready. I still looked like Mom, I realized as I looked at myself in the mirror one last time before going downstairs to greet my date. "Old as a rose in bloom, and as beautiful," I whispered, and felt a warm glow of love envelop me.

❧ My Possession ❧

by Simon Sheppard

When we first met, we "met cute," as they say in Hollywood. You were tied down to the rack in my friend Allen's dungeon. I was late getting to the party; perhaps 20 men were already there. You were naked, on your back, restraints around your wrists and ankles, a few ropes around your arms and legs, gas mask over your face. My pal Berkowitz was standing over you, his shiny black rubber suit showing off his notoriously big cock. When I approached, he smiled. "Want to try some rope tricks on him? I'm bored."

I took over, never even looking at your eyes through the shiny faceplate of the mask. I think that's why I fell for you: the sheer impersonality of the play. At that point, you could have been any-one. Anyone with great legs and a fat, uncut dick.

Unlike Berkowitz, with his desultory style, I went to work on you for real, feeding soft, white rope through the rough cord webbing of the rack. Entrapping you in a web which, even then, you, face-less, theoretically submissive, were willing into being. When I tight-ened down the ropes around your hairy upper thighs, cinched them down and knotted them, your dick sprang to its full hardness. Your long, tight foreskin never retracted. Glistening precome pooled at its tip.

Watching your trim, naked body strain against the ropes gave me the deepest pleasure. As is often the case in the best of scenes, *time* ceased to mean anything at all. An hour, perhaps two, had gone by when Berkowitz returned. "Gotta go," he said. "Work tomorrow." He smiled. "Gotta take my gas mask."

Your face, when I saw it at last, was perfect. Our first ferocious kisses tore through my soul. Though the party broke up, we remained in the dungeon, playing until the unseen break of day.

Words are slippery things at best, so it's damn near impossible to put into language what happened between us in the dungeon that night. I'd never known such mastery in a scene, nor received such a gift of absolute surrender. You swore to me your trust was complete; I took you at your word. In one position, then another, coils of rope always tight against your tender flesh, you went further and still further into the welcoming dark. And you took me with you, to where we both hungered to be. And then sometime near dawn, with wrists and ankles securely bound, you curled up to sleep in my arms.

Your first letter read:

> The few days I spent with you were among the greatest times of my life. You taught me what submission truly is. You touched a deep, deep part of me, and I'm forever in your debt. I am yours, entirely yours.
>
> I can't believe that you're now thousands of miles away. Returning here to my home was so difficult. I feel so empty. But I'll be back with you when I return in the fall. And I know that, no matter what, I'll never forget the time we had. Dearest Master, in a very real sense, I'll always be with you.

Our short time together had been intense for me as well, the kind of scene I'm always searching for but so rarely find. Just reading and rereading your letter made my dick hard. I'd load the video into the VCR, watch you in close-up, in slow motion, hungrily licking my stiff cock. You in the bed of your hotel, enmeshed in a web of ropes, your wrists and ankles anchored firmly to the base of your swollen dick. Your moans when I tweaked your nipples. You gazing at the camera, at me, in what looked like absolute surrender.

But…something in the tone of your letter was excessive. Too much commitment, too much devotion. In the back of my mind, a caution light was flashing. Even then I began to suspect that you were addressing not me but your own desire.

When I wrote back, I tried to be totally honest. I realize now that that was, in some respects, a mistake.

The months went by. From time to time, I played with bottom boys, boys who were maybe substitutes for you. Some were generous and honest in their submission. Others were self-absorbed little pricks who just wanted to be entertained. Always the shaky promise of your return was there, waiting.

Your letters kept coming, each more slavishly devoted than the last. You longed to be my property. To sleep at the foot of my bed. You were telling me what you thought you wanted me to hear. I knew you were. I fell for it anyway.

On nights when I had trouble getting to sleep, I thought of us in the dungeon, after everyone else had gone. You were wearing my black leather collar, being my puppy. Walking on all fours. Licking my hand. Taking my commands. Wagging your beautiful, naked butt. "Roll over." Yelping happily, you got on your back. I scratched your hairy belly. Your doggy dick was hard. Your pink tongue lolled out. I hoisted your hind legs over my shoulders and drove my dick deep into you. "Good boy. Good dog," I'd said.

I went to work for Doppelgänger Press, specialists in transgressive postmodern literature. *Vertiginous Desires* was the latest book by a hot

French author whose pen name was Choderlos de Laclos. Nobody seemed to know who he really was. I set to work translating the French into English:

> Yeah, you've betrayed me. It's why I love you. You, who've given up so much for me. When it started, so simply and cleanly, you were tied up, restrained, me tying the knots. I seemed to possess you. I knew so little. You, in your ignorance, have since taught me so much. At first, it seemed, by going behind my back, seeking out another master though all the while pledging submission to me, it seemed as though you were just another "pushy bottom." As though you were out for power, even the power of slaves. But now, only now, I see the genius of your selfless love. Now, as I stand here, rope in one hand, dick in the other, you are nowhere to be seen. You're with someone else, someone you sought out, as the murderer seeks out his executioner. You giving him your body, your orgasms. He your "master," you his "slave."
>
> But you, stupid genius of desire, have at last given me the obliteration of "you." It's the gift we both thought we were opening when I tied white rope around your arms, your legs, your cock, your cock which is too dark for your body, your cock which can't even crawl free of its foreskin, your ignorant, precious cock. The ritual was supposed to mean you were giving up selfhood and will. To me. For me. But let's face it, you in your pride couldn't ever give me the true gift, as I in my pride couldn't accept it. Until now.

And so on. I was struck by the parallels between *Vertiginous Desires* and the story of me and you. It even sounded like your dick. Still, the narrator's affair had gone terribly wrong. Ours hadn't. Not yet.

For some reason, we never once spoke by phone. Transatlantic calls don't cost that much. I suppose I didn't want to be pressed for an immediate response to your pledges of devotion. I suppose you feared that your voice might give the game away. It's easier to lie when you're doing it on paper. "I want you to know, to believe, that there are truly no limits between us, that my trust in you is absolute." I read it again and again, let it roll around in my brain. What was I going to do with you? How could I live up to what you believed me to be?

The last days of summer faded into fall. You were due to come back soon. I sat before the VCR more and more, stroking my hard dick while I played and replayed the tape, watching the interplay of flesh and muscle, trying to decipher your face. My hand reached into the frame and pulled off silvery titclamps, leaving dead-white indentations in your pink nipples. Circulation returned to bruised flesh, painfully. You moaned and writhed. Looked straight into the camera. Aware of the effect. As though you were acting for the eye of an observer. As though that observer were you. Not me. I leaned into camera range and spat in your face. And again. The moment when you closed your eyes, licked my spit from your lips and said, "Thank you, sir," almost always made me come.

Two weeks before your plane was due, I received your final letter:

It's so hard to write this. I am sorry to have to tell you that I have signed a full-time slavery contract with a man I met through an ad on the Internet. I'm afraid I won't be able to let you play with me during the next year, until the term of the contract is up.

It seems unfair that you, who taught me what submission really is, should end up the loser. But I felt in need of something bigger. Though he and I haven't yet met face-to-face, I know that Master John is the man I've been seeking.

Please don't take this as a rejection. I hope we can still be friends. And I'll be free again in a year. I know I'll be worth waiting for.

I've always had problems dealing with people who deal in bad faith. It makes me want to scream and throw things, but besides being undignified, it never does any good. Which is why I sent you a note saying only "Good-bye and good luck." Anything more would have been self-indulgent.

I would have let it go at that, or at least would have tried. But when you got back to the States, you made that damned phone call to me. For the first time in months, I heard your voice: "I can't believe the brusque tone of your note. You're not the man I thought I knew. I thought I meant more to you than just sex."

I responded: "I would have settled for less than a pledge of total submission. I would have settled for honesty."

You said: "Why couldn't you have written what I needed to hear? You never once wrote that you wanted to own me."

I said: "Listen, at the same time as you were telling me there were no limits between us, you were auditioning Master John and who knows who else. I can forgive your wanting to play with some-one else. But you lied. You're like some little kid who doesn't know he's doing wrong because he can't distinguish fact from fantasy. And you still want to be friends? Drop dead."

And that was that. I wish I could say I didn't think of you again. I wish I could say I didn't jack off to your image any more. I wish that *Vertiginous Desires* didn't make so much sense to me:

What a stroke of brilliance! What ascetic glory! Through your betrayal, you've discarded all the pleasures I gave you. Robbed yourself of my adoration. My very presence. Through your treacheries, you've made yourself worthless, lower than low. Valueless as shit. You, miserable little trai-tor that you are, lying, groaning, sweating, stinking in the bed of some brutal man too stupid to know what he's got, you've given me what I always knew I wanted.

You've made yourself the dirt beneath my boots. How then can I do anything but love you? You, who've made yourself repulsive to me while I watched, you've allowed me not to be merely a "top" in the shabby little bedroom-games sense. Oh, I worried I was weak, but you've shown me, by your cowardice, your blinding insincerity, how strong I truly am. You've allowed me to tower high above you. You've abased yourself so thoroughly that nothing, nothing will ever obliterate your shame. How then can I do anything but burn for you? Burn for you with the terror of the dying sun? You've destroyed me utterly with your faithless dick. And I, who longed to know the dark of death yet still live, I'm gone but still here, you arrogant bastard. I can taste the juice of immortality, while you, you've vanished without a trace. No, wait, that sticky-sweet, slightly rancid taste—*it's you.* I've gulped you down, you're part of me, my nourishment, my poison. Drinking you to slake my thirst. Pissing you out again. My love. I burn for you. Even as I, in the very act of writing this, showing it to strangers, I betray you. Risking all, even my freedom, I lower myself to you. My love. My deepest, worthless love.

I turned off the computer. I went to bed. I slept fitfully, as I often had since your last letter. I woke up in the middle of the night. You. You were standing, naked, at the foot of my bed.

"Use me, sir, I'm yours."

"How the fuck did you get in here?" I said.

"Whatever you want to do, sir."

"How the *fuck* did you get in?"

You were peeling back the covers, kneeling between my legs. Your mouth closed around my dick. Slight surprise: your mouth was wet but cool, as though you'd just finished drinking iced tea. Your chilly tongue played with the underside of my dick until I swelled to fill your mouth. I lay back and stared at the blank ceiling as you sucked me deep into your mouth. Cool, with the force of a vacuum. You brought me really close, really quick. I reached down, tried to pull your head off me, tried to get you to back off for a minute. You hung right in there, took my dick all the way down your throat. Your hands reached around, grabbed my butt. Your fingertips lightly brushed my hole. I couldn't help myself. I shot, yelling as I came. You gulped down my spunk like a starving man.

When you'd swallowed the last drop, you let me have my dick back. "I'll be right back," you said, leaving my bed.

I lay back and drifted off to sleep, the soundest sleep I'd had in weeks. When I awoke, it was midmorning. You were nowhere to be seen. The door to my apartment was locked. From the inside. As though none of it had happened. As though it had been a dream.

In the days that followed, I wrapped up the translation. Though I'd previously worked in fits and starts, agonizing over every line, I now ripped through the rest of the manuscript at fever pitch and sent it off to Doppelgänger. And all the while, I thought about you. At the oddest moments— waiting on line for a cappuccino, working out at the gym, watching *Jeopardy!*—your face appeared before me, and I wondered if and when you would return. Each day, I impatiently waited for the postman, hoping for a letter from you, and felt pathetic in my daily disappointment. I toyed with the ache of desire like a child whose tongue can't keep from worrying a loose tooth. Loving the discomfort. I was, beyond a doubt, being a fool.

And then, in the second week, I was awakened by your voice. In the dim light I saw your naked form kneeling beside the bed. You said, "After we talked that time, you never wrote to me."

"I—I couldn't."

"Pride?"

"More like needing to know that if you came back, it was because of your need, not my persuasion."

"Pride."

"Maybe so. But did you expect to rob me of everything?"

"Tie me up."

"What about John?"

"John is gone. There's only you. Tie me up. Please."

You were mine again. Mine. Your body belonged to me. I circled rope around your torso, brought it from the sternum back over your shoulders, gathered your hands behind your back and wrapped the cords around your wrists until you were firmly restrained.

"Facedown on the bed."

You knelt on the mattress. I helped you lower yourself down. I wrapped rope around your ankles, cinched it down tight. Tied the ends to the windings of rope around your wrists. Securely hog-tied, you started humping the mattress. I reached between your thighs and grabbed your dick. Your faithless dick. Even there, your flesh was cool to the touch.

I looped a cord to the base of your balls and wound it around soft flesh until your ball sac was taut and shiny. I flicked my fore-finger against your balls. It made me happy to watch you jump. And then you looked back over your shoulder at me. The same look that the video had caught. The actor, supremely self-possessed, pre-tending to surrender for the sake of effect.

I roughly grabbed hold of your hard, dark shaft and tried to peel back the tight foreskin. As I worked to stretch it back over your swollen dick head, your discomfort was real. I hope. Finally the foreskin gave way. Your shiny purple dick head, slick with precome, burst forth from hiding. I had you. You were mine. My possession.

"That's enough for now. You'll sleep at the foot of my bed." I freed your hands, put locking restraints around your wrists. Tied the restraints firmly to the legs of the bed. You'd have a hell of a time if you tried to get loose. You'd have a hell of a time just try-ing to get to sleep.

You'd gotten off easy, though; part of me wanted to rip you apart.

In the morning you were gone. The empty restraints lay on the floor, still tightly locked. There was a limp pile of ropes where you

157

had been, And the front door, when I checked it, was locked. From the inside, of course.

For weeks, there was no more sign of you. I started on a new translation. I should have been writing a story about you, about us. It's the only way I had to try and master you. *I'm getting a little old for this sort of obsession,* I thought. It didn't matter. You ruled my thoughts. *Maybe all I want is to be able to say "I love you" to your face and mean it. Or maybe I want to pierce the hidden head of your dick, slip a silvery ring through the hole, feed a rope through the ring and tie it to a stake through my heart.*

My VCR went on the blink and ate the tape of you. I was robbed even of your image.

Finally, I gave up. I swallowed my pride and wrote you a letter. It said:

> I know now that my desire for you is real, that it exists not *despite* what has happened, but *because* of what has happened. Your lies and your betrayal have brought us to a point beyond mere bedroom game-playing. And your knowing that I am not the Master you've fantasized, but only the man I am, will make your submission, if it comes, riskier, more radical and more filled with love.

I signed it "With much love" and dropped it in the mail. For weeks, it brought no answer. *Typical,* I thought. And I knew that, whatever my faults, you were unworthy of me, of what I had to give you. My friends, when I told them the story, all had the same response: He's a fucked-up, confused little liar. Forget him.

But by now, with the force of a brick to the head, the words of *Vertiginous Desires* had become real to me. I could have written them myself. All that transgressive, postmodern stuff wasn't just pretentious bullshit. It was realer than real. The struggle between irony and lust was over. Lust had won.

My new translation was going nowhere. I couldn't get to sleep. You. You were possibility, promise, the threat of closing doors. The uncertainty tortured me. Fucked-up, I was real fucked-up. I needed resolution, any resolution. Then one day I received a letter in an unfamiliar hand. It was from Master John:

> There's no easy way of saying this. I'm sorry to have to tell you that your friend is dead. It happened just days after we first met. We had played most of the night. He turned out not to be the boy I'd hoped he'd be. Too controlling. I had to work hard to show him who was boss. Finally, finally, I broke him down. When I was done, I tied him down to the bed. I was dissatisfied, restless. I went for a walk. I don't know what happened. When I got back, fire engines were there. The house was in flames. He died there, tied naked to my bed.
>
> I'm torn up about this. I just can't tell you. I'll never forgive myself. I tell myself it was an accident. It doesn't matter. I failed in my responsibilities, and now he's lost. Lost to both of us. And he seemed like a real nice guy.

Failed you. We both failed you, I as much as Master John. More. If I had only been what you needed. And then I realized how stupid it was to think that way. Still, if only…

I drank myself to sleep. And in the middle of the empty night, I felt you crawling into bed with me. "I'm here," you said, and I was terrified, though not of what you'd expect. Death I can deal with. I've lost plenty of friends, we all have. I was terrified of how much I needed you, of how glad I was to see you again.

"I know all about you now," I said.

"You don't know what I am. You never did. I'm a mystery. A fucking mystery." You pressed your body against mine. I grabbed your hard, uncut dick. "But whatever I am, I belong to you." You smiled. A smile for the camera.

"I love you," I said. "I need to possess you."

"Just lie back," you said. Commanded.

You started at my feet, running your cold tongue between my toes. You worked your way up my calves, licking behind my knees, then up my inner thighs. "I exist only to serve you. There are no limits between us. No limits." Your voice was coming from everywhere and nowhere. I ached to have your mouth on my dick. Instead, you threw yourself upon me, grabbing my wrists and pinning them to the bed. "No limits. Not ever again," you said, your eyes full of chill blue fire. Your body felt weightless, but I couldn't move. You kissed me, hard, shoving your tongue down my throat, filling my mouth with an odd taste, a not-unpleasant taste of earth and decay.

You slithered back down my body. Grabbing my ankles, you pushed my knees to my chest. "I need you in order to be real," you said, and plunged your tongue into my ass. It had been a long time since I had been rimmed. I'd forgotten how great it felt. I started to worry that it was unsafe for you, till I giddily realized it didn't matter anymore. Inside me, your probing tongue felt like cold fire. Though the tip of your tongue was buried deep, your voice was distinct. "I'll never leave you again. Never again. I'm yours forever. No limits." My body began to tremble, then shake uncontrollably. The room became filled with cold blue flames.

At first you used your fingers to open my ass wider, so you could bury your tongue deeper inside. Your sharp, icy teeth pressed against my tender flesh. Then your mouth was replaced by fingertips, then fingers. I'd never been opened up so wide before. You moved your bloodless hands inside me, spreading me, opening me for you. Surprisingly, there was no discomfort, but there was no pleasure, either. The blue flames grew brighter. I closed my eyes. "No limits," I heard you say. And then you entered me, headfirst, sliding up inside me. Shoulders. Torso. Butt and hard dick. Giving birth in reverse. But slithery, silky-smooth. Your legs gliding into me. Then your feet. Your toes. I felt myself close up again. Your shape shifted, stretched, filled me entirely. I looked down. Your body was gone. My skin had an eerie blue glow. You were mine. All of you, mine. And as you filled me, I experienced something so near to ultimate joy, yet so close to death...

I came, in big, shuddering spurts. And when I looked down past my come-spattered belly I saw, not my pink dick, but your dark, uncircumcised cock.

And now you've taken over. You're with me everywhere. When I look into the mirror, I see your eyes staring from my face. When I flog a tied-up young bottom boy, I feel your hand guiding mine. When I come, it's your cock that shoots. And when I finally get to sleep, you wait implacably for me until morning comes.

There are no limits between us. No limits. You own me completely. For now. Maybe forever.

⇥ Moving Into a New Place ⇤

by Regan McClure

They only did it once. Tar and Emily just wanted to get off to a good start in their new place. After some clumsy research in New Age books, they began with the "unbinding" that dislodged what the book called "the unwelcome presence of former entities not working for your Higher Good." In the bustle of moving, it was a whole week before they belatedly finished the ritual, "giving welcome to spirits who come for your Higher Good."

"It sounds like their spunk has some healing powers," said Tar, who was less than reverent about the process. Emily smiled and managed a self-conscious finish to the ritual, winding her way through the maze of narrow halls in the old Victorian house, focusing on positive, healing thoughts.

Magically speaking, a week is a long time to allow entities who couldn't care less about your Higher Good to drop into your life. To top it all off, Tar and Emily never did ground the ceremony properly—they never got as far as chapter 12—quite a no-no for would-be witches. Their carelessness left a swirling brew of energy around their house, built up by the sweaty effort of hoisting the accumulated possessions of three years and two packrats into a new place.

So many actions, however, are only recognized as pivotal (or even relevant) in retrospect. And finding the right event from which to take a retrospective look is sometimes difficult. Like plotting orbits of a moon, one must first identify which objects are connected. The first less-than-ominous outcome of Tar and Emily's less-than-ideally-executed ritual was the incident with the red shoes.

"Where the hell have my shoes gone?" said Tar, rummaging in her closet. Everything seemed to go missing those days—which is about what you'd expect when you've just moved into a new place. With more rooms to lose things in and rummaged boxes spilling everywhere, chaos-besieged Tar had only enough energy to search for a moment before passing onto other concerns. *What the hell,* she thought, *the shoes will turn up eventually.*

They did. Eventually. Under the stairs in the basement and much the worse for wear. Tar couldn't remember how they'd gotten down there, but the busy moments of setting up house were continually producing surprises.

In truth, Tar's memory was working just fine. She hadn't taken anything down the stairs, and neither had Emily. No, not the cats either. Maybe it's not the most exciting mystery you've ever heard of, but even smaller mysteries should be filed away as clues to larger ones. Everything is related to everything. The path of a butterfly you saw last year in the park exactly mimicked the chaotic whirling of the Hugo Nebula, and you don't want to know what happened after the butterfly got caught in the grill of a passing car.

Don't believe me? Perhaps it would help if I said the basement was really more of a cellar—short, dank-smelling, and windowless. The oily darkness of the place could not ever be cheered by light bulbs. After Tar picked up the shoes she installed a 100-watt bulb, stacked up rows of empty boxes and a toboggan for winter sledding, and left the basement with no intention of going back until the snow started falling.

Nothing else happened. Not until the snow fell and Tar went to look for the toboggan. The cardboard boxes had rotted in the humidity and crumbled in sagging disarray, and the toboggan was gone. That night, Tar asked Emily about it.

"I haven't touched it," Emily said, surprised. "I was just thinking about it, though. I thought maybe we could go sometime this weekend."

Together they went into the basement the next morning, only to find the toboggan where Tar had put it six months before. As they dragged it upstairs, they noticed the bottom was all scratched. It would have to be re-waxed to become usable again. It looked like someone had dragged it over sand or a pile of rocks exposed through snow. An unbidden sensation came drifting into Tar's mind—the gritty feel of sand in her red shoes before she had washed them clean after recovering them from the basement. When the cat saw the toboggan she spat at it, and if that doesn't tell you something, it should.

That night, Tar dreamed of running across a desert. She dreamed of the tang of the dry night air in her nose and the dead chill of sand. It felt odd to touch sand like this; sand was something she had only felt in the summer warmth of a day at the beach, something so hot it burned her soles as she walked to her beach towel. But in her dream, the lifeless, cold sand smothered her toes with subtle pressure. She felt a shimmer of inexplicable fear. She realized how you could suffocate in sand, desiccated and shriveled as its implacable weight sucked the moisture relentlessly from your skin. She broke into a run, pushing off desperately with each stride from the soft sand.

That weekend, Tar was shopping up a butch storm in the Canadian Tire hardware and sports department. She had gone with the intention of buying some skates, but instead found herself pausing at the rows of snowboards. She picked one, thinking "this will be more useful." Useful for what she didn't know. She had never been snowboarding and didn't really want to try it. But in that simplifying way that denial can electrocute rational thought and hold it stuck to the live wire until the deed is done, she walked happily out of the store with a snowboard under her arm.

Emily was cooking dinner when Tar got home and perhaps didn't notice the snowboard tucked under Tar's arm when she kissed Tar hello. Tar got a big jug of water and started to water the plants, then suddenly decided to leave the snowboard out of the way in the basement. She "forgot" the half-full jug of water there as well. As she got to the top of the stairs, she looked back to fix the image in her mind. *I'll just see what happens,* she thought, and then forgot all about it.

That night Tar had another dream, running to the top of a sand dune and then sliding down the other side on her snowboard with a smooth glide she never thought possible. Her body felt longer than normal. A sense of relief bubbled through her dreams. She realized wheels were useless, that sliding was smooth and fast and freed her from the suffocating sand. When she woke she couldn't remember anything but this determined, exhausting movement— no sun, no sounds, no end to the sand.

The snowboard and water had disappeared when she checked the next day. Tar made a mental note, and then forgot about that too. They were back again the next morning, and finally Tar had had too much mystery for one person to forget. She dragged Emily out of bed to show her the heavily worn snowboard and the empty jug of water, and to tell her about the sand dreams.

"Ohmifuckingod" said Emily, who seemed to have no difficulty believing Tar's story—but she was always interested in things like that. Finally, something "like that" was really happening, and Emily had to sit down for a little while. It wasn't a scene from a sci-fi movie with explosions or bright lights. But like the softening smile of your lover, it's not the surface of the event that moves you, but what it means.

Tar began to leave things in the basement. Just ordinary household items that someone might find useful on a desert trek. Emily read books about the Mojave desert and Tar kept having anxious dreams of cold, dark, endless sand dunes. Water was always welcome, it seemed, as were bandages, antiseptic, and shoe pads to stop you from sinking in the sand. An experimental sandwich was returned uneaten. The bug spray was also unused.

"I hope they didn't try to drink it," said Emily, flipping through the pages of *Explorer Magazine*.

"Nah, she's smart," said Tar, collecting the evening's provisions. "At least I think so."

"Smart?"

"No, I mean a 'she.' It feels like me, but different. Really different."

"How?"

"Well, taller I guess, and she has to keep moving, but I don't know where." There was more to it than that, but Tar couldn't really explain how it felt.

Tar was the one to take the supplies down to the basement. "Always happy to help a transdimensional-being/alternate-self/ghost/alien/friend-in-need," Tar would gasp in the same voice she used as a child going into her grandma's basement, announcing to the monsters that small children tasted bad and the dog was coming with her. Then she'd swiftly place some water on the floor like an offering at the temple of an avenging god, and scuttle back up the stairs.

Tar and Emily were closeted about their basement; when a visiting friend sniffed over her coffee that they should really keep the kitty litter downstairs, they offered no explanation. They did move the litter out to the back door.

Sometimes at night Emily would wake up under Tar's casually outflung arm and watch her while she slept—dreaming of strange landscapes, walking under unrecognizable stars, moving in endless motion. It felt strange to be lovers with someone who was haunting another place. Often, Tar would frown or moan in her sleep and Emily would gently untangle her from the twisted blankets, kiss her, and stroke her cheeks until she slept peacefully again. Emily never quite admitted how she felt—jealous and relieved at the same time—safe from the unknown, yet removed from the profound. Somehow, she had been given a bit part in the test of her own slippery faith. But she had to admit that Tar was coping with it better than she could have. Emily reconciled herself to being the historical witness who anchors the event in reality.

It's odd to think that their actions could have led to such events. They may have wanted wonderful things to happen in this house, but they were thinking of sexual athletics or maybe a nice dinner party. They couldn't quite have believed in these New Age rituals, or they never would have been so sloppy with them.

Tar and Emily never did solve the mystery entirely, although they reasoned that during their unfinished ritual when their home was a wide-open pool filled with physical energy, they must have attracted someone who needed some help moving into a new place of her own. They never knew the purpose of this constant effort, but perhaps their own lives seemed just as odd when viewed via a transdimensional perspective. Tar only knew that someone or something needed her help to escape the sand. Emily only knew that Tar needed her.

One day in early spring, Tar was taking the water bottle and a new pair of shoes to the basement when one of the cats ran ahead of her and ducked through the door. She stopped, surprised, and slowly peered around the door frame. At the foot of the stairs the cat was cautiously sniffing a bouquet of flowers. Tar brought them upstairs and shouted to Emily. They put the flowers in a vase. Even their coffee friend couldn't say what kind of flowers they were. She'd never seen their like.

That night, Tar had one last joyous dream of a sailing boat in a blue-water bay on the edge of the sand dunes with green, green growing things all around—the boat skimming past a field of heady-smelling flowers, floating effortlessly toward the ocean.

Emily watched Tar smile in her sleep for the first time in months. She smiled back at her sleeping lover, kissed her forehead, and then settled down to get some rest.

⊰ Simon Says ⊱

by Marshall Moore

I'd have expected someone who had grown up seeing ghosts to dress in black every day. I'd expect him to be gaunt and to chain-smoke foreign cigarettes, Gauloises maybe. The kind wrapped in black paper. Strong. Two puffs and you've got throat cancer. I'd expect him to have…well, never mind what I would expect. Simon was none of those things.

He did see ghosts, however.

Starting almost at birth, he told me. They'd swirl around in the air above his crib, sometimes trailing ectoplasm, sometimes not. Supernatural mobiles. Baby Simon would stare at them, eyes wide, and gurgle. They'd gurgle back. Other people in the family had the ability as well, but to a lesser degree. Simon's mother told me she saved a bundle on baby toys, since a half dozen pesky poltergeists amused him far more effectively than anything manufactured by Fisher Price.

The ghosts taught him to speak, to read, and to write. When Simon told me that, I had to raise an eyebrow. But by that point I was convinced he really could see specters, and was head over heels in love with him. So who was I to argue? Before most other kids could write their names, Simon had developed a beautiful cursive. He could speak English, Italian (the language of his paternal forebears), German, French, and Russian. Simon's mother had sense enough not to call in priests, attempt exorcisms, or conduct seances. She concluded there was nothing wrong with free education, regardless of its source.

Rather than fostering dependence, Simon's ability produced the opposite result. He charged through life grimly determined to succeed on his own merit, as single-minded as a spermatozoon. Had he wanted them to, his ghosts could have solved all sorts of problems for him—getting even with bullies (any gay child is fair game for his peers), providing answers to test questions, that kind of thing. Somehow, though, Simon sensed he'd never amount to anything if he allowed this to happen. In grade school, he gave himself headaches from studying into the night until his parents finally sent him to bed. He took up the piano and practiced for hours, not recognizing his lack of a gift for music until high school. He locked himself in his room and wrote poems he'd later burn. Everything he did, he did with abandon.

Here's where I come in.

Until recently I had never seen a ghost. Or, rather, I had never seen one and known what I was looking at. As a child the idea of ghosts fascinated me. I checked out all the occult-related books the library had, and skulked around graveyards hoping to catch a glimpse of something supernatural. I expected transparency, shrouds, tendrils of fog, moans and groans. I got nothing.

Growing up in the South contributed to my outlandish expectations. Southerners take for granted things people from other parts of the country would never even consider. My own mother and grandmother, born and raised in coastal North Carolina, superstitious to their cores, scared the piss out of me time after time with their ghost stories: The Devil's Tramping Ground, a patch of sand where no grass would grow because Satan liked that spot to pace and think; The Phantom Engineer, decapitated by his own train, forever walking the tracks on foggy nights, swinging his lantern, searching for his head; The Hitchhiker in the Darkest Part of the Forest, a girl who would ask for a ride home, arrive, wait in the car for the driver to knock on her parents' door, and then disappear while the person answering the door explained how his or her daughter had been killed in a wreck years before. I believed every word, but never saw a thing.

Simon thinks we met once, in junior high school, when he visited cousins in North Carolina. I disagree. I think I'd remember a boy with dark red hair and brown eyes. By that age I felt pangs of interest in other boys and would have had a crush on Simon at first sight. In any case, when we allegedly met, Simon's ghosts were there. He says he was sitting in a park talking with two of them, a great-aunt who died in Ireland (the other half of his lineage was Irish) years before his birth, and Oleg, a man from Russia who liked to follow him around. I walked by, stopped to say hello, noticed nothing unusual about the boy on the park bench talking to older relatives, and kept going. The Russian, who could see parts of the future, told him who I was and what my role in his life would be. Simon tried to run after me, but I had already disappeared around the corner.

We met again 13 years later.

Living in Baltimore, slogging through my second year at Maryland Law, not entirely sure what I'd do when I graduated—or even the next week—I managed to hold onto some kind of social life. My friend Mark Tucker, from undergraduate days at Rutgers, had moved to DC and gone to work for some agency that contracted with the federal government doing something with computers. He earned obscene amounts of money. He told me several times what he did for a living, but I could never remember. I look at computers as just another appliance, like a toilet or a fax machine. When Mark and I were seniors, he met Jeremy Glass, then in his first year at Penn Law. Love at first sight. They spent their extra time (Jeremy didn't have much) on the phone, swapping e-mail, or commuting first between New Brunswick and Philly, then between DC and Philly. Jeremy finished Penn and took a job with the Department of Justice. They bought an old rowhouse on Capitol Hill and restored it. Marital bliss.

My second meeting of Simon was at their housewarming party.

"Drinks are in the kitchen," Mark said after we kissed hello. "Get a beer or a glass of wine, say hi to everybody you know, and meet me on the deck around back as soon as you can, OK?"

Off to my right, in the kitchen, I heard someone trying and failing to open a bottle of beer. "Where is the fucking bottle opener? God damn it, where did that thing go? I just saw it not three minutes ago. And these mother-fucking imports do not have twist-off caps."

Mark propelled me in that direction and slipped into the crowd.

The music got louder. Somebody shrieked.

I found a Michelob Dry and gloated discreetly as I twisted off the cap and threw it into the trash next to the guy who was still swearing at his bottle of Amstel Light. Didn't even miss the garbage can. I felt so manly I scared myself.

Mark materialized again.

"Get your ass out here now," he hissed in my ear.

I followed him outside.

"Is something wrong?"

"No, you just live in Baltimore, that's all. I never get to see you, so I'm being selfish. It's my prerogative because we're in my house." He kissed me again.

"Careful, bud, you've got a husband."

"John, come on. Jeremy's not insecure; he doesn't have self-esteem issues; he wouldn't keel over dead if he saw me kiss my best friend that I used to sleep with at Rutgers."

"No?"

Mark swigged his beer and shook his head. "His head's screwed on too well for that. Besides, he likes you."

"Things are going well, then?"

They were, except Mark confessed to jitters because he and Jeremy were the couple everyone said had been born for each other. This led to a certain pressure to be "on" all the time, to be perfect, to never argue, never fight, and to make wild love five times each night. Mark loved Jeremy and loved being half of a pair of bookends, but felt a little puzzled at the same time. They had the house. They had a black Lab named Sam. They had year-old European cars (a Volkswagen GTI and a Saab). They made a lot of money and invested it well. What more could anyone want? Or, now what? Mark didn't know which question to ask, much less what the answers might be.

I told Mark he worried too much, shivered, and drank more beer. Sooner or later the alcohol would kick in and I wouldn't notice the chill. Mark caught my gaze wandering and changed the subject; he knew me well enough to know when I'd maxed out on something. Come spring, he and Jeremy intended to landscape their backyard plot. Their south 40 comprised a paved slab where they parked their cars, a narrow strip of earth next to the fence on each side, and the deck off the kitchen where we stood leaning against the balcony. My nose kept threatening to run. I wanted to move the conversation to a quieter spot, but Mark seemed to pre- fer talking outside. Inside the house, "Regret," the new New Order single, started pounding the walls.

Then Simon walked into view.

"Thank God you were finished with that," Mark said when the beer bottle slipped from my hand, bounced off the wooden deck, and shattered on the pavement under the front bumper of his GTI.

"He's beautiful," I said. Maybe that's not exactly how I put it, but I know I said something just as inane. "Who is he?"

"Simon Rossi. He's not your average gym-polished Ken doll, but you can't take your eyes off him, can you?"

"Italian? With red hair?" In the age of Caesar cuts and goatees, Simon wore his hair long and in a ponytail.

"Half Italian, half Irish. And I'd call that auburn, not red. Jeremy knows him better than I do. He says it's not from a bottle."

I wanted more beer to swallow, another bottle to hold, something to do. Mark laughed when I grabbed his half-full Kirin and drained it dry.

"He's single, you know."

"With his looks?"

"This is a brainy town, but most of the fags here still chase after gym clones."

Beyond belief.

"He's had an interesting life, John. You should talk to him. You might hit it off."

For some reason the idea terrified me. My heart raced. I fidgeted and, when I took a step away from the balcony, I realized it had pressed a wet line across the seat of my pants.

"I should have mentioned it rained here this afternoon," Mark said. "I take it Baltimore was dry?"

"Never noticed." Simon was making his way through the crowd in the kitchen. I can't exactly call what I felt love at first sight, but I knew I was intrigued. Knowing what I know about Simon now, I don't mind labeling this a premonition of the most basic kind. Destiny in Levi's and a heavy wool sweater. Coming my way.

"I'll introduce you," said Mark.

He did.

Like Bambi in headlights I stared at Simon when he stepped toward me and offered his hand to shake. Mark gave me a mischievous wink and disappeared into the house for fresh bottles of beer. When Simon and I attempted conversation it limped along on crutches: "Nice place." "They've done a lot of work." "Where did you go to school?" "What do you do?" If our first words to each other had been a car, I'd have been afraid to drive it. I'd have traded it in on something sleek, reliable, fast, and new. But it doesn't work that way with conversations. I'm surprised he didn't think I was as boring an asshole as I thought I was at the time.

Mark returned with Jeremy and more beer.

Jeremy was already drunk.

"You're both tongue-tied," he announced.

Simon and I blushed. His face turned as red as his hair.

Jeremy continued, "Stick out your tongues and compare knots. If you're both into bondage we've got a guest bedroom."

He and Mark exchanged a glance and nodded. They communicated on a level I couldn't access, although I could guess where their thoughts were going; Mark and I went back a long way and had our own private channels. When he and Jeremy talked on their secret frequency I could often get the gist.

"You're not," I said.

Mark and I lived in the same dorm as freshmen. Although the honors dorm was designed to be a quiet, bookish sanctuary free from standard underclassmen's antics, we partied as hard as anyone else. One popular trick involved pennies: three or four of them, wedged between door and frame, no exit for the occupants of the room.

"C'mon, don't protest," Jeremy said. "You two look as good together as we do. Step inside and go upstairs or I'll get out my cattle prod."

"Cattle prod?"

"For the tourists," Mark explained. "And people in malls at Christmas. Now, go."

Half the people at the party got involved. Simon and I were herded into the guest room and pennied in; the party-goers cheered when the deed was done.

When Mark and Jeremy returned two hours later Simon and I didn't want to be bothered. Somehow a real conversation happened. Simon told me he had seen ghosts. He could speak German, the one language that makes me weak in the knees. He warmed up to me when he found out I knew Latin. My Southern origins fascinated him; growing up in Manhattan and Connecticut, he had read books about the South, imagining the sultry weather and magnolia trees. For me, the South was more about mosquitoes and segregation. Every day I felt a twinge of relief not to be living there, but I didn't want to argue the point with this beautiful man, especially when he had stretched out on the floor with his head in my lap.

I stayed at his place in Adams Morgan that night. He wouldn't hear of me driving back to Baltimore at 3 in the morning. The next night he drove to my place. That's how we got started.

We moved in together a year later. I had just graduated from law school and had the bar exam to prepare for (and dread), plus the rounds of interviews my headhunter and the school placement office had arranged. Simon and I found a little tract house to rent in Aspen Hill, a suburb about ten miles north of DC, up Connecticut Avenue and accessible to nothing. We moved in during the narrow gap between the end of finals and the beginning of interviews. I would have taken the plunge sooner, but commuting between DC and Baltimore while keeping a law student's hours is only for masochists.

We got through the standard newlyweds' arguments about whose sofa to keep (mine) and whose to discard (his), where to shop for a coffee table (he didn't want to default to Ikea like every other gay man from DC to New York; I couldn't see why not), whether to buy groceries at Giant or Super Fresh (neither of us cared enough to bicker for long). We bought furniture. We filled in the empty spaces. We used one bedroom and had two left—an office apiece. We shopped together for an aquarium (hexagonal), and managed to agree on which fish should occupy it (a pair of kissing gouramis, some barbs, and a catfish we named George Bush). We lovingly Windexed birdshit off each other's car windows. When I passed the bar Simon surprised me by baking a chocolate cake. When I got my first job he surprised me with a week in Provincetown. At home, we woke every morning, blearily made coffee, stumbled downstairs to Soloflex and NordicTrack ourselves into something like wakefulness, performed the morning rituals, kissed long good-byes at the door before leaving for our jobs, mine at the law firm downtown, his at the World Bank. I found I liked my life—our life.

Then dead people got our phone number and started calling at all hours.

The first time, I didn't know anything odd was happening. The phone rang just as we had finished playing around on the sofa. I had gone to grab a towel from the linen closet. Simon lay still to avoid creating a stubborn stain on the upholstery. The phone rang. Out of the corner of my eye I saw Simon reach carefully for the cordless handset.

"Hello? Oh, Hans." His voice hardened. "*Guten Abend.*" That was the only part I understood. I recognize German when I hear it and can pick out words here and there, but I can't follow a fluent speaker, especially when he is pissed off. Simon unleashed what sounded like a reproach and a string of invective, then dropped the phone on the floor.

"Hurry up before the come runs off my chest," he said, voice still tight.

I tossed him the towel.

"Who was that? I didn't think anyone you know in Germany had this number yet."

"My, umm…that was Hans."

The phone rang again.

The aquarium aerator stopped bubbling. Power outage, I guessed. All the lights in the house switched off at the same time. The refrigerator's faint mechanical humming ceased. The green numerals on the VCR disappeared. I looked out the window to see who else had been affected.

"The lights are on down the street," I remarked.

"I'm not surprised. I think Hans is having a tantrum."

"Are you going to answer it?" was all I could think of to say.

"I might as well."

Simon picked up the phone. More German. He absently toweled away our post-conjugal stickiness and scorched this Hans person's ears. Then something happened I couldn't quite follow. In the middle of what I assume was a sentence, Simon paused. "Oleg?" He switched to Russian, smiling now. The lights came on. Simon and Oleg talked like old friends. I understand even less Russian than German, but I knew Simon's vocal inflections well enough to discern he was now talking to a friend.

After a few minutes he rang off.

We stared at each other, still nude.

"Oleg wanted to congratulate us for moving in together. I haven't seen him in something like fifteen years. Well, once in a while, but not lately."

"Oleg?"

"He's Russian. He was with me the first time I saw you."

"At Mark and Jeremy's housewarming party?"

"No, in North Carolina, when we were both in the eighth grade."

"I love you, but you're a nut sometimes. An adorable nut, but still kind of a nut. Have I told you that before?"

He nodded.

"Oleg was born in a village near Tashkent. He's Uzbek but speaks Russian. During World War II he was conscripted…"

"Wait a minute, Simon."

"Believe me," he said, looking me straight dead in the eye. "This isn't an episode of *The X-Files*. You are not Agent Scully." He paused for effect. "The ethnic Russian officers conducted a sort of ethnic cleansing long before the Yugoslavs got around to it. They'd march regiments from the Asian republics across minefields, to clear them, to keep their precious Russian and Ukrainian soldiers from being blown up. Oleg stepped on a mine in what is now part of Belarus."

"That's a hell of a long-distance call," I said. It was the first thing I could think of.

Simon nodded.

"Hans is from the same time period. I don't like him as much, but he has his uses."

"Uses?"

Simon sat up, noticing (I guess) for the first time that we were having this completely whacked conversation while sitting stark naked in our living room after sex. He pulled on his boxer briefs and stared into the aquarium, where our gouramis wrestled in a passionate liplock.

"Hans can see the future, up to a point. Mostly he gives me stock quotes. With his help my investments have outperformed the market average by over a thousand percent in the last ten years. He warned me to get out before the crash in 1987. He told me about Microsoft and some of the other technology stocks. I didn't inherit as much from my grandmother as I allow people to think."

I searched the pile of clothes by the sofa for my underwear. Though I had accepted what little I had been told about Simon's lifelong contact with ghosts, I was still struggling with this. To accept that a dead Nazi gives your boyfriend great stock tips is difficult to swallow under any circumstances, let alone while half-naked and sex-sticky in your living room. This is more or less what I said to Simon.

He blinked at me. I had never seen him look more haunted.

"I haven't seen ghosts since we moved in together, for the most part. Usually they are respectful enough to allow me some space. Except Hans. Hans was on the crew of a U-boat. A Nazi. Claims he sank the Lusitania. He has a lech for me."

"Then I'm calling him back and telling him if he lays an ectoplasmic finger on my boyfriend I'll come after his ass, dead or not."

"What?" Simon actually looked alarmed.

"Star 69," I said.

The phone rang a couple of times on the other end. I expected but didn't get the canned recording, "We're sorry. This service is not available for the number of your last incoming call." Instead the ringing stopped and I got silence. Dead air. I pressed the phone closer to my ear and squinted, listening to the silence. I heard voices in the background, very faint, speaking languages I didn't recognize.

"Hello?" I asked. I didn't like this. Too real. "Is anyone there?"

Simon reached up and took the phone away from me. He turned it off, retracted the antenna, then crossed the room and turned off the ringer. His normally olive skin had gone a shade of pale whiter than any I had ever seen. His eyes were huge. Sweat shone on his brow.

"It's real, John. I'm not making this up." Simon looked scared.

I knelt on the carpet next to the sofa where he had stretched out, and cupped his face in my hands. I kissed him. "What do we do now?"

"We get dressed and fix something to eat, we brew a pot of coffee, and I tell you the rest of the story."

We talked late into the night. Our kitchen with its cheerfully dowdy yellow wallpaper, its refrigerator covered with magnets shaped like farm animals (cows amuse Simon to no end), the smell of the vegetables I stir-fried, was no place for a story like this, I thought. Simon filled me in on the history of Hans and Oleg and the many other ghosts in his life. With the exception of Hans, none seemed even remotely scary. And Hans gave good stock tips, so maybe even he wasn't all bad.

I know more now than I did then.

One weekend a few months later, Jeremy, Mark, Simon, and I decided to drive up to Philadelphia for a change of scenery. After the initial phone call from Hans and Oleg a certain equilibrium returned to Simon's and my life. Simon's ghosts were back, but they kept a low profile. I could sometimes tell he saw something I couldn't; he'd stare at a point in space, occasionally making a face but never speaking. To his credit, I never heard him talking to thin air. A fractured sort of peace reigned, but I had a sense that something was about to happen. And I'm as psychic as your average two-by-four. Simon's ghosts (Hans, I assumed) weighed in with the occasional forecast about which stocks to buy or unload, which roads to avoid, and the like. Benignly unobtrusive. Simon and I grew a bit wealthier. He traded his Saturn for a blue BMW. We got a cat and named her Bicker because that's what we did for two days, trying to settle on a name. Simon rarely mentioned ghosts, and if any otherworldly activity was taking place it was too discreet for me to see. I suppose this is what it's like to live with HIV; you get on with your daily life but in the back of your mind you remain vigilant.

South Street is Philadelphia's urban hip strip. Funky shops proliferate. Pierced 20-somethings browse in thrift shops or buy CDs next to buff gay boys and middle-aged tourists. Lines form at the cheesesteak restaurants. None of us had been there since Jeremy graduated from Penn Law. Simon had never been at all.

"You'll never find a parking spot in this crowd," Jeremy said.

He thought Simon was either naive or crazy to drive into the one-way congestion on South Street and expect to find a place to leave his car, and had said so twice already.

"Oh, I think I will. I'm lucky that way."

Simon winked at me.

I mouthed, "Oleg?"

He nodded.

True to form, Simon found the perfect spot in front of Tower Records. A man with wild curly hair carefully squeezed a mammoth blue Mitsubishi 4x4 out of the slot just ahead of us and to the right. Simon claimed the spot and graciously did not gloat over it to Jeremy.

We spent the next few hours browsing, relieved to be away from Washington for the day. The plan was to spend the afternoon on South Street, have a late dinner, go dancing, then find a hotel to crash for a few hours. Of course it didn't happen that way.

In the depths of an antique store, where Jeremy and Mark had dragged us to look at fixtures for their house, my cell phone rang. This wouldn't have raised any red flags, except I always kept it turned off until I wanted to make an outgoing call. Always. "This is probably for you," I said, handing the phone to Simon.

His eyes widened and he looked over my shoulder, not at

Jeremy, Mark, or their window, but at something only he could see. His face darkened. "Oh, shit." He took the phone.

"What is it?" Mark asked, putting the window down with a grunt.

Simon's voice broke. "My mother and sister were killed about an hour ago. It was a car wreck. I saw them just now. Before your phone rang, John."

"They were here?"

He nodded. His chest hitched; he was trying not to cry.

"We need to go home," I said, trying to take charge of the situation before it slipped into the Twilight Zone. Jeremy and Mark politely did not ask Simon to clarify what he meant by seeing his mother and his sister.

Walking back to the car, Simon leaned over to me and whispered, "It's worse than you know. Hans did it."

"What?"

Simon nodded. His eyes welled with tears; one broke free and ran down his cheek. I squeezed him tightly.

"You think I'm insane," he said.

I shook my head no. "My cell phone was off, Simon."

He nodded.

"This isn't easy," I said. "This isn't how we're taught the world works."

"Surprise, surprise." He barked a short laugh. "Ever wonder which other basic truths aren't really true?"

"Every day. Here's the car. Give me your keys; I don't want you to drive back."

He agreed he shouldn't drive right now. Jeremy and Mark huddled together, saying nothing, obviously sensing something wrong beyond what they already knew. I promised myself I'd find some explanation by the time we got home. Driving would help clear my head.

Simon's new car permitted me to make better time than I would have made in my practical little Toyota. I had us home in two and a half hours, most of which passed in silence. I noticed Simon seeing things whose nature I could only guess. My stomach and bowels lurched and knotted in fear of what revelations he'd have for me after Mark and Jeremy left. They offered to stay for moral support, but Simon declined and kissed them good-bye. We promised to keep them posted.

Finally we were alone.

"Some of this won't make sense," he said, "because you can't see Hans and the others. But trust me."

I started brewing a pot of coffee to keep my hands busy. If I was a smoker I'd have lit a cigarette.

"I told you he has kind of lech for me?"

I nodded.

"Well, it's a bigger lech than I thought. My mother came back to warn me. He'll come after me now. Today was an experiment. He scared the driver of an oncoming truck; the guy lost control and hit my mother and sister head-on. Now they're in the same place as Hans. I don't know how or why, but they are. I thought they'd be somewhere else, but…"

I sat on the kitchen floor and traced the patterns in the linoleum. I didn't want to be having this conversation. My stomach writhed like a vat of eels. I wanted to vomit, to run outside so the cold air could shock me back into the real world where ghosts didn't exist. My head started to pound, a baby migraine taking its first faltering steps; I figured I had half an hour before it reached full gallop.

"Hans always said he wanted me to be with him forever, but I dismissed it. I never thought he'd be able to do anything about it."

"What can we do?"

Simon looked bleak. "I don't have a clue. I've always tried to minimize the impact the ghosts would have on me. Maybe I should have been paying more attention."

"We have to do something," I said.

"I know."

We sat at the table drinking coffee laced with Bailey's, waiting for the phone to ring. Over the next few hours Simon's father and brother called from Hartford and Chicago. Relatives were already on planes from Ireland and Italy. Arrangements were being made. Simon refused to fly or drive to Connecticut; he insisted we take the train. He thought he had a better chance of surviving a train trip than a drive or a flight.

"I think I need to spend a few hours in the office with Oleg and a few of the others," Simon said after the last call from his family.

I nodded and kissed him, then followed him through the house to his office. He closed the door and shut off the light. I heard a match being struck—candles.

That was the last time I saw him alive.

I fell asleep channel-surfing. When I woke a talk show blared from the TV, some asinine story about trailer park dwellers who kept large pets. A big-haired woman named Gert from west Texas lived with two goats in her mobile home. I imagined the smell during an El Paso summer and almost puked. Coffee and Irish Cream roiled like lava in my stomach. I switched to the Weather Channel, my favorite soporific, and wondered whether I should knock on the door to Simon's office.

I did. He didn't answer.

I opened the door, saw him on the floor, not breathing, and screamed. I'm not really sure what happened next. 911? At some point I must have called Mark and Jeremy, because they were there. And the EMTs, the ambulance, defibrillators…

That night I saw my first ghost. I expected my first sighting to be accompanied by feelings of encountering something alien and bizarre, but that's not what happened. The experience felt so normal. The ghost was Simon, of course. I was so glad to see him I forgot he was dead.

"You're here," I said, reaching for him.

He lay next to me in bed. He felt solid and as warm as real life. "I'm here."

I started crying again. "I can't live without you. I don't want to."

He held me. "John, don't."

For a long time we lay like that, his arms around me, him dead, me alive, until I had cried myself out.

"I took care of Hans," he said. "Hell doesn't exist—not the way the Baptists would have people believe—but Hans is in the closest thing there is. He'll never be a problem again, not for me or anyone."

"Why did you leave me?"

"It was the only way we could think of to stop him. Oleg, the aunts, a few others. We made plans for hours while he laughed at us. He didn't think it would work, but I surprised him."

"Can't you come back? That's the only part that matters now."

"I wish I could. But it doesn't work that way. You know that."

"I don't know anything anymore."

Simon said nothing.

Eventually I fell asleep.

Simon and I talked for hours in the morning. I had an idea and convinced him of its merit. He cried this time, as did I. But there was no other way. I didn't want to spend the rest of my life sleeping with a dead guy, and I didn't like the idea of waiting for him to reincarnate and me becoming a pedophile, or even worse, him coming back straight. That left only one option.

I called in sick to work. I put my affairs in order.

Remember high school, when you read Poe? "We loved with a love that was more than a love." Only I didn't have to dig Simon up to be reunited with him.

He came back for me at midnight. He did it for me the way Oleg did it for him. I just closed my eyes. There wasn't any pain.

My ashes are scattered in the same place as his.

Together forever.

Marital bliss.

⤙⇒ Paisley ⇐⤚

by Jessica Kirkwood

"Go ahead, Charlotte. The first time is always the hardest."

Lynn lifted her flashlight behind me. The movement of the harsh light caused the long shadows of the trees to dance madly around us, giving the illusion that the ground itself was moving. I swallowed.

"It's OK. I know what you're feeling. I remember my first time."

"Did we have to wait until after dark to do this?" I asked.

"We'll go home right after this one."

The casket on the ground in front of me hardly looked like it could have held an adult, but Lynn had explained that people were taller now than they had been 200 years ago. Above us, tree limbs knocked together, sounding all the world to me like rattling bones. "I'll do it tomorrow," I said, backing away.

Lynn grabbed my elbow and pulled me back. "Just open it, Charlotte," she said. "It's better just to get it over with. I promise. Then before you know it, it'll be just another job."

"Right," I said, my mouth dry. "Just another job."

Three days of rain had caused the ground to get soft, causing my feet to sink with every step through the cemetery. And I had thought *that* had been unnerving. I got down on my knees and felt for the casket lid, muddy fingers against the slick muddy surface of the wooden box. In one flash I thought about all the things I swore I would never do in my life—like, for instance, skydiving. The experience was fantastic, friends had told me. But personally, I knew that if *I* ever tried it, I wouldn't live to tell anyone about it. And that had nothing whatsoever to do with whether or not my parachute opened.

I closed my eyes and exhaled, hoping that when I opened them, I would discover I had a parachute strapped on my back. But no such luck. The casket was still in front of me.

"What can I expect to see in here, Lynn?" I asked.

Lynn shuffled impatiently beside me. "Bones, mostly. But more is intact, sometimes, than you would imagine. The clothing will probably still be in pretty good shape. I've seen remains from the early 19th century—like this one—where there are still bits of skin and hair. The skin will be darkened, of course, but…"

"OK, OK, OK…stop…" I interrupted. "I'm sorry I asked. I mean, I am *really* sorry I asked."

"Sure. Too much information. I understand." Lynn quieted next to me.

I worked my fingers under the lid, feeling 200-year-old mud seeping beneath my fingernails. I paused. Maybe if I waited the courage would just come to me.

"Charlotte…" Lynn said.

"Yeah?" I answered, my body paralyzed with fear.

"Just open it, hon."

I lifted the lid in one full motion.

Lynn raised her flashlight above us, revealing the contents of the coffin. Terrified, I couldn't focus my eyes. There seemed to be not one, but two figures within the coffin. Somehow the fact that they were both women, locked in a kind of embrace, seeped into my consciousness. One of them wore a pale blue dress. The other seemed to have bits of red...or was it auburn?...hair, and she wore a dress of...now faded...paisley? Yes, paisley. A paisley print. And out of a sleeve there was such white...bone...

I stepped back, looking away, my knees weak. Suddenly flashlights lit the trees around us and whooping noises went up through the cemetery. I turned to see the whole archeological team running toward me.

"You're initiated!" someone yelled in my ear.

Jeff slapped me on the back. "Sorry, but we always have someone do it the first time at night. That's part of the initiation."

"Oh," I forced a smile. "Did you say initiation? Or hazing?"

"Doesn't matter, girl. You're in the club now." There was a loud pop and Dale held up a bottle of foaming champagne.

"Great. Great. Thanks, guys," I said, grinning weakly. "I guess that means I'm really cool stuff now. Yeah. I feel really cool. Really."

I thought I was going to throw up.

Halfway home, I stopped at an all-night diner tucked between two big Appalachian mountains. No way was I going home alone to that trailer after what I'd just been through. Perhaps if I ate apple pie long enough I would shake this severe case of the creeps. At least it was worth a try.

This whole thing was my own fault. I was a math teacher. I usually spent my whole day teaching teenagers and spent every evening preparing to teach them. It didn't leave much time for a social life, and I hadn't put much effort into anything but my job.

For whatever reason, deep down, I had always expected that if some woman was meant for me, she would just appear. Then I would recognize that she was The One, and we'd live happily ever after. But now, in my 30s, I had to wonder if that had been a realistic strategy. There had been three important women in my life, all of whom had gone out of her way to meet me, but none of whom had been the person I knew was meant to be my "everlasting love."

Jessica Kirkwood

I was now getting old enough to struggle with the questions: Was there really one woman meant for me? Had I met her but hadn't recognized her yet? And would this—gasp—require that I take the first step and put out some effort to find her?

I decided to switch strategies and actually go out and meet people. That's when Lynn, a.k.a "Dr. Lynn," asked if I would volunteer my summer to help with an archeological project in the Eastern Kentucky Mountains. At the time, it had seemed like a really cool idea. I would be the female Indiana Jones. I even went out and bought a hat.

The reality turned out to be long, hot days of filtering through what was considered "my" square yard of dirt. When it got too late to work, we would quit, and I would drive my aching back to an old trailer that served as my summer housing, where I would crash from complete exhaustion. When Lynn finally announced that some of us would be moving to a different site, I volunteered to go, thinking that anywhere else had to be a better assignment. It wasn't better. It was the cemetery.

Lynn had tried to keep me motivated with the mystery of it all. "Think, Charlotte," she would say. "A whole community disappeared up here—suddenly—almost 200 years ago. Nobody knows why. You may be the first person in 200 years to know the answer. Don't you find that fascinating?"

Paisley print swam before my eyes; paisley swirling in front of me, moving and swaying, as if on the body of a dancer. Paisley, and what was that? Auburn hair?

Somebody shook my shoulder. I looked up through blurry eyes to see the waitress standing over me.

"I'm sorry, sugar," she said gently. "But sleepin' isn't allowed in the booths. The manager says you gotta go on home."

Back at my trailer, I turned on all the lights and went to bed. I was exhausted. I fell into a deep sleep for nearly eight minutes until I awoke with a start.

My dream had been vivid. An auburn-haired woman in a paisley

188

dress had been standing in my room, calling someone's name. I struggled to remember. Shannon. Shannon had been the name she called.

"It's amazing, Charlotte!" Lynn patted my arm with excitement the next day. "Amazing what you found. Two females buried together. Very unusual. Not unheard of, but very unusual."

"Who are they?" I asked.

"I don't know. I'm guessing a mother and a daughter. Perhaps sisters. Evidently they died the same day. Perhaps it could indicate the family didn't have the money to buy two caskets—although the dress of the women seems to suggest they were well off. Or perhaps the community began losing people so fast that it began to get difficult to bury them all."

"So, which is it?"

Lynn shook her head, clasping her hands together. "Well, we don't know yet, Charlotte. The important thing is, a find like this begins to suggest scenarios."

I managed to fall asleep with the lights off in my trailer that night. A big mistake. At 3 in the morning I awoke. The woman in the paisley dress was leaning over me, close as a kiss. My skin began to prickle.

"Shannon…Shannon…" she repeated.

Her face was beautiful. Her long auburn tresses—there was no other word—fell across my breast. Her eyes were as blue as any I had seen in my life; her lips full, inviting. Yet she had no…substance. I broke into an icy sweat.

"I knew you would come for me, darling. You promised."

I came fully awake with a start, pulling myself up in the bed, still seeing the specter leaning above me. Wildly I reached for the lamp, turning it on.

But there was no one there.

"Lynn—what were the names on the stone?"

Lynn was in the tent, cataloging things. She spent a lot of time cataloging things, whatever that meant. She looked up. "What stone, Char?"

"The headstone over the grave site that held the two women."

Lynn sighed heavily. "I'm swamped with stuff to do. I'd love you to tackle that one."

"What?"

She yelled past me. "Jeff? Jeff! Come here a minute."

Jeff crawled out of a pit and came into the tent. "Jeff—take the suitcase. Charlotte'll show you where."

"Sure." He grabbed a battered suitcase and followed me out of the tent. I hurried over the soft ground, slipping in the mud under my feet. When I got to the site, I looked around until I saw a small stone close to the women's grave.

"This one, here," I said, kneeling to touch it. "But why was Lynn so mysterious about this?"

"Because of this," he said, raising the fallen stone so that it faced me. The stone said nothing.

"What? They were buried without their names?"

"No; no," he laughed. "But this mountain gets a lot of weather, so to speak. The headstone was carved out of a soft stone. After a hundred years or so, the wind and rain start wearing the names away."

"So we'll never know?"

"Not necessarily. You can do a rubbing."

"How?"

Jeff pulled a large sheet of thin paper out of the old suitcase. He spread the paper over the face of the stone, described to me how to get a rubbing off the tombstone, then left me. Highly motivated, I went to work. The stone was so smooth on both sides I wasn't sure which side might hold the information I was looking for. I did rubbings on every part of the small stone, and then did them again. A half hour later Jeff wandered by. "What'd you find?" he asked.

I fished through the several sheets of used paper stacked in the suitcase. At the edge of one, I pointed. "Right here," I said. "It's all

I could get."

1810, it read.

I decided to just stay awake all night. It must not have worked, though, because at some point I woke up. The nameless woman in the paisley dress was calling to me again. She stood at the foot of my bed. "Shannon," she called, as if she meant to awaken me. "Shannon…"

For the longest time I didn't move, afraid even to breathe. Maybe if she thought I was dead she would go away. But she didn't. She just kept calling me Shannon.

I raised slowly to my elbows, and our eyes met. "I'm not Shannon," I managed to whisper hoarsely. "Please go away. You've made some kind of mistake. You have me confused with someone else."

She smiled, as if a four-year-old had just said to her, "Go away. I'm not Shannon. I'm Batman." She raised her hand to her cheek. "Come now, darlin'," she said, with an accent I couldn't quite recognize. Something…not quite…British. But certainly not American. Now I really was sure she had made a mistake. After all, I had spent the week digging up Americans.

"I'm not…" I started to protest.

"Shannon," she chided. "you done what you promised. You came back for me. Now it's time for you to go with me."

I started to argue again, forgetting I was arguing with someone who wasn't there. But the words hung up in my mouth. Because, for the first time, I realized how perfectly beautiful she was—the fair skin, the auburn hair, the high cheekbones. And, though I didn't want to admit it, there was something darned aggravatingly *familiar* about her.

"Shannon…" she said again.

"I'm not Shannon!" I whispered, as the vision faded. "I'm not Shannon…" But for one sudden, awful, moment, I found myself wishing I were.

I woke up thinking about the nameless woman in the paisley

dress. I dressed thinking about her. I ate breakfast thinking about her. I stomped through the cemetery, searching for Lynn, thinking about her.

Of *course* she had looked familiar to me, I reasoned. She had been in my trailer every night now for three nights in a row. And of course I was beginning to think she was beautiful. We were very nearly living together.

Lynn was kneeling beside an open grave, making notes on a clipboard. Her hair was pulled back from her face in a little bun, and she was wearing her wire frame glasses. I sat down beside her.

"Lynn," I began, "do you think that—just maybe—some people aren't, well, psychologically prepared for this kind of work?"

"What do you mean?" she mumbled without looking up, while she wrote something down on the clipboard. Then, without waiting for an answer, she looked up at me through her glasses. "Do you want to hear the DNA results?" She asked.

"I…sure." I sighed.

"Not related."

"So? What does that mean?"

She shook her head, pulled her glasses off and set them on the clipboard, then smiled at me mystically. "Well, it just means that the two women whose bodies we found together in that casket weren't related by blood. Of course, that doesn't rule out related by marriage. They could have been sisters-in-law, or something."

"Maybe they were friends."

She looked at me. "And were buried together?"

"I meant, lovers."

Lynn frowned. "Char, we're talking 200 years ago…definitely pre-Stonewall."

"Lynn, we've always been around. Just out of sight to most people's eyes. You know that."

She squatted back on her heels, thoughtfully, then smiled at me. "I knew there was a reason I invited you along. You're right. I have to consider it." She tapped her pen on the clipboard, then shook her head. "You know what, Charlotte? I've taught too many classes. I've started to think from the point of view of a scholar, and that world-view has rarely taken into consideration...our worldview." She shook her head. "That's what I get for being married to my job."

She reached over and lightly tapped me on the head with her pen. "That was good thinking! Although, I have to tell you, it would be a real long shot if they were lovers. I mean, to be buried together. That would indicate someone else knew and supported them. That's still very...anachronistic."

"I know, but..." I desperately wanted to tell her about the ghost in the paisley dress. But I wasn't about to let on that I was out of my mind right after she had compared me to Einstein.

"But what?"

"Never mind."

She stood up and stretched her slender body, then reached over to help pull me to my feet. "The people here," she said, "migrated into Eastern Kentucky from Virginia. They were mostly descendants of English, Irish, and Scottish. Still are..."

She mumbled on, but I was remembering the accent of the nameless woman in the paisley dress. That was it. Scottish. The accent hadn't been not quite British, it had been not quite Scottish.

Why had I ever thought that Americans 200 years ago would talk like Americans today? Of course they wouldn't. They were closer to their native roots. They would have still retained much of their native accent.

And paisley. A print named after a town in Scotland.

I wrapped my arms close around my body. That would explain it. I must be a very lonely person and, although I thought I had forgotten, deep down my subconscious remembered that paisley was Scottish, so my mind has pieced together this woman with a Scottish accent who comes to my room every night and calls out for someone named after a river in Ireland.

Geez, I thought. *I must be* very *lonely.*

Somehow, I had thought that night, when she appeared, I would be happy to see her. After all, I had thought about her all day. Instead, I couldn't move.

"Shannon...Shannon..." she called to me.

I knew if I could just turn on the lamp she would disappear. But I was too terrified. I felt like a child being awakened from a nightmare—wanting nothing more than to run and get her parents, yet being too terrified to even pull the covers over her head.

"Shannon..."

"I'm not Shannon," I managed to whisper. It was as if the room had become too cold to breathe.

"Shannon," she called to me. "It's time to go home, darlin'?"

"But...I can't. I mean, how?" I could barely manage a whisper.

She laughed, a low, lilting laugh. "You're always like that, Shannon. At once you're brilliant, then the next you can't see what is right in front of your face."

I wanted to tell her she was the most beautiful woman I'd ever seen. I wanted to tell her that—somehow—something felt familiar about her...something that felt like home. I wanted to tell her that I wished I could be her Shannon, and, crazy as it seemed, I was beginning to think that she was The One.

But I couldn't. She was dead. Or, at least only a figment of my lonely imagination.

"Shannon? Shannon..." she called sadly. Again, I hadn't responded in the way she was waiting for me to respond. She began to disappear.

As the vision faded, a tremendous sense of loss welled up in me—a chasm of loneliness opening in my chest. As the last bit of paisley print disappeared into thin air, the loneliness overwhelmed the fear and I sat bolt upright in bed. "Eleanor!" I cried out.

My breath caught in my throat. Who the *hell* was Eleanor?

I pulled the truck up against the curb and parked by the storefront. Lynn was using this as her home base in town for some of the more delicate operations related to the dig. When I stepped through the door, there was hardly room to move. Strewn about the floor were hundreds of objects of various sizes, all from the dig, and all with tiny numbered tags attached to them.

"Come on in," Lynn called from the other side of the room. "But be careful where you step!"

She was boxing things to ship back to the university. I picked my way to her side of the room. "Can I help?" I asked.

"Sure," she said. "Hand me that."

I handed her what looked like a broken piece of porcelain. She wrapped it in paper and fitted it down into the box.

"You going to piece all these things back together at the university?" I asked.

"Like a jigsaw puzzle," she grinned. "But, not everything. And not me. That's something to keep the grad students busy. Wanna see something?"

I shrugged. "Sure."

She brushed off her hands on her flannel shirt and motioned for me to follow her into the back room. "I've had students going through archival records in the surrounding towns, looking for evidence of anyone from 200 years ago who might have escaped whatever wiped out the town we're digging up. They found a couple of references that nobody has recognized before." She turned to me. "It was cholera. Apparently the well in the center of the town became contaminated. It took such a heavy toll on the population that the few who were left just moved away. But I wanted you to see this…"

We moved to a back table on which sat several skulls from the cemetery dig. Some of them had been mounted on stands, and clay was being applied to them, returning to the bones an image of the faces they once wore. "We have a forensic anthropologist, a grad student, with us. She's been working on the skulls of the bodies you found in the casket. She's just finished this one. Look…"

She turned the clay model to me. The room went cold and I couldn't get my breath. I knew that face.

"Can you believe it?" she smiled gleefully. "We call her Charlotte."

I was staring into a clay mirror image of myself.

That night at the trailer I tossed and turned, thinking Eleanor would never appear. But right before dawn, I was awakened to her voice.

"Shannon? Shannon? Time to go, sweetheart…"

I crawled out of the bed, fully dressed. "I'm ready," I said, less romantic than I had hoped to be. "What do I need to do?" I asked. "Am I…am I going to die?"

"Just come take my hand," she said, reaching out to me.

I stepped forward, but the moment was surreal. A leg that was not my own extended from my body, the foot touching the floor in front of me. A roaring sound raged in my ears as a head that was not my own peeled from mine, the head bowing from my neck. Then a torso turned sideways and moved out of my body, until I found myself standing behind a translucent woman in an early 19th century dress—a blue dress, like I had seen in the casket with the paisley. And the woman in it looked spookily like me.

"Eleanor!" the ghostlike woman said with a cry, rushing toward her.

"Shannon!" She had barely said the name before their lips met in a kiss.

All at once I felt the warmth of Eleanor's mouth on my own, just as if I had kissed her myself. I stumbled backwards. As Shannon's mouth moved away from Eleanor's, the sensation disappeared from my own lips. "Eleanor…" I said in a whisper.

The two women, embracing, turned toward me. This was not going at all like I'd planned. Suddenly I felt very, very alone.

"But I thought…" I stopped. I didn't know who this other woman could be other than me. At this moment, I felt Eleanor in my arms as Shannon held her. I felt Shannon's feelings; I thought her thoughts. I *was* Shannon, but I was also me. I finally held Eleanor in my arms, yet I stood here as alone as before. I struggled between jealousy and overwhelming happiness.

"Shannon," Eleanor began. My eyes darted to Eleanor, but she was addressing me, not the other woman.

"I'm losing you, aren't I?" I blurted out.

She held tightly to her Shannon, which I felt, but spoke to me. "I…I don't know, Shannon. But perhaps the world is…woven like an intricate pattern in cloth. You know it repeats itself, but it's difficult, unless you look very close, to see where the pattern ends and where it begins to repeat again."

"What? What do you mean?"

She sheltered herself further in Shannon's arms. "Oh, Shannon," she said to me. "You're so brilliant. Why is it so hard for you to see what is right in front of your face?"

"But I don't understand! I don't…" They faded from view.

Pink was just coloring the morning sky. I ran blindly along the side of the mountain and into the cemetery, not sure of what I was looking for. I reached the grave site where I had first opened the casket and stopped. The smooth, anonymous headstone lay to the side of the grave. Panting heavily, I stood and looked out over the mountains.

The view this high was breathtaking with the coming dawn. A heavy morning mist hung in the mountainscape below me, and thick, towering trees canopied over me. Beyond the mountains, a sky bigger than all of us was beginning to turn a shade of warm gold. I took a moment and inhaled the clean mountain air, trying to get my bearing.

"You're here early," a voice said from behind me. Thinking it was Eleanor, I turned quickly. It was Lynn. She stepped up next to me. "I come up here every morning to watch the sun rise," she said, "before things get crazy with all the digging and the questions. The natural world helps to put things in perspective, don't you think?" She pulled her sweater around her with the chill of the morning air. "Why are you here?"

"I…I was looking for something." I was hoping she wouldn't ask what, because I didn't have a clue.

"The headstone?" she asked.

I gently kicked the smooth stone that lay by the side of the grave. "No, no. There's nothing on that."

Lynn smiled. "I know. I mean the headstone for the first grave you uncovered. The one that held the two bodies."

I looked at Lynn. "You mean that's not it?"

She laughed. "No! That was the footstone! Look…" she pointed to my right. "There's the headstone. It just rolled down the hill a few feet."

At the risk of losing my balance, I nearly threw myself down the steep slope. Coming up next to it, I reached under the stone and gently turned it over. There was no need for a rubbing; the names were clear: Shannon McAfee and Eleanor Duncan.

I looked up at Lynn. She was shaking her head. "Charlotte, honestly," she said. "One moment you're brilliant, the next you can't see what is right in front of your face!"

She laughed, and it was low, lilting. I felt strange, as if I were in two places at once. I came back up the hill, and her eyes followed me. Walking to her, I touched her soft cheek, then reached up and gently took the wire frame glasses off her face. Looking into her eyes, I saw something I recognized. The intricate pattern was repeating itself.

"What are you doing?" she asked, and I could hear the emotion in her voice.

I should have seen it from the beginning. After all, she had been the one who had opened the casket with me. But this close, I knew. I ran my hand through her soft hair, drew her to me, and kissed her. It was warm and familiar.

"Why didn't you tell me how you felt about me?" I asked.

She shrugged. "I don't know. I guess I was waiting for you to take the first step. When you were ready."

She knows me well. I guess she always has. Sometimes I can't see what is right in front of my face.

‡ Remembrance of Tom Purdue ‡

by R.E. Neu

Last night I dreamt I went to Bannerjee's again.

And the bed-and-breakfast looked exactly as I remembered, a small, ramshackle tumble of sea-weathered wood nesting cozily in a clearing just a short path from the seaside, encircled by 200-year-old pines. I could see the bentwood rocker on the trellised porch and the blazing red geraniums that overflowed the second story's flowerboxes. I could hear the wind scratching the needled branches against the dilapidated structure, and the rhythmic squeak of the old swing that hung from a twisted red branch of the largest tree.

Bannerjee's is an establishment frequented primarily by gay men, so the less said about this swing the better.

For some reason in this dream I wasn't in the Jean Genet room, but the Martina Navratilova. At least I assumed it was the Martina Navratilova. The wallpaper was a tasteful, cream-colored racquet-and-ball design. In the bathroom the towels were inscribed HERS and HERS. And in the morning what I thought was a newspaper slipped under my door turned out to be a stack of florid notes from lovelorn women golfers. Still, in these unfamiliar surroundings the Captain found me. I remember trying to stay awake for his arrival, but without thinking I had taken the welcome Xanax the maid left on my pillow and within minutes I was dead to the world.

Initially I slept quite soundly, but as night wore on the wind intensified and the ceaseless battering of branches against my window roused me back to wakefulness. I laid there watching the dappled moonlight play across the room when, with a whoosh, the window burst open and a piercing gust of wind blew in. The curtains billowed out and snapped at the air, whipping and gyrating like Michael Flatley in beige damask.

Stumbling my way toward the window was when I heard it. Like a rumbling train or a scratchy radio, it seemed less like a voice than the wind trying to speak. Its low, scratchy monotone was intermittent and expressionless—like Stephen J. Hawking falling down the stairs. The idea struck me that perhaps someone downstairs had found a copy of "Chant" on vinyl. But then, as I finally deciphered the voices words, the hair on my arms stood straight on end.

"Sea Biscuit... Sea Biscuit..."

The Captain had always called me "Sea Biscuit," for reasons unknown. While I found it simultaneously endearing and embarrassing, my suspicious friend Chris ventured it might foreshadow an attempt to smother me in clam gravy. Following the voice came the cool salty scent of the sea—not that surprising since it was roughly 12 feet away. The center of the room started to swirl with steam and fury and incoherent noise like a tornado at the Republican National Convention. And then he was there.

At first glance he looked exactly like he had some ten years prior in his black knit hat, yellow rain slicker, and old leather boots. But there was an unsettling feel to him: the corners of his mouth no longer curled up in humor, his eyes didn't twinkle with warmth, and his thin, shaky form looked as hopeless as a new Tony Danza sitcom.

"Captain!" I yelled, not knowing how my voice would carry

across the great divide, and not wanting our time together to be punctuated by lots of "Huh? Is that you?"

"Aye, laddie."

I'd always been a bit self-conscious about how the Captain's speech seemed to trace directly back to men's soap commercials, but reassured myself that it was just another case of art imitating life.

"Laddie, you've got to come quick. To Bannerjee's. *Quick!*"

And as quickly as it had appeared, his form began to fade, as skittish and shaky as Clarence Thomas meeting Malcolm X in a dark alley. His new molecules sank into grays, and tiny bits of the picture burnt out like bottle rockets. Within a second every trace of him had vanished.

"I'll come, Captain," I promised the empty room. "I'll come."

And so the next morning I wrenched myself out of bed at dawn, called in sick to work, tossed a few days' worth of clothes into a suitcase, and hit the road for Bannerjee's.

I spent most of the journey up the coast listening to the wind, and reminiscing about my first trip to Bannerjee's. I'd loved the sea since my first visit to North Beach as a child, when I saw a riptide drown a tanning televangelist who'd gone in to rinse off sweat. In most cities the sea seems reined in like a trained bear for the entertainment of tourists. In San Francisco, though, it refuses, remaining ominous and imposing. As I grew older and watched the teal tide of yuppie gentrification wash its way across my home city, the shore soon became the last refuge where I could rest without fear of waking in the shadow of a tangerine-and-melon Marriott.

Mostly, though, I loved the men who loved the sea. Ordinary men are content to recline at home with beer and Cheetos and unsettling dreams of Bob Vila, but there once were some adventurous souls who would have considered this life to be hell with upholstery. To these men happiness meant packing everything they needed into one bag and congregating in confined, filthy spaces with little to eat or drink and nothing but themselves and other

201

salty lads for entertainment—sort of a 19th-century health spa.

And so finally in my 30th year I toured the northern Pacific Coast, with plans to visit every maritime museum, old sailors' home, and shipwreck site from San Francisco to Nova Scotia. If everything went according to plan I would return home a month later to write the first book about gay sailors that didn't include a leather-clad Captain, a lithe blond cabin boy, or a salacious double entendre involving the term "white whale."

And so one inhospitably rainy night I was driving a deserted stretch of the south coast of British Columbia when I found myself falling asleep. I'd hoped to reach Gloucester, a tiny fishing village which, despite having the oldest lighthouse on the West Coast, had witnessed some of the most disastrous shipwrecks in history. The drone of static on the radio and the rhythmic beat of the windshield wipers, however, lured my eyes closed. I decided I'd better stop.

I had just about resigned myself to sleeping at the side of the road when I passed an announcement that I had reached Gloucester, population 912. A few hundred yards later I followed the instruction of a sign pointing toward the coast and a gay bed-and-breakfast. Two minutes later I was in a small clearing. As my headlights swept across the building a light came on. Even before knocking I was met at the door by a tiny old man in a blue bathrobe; he seemed surprised to find me bearing luggage.

"We don't get too many guests in the winter," he said, leading me into the kitchen while spraying the air with a scent that might have been Glade's new Cinnamon 'n Crap. "Fact is, last time I had any guests it was 80 degrees out. August. Place was filled to the rafters with a gay softball team. Nice bunch of guys, stayed here two weeks. Played the local police department. I've never seen so many shaved chests slathered in baby oil. And that was the cops."

His smile faded as a middle-aged woman with the face of an annoyed dachshund entered, pulling a tattered pink robe tightly around her. "This here's my sister Edna. If you'd like a snack or anything I'm sure Edna would be happy to—"

"All we got is leftovers from dinner. Spaghetti." She veritably spat the word at me, then expounded as if the concept of spaghetti was beyond me. "You know, long thin noodles and crimson meatballs the size of your fist." I declined the offer and she left the room as quietly as she'd entered.

The owner gave me an apologetic look. "Most of our guests try to give Edna her space. She don't like gays too well. Fact is, she wouldn't be here if she had anywhere else to go. Her husband was killed in a car accident a few years back. She claims it was a gay man who killed him, only because it was a single guy driving alone and the cops didn't find any beer cans."

He led me up a winding flight of stairs and down a darkened hallway to a wooden door chiseled with the inscription, "The Jean Genet Room." He pushed the door open with a squeak and switched on the light, illuminating a large, simple room with light gray walls and an unfinished wooden floor. In one corner was a wooden chest of drawers topped by a rectangular framed mirror, and against the far wall in the center was a large bed with an inviting comforter. I okayed the room and, after brushing my teeth and hanging up my clothes, decided that Genet must have spent the night there because there seemed to be no other connection between this attractive, cozy room and the seedy French jailhouse writer. This room differed from the ordinary only in that it lacked the usual small ceramic dish of potpourri, the toilet paper wasn't decorated with pastel flowers, and the little wicker basket for toiletries contained only a small bar of Ivory soap and a sample tube of Prell.

Just as I was settling into bed I heard a knock at the door—the owner proffering a mug of hot tea. "A lesbian who stayed here last year left it," he explained. "I think it's supposed to be good for women's problems but I figured you'd enjoy it anyway." I thanked him, said good night, and drank it in bed. Through the window I watched the waves crash against the shore, and soon the rhythm of the sea and the warmth of my drink sent me off to sleep.

I didn't sleep well, despite an odd feeling that my uterine tissue was now completely nourished. When I awoke I wasn't sure I was awake, as the difference from the previous state was not that pronounced. I repeatedly clicked the bedside lamp but it refused to illuminate. As my eyes adjusted, I began to see a shadowy figure standing at the foot of the bed. At first I thought it might be the owner, but this man was younger, with warm eyes and shock of dark hair jutting down across his forehead. As we stared at each other I realized his face looked familiar to me. And so, while under any other circumstances this apparition would have caused concern, in this instance it invited more than frightened.

We remained motionless, each absorbing the details of the other. Two facts became obvious: 1) this was a very handsome man; and 2) judging from the style of his apparel, he hadn't been to a store in the last hundred years. I nearly got up to get a closer look, but stopped when I realized that while I was naked he wore enough clothing for three or four. I try to make it a practice not to be the only naked person in the room. I gathered the bedcovers around me, then waited for him to approach, which he did.

"Ahoy there, laddie." While he spoke the wind blew the branches away from the window, momentarily allowing more light, and I could see him more clearly. He wore a heavy rain slicker, a thick knit cap, and battered leather boots. But what struck me most was the water—everywhere—coalescing in his cap, clinging to his whiskers, sliding to the wooden floor from his boots. Even his face glistened with moisture.

"Hi," I said.

"I haven't seen your likes in these parts before."

I was momentarily tempted to explain the concept of "hotel," but decided not to risk irritating a man I was so clearly attracted to, a man who had 5 o'clock stubble you could clean lasagna pans with. "I've never been here before," I said.

He sat on the edge of the bed and pulled the covers off me,

exposing me to the waist. He looked me up and down with a glance that told me he liked my rigging.

"What brings ye to Gloucester?" he asked, without taking his eyes off my body.

"The sea."

He reached over and lightly ran his fingers over my chest. "Aye, she brought me here too." His fingers veered to starboard and found a nipple, where they circled repeatedly, as if they were an airplane waiting for clearance to land.

"I hate to be rude," I said, "but I've been driving all day and I'm pretty well exhausted."

He slowly pulled his hand back and lowered his head.

"All right. I'll leave ye alone, laddie. You gets your rest." As he stood I watched water droplets on his slicker slide to the ground.

Then it hit me. I *had* seen him before—earlier that day at the Maritime Museum. There'd been some pictures of men lost in shipwrecks. One in particular stood out—a swarthy, 40ish man, clad as my specter and similarly rough-hewn, bearing the same look of passion and determination. And underneath the print, I remembered, was the spidery, handwritten notation, "Tom Purdue, Captain of the Mary Celeste."

Who had almost completely vanished from view.

"Captain?"

I could hear the voice before the silhouette reappeared. "Aye, laddie?"

"You were on the boat?"

He smiled. "The boat? It's safe to say I was on most of them, one time or the other. But I suspect you mean the Mary Celeste." He gestured towards the window. "You can see the rocks just outside. Them and myself are all that's left." He came back to the bed and sat down again. I took his hand and began to stroke it, and finally he began to smile. "Now you know my secret, laddie."

He slowly pulled the bedcovers back and this time I didn't stop him.

I don't want the disclosure that I made love with a ghost the first time we met to make anyone think I'm sexually indiscriminate, because the fact is I hadn't been with another man for probably eight years, though less out of a quest for celibacy than simple lack of temptation. But something inside me said to go after him. Scientists say genetic fitness causes sexual attraction, with the brightest peacocks the most sought-after. I found myself feeling like an anxious peahen. Something inside me said this was the man I wanted to reproduce with, and though I knew that no matter *what* we did we wouldn't be reproducing, I still couldn't diminish that resolute inner voice.

He made love like you'd imagine an old seaman would, with a stout heart, a firm hand, and a wariness for splinters. But also it seemed he had harnessed within him all the power of the sea, and then distributed it rather nicely through the important body parts. We rocked and rolled and grappled and wrestled, intensity building with every embrace. And finally, when the fury of our passion gave way to exhaustion, we slept. When I woke the next morning he was gone.

I remembered the last words we spoke:

"It must have been horrible," I said.

"Ah, no laddie," he said, with a twinkle in his eye. "That's the best I've had in years."

I ended up spending a month at Bannerjee's, and each night my Captain reappeared. His name was indeed Tom Purdue. He was born in 1824 on the south coast of Africa. His mother was a poor young Italian peasant, his father an itinerant onion seller who left her with a child, a mortgage, and a bad case of shallots. The lure of the ocean called to the Captain when he was scarcely 12; he sailed off with a ship carrying spice to the New World. This voyage so excited the young lad that for the rest of his life his sole passions would be the sea, other men, and nutmeg. After that he sailed everywhere from Africa to Asia to Antarctica, and rose in rank from cabin boy to captain.

Ours was a rough, tumultuous affair. Though we never wandered out of the view of those rocks, before the month was over I knew I loved my Captain with all my heart and soul. But I also knew I'd have to leave. I listed the positives and negatives in the back of the guest book I'd found by my bed, positive column containing words like love, fulfillment, and fate, negative column with only one entry, "Ghost." Sufficient to send me home.

After spending the next few days in a haze of despair and denial I made the mistake of unburdening my experiences with my suspicious friend Chris, and while his primary response was to express concern for my sanity he also reinforced the wisdom of my decision. Though I spent hours recounting both 19th-century life and the wreck of the Mary Celeste with the detail of an eyewitness, his logic and skepticism soon had me wondering if the entire experience wasn't the product of a forlorn soul and a few dozen helpings of bad fish-and-chips. About the ghostly manifestation: "This place was a bed-and-breakfast, not Fort Knox. It wouldn't have taken James Bond to get your room key." About his attire: "Yellow rain slicker, knit cap, boots. Why does this say '19th century' to you? To me it says 'Paddington Bear.'" About the Captain's scent of the ocean and tides: "And this differs from a tuna sandwich exactly…*how*?"

And so, within a few days of my return, I quietly surrendered my love to improbability.

Until my dream last night.

I finally reached Bannerjee's, looking exactly as I'd left it, except the word "gay" had been erased from its sign. This time the owner's sister Edna answered the door, ten years later looking like an older and even more annoyed dachshund. She led me in and explained that she'd recently taken ownership of the establishment after the unexpected death of her brother. It was clear she didn't recognize me. She led me down the same path her brother took on my previous visit, stopping at the same door. To my horror the chiseled inscription was now covered by a blue plastic placard announcing this was "The Chuck Norris Room."

She flung the door open, revealing an interior that screamed from its every square inch the inhumanity of bad decorating. The walls were covered with photos, and newspaper and magazine clippings illuminating the minutiae of Mr. Norris's life, yet the room carried an unspoken theme: faded blue denim walls; rust-orange shag carpeting; flesh-colored bed poking out from a ginger headboard. The room was a giant replica of Chuck Norris's exposed groin.

There was no way I was going to sleep that night. I paced the perimeter of the room for as long as I could, but after my legs began to swell I gathered the courage to sit, and then a few hours later to lie down. Thoughts of Chuck Norris, inescapable here, mingled with my recollections of the Captain, which in turn evolved into visions of Paddington Bear and tuna sandwiches. I began to fear I'd traveled 500 miles to a heterosexual hellhole to restore a relationship that had probably never occurred. Finally, curling into a ball atop the giant penis bed, I slept.

Some time during the night I heard the wind rise, and what sounded like the cries of men. I heard a wrenching, a scratching, distant shouts. Then I heard the sound of something substantial smashing, followed by anguished groans and inhuman screeching, as if someone had dropped Richard Simmons from a great height. I pulled on a bathrobe and ran outside, where I saw a small fishing boat foundering on the very same rocks the Mary Celeste had foundered upon. I watched a wave roll in, further damaging the now sinking vessel.

I raced down the sand, hopped into the bed-and-breakfast's rowboat, and begin to paddle. Though my boating skills had heretofore been limited to brightly-colored watercraft bearing names like "Mole" overseen by girls in gingham and guided by hidden tracks, I soon found myself in the sailors' midst, whereupon I wrestled them aboard like large fish. I ferried the men to shore and began a second search to see if I'd missed anyone. The moon disappeared behind a battered black cloud, so I really only saw a sliding silhouette of the leviathan wave that flipped my boat, spilling me into gauzy froth and smashing my boat against the rocks.

When I woke I thought I was dead because all was black. I also thought I must be in hell because I was wet and cold and felt the distinct scratching of sand in my underwear. Then something large and furry rubbed against my face and I wondered if perhaps I'd been reincarnated as either Siegfried or Roy—until I heard the low, warm voice say, "You're safe now, Sea Biscuit. You're safe with me." When I opened my eyes I saw I was covered layers deep in 19th-century clothes, topped by a yellow rain slicker, and that it was not the sea that held me now but the Captain.

"Captain," I said, "I've missed you."

"Aye, laddie. I've missed you too."

"Am I here for the shipwreck or for you?"

"A bit of both," he said, the familiar twinkle returning to his eye. "I know how much you like your sailors." He pulled me close and gave me a kiss that made me realize how much he loved me. And I gave him a kiss that said how much I loved him, and then another that told him how stupid I was to have left. And then one more, spotted by Edna.

She had been content to watch the disaster from the comfort of Bannerjee's but our kissing had brought her to the water's edge, a hair's breadth away, holding a large Ginsu knife. "Faggots," she spat, tossing the knife from one hand to the other.

Now I was mad.

Partly I was mad that this woman was threatening my long-lost lover and me with a knife that could cut through a tin can and then a tomato, but mostly I was mad because she'd called us faggots. Somehow it seemed understandable this woman could be psychotic, that she could redecorate a bed-and-breakfast so that each of the rooms would resemble the genitalia of an (allegedly, at least) heterosexual TV star, and that she could now want to chop the

Captain and me into tiny bits. But *bigotry*? That was just plain rude.

"God made Adam and Eve," she muttered. "Not Adam and *Steve*."

I pushed the Captain behind me and slowly approached. "Then who made Steve?" I answered, diving for the weapon. We tumbled to the sand, the element of surprise enough to win a moment of safety. She smashed her knee into my groin and the pain gave her an opening. She slammed her fist into my face with the kind of strength a thinking God wouldn't have given the insane, and then sat astride me, knife above her head with both crazy hands.

"It's an abomination to the Lord for men to lay with men," she hissed.

"The Bible also says it's an abomination to eat shellfish," I spit back, "but I don't see you stabbing Mrs. Paul!"

She gave me a bitter, confused look and then fell forward on top of me, dropping the knife on the way down. Behind her stood the Captain, holding a large rock.

"You took your own sweet time," I fumed.

"You didn't need my help at all, laddie. See that knife? The scratch marks along the edge? She tried to sharpen it."

"But it's—"

"Exactly. Now it's probably dull as dishwater."

I ran my finger along its edge and watched a thin streak of blood form. I also watched Edna reassemble and propel herself toward me. I darted out of the way and she hurtled past. I took inventory and realized I was knifeless.

Edna wasn't. The Ginsu had plunged through the center of her ribcage and into her heart. A pool of blood formed in the sand, marking her death.

"What do you know?" the Captain said. "Those things really *can* keep an edge."

The hardest part of the next few days wasn't deciding whether to stay at Bannerjee's, or convincing the police I'd killed Edna in self-defense (the sailors I'd rescued corroborated my version of the events), or even scraping together the down payment needed to buy the bed-and-breakfast. The hardest part was removing all vestiges of Edna, restoring Bannerjee's to how it looked when I first visited. But now, finally, all traces of supersized genitalia have been vanquished. The Genet Room has been reborn, although this time with quality toiletries since this is the Captain's and my room.

The Captain proved invaluable to the research and writing of my book, and proudly accepted the first copy, smiling at its sappy dedication.

It seems ironic now that the Captain and I have found each other, that we're content to recline at home like the men I castigated earlier—though with imported beer, tastier snacks, and a mutual distrust of all things Bob Vila. And so we now live and love in a state as near to bliss as you can get without either a lobotomy or a housekeeper.

❧ There With Bells On ❧

by Julia Willis

You couldn't quite call it a nightmare. I didn't wake up screaming. But it was the sort of dream that leaves you with an odd, queasy feeling—like the one you get when you answer a ringing phone at 3 A.M. and no one's on the other end of the line. There's probably nothing to worry about, it was likely a simple dialing mistake, but all the same you wish it hadn't happened, that no one had called, even by accident, and you can't go back to sleep right away because you're waiting for them, whoever they are and for whatever reason, to call again.

"Honey?" Lucinda asked patiently. "I said, 'what was it about?'" Although it was still dark out, she was already dressed and hovering over her earring tree, picking out one to match her sneakers of the day.

Blinking and groggy, I sat up. "Hmm?"

"Your dream. You were dreaming."

"How do you know?"

"I had you hooked up to that big nasty machine I keep under the bed to monitor your brain waves—how do you think?" Holding the pink enamel earring she'd chosen between two fingers, she came over to the bed and sat with her leg snuggled against me. "After all this time—"

"Not all that long," I complained, yawning.

"However long, a smart girl like me learns to pick up on the smallest of nuances when it comes to the sleep of the woman she loves. The moans, the rapid eye movements, the flailing arms and thrashing around—" She leaned over, kissing my chin with my mouth still open from the yawn, so my upper teeth closed on her nose as she withdrew. "All those subtle cues—ow, watch the nose, even if it is paid for."

"Nuances, subtleties," I sniffed. "You sound like someone who lives with a writer."

"See? That's what happens—"

"—after all this time," I finished for her.

"Right." With a caressing hand she smoothed the blanket over my breasts. "So you gonna tell me what it was about? Fast, before I run out the door to meet my boss for breakfast?"

"I'm not sure I can." Some dreams can be summed up in a sentence: "I was in a train station with this huge box of kittens," or "I was in my mother's kitchen and all the appliances were green and all the food was sitting out on the counters, spoiling," or "You and I were making love, only strange people kept coming to the door and interrupting us." But this dream wasn't like that.

"Anxiety dream?" Lucinda guessed.

"In a way," I said. "But not really."

"Know what I dreamed?" she asked, telling me quickly without waiting for a reply. "That I was back in that awful band."

"Which one? You were in several awful bands as I recall."

"The Flaming Femmes—*that* awful one. And when we got to the club and opened the back of the van all the equipment was gone."

"Haven't you had that one before?"

"Only about 50 times. But there's always a new twist. You know, a variation on the theme. This time the club owner said we'd missed the sound check but we had to go on anyway—so she hands me this tin pie plate and a wooden chopstick to beat it with and points me toward the stage."

"Was your audience into pie plate drumming?"

"Can't tell you. That was the end. I woke up." She kissed me again, much better than before, and stood up. "Gotta go. But can you believe I'm still dreaming about that fucking band—"

"—after all this time?" I said. "Sure. When she was 92, my grandmother was still dreaming about losing her Latin homework."

"Whew—lucky her." Lucinda lingered by the dresser mirror to slip in the earring and fluff her bangs. "Well, if it's bothering you, your dream, maybe you should write it down." She clicked off the little lamp on the dresser. "That's what Jackie's therapist has her doing. Writing down all her dreams. In a dream journal."

Jackie was Lucinda's upscale sister. I tried to picture her dream journal, a clothbound affair with marbleized end pages and thick white paper edged in gold. Fortunately, Jackie had the practiced penmanship worthy of a fancy book like that. My hurried scribblings, on the other hand, deserved nothing nicer than a spiral-bound memo pad with blue-lined pages and a Looney Tunes cover. But I wasn't feeling the need for a dream journal. "I won't have to write this one down. I'll remember it."

Lucinda paused in the doorway, framed prettily by the light from the stairwell. "Yeah, well, that's what you think now. But I bet if I call you later you won't remember a thing. Bye."

She switched off the light on the stairs on her way out and left me in bed, wide awake and staring at the ceiling, watching it slowly turn white and blank as an empty page while the sun rose and I thought about my dream…

I had gone to a place in the country, one of those writer's retreats that are always in the country. Rustic solitude is supposedly conducive to good work, though I've heard that city writers cast adrift in a hundred secluded acres can undergo sudden, severe cases of urban sensory deprivation. After a few days of maddening peace and quiet, they go scampering back to their noisy rooms in Manhattan. Of course, I find that whenever I attempt to escape civilization, it never fails to follow me: buzzing chainsaws, incessant hammerings, and small low-flying planes with unmuffled engines can and do track me to the ends of the earth. But this doesn't stop me from seeking occasional bouts of woodland tranquillity, especially if the room and board are free for the taking.

So there I was, with nearly a dozen other writers—some men, some women, all presumably straight and none of whom I'd ever met before. We had arrived in the afternoon, settled into our respective cabins, and finished our first dinner together in the main building's dining hall. We were lingering over coffee and the remains of a gooey chocolate dessert when a strange note was delivered to our table by the puzzled caretaker who had found it tacked to the front door of his lodge. A graying novelist named Gilbert, whose place was at one end of the long oak refectory table, stood and read its curious message aloud.

The note was impersonally addressed to "The Writers" and handwritten in large, block letters. Considering its content, I was surprised it wasn't made up of those cut-and-paste magazine letters that movie kidnappers always use in their ransom notes. Because the gist of it was that someone was threatening by some undescribed means to take all our writings, rip them into shreds, and "scatter them across the meadow like a sack of paper wildflower seeds."

A quick shudder ran through Gilbert as he paused, gripping the note tautly in both hands like a shoeshine rag. Several of the other writers gave nervous chuckles, and a tall woman with a colorful Guatemalan shawl across her shoulders and a strong hint of contempt in her voice said, "And I suppose we can expect this outrage to occur on the precise stroke of midnight."

Gilbert adjusted his reading glasses before continuing. "No, no—it says, 'A bell will ring once, as a warning for you all to clear out.'

Wants us to leave, apparently."

"We just got here," someone at the opposite end of the table complained.

"Go on, Gilbert," said a woman poet beside me.

"Yes, well, after that warning bell, let's see—'a second bell will ring. Maybe a minute later, perhaps an hour. But whenever that second bell rings, then shall I come, like an evil wind blowing up from Hell, and destroy all you have, every written word.'" Gilbert turned the note over and back again. "That seems to be all. It's—unsigned."

He dropped the slip of paper on his refolded linen napkin, and as if by prearranged signal the table erupted in an animated display of wild speculation regarding the note and its contents. Where had the thing come from? Who had sent it? Was it merely someone's stupid idea of a joke, or should it be taken seriously? And if we proposed to accept it at face value, what then?

Everyone tried to talk at once, with the exception of myself and the woman poet sitting beside me. I don't know what she was thinking, but I know I was momentarily struck dumb by the speed with which such an ominous announcement was being transformed before my eyes into an intellectual parlor game. Not that I didn't have those same questions, but there was an almost manic eagerness at that table to deflect the alarming consequences of the situation by endless rounds of questions and light-hearted banter. Within minutes the group had divided itself into three camps.

First there were those who saw the note as a test, an experiment devised by an unknown party to see how we'd react to the threat of our work being destroyed. A second faction concluded it was simply a cruel practical joke being played upon us, either by some bitter outsider who had not been invited—or by one of us at that very table, a prospect that made everyone distinctly uncomfortable. Then there was the third contingent, which included noteholder Gilbert, who kept bringing the paper up to the light, turning it this way and that and squinting. This little coterie never arrived at the who, what, or why, being too caught up in the minutiae of (a) whether it was a woman's or a man's handwriting, (b) if the phrase "all our writings" in the threat referred only to our writings-in-progress and what notes we'd brought with us or would also include any printed copies of our work that happened to be lying around the place, and (c) how the actual seriousness of the situation might be determined by the particular way the note had been fastened to the caretaker's door (with a dagger—chilling, with Scotch tape—negligible).

"What do you think it means, Barbara?" someone from Gilbert's detail-fixated quartet finally inquired of the quiet woman poet.

She smiled at me and rose from her chair. "I believe," she announced, the smile dropping off her face as her napkin fluttered to the floor, "it must be a communication from a dark force dwelling within this place, and I believe that force is capable of anything."

To confirm Barbara's belief, no sooner had she finished speaking than the six tall candles on the table flickered once and went out, plunging us into a shadowy semidarkness lit only by short streaks of light spilling in from the kitchen on one side and the hallway leading to the game room on the other.

"Good Lord," said Gilbert in a hoarse whisper, "if that were to be the case, this thing could conceivably destroy every word we have ever written."

"Or all the words we ever will write," someone else added.

Before we could contemplate the likelihood of either of those unpleasant suggestions, the first bell rang—a soft but resonant tinkling that filled the room. We received our fair warning, and I woke up...

Shivering, but not with cold, I threw off the covers. Thinking over my dream brought back that same stifled, light-headed feeling I had when I earlier awakened to the sound of that warning bell. And a part of me still clutched at the dream as it dangled there in the air, unresolved, unfinished.

Our bedroom was drenched in daylight now, and a faint whiff of exhaust fumes let me know the morning traffic was backing up at the stoplight on the corner. Time to get up and put on the coffee and walk the dog. I resisted, closing my eyes again and resuming my seat in that shadowy dining room with the faint echo of that first bell ringing in my ears. What should I do?

Supposing it were a test, some insidious pop quiz my unconscious had arranged for me—would it be cowardly to run back to my cabin, toss my clothes, file boxes, and notebooks into my truck, and make a run for the border? Or would it be foolhardy not to? But if Barbara and Gilbert were correct, if supernatural forces were at work, what would it matter what I or anyone did? Go or stay, flight or fight, that second bell would certainly ring, unleashing a destructive power to reduce all our fine efforts, our years of desperate struggle with an untamable language in an unsympathetic culture, to nothing—or, as the note had said, to a scattering of "paper wildflower seeds." Was that the dream's lesson, then? To imagine how it would feel to have "writ in water?" To mourn in a place where no words of grief exist? To be a speechless soul, doomed to mute agony for all eternity—

The doorbell rang and I bolted out of bed, my heart racing. If the cosmic word police had arrived, it was too late to hide that half-written novel under the attic floorboards. Quickly pulling on a pair of jeans, I ran downstairs where Moondog was pacing and a dark figure loomed behind the front door curtains.

"Who is it?"

"Package—Lucinda Doyle?"

I opened up for the UPS woman, signed her clipboard with Lucinda's name, and took the small brown parcel she handed me. Before closing the door I glanced at the return label and burst out laughing. The delivery woman stopped on the steps, cocking her head sideways at me.

"Wildflower seeds!" I shouted.

"Uh-huh," she said, nodding, and picked up the pace to her truck parked on the corner.

"Wildflower seeds," I repeated to Moondog, who didn't care one way or the other as long as she got her walk in the next five minutes. So she did.

After our brisk jog around the block, I made a pot of coffee and carried my first cup back to bed. I couldn't go back to sleep and continue the dream, but maybe if I sat with it awhile I could figure out who had sent that threatening note, and why. I closed my eyes for the third time that morning, relit the tall candles on the dining room table, and looked around it at my fellow writers. They were such familiar strangers.

I began with Gilbert, whose air of endearing befuddlement stemmed from the fact that for the last 30 years he'd been writing different versions of the same tired novel: the story of a clever, rebellious, young-to-middle-aged white man tilting his phallic lance quixotically at the academic or corporate institutions of other not-so-clever or rebellious white men, while a series of vacuous and needy wives and girlfriends alternately succored and tormented him. Having made a pretty fair living and a name for himself this way, Gilbert was puzzled and somewhat annoyed these days by books whose characters weren't white or whose women weren't needy. Happily for him there still weren't too many of those, not from the major houses, anyway, so they could usually be avoided.

Seated across from me was Francine, a statuesque woman who, well along in her life of privilege, had traded her mink for Third World apparel, leaving her investor husband and college-age children to fend for themselves as she traveled extensively, writing and self-publishing commendable chapbooks of essays on the hardships of peasant women and the tragedies of a shrinking rain forest. They were beautifully made volumes, critically well-received and primarily read by editors of the best eco-journals and a select number of her friends. No one could ever accuse Francine of being ill-informed; yet her money would always give her the perspective of someone examining the world carefully through the wrong end of a telescope.

On my right was Barbara, a poet acquainted with all forms of personal tragedy, from two bad marriages to the loss of her only son, from breast cancer to alcohol addiction, from rape to recent recollections of childhood abuse. Her work brilliantly reflected every ounce of her pain with the clarity and strength of a true survivor. She had come to understand and count on the tremendous power of the human spirit, but she remained haunted by visions of the next round, the ensuing demon, the final battle she won't win. Consequently, she was prone to sudden outbursts and violent mood swings, preferring to spend her days and nights alone.

Also arranged around the table were the rest, those I didn't know by name but recognized nonetheless. Flanking a young red-headed woman at the far end of the table opposite Gilbert was a matched set of young men fresh from graduate school, both of whom had written their coming-of-age-in-a-dysfunctional-upper-middle-class-family novels before they even *came* of age, both of whom now found themselves desperate for ideas and experience, and both of whom were presently competing for the aforementioned young redheaded woman, whose own coming-of-age-novel-with-a-twist (the dysfunctional family belonged to the narrator's best friend) had been optioned by Paramount while it was still in galleys.

Beside Barbara the poet sat the self-effacing daughter of a famous writer parent. Her books were always better than she thought they were but never quite as good as was expected of her by a reading public who simply adored her mother. Next came the playwright whose characters' dialogue crackled with wit and sparkling repartee, though in ordinary conversation he himself couldn't manage to string more than half a dozen words together if his life depended on it. Across from him was the pink-cheeked, white-bearded writer-illustrator of children's books who, beneath his Saint Nicholas facade of mellow professionalism, ached with longing for the "important" book which had somehow never materialized.

The former foreign correspondent beside Good Saint Nick was so indoctrinated by his years in journalism to think in words per minute that he was compelled to announce when he first sat down to dinner how he'd unpacked and written six pages since 4 o'clock and definitely planned to complete his chapter before bedtime. (If this dream were a murder mystery, he would surely be the first to go.) And finally, there was the 30ish black woman writer who had worked her way through business school, trained herself to write from 4 to 6:30 every morning, taken five years to write her autobiographical novel, and then engaged in a campaign of tireless self-promotion to turn it into a bestseller. Her novel had indeed made the pages of "The New York Times Book Review," so now she was seated between the journalist and Francine; their exaggerated attentions made her feel like a rare exotic specimen wriggling on a collector's pin.

That made us an even dozen counting me, the retreat's token lesbian, who could expect to go under the microscope as soon as the assembled company tired of poking, prodding, and patronizing the black writer just to show her they weren't prejudiced. While some of us, in twos and threes, would connect and perhaps become friends, the idea of all of us in the same room, much less breaking bread and peacefully co-existing for weeks on end, was mind-boggling. Any one of us had several sworn enemies at that table. There was enough professional jealousy and political disharmony to keep us permanently estranged. So why should it be surprising that someone sent a vicious note, hiring a confederate to ring a hidden bell? If caught it would be easy to deny malicious intent by claiming that "learning experiment" defense. The right to observe was any good writer's prerogative. No, never mind the caretaker, or some nebulous unknown trickster—our note writer was sitting right there at the table all along.

But who would have done it? And since it was my dream, which of those writers would I have chosen to be the culprit? I began by weeding out the most obvious suspects. Gilbert, the bearded children's writer, the journalist, the two boy writer clones—they were all driven, and to some extent disillusioned, by their careers. They presumably shared the dark secret thought that a literary life was somehow less than manly, trying to compensate with Hemingwayesque touches like facial hair, fly fishing, or consistent overindulgence in alcohol. Control games and frat house pranks seemed so fitting, so in character for this bunch, choking on their own testosterone, that surely I had more imagination than to pin the crime on one of them.

Women on the fast track? They frequently took the rap in mysteries, didn't they—the ambitious bitch prototype being the modern-day equivalent of the woman scorned? Maybe the young redhead realized she was peaking at 25, or the older black woman could feel her head bumping up against status quo publishing's glass ceiling. No, count them out. Again, too obvious. Also too sexist and/or racist, not my style at all.

Having narrowed the field considerably, I paused and opened my eyes. My coffee was cold. "If I were Sherlock Holmes," I said, "I'd only have to ring for Mrs. Hudson to bring me a fresh pot." But I wasn't and she wouldn't, so I took a cold sip and a deep breath instead. Let's see—the quiet types, the tongue-tied playwright or the modest daughter. They were so accustomed to moving practically unnoticed through life's shadows that either might assume he or she could plan and carry out the cruelest hoax without suspicion pointing in their direction. But it was hard to imagine them doing anything to risk calling attention to themselves.

Whereas everything about Francine—her voice, her manner, even her height, an Amazonian 72 inches—cried out for the world to sit up and take notice of a woman with something important to say. Could the note have been a sneaky guerrilla tactic to make everyone see that time was running out, not only for a pack of writers and their silly words, but for natural resources, indigenous cultures, planet Earth herself? No—too far-fetched. Francine always spoke right up if she had something on her mind; a Sarah Lawrence girl, she had nothing to hide.

Neither did Barbara, not anymore. She'd told the whole truth and let the chips fall often enough. Our eloquent doomsayer, she was willing to predict an after-dinner calamity at the risk of being labeled a paranoid Shirley MacLaine. In fact, she was so damned honest, so beyond reproach, that she could be the logical suspect beyond suspicion, the long-suffering victim no one would guess was actually the scheming perpetrator bent on revenge for the long years of hurts, real and imagined, life had heaped—wait a minute. This began to sound like just another case of blaming the victim, and I was certainly not prepared to be accused of that.

Then what could I be accused of? If Barbara hadn't sent the note and I had edited out everyone else, I was the last suspect left standing. Could the angry part of me, aware the LESBIAN badge I wore so proudly was keeping me in a box of small presses and out of the mainstream where the big deals were made, be that resentful of these other writers? Writers I had specifically selected to populate this dream, all of whom by luck, gender, accident of birth, or sheer perseverance tended to be—for the moment, anyway—more financially successful than I was? Did I really wish them harm?

Taking another deep breath, I looked at the clock. It was already past time for me to start work, and if I didn't sit down at my desk soon I'd find all sorts of excuses to delay finishing that story today: letters that needed answering, errands that needed doing, laundry that needed sorting—there was always something else I could be doing. Something so much easier. Because it was never easy to face that first blank page in the morning and convince myself the job of filling that page was the *only* thing in the world worth doing. And always, in those first few minutes, before the words began to flow, when it appeared as if they had abandoned me and were never coming back, as if they'd never belonged to me at all—

"Of course," I said, "the note." What was it Holmes told Watson about the truth? That once you've eliminated the impossible, whatever remains must be true? Well, it was. I *had* written that note. I was guilty, and everyone else seemed guilty because they were too, but not for the reasons I thought.

Taking one more cold sip of coffee, I let my mind's eye wander one final time over the group around that dining room table. Freezing on the moment before I awoke, just as that first bell rang, I searched those faces and found panic, shock, dismay. In the next millisecond such terrified expressions might revert to blank stares or nervous grins or the ultimate gaze of supreme indifference, but for one brief instant we were united in our overriding fear of losing a precious gift. We shared the same crazed, compelling desire to make stories and put them down on paper and send them out to live in the world. Whatever our separate, selfish reasons for coming there, to see our stories destroyed, to lose our ability to make more, would be equally devastating to any one of us.

Yes, I had written the note. So had Gilbert, Francine, Barbara, and the rest. In the dream's reality we saw only one note, when in truth there were twelve identical notes delivered to that table, one from each of us to ourselves. Because we all knew if the power to create could live within us, so could its opposite, and whenever we confronted another pile of notes, another incomplete sentence, we renewed that battle within. Every day we faced the horrible fate of running dry, or of writing the very words that would someday destroy us.

However we worked through our fears, covered them with smug pretensions, or cranked out the prescribed number of pages per day, we were so alike in spite of our differences. We wanted the work we did to mean something, and to last. We were poised and waiting for that second bell to ring, while hoping against hope it never would…

The phone rang once, sharply, and I jumped. Lucinda was calling from work. "Figured out that dream yet?"

"Uh-huh."

"Yeah? What did it mean?"

"It was sexual," I lied in a deadpan monotone.

"I should've guessed."

"You got a package. Seeds."

Her enthusiasm almost rattled the receiver. "Oh, great! Will you help me plant them this weekend?"

"Is that a come-on?"

"You bet."

"Sure I will," I sighed, "if I'm not too busy planting my own seeds."

"Why is it," she asked, "you make every conversation I have with you seem to be about sex?"

"Sex? I wasn't thinking of sex. I was thinking of art."

"Oh, well—sex and art, what else is there, right?" In the background I heard the ding of a microwave. "There's my coffee," she said. "See you tonight."

After getting myself a fresh cup of coffee, I went to work too. And I stared at that blank sheet of paper for a full five minutes before I remembered to turn down the bell on the phone, just so I wouldn't hear it ring.

⫷ Closer ⫸

by Andrew Berac

October 18

Winter sucks. OK, OK, so it's not exactly winter, but you can tell it's going to be. Great time to get booted out of your own house. Yeesh... Get real, Walker. Three months in a rental due to extensive renovations does not a tragic movie of the week make. This place does look like something *The X-Files* would use in a location shoot though. One of its more redeeming qualities really. Better thing to concentrate on than the fact that the bathroom smells obscurely of old lady and the curtains look like they were purchased by the Brady Bunch. I'm sure I'll get used to it. I'll have to; no way am I putting any effort into upgrading this place for a landlord. It's only three months, right?

October 20

I saw a kid fall down the stairs today. Here. In the house. Now, a kid in my house would be strange enough on its own since I don't know any kids and I certainly don't hang around with them, but once this kid made a point-blank landing on its head, it disappeared. And this was *before* the trip to the cold beer store, so I can't put it down to an altered state of consciousness. Don't know why I'm writing this all down in the first place—God knows I've never felt compelled to keep a journal before—but it's something to do, and it's not every day you see a 6-year-old kid fall soundlessly down your stairs. Yep, soundless. Took about ten seconds. Couldn't tell if the fall was fatal or not, since the whole scene ended like someone had turned off the VCR. I glanced at the stairs and there he was. He fell, he hit bottom, and then he was gone. This is taking that *X-Files* comparison I made the other day a little too far. I think I have ghosts.

October 23

Thought about telling Kevan about the kid when I talked to him today, but it sounds too stupid. I can just hear him: "Oh, fuck, Curtis, you have truly lost it now." Or something to that effect. He's my best friend and occasional fuck buddy (though I get the distinct impression that he's in the process of getting himself a serious relationship these days), but he thinks I'm as whacked as everyone else does. Well maybe not *as* whacked, but he definitely thinks I'm twisted. He's told me so more than once.

November 1

What a disappointment. Halloween last night and not a ghost to be seen here. Not that I was home for much of it. Went out for a drink, ran into Roach (I have no idea what his real name is; sometimes I wonder if *he* does) and spent the bulk of the night having some consensual fun at his place, as a result of which moving from my bed to the couch this afternoon was an effort. I can only imagine what he feels like at the moment. I am going to stay on this couch, watch mindless TV all night, and order take-out food. The kid can fall downstairs without an audience.

[later...3 A.M.?] So I'm watching *Total Recall* for the millionth time, not having a care in the wicked world (except for the fact that this is the most uncomfortable couch I've ever sat on), and suddenly Trevor walks into the living room, throws that ghastly brown leather jacket of his onto a nonexistent piece of furniture, gives me one of his patented puppy-dog looks, and promptly disappears. After the initial shock (yes, boys and girls, even Curtis Walker is shockable on occasion) my first thought is that I didn't have any idea he was dead. I haven't seen Trevor in over a year. We had what you might call a love/indifference relationship. He thought he loved me. Crass as it may sound, I just wanted in his pants. But since it was much more effective to play along, I played along. I've never understood these feelings of "love" people profess to have for one another, but over the years I've gotten damn good at being charming. So I made all the right facial expressions and all the right noises and Trevor gave me everything in perfect confidence that we'd be together forever. Forever turned out to be six months. He'd started to bore me both intellectually and sexually. There were just too many things he wasn't willing to think, willing to do. And his taste in music was abysmal. So I broke it off, but in a tortured, angst-filled way that had him convinced it was *his* fault our everlasting love went down in flames. It was all a rather neat piece of work. But I don't like the thought that he might be dead. I wonder if I should get tested for AIDS.

November 5

Saw the kid again today. In fact, this time I walked through his head as he fell sprawling on the landing. He's like a 3-D videotape loop playing endlessly on the stairs. Trevor's ghost still bothers me, and the results haven't come back yet. I'm at loose ends. Can't go to Kev to relieve a little tension. Not until I find out if I'm clear. Of course, I'm not even sure if Kev would welcome me right now. This new boyfriend of his has been occupying all his nights lately. Looks like me and a case of beer tonight…and maybe my knives. Better go get the beer and rent a video or two. There's sure as hell nothing on TV, and I'm not in the mood for socializing.

November 9

Now this is getting weird. Still no word on the test, but that's not what's weird at the moment. I'm pretty sure I have nothing to worry about anyway. Get this (he says to his faithful laptop; why the fuck am I writing all this down in the first place? I'm not even being Mulder, looking over my evidence and coming up with some strange but brilliantly correct answer to what's going on. I'm being Scully, conscientiously making notes about it all)…I get up this afternoon, have a coffee or three, jump into the shower in the bathroom that still smells faintly of old lady…business as usual, right? Well. I get out, dry off, and wipe the steam off the mirror, looking closely at myself for signs that something's not right. (OK, so I'm a little paranoid after all.) I look just like I always have. Same black hair that's so determinedly thick and unruly my mum used to have to practically shellac it to get it into some semblance of order till I put a stop to her efforts. Same dark eyes. Same tan-resistant skin (though sunburns are another story). Same body that refuses to put on anything resembling muscle mass. Hell, I had that pale, anorexic Goth look before anyone decided it was fashionable. Just a fortunate thing that I'm naturally nocturnal, love the music, and even have the blood fetish. Still a few battle scars from Halloween night, but that's nothing new. For me, I'm the picture of health. Still naked, I leave the bathroom and practically walk through the ghost of Leanne MacDonald. I stop before I do, and look closely at her. She doesn't seem as inclined to disappear as Trevor and the kid on the stairs. She's leaking tears, which streak her mascara unattractively. She spits something undoubtedly uncomplimentary at the empty space behind my left shoulder and spins around, flouncing into nothingness. I blink, wondering what to make of it. She's dead too? Leanne was one of my few forays into the world of hetero-sexuality, back when I was about 17. Not for any of those typical reasons. I wasn't in the least confused about my sexuality, or trying to deny it, or trying to make people *think* I was straight (truth is, no one thought I was queer; they were all too worried with the thought that I was psychotic). I'd gone after her out of pure mal-ice; an unsolicited favor to a friend of mine (who was all too obvi-ously gay) after she'd made about a thousand too many snotty comments and sicced her football-player boyfriend and his yard-ape buddies on him. Well, that and I just thought it would be amus-ing. So I sweet-talked her, I charmed her, I let her think I was the quintessential bad boy with a heart of gold that only she could reach. I dated her on the sly. (After all, she couldn't be *seen* with a freak like me.) I acted like a puppy dog who couldn't believe his good fortune at getting the attention of one of the prettiest, most popular girls in school, and in a surprisingly short amount of time she fell for it. Even said she loved me. Then I fucked her, the first time nice and sweet and hesitant and everything she ever dreamed of, the second, letting my natural inclinations show, not to the point that *I* like but enough to freak the fuck out of *her*. Then I dumped her as hard and cruel and publicly as possible. Have I mentioned that there are those who would say I'm not a nice person, myself among them? See, it's not easy to care when deep down you never have, so I simply don't bother. And now here she was, five years later, playing ectoplasmic games outside my rented bathroom door. *Is* she dead? Am I supposed to gather from this that I caused it? Is that supposed to jolt me into caring about something, feeling some sudden remorse for my dastardly behavior? If it is, it's not working.

November 15

The kid made his usual appearance today (he seems fond of 7:15 P.M.) and this time I even had witnesses! Bob and his date-of-the-week were over, and just on the off-chance I dragged them to the landing at the appropriate time. Sure as shit, there he was. Both Bob and The Date were appropriately impressed. The Date suggested I get an exorcist, but I don't see the point. I've never seen any level of intelligence in the one-act tragedy on the stairs. He shows up, he falls, he disappears. It isn't a possession; it's an ecto-plasmic 8-track. Bob seemed to understand. Went on a lot about hearing about this sort of thing on the Art Bell show. (He works nights, so he's very up on late night radio.) But he didn't have any suggestions as to what I should do about it other than try to doc-ument it on video. I thought about mentioning Trevor and Leanne, but it didn't seem worth the effort.

Happy birthday to me. I shouldn't sound so bitter. Not only did the test come back as negative as ever, but Kev and Ian stopped by with gifts and a two-four of beer and we actually had a pretty good time. I think I'm just feeling sorry for myself because not only could Kev not quite shut up about this new love of his (and Ian had oh-so-thoughtfully brought over some godawful disco shit of his to put on *my* CD player), but after they'd left and I was well and truly buzzed, who should show up on the ghostly hit parade but Victor. There I am trying to coffee my way out of an alcoholic haze, listening to a little Front Line Assembly, and in he walks. Gives me his patented green-eyed "here I am" smirk, settles into what should be a chair, and disappears. This one bothers me more than the oth-ers. I *know* he's not dead. He's too smart and too much of an ass-hole to be dead. Our problem was we were just a little too much alike. We started out trying to use each other, and when it became evident we were starting to feel a little more than that (not *love* or anything, you understand; more of a mutual giving-a-shit about what the other thought) we both panicked and broke it off. But if he's *not* dead, why is he haunting my living room?

Andrew Berac

November 29

OK, this is getting stupid. I saw *Ian* in my hall closet today, and I *definitely* know he's not dead. He was at my house just a week ago and I would've heard if he'd kicked it. I'm feeling very poorly done by in the haunting department. From everything I've ever heard, ghosts are supposed to be extremely dead. Whether you think ghosts are people who haven't been able to accept that fact, residual echoes of strong emotions, whatever, the one thing all the theories have in common is the discontinued physical existence of the ghost in question. It's bad enough living in a house haunted by dead people; at least there's a certain classical glamour to that. You can invite paranormal research teams over, use it as an ice-breaker at parties, feel slightly smug that you've seen evidence there really *is* an afterlife.... But no, I have to be haunted by *live* ones! You'd think the living would be too busy doing just that to waste time manifesting themselves as life-size 3-D tape-oops for my viewing displeasure. And the second part of the question is, if I'm being haunted by the ghosts of very alive people who I've been personally acquainted with, where does the kid fit in? I know I've never seen him in my life, and that fall looked possibly lethal. I know I'm not becoming delusional. I only see things in this house, and besides, Bob and whatshisname saw the kid too. Maybe I'll do the next classic horror novel move and see if I can find any answers to this at the library.

December 3

No new ghosts the last few days, though Vic sauntered through the living room again. Oh, and you could set your watch by the kid these days. The library was a complete waste of time. Every book I looked in was as convinced as I used to be that in order to be a card-holding member in the ghostly Union you have to be dead.

Closer

December 9

Yet another Trevor-in-the-living-room. And a new one. S[...]
man by the back door. He looks a little familiar but damned [...]
place him. I'm getting real tired of not knowing when or wh[...]
next new ghost is going to turn up. Correction—I'm gettin[...]
tired of ghosts, period.

December 15

I heard something interesting on the radio today. It might eve[...]
partially explain my unique pest problem. (Speaking of which[...]
Leanne was blubbering at me outside the bathroom again; [...]
walked through her this time. Didn't seem to make any impression,
which makes me think I was dead right about there being no
intelligence behind these manifestations.) Ha! "Dead right." Get it?
Anyway, one of those radio psychologists was saying (in reference
to dating, but I think it sort of applies to more than that) that when
humans try to get to know you they send out little "tendrils of emotion," which they hope will attach and take with the tendrils that
you're supposedly sending out. So I'm starting to wonder…could
those tendrils have an afterlife? I'm gonna try something, if I can
figure out how to go about it. Good thing I've watched the right
movies and I'm on the morbid side to begin with. Otherwise I
would've run out of here screaming by now.

December 23

Well I'm certainly in the mood for the test I've come up with. I
hate this holiday crap. And don't go thinking it's because of some
traumatic thing having to do with my childhood or my parents
being dead. It's just that seeing all these people forcing themselves
to pretend to be jolly and charitable because it's That Time of Year
makes me want to smack them upside the head. Incidentally, it was

ome old
if I can
ere the
g real

ed me to try this test. See, I fig-
who'd felt emotionally attached to
wn up *first*, especially since they *are*
picuous in their absence. Whereas the
for a solid year before I "accidentally"
cer game in tenth grade Phys Ed walked
d glared at me a few days ago. So I'm think-
eing is some kind of... emotional dandruff,
severs it. We'll see...

December 24

definitely onto something. It was a long shot, but like
as in the mood anyway. I've mentioned I have a blood
ght? And the way things are these days, satisfying that is a
solitary activity. In other words, I cut myself. It's not a "cry
elp" or whatever else the pundits that preach from the pulpits
Oprah and Jerry Springer would have you believe. It just plain
ets me off. But there are a hell of a lot of people who've bought
the Cry for Help theory of Self-Mutilation hook, line, and sinker.
So I figured what the hell. I was in the mood, and if anything man-
ifested it might help back up my theory. Worked better than I could
have hoped. I'd made no more than a few shallow cuts when who
should appear but my junior high school psychologist (the appropriately named Mr. Dyck), complete with that earnestly baffled
expression he always had when he was dealing with me. He'd
thought I was crying for help when he saw the admittedly gruesome state of my arms, and since I didn't exactly want to tell him
that the shock of controlled pain and the sight of blood give me a
hard-on, I'd blamed it on the family cat. Then there'd been a big
soap opera with him trying to get me to admit I was emotionally
fucked up while I stuck to the cat story (which had always worked
before). It came down to me not budging and the parents siding
with me. Again, it was a story of long standing so there wasn't a

damn thing he could do about it. But I do think there's something to the fact that his ghost appeared to me during that particular activity. The question now is what can I do about it? Or should I do anything? After all, I only have another month to go here, and since I've never seen ghosts before I'm assuming it's a phenomenon unique to this house. And what the fuck does that kid have to do with it all?

January 3

New Year's parties are definitely overrated, whether they be the overpriced arranged ones throughout the city or the private parties. I suppose I sound jaded, but the fact of the matter is I find most people tiring and incomprehensible and parties just seem to bring that home more and more these days. Ha! "These days"... you'd think I was 43, not 23, eh? Could have something to do with the fact that ever since I was a kid I've never quite been able to shake the feeling that almost everyone and everything around me is fake, if that makes any sense. Still, I made the effort rather than sit around waiting for the next ghost to show up. Not that they wasted any time once I got home. The newest one is a rather sweet, pudgy girl trying desperately to look mysterious and vampiric who spent the better part of one night a few months ago talking to me quite earnestly about the merits of inducing a near-death experience through auto-asphyxiation. If my Emotion-Tendril theory is right, she thought it was a way of coming on to me and that's why she's shown up in my kitchen. Problem is, I found it and her rather dull. Just because I have a penchant for black clothing doesn't mean I have a fascination with near-death experiences, even if she *was* my type. Which she most definitely wasn't. This is starting to get irritating. If I stayed here long enough would every single person who tried to make some emotional connection with me show up? Since I can't think of one person who ever has made such a connection, I suppose I'd have a houseful before the year was out. I've decided

I don't know who the old man was. Maybe he's another one like the kid, just comes with the house.

January 10

I wonder if this living-ghost thing has happened to everyone who's lived in this house, or if it's some special treat just for me. And if it's the latter, *why* me? If I'm supposed to be learning something from this, the object of the lesson has escaped me entirely, unless it's that hauntings aren't nearly as exciting as Hollywood makes them out to be. Mr. Dyck popped in again just a few minutes ago, but he disappeared before the couch pillow I threw at him could connect. I'm wondering now...I know the kid can be seen by other people, but would they be able to see the *living* ghosts, too? At least I'm outta here in a few more weeks. Then I can stop worrying about it.

January 12

HA! That's one question answered! Kevan came over last night and while we were talking in the living room Vic put in his semi-regular appearance (funny how he and Trevor never show up at the same time). Kev nearly jumped out of his skin. Once he'd calmed down—after a good 15 minutes of "What the fuck was that? Did you *see* that? A fucking *ghost* just materialized in your *living room*, Curtis! How can you just *sit* there?"—he finally realized that not only had a ghost appeared in my living room, but he'd recognized it. Which freaked him all over again, so I finally ended up telling him the whole story. To tell the truth, it was a relief to finally be able to discuss it with someone, and a relief to know that those personal tape-loops can be seen by other people. Guess it's all been bothering me more than I thought. He didn't say much, just listened to me seriously and asked a few questions, then—typical Kevan—said he wanted to think about it. Then he broke that monogamy rule he seems to have made for himself since finding True Love and helped me take my mind off this whole damned ghost business for the rest of the night. Afterwards I had the best sleep I've had in weeks. You know, I often wonder why he likes me so much, especially when he's the first who'll tell me what a self-absorbed bastard I am...

January 16

Another day, another new ghost. Can't even remember this one's name. From what I recall, I'd made nice to him so he'd take me to a Nine Inch Nails concert instead of the guy he was dating at the time, since the show had sold out before I'd managed to buy a ticket. It worked, too. Talked to Kevan today; he thinks maybe the kid falling down the stairs was the trigger for everything. I'm not sure how he came to that conclusion, but it's as good a theory as any. I could wish that with the number of ghosts hanging around here these days, one of them would take a break from doing mindless tape-loops and do my dishes.

January 17

Ugh! I cannot *wait* for this week to end so I can get the hell out of this place for good. Kevan just left. He thinks he has the answer to my pest problem, including the nice little moral lesson I should learn from it all—and that's what makes me want to hit him. He should know me well enough to...well, if I'm taking the time to write this all down I should do it properly. He agrees with my Emotional Dandruff theory, that it's the only explanation that makes sense for why I'm being haunted by people who are alive. The salient points of the conversation went something like this:

"What's the one thing all these people have in common, Curtis? They all tried to reach you, to connect with you in some way."

I shrug. "*I* figured that much out."

He sighs a little impatiently. "Yeah, but take the next step. They all *felt* something for you, but you didn't feel a damn thing for them. So those tendrils of emotion you were talking about just...stuck, with nowhere to go. And for some reason they're...they're physically manifesting here."

"I liked Vic," I point out.

"You cut it off with him the second you thought you *might* start to feel something for him, you mean."

"It was mutual and you know it," I snap. He does know it.

"Well maybe he felt a little more for you than he let on."

I roll my eyes. "Then how do you explain whatshisname? The goof whose ankle I broke in tenth grade? The only thing he wanted to connect was his fist with my face."

He's ready for that one. Gives me a smug look and says, "I seem to remember him *trying* to talk to you at the very beginning and you being a complete bastard to him because he was on a couple of sports teams."

"I hate sports. Besides, he made my life a living hell."

"But he did try to connect with you," he says triumphantly.

I glare at him and try to change the subject. "So how do you know these tendrils have been sticking to me ever since these people tried to connect with me?"

"Simple. Do the ones from years ago look the ages they are now, or do they look the same as they did then?"

I have to give him that one and I say so. I'm finding the thought of all those emotion tendrils sticking to me for years vaguely disgusting. "So why haven't *you* showed up as a ghost?" I ask.

"Because," he smiles a bit, "I *do* connect with you a little, and *you* know it."

I hate it when he's right. I sigh. "Well, this is the lamest haunting I've ever heard of."

He gives me a look. "That's all you think?"

"Huh?" What does he *want* me to think?

He looks at me impatiently. "It doesn't occur to you that if you weren't so self-absorbed this wouldn't be happening to you? That maybe if you gave a shit once in a while…"

I snort. "Oh, please. If I wasn't in this house this wouldn't be happening to me. It's not *my* fault everybody's been emoting all over me."

He gives me that look again, like he finds me utterly unfathomable. Well, the feeling's mutual. I never claimed to be the warm, fuzzy, caring type, and I don't appreciate some lousy house trying to convince me I should be, any more than I like people doing it.

Since I don't feel like arguing the subject, I change it again. "So where's the kid fit in? I never saw him before in my life. And all he does is fall down the stairs."

Thankfully he goes along with me. "I'm not sure, but since you say that was the first thing you saw…maybe he really did die in that fall. Like, he's a real ghost, and that somehow triggered everything else that's been happening."

"Well if he *is* a real ghost, he has no more imagination than the others. He just does the same thing over and over again."

Kevan shrugs. "Just a thought. I never claimed to be an expert."

"So you can't explain why the bathroom smells like an old lady?" I grin.

He laughs. "Maybe *that's* the real ghost. The malevolent remainder of an old lady who's determined to teach everyone who moves in here a lesson." Then he goes all serious again. "But, Curtis…it would be nice if maybe someday you'd care about something. You might even surprise yourself."

Perhaps. Fortunately my sarcastic comeback was cut short by Trevor doing his ugly leather jacket routine. It seemed to break the mood and we spent the rest of the time before he left talking about everything *but* ghosts. All in all I think I'd rather have roaches.

January 25

Last day; I'm finally out of here! Everything that didn't come with the house is already gone. I just figure I should make one last entry seeing how much time I've wasted writing all this down. Can't say that I'll miss the ghosts, but at least I can now say I've had an Authentic Paranormal Experience. The ghosts are on their own, though I suppose without me around my personal bits of emotional dandruff will disappear. That leaves the old man in the kitchen and the kid. I wonder…once I'm gone will the kid stop falling down the stairs? Yeah, right. And maybe someday I'll care about something.

Retrieval

by Carol Guess

The animal shelter where I finally found work was on a narrow strip of land, overlooking a farm: corn and cattle. We all called it The Bean, but its full name was the Mary Bean Breckenridge Shelter for Animal Retrieval. Mary Bean had been the Breckenridges' oldest daughter; when she was killed in an accident up near Omaha, they donated a bit of their land to set up a shelter in her memory. Back in Bamberg dead people were always having plaques and memorials donated in their names—dead things, all varnish or stone. But the shelter was living, and the Breckenridges stopped by fairly often to say hello. The shelter vet, Karen, had known Mary Bean; they'd been in vet school together. She talked about her like she'd been some kind of rugged saint. It was the one thing she and her husband Jake agreed on—how perfect was Mary Bean.

"She could ease any kind of animal by looking in their eyes," Karen would say, and Jake would nod agreement. "They'd show their bellies the minute she stroked their backs."

The irony was, she'd died tending to a creature. After vet school she'd rotated around some, then got a job up at Pioneer Park in

Lincoln, working with the animals in the nature center. It was bison she was tending to when she died; one of them was sick, and wouldn't take comfort, and kicked her when she went in for an injection.

"She would've been OK if she'd hadn't have hit her head up near the stair," Mr. Breckenridge explained the first time we met and he told me the story. He and Mrs. Breckenridge were always telling the story, to anyone who would listen: over and over again, nonstop Mary Bean. I'll admit I was fascinated, especially since everyone said she looked like me—so much so that when I first met Karen, and later the Breckenridges, that was the first thing they said.

"You and Mary Bean might've been twins," Mrs. B told me, getting very huggy. I usually don't take to touchy-feely stuff from strangers, but somehow with the Bees it was OK. What I liked about them as their history unrolled was how they'd made space for their daughter's ghost on their land. Usually when someone's haunted the ghost just bumps around inside them, rattling like a pinball. But they were smart, the Bees; they knew they'd want to visit with her and be reminded, only not too much—not with pictures and knickknacks and such, and not in their house, disturbing their sleep.

"She's alive for us in the animals," Mr. or Mrs. B would say, coaxing a cat from its cage and cradling it. You could see where Mary Bean had picked up her gentle ways. So I liked working in the Mary Bean Breckenridge Shelter, and I liked knowing Mary Bean had looked like me, that maybe I was a reincarnation of sorts, only off by about ten years. I specially liked knowing that maybe Mary Bean had been a dyke, which was the bottom layer of the story I picked up, though I was never sure whether folks knew it and didn't say, or didn't know, and so said whatever the hell in their unknowing.

Tacit was like that.

In Bamberg, and in New York City, where'd I'd gone once on a field trip with Bamberg High to see *Cats,* and in Charleston, where we'd gone a whole bunch of times, Mom and I, to sell the jewelry Mom made in her spare time in the old slave market, this little noise—my clicker, I called it—would go off when I saw someone who might be kin. I'd look them hard in the eyes and they'd look back and we'd know we were the same in that one way, if not in others. But Tacit, and Nebraska generally, was different. My clicker went off all the time, but it was almost always wrong. This maybe should've started me wondering if I should pay attention to girls who didn't set off the clicker, but those girls weren't interesting to me in the first place, so it was what Mr. Taffy in seventh grade would've called a paradox, and I decided I didn't want to know. I just kept those feelings to myself, and let them fuel me. Energy's energy, is my theory, and what you don't use in bed you'll use to mow grass, or cook fancy dinners, or, if you're a schmoo like me, scoop dog poo and walk all those wagglers. It was fine, having energy to burn; I was the shelter's best asset, everybody said so. I liked being best at something, and I liked the Mary Bean Breckenridge story, and the Bees, and their daughter's ghost, who I felt sometimes, especially in the rabbit area, so I wasn't surprised when I found out that rabbits were her favorite dears.

Got to where I wanted a picture.

But I never asked for one, first off because if she was supposed to look like me but then the picture was ugly, I'd feel like a loser, and second off, because I was afraid I might fall for her, and then where would I be? It was the sort of thing that would happen to me, loving a dead girl, getting all revved up every morning, dressing to court her ghost. Bad enough that I ate my lunch among the rabbit hutches so I could feel her brush past, the way she did—not a body, not a shape even, but a wind that tickled the rabbit's ears and calmed their twitchy pink velvet noses. A carrot-scented wind; sometimes when I fed them nibbles of my lettuce or bread I could feel the stroke at my back. Even in winter it made for pleasant shivers.

So Mary Bean.

I will say I'm grateful. Not just for the wind, but because it was my crush on her that led me round to asking Leda for a date.

Leda was the secretary at Tacit Vet. She and Karen were pals, so she hung around the shelter quite a bit. When I met her I wanted to know her name. She hid her eyes behind her hair but her lips said *tell*. We started talking; after that she'd walk the dogs with me when she got off work early.

I thought she was like me, but I wasn't sure. Visiting the bison seemed one way to learn.

"What should we do?" Leda asked after I made my offer. We were outside the shelter. She'd stopped by to see Karen, or so she said.

I knew just what. I'd been waiting months for someone to ask me that very question; months, because I'd had in mind a road trip since meeting the Bees for the very first time. My dream was to drive out to Lincoln, to Pioneer Park, and visit the spot where Mary Bean was kicked by the bison and split her head open. I thought maybe I could summon her ghost, and learn more about her than I'd ever know from the carrot-scented wind that blew through the hutches. So I told Leda *Lincoln;* I told her, *Pioneer Park,* though I didn't tell her why. Later we could talk about ghosts and visions, telephones that rang outside of wiring, shiver-winds. But not until I knew what she believed in, and how far I could go before she'd roll her eyes.

Leda unclasped the barrette holding back her hair; the curtain covered her eyes. "I was thinking of a film. Or dinner."

"We can picnic. And watching the bison will be like watching a movie."

"OK." Her voice made her hair's lights go out. Maybe she'd been wanting a real date, fancy and such. But I knew enough of Mary Bean's story to know Leda wouldn't be disappointed. And all that time together on the road—sure to be romantic. Either that, or we'd discover we couldn't keep time together. Either way, we'd know the score.

The day came, and I opened the door for her. Four hours passed like an October wind. Then the sign: *Pioneer Park*. Then the park itself. We drove and drove, circles on coils, before we found signs for the nature center. Up a hill, then a curve like a breast, and then the moon: huge, gold-orange, impossibly close.

"Harvest moon." Leda brushed her hair from her eyes. "Have you ever seen one before?"

I paused the car at the lip of the embankment by way of an answer. We sat very still while I thought about two ways of going crazy. There was the usual—what a full moon meant—and the specific—Leda's profile, her lips as impossibly close as that moon, silhouetted against the blue beyond her open window.

When my eyes were too full of her, I started the car again, and poured us toward the belly of the hump.

"Bison," Leda said; I could see their shadow-shapes beyond a lattice of barbed wire. One was sleeping: pillow. Another stood, a great shaggy beard; another, a violet waterfall. But as the car rounded the circle, our two-ness smashed into a thousand pieces. Teenage boys—a pickup truck full. And full of secrets—I could tell.

I felt Leda strap on her seat belt, which she'd taken off while we were moon-gazing.

"Should I keep driving?"

She didn't answer, just snapped the clasp of the buckle open and then shut it again.

"Let's pull over." I parked in front of the truck, got out, and walked around to Leda's door. Then I held it open for her while she sat and sat, gazing not at the harvest moon or the bison, or even behind her to the boys, but through the windshield at the road in front of us, winding restlessly downhill.

While I waited, one hand on the door, one jangling my keys, I looked at the barbed wire fence separating us from the bison. I'd never thought long and hard about barbed wire before, so I was grateful to Leda for giving me a chance. Maybe it was even on purpose; maybe she wanted me to see us in the bison, bleeding between themselves and night, their edges shaggy as their fur, their shapes indistinct as they separated and came together. Grazing at night; what was it that I understood? Hunger, and how it could break you as the moon rose.

From behind us a purr, then a crackle as the truck's wheels spun off the gravel lot and onto asphalt. Two boys rode in front, two in the truck bed; all four waved as they drove away. "By-y-ye!" one of them called as they rounded the curve and clunked downhill. They'd left behind an empty package of Camels, six Bud cans, crushed, and a view of the sunset beyond the bison's hutch: pink and orange following the land line. We couldn't see far; the land was flat, and we weren't specially high up. It bothered me, the flatness; it was the thing about Nebraska that was most foreign to me. No place was a lookout; beauty was always only about what was most directly nearby. So I shifted my gaze from a hidden far-off to the nearest at hand: the wire, struggling to separate us from our beast selves, nervous circles and pinprick knots done over and over to keep us from knowing who the bison were.

I heard Leda's skirt rustle through a scrim of crickets, and then she stood beside me, her hand on my back. "Let's see," she said, gravitating towards the bison. The boys' absence had left us with more quiet than we knew what to do with, but the crickets quickly filled it, and our shoes on the gravel, and then the faint call of a far-off owl. Close to the fence, and closer: then we were peering through, playing with wire like it couldn't hurt, calling to the bison like they were pets because we couldn't help it: "Here, bison, bison, bison! Nice bison, here girl. Boy. Girl."

None of the three big lunkers flinched. One was eating, one reclining, and one nuzzling a baby bison, only slightly less shaggy though considerably shorter. They had so much hair; I wondered if winters were bearable. How had they ever survived way back, before people came along and built hutches for them? Thinking that way made me laugh: before people came along, and killed them, caged them, till only a handful were left, and those in camps, like these.

"I bet they hate us."

She was thinking as I was, the crickets' chirrups a thread between us, and the sunset, its wings soft on our shoulders. I couldn't see Mary Bean's ghost, as I'd hoped, but I could feel her laughter within myself: laughter at the two of us, trying to understand animals, who were anyway smarter, and the great long flat land we stood on, which had lived so long before us and would go on more. The sunset too, each night the same but a little different, and, come the season, the harvest moon, gold as if it had been dipped in the fires Native dwellers had built on this very spot. It had been Native land; I knew that; every schoolchild knew that. We just never spoke of it, because that was over now, and it was time to move on.

To strip malls, burger joints, and overnight dry cleaning.

To bakeries selling three-tiered wedding cakes, with plastic people holding hands atop sugary swags.

To stoplights and churches that separated themselves from the land they were built on, that rose away from it, spiraling up instead of nestling or complimenting the long stretches of brown earth that had once been fields: wheat and corn and wheat and corn.

We watched the bison for a very long time. While the young one snorted into its elder's coat, we held hands, but then we let them drop. It wasn't romantic, what we felt, just comfort. Our palms fit together, but so did the wire coils: circle on circle, keeping us here, keeping the animals back. When Leda dropped my hand, I felt my own hand shiver: Mary Bean. She took up where Leda left off, and I had, while time stopped, the thing I'd come for.

After that I didn't care.

The ride home was long. We even ate in the car. I'm good at driving and eating; I love the feeling of fullness and speed both at once. It's the closet to sex driving comes, and driving often comes close; other people think so too, which is why there are so many accidents. Forgetting, losing yourself in motion. So driving, and nibbling, though it wasn't a specially sexy meal; we joshed about not breathing on each other. I wanted to say *kiss,* and *kiss* almost slipped out, but instead we both said *breath,* which was different, though somehow felt like what we couldn't say. While I drove, and ate, and listened to Leda's sniffling (allergies), and tried to see through the soupy dark far enough ahead to keep leaving Lincoln, I searched my skin for the remnants of the ghost. But ghosts aren't puppies; they don't come when you beckon. You can't coax or cry them home, and you can't shoo them away when you're good and done. Mary Bean was gone, and I knew somehow that she was gone; gone, for me, for good. It was OK; we'd had our time. But I missed her already, the way I always missed the ones who'd chilled me, in a good way, their ghostie-bones sweet clouds that passed through my own like a hand through water: the slight tug, the closing-over.

Suture.

After awhile longer, I started to get droopy. Leda was sleeping, her head wobbling against the glass, her hands curled against her belly, keeping her secrets in. My eyelids grew heavy, and you know what? I actually closed my eyes for a couple seconds, jerked awake, closed them, jerked awake: the most dangerous weaving a driver can do. A blanket of startle; when I came to the second time, I knew it was serious. The road stretched, dead flat, before us—over an hour of night, and nothing, and no one else, my lights painting only a few feet of the flat as my wheels spun on. Because I could feel a third sleep coming on, because my body wasn't ready to resist, and my mind giving in, I pulled over, shut down, and slumped, and slept.

When I came to it was another day. Night had escaped; I'd lost time again. It was always happening. Now I was one day closer to 27, to 40, to 72. To the future that seemed impossibly complex, ever since I'd realized I would never follow the usual path: the long road stretched dead flat, the husband, children, fenced yard with sweet flowers growing come spring, and snow angels before the blizzard. Who did I have to follow but my instincts and the ghosts

I most trusted? And the animals, who didn't marry but kept right on, making cycles of their own, even captive as they were under our hands, and fenced by fences, asphalt, cars.

Usually I didn't mind having no one else to follow.

Usually life felt as if I was following myself.

Once in a while, though, the headlights went out; that was when things got difficult. For het girls, at least when their personal timing was off, they had the world to model options. Me, I had to take care of it all myself, myself my own history, present, future. My own precedent. Leda was still sleeping; the temptation was to stroke her cheek, a little wet from where her eyes had cried in the night. But I don't touch unless touch speaks back. I turned on the engine, and started back: on the road, now illuminated up to the vanishing point.

We passed vanishing. We passed the tip of the V till it became some other letter.

Then Tacit, and Leda stirring restlessly, as if on cue, blurting something as she rose from sleep, shaking dreams off like droplets.

"Where are we?" she mumbled.

"Not quite home," I said, though I doubt she understood.

⇢ amat67.jpg ⇠

by Hall Owen Calwaugh

Something about the eyes. The set of the jaw. The pale flesh. The curious tattoo above the left nipple. The round face, full-lipped—boyish but tattered. The irrepressibly impish grin. The mixture of innocence and sleaze. Definitely hot. All right, so he had Alfred E. Newman ears, but Keith got off on that. Oh, yeah, and the red hair. *A natural redhead, no question about that,* giggled Keith. Not too amply provided for downstairs, but that wasn't a major issue in Keith's book. No, faces were his body part of choice. Faces like fine liquor. Faces you could riff on. Faces you need to revisit. Over and over and over again. And this one's face—well, it was a piece of work. Not handsome, per se, but arresting. Yeah.

The eyes. Windows of the soul. They glittered darkly, those bottomless eyes. They laughed at the pomp and foolishness of the world. Danger sparked in them. Compelling. Eyes that jumped off the screen and grabbed at his soul. Eyes with a hint of a sneer through the laughter. A *shared* sneer—that was it! "It's all bullshit!" they seemed to snigger and caress all at once. "You know it. I know it. Bullshit, babe!" Keith could drown himself in those endless, now-and-forever eyes—lost in the rich, amoral laughter that exploded out of them. God, he was hot!

Butting into his rapture, the phone bleated at him. Irritated at the interruption, Keith let the answering machine pick up. While it screened the caller, he took another look at the jpg before him. A tad more clinical a look. Dispassionate. Professional. The original photo was seriously grainy. Overexposed. Bad lighting. Clearly a self-made photo. Amateur. No professional photog on this gig. And yet how could an amateur *by accident* capture such an expression of—well, Keith didn't know what. Hunger? No, not that. But something very like it. Damn, it was exciting! Who *was* this guy, anyway? Why hadn't he read the message that went along with it?

"Hey, Keith, you home? Come on, come on, pick up. PICK UP ALREADY!!! I know you're there…" Ah, the delicate bouquet of Jody's fine whine. Keith had to succumb to his odoriferous slosh and pick up or Jody wouldn't stop. Persistence was Jody's middle name. "K-E-E-EITH!!!" Still, he'd managed to say no when Jody propositioned him last year. No, let's remain friends, he'd told him. Ah, the look in Jody's eye—scary. In the end, Jody had forgiven him. They were fast friends now. Whatever that meant. "Are you going to pick up or what?! I'm w-a-a-aiting…!"

"It's late, Jody." Keith carefully let the tiredness show. Hell, it might even work this time? He really didn't want to talk to Jody tonight. Not with this incredible face staring at him, calling out to him, making the room—his whole life, what there was of it—go dark in comparison.

"You're on the web, aren't you?"

"Now what makes you think— "

"Oh, admit it. I am too. I have one word for you: amat67.jpg. You know what I'm talking about. Come on, come on?!" Jody was even more excited than usual, and that was saying something.

Keith glanced up at the gray bar stretching above the face that roared out of his monitor—it read "amat67.jpg." *Damn that Jody,* he bristled, *how dare he presume to tell me who I'm attracted to? And how dare he be right!*

"Alt.binaries.pictures.erotica.amateur.male. You've seen him, right? He is s-o-o-o *you,* Keith. You've just got to see him. I'll E-mail you a copy, if you haven't."

"Calm down. What are you talking about?"

"amat67.jpg—that's what I'm talking about. Get with the program here. Hell-o-o-o! Have you seen him?"

"No, Jody. I gave that up, remember? For Lent. I don't cruise the newsgroups anymore."

"Bullshit. You're on the web right now, I know. You've got the phone cradled between your shoulder and your ear and you're typing—OR WHATEVER—" Jody let fly a salacious snort, "right now! Admit it, admit it!"

"No, Jody. No, I'm not. I'm just about to go to bed. Got a big day tomorrow and I've got to fade or I'll never get it up and on the road in the morning."

"Then I'll E-mail you a copy."

"No, Jody, no. No thank you."

"But—"

"Say 'good night,' Jody."

"Shit. You're no fun."

"Lunch on Friday?"

"Yeah, right… You sure you don't want me to—"

"I'm hanging up now."

"Friday then. You're missing out on this one—amat67.jpg!"

"I hear your mother calling. G'night!"

Jody. What a fucking idiot! Why did he waste time on the little bastard? Was he that desperate for company? "Don't answer that, Keith!" he told himself as he pulled his underwear back up.

Still, Jody could be amusing. "At times…" Keith found Jody's fascination with crystals and astrology and Wicca and all that New Age shit very entertaining. Not that Keith believed in any of it, but that made it all the more entertaining.

Anyway, it *was* true that Keith was going to bed. Yep. He just wasn't going to go to bed *alone* tonight—amat67.jpg was going with him and sleep wasn't the first priority.

"Mm-MMM," he murmured to himself as he sent the jpg to the printer. "This one's a keeper. I could fall in love here! Or a close facsimile thereof…"

"…BzzIP!…BzzIP!…BzzIP!…"

Floating contentedly in a tropical lagoon, wrapped in the arms of a pale-fleshed man, Keith seemed to recollect a distant sound.

"…BzzIP!…BzzIP!…BzzIP!…"

An alarm clock. Just an alarm clock.

"…BzzIP!…BzzIP!…BzzIP!…"

His alarm clock.

"…BzzIP!…BzzIP!…BzzIP!…"

Shit!

How long had it been going off? He pried open one eyeslit. Nine fifteen. *Shit.* Forty-five minutes. *Shit.* He was going to be late. *Shit. Shit. Shit.*

Groggily stumbling to the shower, he seemed to notice a strange smell in his bedroom. Familiar, but strange.

Late again. Shit. Shit. Shit. Ted will just be wild. Shit!

As the hot water revivified his flesh and helped center his consciousness, Keith wondered what had happened. It was as if he had a hangover. But he'd not been drinking the night before? Not as he could remember? He came home, late. Right. Then wrote some checks. Right. Then went on the net. Right. Jody called. Right. Oh, that jpg. Yeah. He'd, uh, spent some time with that new jpg. "Yeah, that." Keith smiled. Then he'd drifted off to sleep. Yeah, that.

Eyes. He remembered eyes.

Sitting on the edge of the bed pulling on his socks he noticed a piece of paper crumpled up under his pillow.

"Oh, yeah…"

He smoothed it out and ran a finger along the line of the jaw and down the chest. He fell into the eyes. Dark. Rich. Bottomless. Irresistible.

Ah, hell, he thought, *if I'm going to be late anyway, I might as well have a smile on my lips when I get there.*

"Nice of you to drop by." Ted shot a significant look at the new receptionist as Keith sauntered in. A brunette with come-hither lips and hips. Ted was such a show-off, thought Keith. Surely she must see through him?

"Yeah, well, the yacht is in dry dock and I ran out of nails to paint." Fuck him. He doesn't own my life.

"Staff meeting in—" Ted made a point of consulting his Hong Kong Rolex. "Ten minutes. Think you can make it?"

"I just don't know, Ted. There's this luscious piece of pastry in the staff lounge desperate for my kind attentions. Sure *you* can appreciate my dilemma?"

"Fuck you, Keith." Ted had no sense of humor. Ted had no sense, period. The receptionist was welcome to him.

Work was more than usually pointless. A catalog for a mattress factory. How many different kinds of mattress are really necessary, he couldn't help but wonder. Five? Ten? Twenty? Sixty-seven?

Amyl? That was the smell. Amyl! Why should his bedroom have smelt of a hungry dance floor? Bizarre. Something else? Armani? Now *that* was just plain silly.

"How're ya doing? D'ya find everything?" White shirt. A tie with tiny cartoon characters bouncing all over it. Too funky. Regulation apron stretched across his middle, highlighting a taut little body. Small waist, wide hips, nice basket. Black Dockers, washed one too many times. He needed a new pair. Long fingers. Gold wedding ring. Shit. Keith could feel the inviting warmth of his flesh even across the checkout counter. Pulsing at him. Demanding his full attention. Keith worked to dismiss it as a pheromones thing. *I mean, the little bastard doesn't even have big ears,* he told himself.

"Yeah. Fine." *No, I'm not fine. I lie,* he wanted to scream. *No, I didn't find everything. No, you randy little fucker with your gold wedding ring, I didn't find anything I was really looking for. I found nothing, all right? Just groceries. Just goddamn groceries.*

"Twenty-three sixty-seven." The checker smiled at him. Licked his lips. They were nice lips.

Keith fumbled through his wallet. "Twenty...three..." Then his coin purse. "Sixty...seven..." He laid the coins down on the counter in a careful pattern. Six dimes. Seven pennies. Sixty-seven cents. Sixty-seven. Keith looked at the copper pennies and suddenly thought of red hair and freckles.

"Whoa! Exact change! Very impressive!" As the checker swept up the coins, Keith noticed he needed a manicure. Other than that and the gold ring, he had beautiful, pale hands.

For a brief moment, Keith looked up and lost himself into the checker's dark brown eyes. *Come home with me,* he wanted to shout at him. *Let me tear that apron off of you. Let me rip those clothes off of you. Let me make you forget that bimbo waiting for you at home. She knows nothing. She is a waste of your time. A waste of your flesh. A man knows what a man wants. Let me take you where you've never been before. Let me—*

"Hey, thanks! Have a good evening." *Yeah, right. Fuck you too.*

Keith woke up with a start. A paper clutched to his chest. That new jpg, of course. Something else though.

The room was dark. But not as empty as it should have been. There was something else...

The smell again. Amyl. Armani. "Oo-ooh, love to love ya baby!" Damn neighbors. But then he remembered. They were gone this weekend. Where was that music coming fro—

He sat up and switched his bedside lamp on. The music stopped. Silence. Had it even been there at all?

He looked around his room. Nothing. Not even the smell anymore. Nothing.

Nothing except that new jpg—amat67.jpg—in his trembling hand. His hand was trembling. He couldn't help but look at it. That jpg.

Who was this guy?

Those eyes. Oh, the hair, the ears, the freckles—all that—but it was the eyes that caught him and held him. Grayish-greenish-blue. The color of the ocean. Keith swam into those eyes with long languid strokes. He tasted the sea salt on his lips and felt the swell embrace him. Swallow him whole.

Goddamn those eyes. *His* eyes. Endless. Bottomless. Laughing. Hungry. Curiously satisfying. Deliciously exhausting. Light. Dark. Everything in the world. Nothing left out. Everything.

Keith shook his head to clear it. It was 3:37 in the morning. He had to get to sleep or he'd never get up in time for work.

He switched off the light and set the jpg on his bedside table. He closed his eyes and imagined what it would be like in bed with good old amat67. He crushed a pillow in his arms and slid his right leg sensuously around a lump of coverlet, thought of red hair and gold rings and squeezed slowly. He drifted off eventually.

Lunch with Jody.

Why did he do this to himself, Keith bitched at himself, walking back to the office in the rain. When he allowed himself to think about it, he had to admit he didn't even like Jody.

Soon enough—somewhere during the salad course—Keith had realized that all Jody wanted to know was whether or not he'd found amat67.jpg. This irritated him no end. So Keith told him he hadn't, but Jody saw through him. Made little piggy eyes at him. It didn't make any sense, but it was desperately important to Jody that Keith find amat67.jpg. And equally as important for Keith to lie about it.

Was this what friendship was all about? Lies over a bad lunch?

To hell with it all, thought Keith as he prepared to shift the point size on the catalog's captions. *It's bad enough I have to spend my days arguing over the best way to display meaningless copy points about mattresses—but to have to put up with Jody's whining and carrying on and weird obsessions as well—it was just too much to ask. What kind of life is this? How did I find myself in this position? If I was smart,* he raged at himself, *I'd just dump Jody.* He was such a black hole, sucking Keith's life and energy out of him. Exhausting. *Fuck him. Fuck everybody.*

Six point seven point is too small to read, but it would allow Keith to fit in all the damn copy Ted was insisting on. Serve him right. His ears were too close to his head. Ted would be much more attractive if he had bigger ears. Six point seven point. That'd show him. Yeah.

Keith had stopped going to bars about six years back. It was so discouraging. Nothing but twinks ravenous for other twinks. Or professional men settling for "professional" men. No thank you. Keith wanted something more. Something that wasn't to be found in the bars. Something special. True love, maybe, whatever that meant. Something special, at any rate. But he'd not found it. Not in the bars, and not anywhere else, either.

He'd tried the chorus, of course, had a middling good baritone—never connected with the in-gang though. Not passionate enough about show tunes. He didn't worship at the shrine of Sondheim, and so was politely passed over.

Wanting to make a difference to somebody, somewhere—he drifted into hospice work, but had to drop out. The emotional demands simply overwhelmed him. After a few weeks he found himself constantly swept along on the edge of emotional collapse. Sucked dry by the patients, the families (those few who deigned to show their faces), the staff, the other volunteers. Keith was just too sensitive. Always had been. Hell, he'd cried in Junior High when Mr. Romar forced him to dissect a worm. A worm, for God's sake! How did he come to think he could work around the dying? The volunteer coordinator had been very sweet. Thanked him, but suggested he take a hike. In the nicest, most affirming way possible. Keith felt like slugging him. Instead, he found a cowboy bar, got shit-faced drunk, told them he was gay, and got himself beat up good. Twenty-three stitches in the emergency room. If he was going to be self destructive, he'd might as well do it up right, he thought at the time. He wanted to die. Still thought it was a good idea, now and again.

Lately, he'd found a kind of solace on the Internet. Traveling from site to site—all around the world. Keith had never left the state in which he was born. Rarely if ever left the town in which he lived. Couldn't afford to. But thanks to the Internet, it seemed the whole world was his—and all the men in it. The Internet. It made him welcome as no one else ever had. CUseeme terrified him, but he did try IRC. That was a sad joke. It was the same inane conversations that he'd run away from in the bars. At least in the bars you could ogle the twinks, that was something. In chat mode, there was no packaging, just content. And what content there was—was nonexistent. Nutrition-free. Taste-free. What *was* the point?

Then he found the alt.binaries. And what a find *that* was. Heaven on earth as far as he could see. Pluses everywhere, relatively few negatives. In the alt.binaries he had access to major ogling, but didn't have to waste time on chitchat with the braindead. It worked. Mostly. Well, it was enough. In his imagination—and he had a vivid imagination—he had sex with hundreds and hundreds of men! Whenever, however, and with whomever he wanted. Everything on his terms for a change. Of course he lost out on any human contact. Any person to person, face to face, body to body, skin to skin connection. But what was that worth? It wasn't worth anything. Not for the price exacted. No, he wasn't missing anything, he told himself.

It was strange, but the alt.binaries made him think of the bars he'd run away from. He brooded on them. It had been years, but he still remembered how the bars smelled. Of cheap beer and tequila. Of department store cologne, snagged on sale. Of denim. Of pretension. Of degradation. Of fear. They smelled of the men who haunted them, night after endless night. The bars smelled of their frantic, pointless search—of their sweat as they danced into the wee hours. The bars smelled of amyl, sweetly medicinal. Of popcorn and pretzels. Of urinals.

Be honest, Keith, he told himself, *what the bars really smelled of was easy, unconstrained, triumphant sex.* Mindless. Soulless. Ecstatic. Like the shot of heroin he'd have turned down had it ever been offered. Like religion and God were supposed to be. Like the music, never-ending, pounding at him. Loud enough to feel through the soles of his shoes. Waves of sound beating at him, washing through him. So loud he could feel it in the air with his bare skin. The bars, the bars! They were the apocalypse, the rapture before the apocalypse. They were like breathing in and breathing out. They were everything he wasn't. Everything he wanted to be. Everything in the world. The universe itself. They were life. Uncompromising. Dangerous. Terrifying. Real.

Too real.

No, cruising the bars wasn't for him anymore. Cruising the alt. binaries was.

Like switching on a light, he was awake. What was the matter? Breathing hard. Couldn't get his breath. Wide awake. Wide, wide awake. Every fiber of his being thrumming. What woke him? A sound? No sounds anywhere. The light from down the hall shone into his bedroom, picking out bits of furniture and bouncing off the dustcovers of books scattered across the floor. Clearly he was in fight or flight mode. But why? What was wrong? He pulled the coverlet up around his neck and suddenly felt an icy-hot hand where no hand could possibly be. It grazed his thigh and encircled his fully erect sex. There was a long, low, throaty laugh coalescing around him like a fog.

Oh, shit, he thought, and screamed his lungs out.

Then he woke up. In a cold sweat.

Hell of a dream. He was even hard. But it was a dream. *Just a dream.* He rolled over, punched a pillow, and tried to go back to sleep. Hell of a dream, indeed.

Clearly this sleeping alone thing was beginning to get to him. Maybe he shouldn't have turned Jody down so fast.

"I mean I coulda done worse," he said out loud. "Hell, I *have* done worse." And yet as he turned the idea over again, he realized he'd made the right decision. Jody was a great friend. Well, a friend. Not lover material. Not a lover, no. Not by a long shot. "Not Jody, *please*…" he growled as he sank back into a fitful sleep.

Even two cups of the strongest espresso from the deli downstairs couldn't keep Keith's eyes from fluttering shut during Ted's endless explanation of the client's desires regarding that goddamn mattress catalog.

"Are you with us, Keith?"

"Yeah. Fine—I'm fine. Sorry. Late night."

Ted pursed his lips with another of his significant looks. *Such a bastard.* Keith's head felt as if it were in a vise. Two more turns of the handle and it would pop like a zit.

Keith hadn't been sleeping well. Horrible dreams. Alternating with wonderfully sensuous ones. And through them all, as a single thread—a lifeline—was amat67.jpg. That face. Those ears. That hair. Those eyes. Oh, God, those eyes. He thought of them, and Ted suddenly seemed so far away. It was such a relief. *Make Ted go away.*

Keith wondered why it was he even came to work. What was the point anyway? How did he end up in this stupid job? He'd wanted to paint, not chase fucking copy around a computer screen.

Was it the first night or the third? Dreams. Perhaps even a week had passed. Or two. It must have been. Dreams more real than real life. It was Friday night again. Alone again. "Naturally…" Except for amat67.jpg. Dreams of amat67.jpg. Waking dreams and sleeping dreams of amat67.jpg. They were the only pleasure in his life anymore. They were the only life in his life anymore. "Dreams more real than real life." What wonderful eyes! Why couldn't he ever meet someone like Sixty-seven? Instead of losers like Jody. Nice enough guys, but losers nonetheless. Just like himself, Keith. Keith was a loser, he knew it. A goddamn loser and there was nothing for it.

Jody had asked again if he wanted to go dancing tonight or to a movie, but he'd begged off. Jody had been unusually insistent—he looked as if he hadn't been sleeping much either—but Keith turned him down flat. It had been week from hell at work. Not because of Ted's mothering the new catalog—all account executives deserve to be shot dead at least once in their beady little lives—no, it was that he couldn't really concentrate on the—

Amat67.jpg. He found himself sketching Sixty-seven at work. Doodling the line of his jaw. The curve of his lobes. The eyes. His endless, oceanic, insatiable eyes. Damn those eyes.

"Are you with us, Keith?"

"No, actually. I'm not."

Did he really get up and come home? He must have done. Here he was and the answering machine light was blinking.

"What the hell do you think you're doing, you little—"

Yeah. Must have walked out on Ted. *That's pretty funny,* he thought, *who *do* I think I am?* Keith giggled for a while about that and then stopped.

Made himself something to eat. A sandwich or something. Something, at any rate. Had to eat. Was supposed to eat. He'd been losing weight. Looked good on him. Off him, actually. Someone—the receptionist?—had commented on his losing weight. He didn't believe her. So he made himself a sandwich.

Threw his mail on a pile of letters, unopened. What was the point? Flipped on the television—cartoons, noisy—but all he could think about was Sixty-seven. How could Jody or Ted or that fucking supermarket checker with the gold ring hope to compete with Sixty-seven? How could anyone?

He didn't need the printout anymore. Just close the eyes and there they were. *His* eyes. Dark, rich, intoxicating. Endless. Bottomless. Ravenous. A black hole. Rich, throbbing, incandescent sable. *Oh, God, just let me slip into them and never have to—*

The phone was ringing. It was Jody. Shrieking. Begging for something. Sorry, so sorry. "I'm so sorry! Forgive me! I should never have sent—" Boring. He turned the volume down on the answering machine. Jody disappeared. Way cool. Had it always been that easy? And he never knew?! Sheesh! Was the television still on? He switched it off and went to the bathroom.

That taken care of, he went to bed. He looked up at the ceiling. It was covered in bits of paper—amat67.jpg carefully tiled to cover the whole ceiling. He'd moved the bed to the center of the room so he could lie underneath those eyes. So he could be sucked up into them. The center of the universe. Those eyes, those eyes, those eyes…

He didn't even need to touch himself anymore.

Someone was pounding on the door. He ignored it.

He wasn't hungry anymore, which was nice. He hadn't gone out shopping for a while. There wasn't much left to eat. He lay in bed looking up at the ceiling. That was all that mattered anymore. Those eyes. *Mmm…*

A terrace. He was on a terrace. It seemed to be his? Was it real? Ah, who cared—it was summer. Early evening. Best part of the day. The terrace—his terrace, surely—was in shade, but the park across the way remained in bright sunlight. Long strands and lovely liquid swashes of sunlight cutting through the trees and illuminating the picnickers. Great time of day for sitting and watching the boys go by. Frisbees. Catching Frisbees. Playing catch with Frisbees. Short shorts. Long hair. Short hair. Tank tops. No tops. Legs. Frisbees. Too far away to look into their eyes.

Eyes…

Perched across the white plastic table from him was Sixty-seven. Lusciously naked. He was naked! So was Keith. Sixty-seven wasn't saying anything, he was just sitting there. Thinking. Looking at Keith with a curious expression in his eyes.

Those eyes. Endless. Bottomless. Hungry. Sad.

Sad? This was new?!

"Why are you sad?"

Sixty-seven said nothing. Sixty-seven never said anything. He didn't even blink.

"Are you sad?"

Not sad. Disappointed. Sixty-seven stood up and stretched wearily. He was bored with Keith! Sixty-seven frowned and turned away. Turned away! Took his eyes—his dazzling, extraordinary, ravenous, poisonous, endless, bottomless, compelling eyes—away from Keith. How could he? Didn't he know how much they meant to Keith? Didn't he care?

The wonderful, horrible eyes withdrew from Keith, and Keith felt his stomach drop away into the abyss. Panic rose in his throat. Filled it. He couldn't breathe! His heart was pounding!

"Don't leave?! You can't leave?! Pl-e-e-ease!!!"

And then Sixty-seven was gone. Only a waft of Armani on the summer breeze to mark his passing.

Keith had looked pretty good at the viewing. Natural, even. Which was a bit of a surprise. Considering how he'd wasted away. "And in such a short space of time?" everyone was muttering. He didn't look the least bit accusatorial, thought Jody. Though Keith had every right to be.

Afterward, a guilt-wracked Jody, desperately clutching a seedy plethora of protective amulets and talismans, trudged back through the dirty snow to Keith's apartment and burned all the paper copies of the jpg he could find. Deleted the rest. Reformatted the hard drive. Smashed the backups. As he had done at his own apartment. It didn't matter though. The damage had been done, and it was irreversible. Thanks to the wonders of reposting, Sixty-seven said it was conceivable he might not ever have to really die.

"A variation on the 'Clap if you believe in Fairies' routine," he'd said.

The laughter had not been becoming.

A Midsummer's Haunt

by Susan C. Coleman

Her name was Lady Adriana Wexton, eldest daughter of Lord Montagu Wexton, sixth Earl of Leicester. Unwillingly betrothed to the Viscount Farnsworth, Lady Adriana sought daily to escape the arranged marriage. Every flight plan was discovered, every attempt to bribe a servant foiled. The Earl of Leicester was forced to exercise tactical wit day in and day out to outsmart his headstrong daughter. She finally won her freedom on her 18th birthday, June 21 of 1868, when she died after being thrown from her horse during an impromptu race with her cousin.

My first encounter with the lovely and willful Lady Adriana was on summer solstice in 1988. This was two years after I'd bought a big old 1920s California Bungalow on 2nd Street in Long Beach. Attracted by the badly overgrown but potentially magnificent rose garden in the monstrous backyard, I'd seen the house as the perfect sanctuary for an antisocial commercial artist. It was huge and drafty, with tiny bedrooms, an antiquated bathroom that still sported a claw-foot bathtub, and a surprise second floor that I discovered when I found a mysterious staircase in a closet. The realtor knew nothing about the unfinished second floor, but assured me that the old antique furniture stored there came with the house, and therefore belonged to me.

That was where I found the delicate 19th century cherry wood writing table. It was one of several nice pieces that I eventually refinished and put to use. It was her writing table, I later learned, but before that was revealed to me I had moved it to my bedroom and used it as a worktable for my herbal teas and incenses. I like to believe that it was the magic of my herbs, lovingly tended and grown in my own garden, that awakened the Lady Adriana from her restless sleep beyond the Veil and brought her to share my solitary existence.

The moon had been full that particular night, as it frequently must be in tales such as this, while I prepared for the first night of summer. At that little table I worked with my magical concoctions, burning candles of pink and white while I crushed resins between mortar and pestle. Sprinkling that powder over the slowly burning measures of freshly harvested rosemary and thyme, I waved a hand through the wispy blue smoke, enjoying the scent of my personal blend. It was during that private little ritual for summer solstice, which was also my own solar return, that I felt a presence in the room with me.

"This is the time of the rose," I whispered, sprinkling more incense over the charcoal block. "Blossom and thorn, fragrance and blood…"

Like a lover's caress, fingertips brushed my cheek. Startled, I spun about and stared at the room. As I expected, there was no one there. It was my imagination again, which fed my creativity but haunted my solitude. Of course there was no one there. I lived alone. I preferred it that way. A wild and impetuous youth had jaded my senses to romance. I had loved women with a great ferocity, devouring them as one might a sumptuous meal. Yet I'd been a glutton, gorging and never savoring. It was a diet of abstinence in the face of self-growth that I chose now.

Still, that uneasy sense of not being alone persisted. Shrugging off my silly apprehensions as the guilty imaginings of a middle-aged woman coming to grips with her misspent youth, I continued to burn incense and recite my favorite poetry on this, the longest day of the year and the night of my own birthday. Although not an exceptionally religious individual, I did take immense delight in knowing that I was born on a pagan holiday that celebrated Litha, Queen of Summer.

The acrid scent of expired candles mingled with the woodsy smell of burning thyme and followed me into the kitchen where I filled my chalice with a Gray Riesling. With the wine and a plate of sliced apples, I decided to finish my birthday celebration in the garden. The full moon perfectly illuminated the inlaid brick path that meandered through a wild and willful collection of herbs, to the small bench beneath an arbor generously adorned with the passionate profusion of a climbing red rose called Don Juan. Here I curled up on the bench and, taking a sip of wine, glanced over-head at the ethereal wisps of cloud that drifted across the silver face of the moon. Picturesque enough to grace the cover of a Gothic romance novel.

"Do you like Gothic romance novels?"

The chalice leapt from my hand and shattered on the bricks. I was standing instantly, my heart pounding in my throat as I stared at the pale young woman who stood beside my favorite Queen Elizabeth rose. Her hair was long and dark and appeared to be pinned atop her head, with curls cascading down the back. The style favored her heart-shaped face, accentuating the fine arch of her dark brows, the slight tilt of an otherwise too straight nose, and the stubborn set of lush red lips. It was difficult to be certain in the moonlight, but I thought I caught a look of amusement in those heavily lashed brown eyes.

"Who—who are you, and what are you doing in my yard?"

She drifted towards me. Yes, drifted. In an accented voice of lovely resonance that belied the etheric quality of her appearance, she answered, "I am Lady Adriana Wexton, and this is my birthday."

Surprised at the strength of my own voice, I said, "It's my birthday too."

She smiled. "Then let's celebrate."

It was summer solstice, 1993. It was my 43rd birthday, and her 143rd birthday. Although I had to admit that she barely looked a day past 18. She reassured me that I still looked like a woman of 30, and in my vanity, I loved her for that myopic observation. Actually, I found that I loved her for any and every reason: for the way she laughed at her own terrible jokes; for the way she ardently expressed her opinions of my art work; for the way she craved knowledge of my era; and most especially, for the way she loved me without reservation.

Did I say earlier that I disdained romance? Did I admit to being a womanizer, who never once appreciated the charms both subtle and exotic that I sampled? All past tense, believe me. Maybe the depth and breadth of my emotional attachment for Adriana was the result of her most unusual existence, or the fact that she could only appear to me, in the flesh, on our birthday, or it was merely the outcome of achieving a modicum of maturity, a conscience, and a decided reverence for all miracles of life.

"Rene, my love, would you keep an old woman waiting?"

I chuckled at her reference to herself, hefted the wrapped canvas onto my hip, and walked out the back door to join her in the rose garden. She was already sitting under the arbor, sipping from a crystal wine glass. I marveled anew at her fresh English complexion, so smooth and creamy, begging to be caressed even by this callused hand. As was her habit these past years, she had traded in her 19th century gown, with its deadly stays and laces, and donned a pair of my blue jeans and one of my white silk blouses.

"Oh, what have you there?"

I propped the canvas on the bench beside her. "A gift. For you. For me."

Reaching for my hand, she pulled me to her for a long kiss, then, "Mmm, I've a gift for you to unwrap too…"

I grinned, fingering the button on her shirt. "A gift I've waited a long year for. But first, open this one."

Graceful, even in her impatience, she tore away the wrapping in careful strips to reveal my latest painting. It was a portrait of a young English lady, perfectly gowned and coifed, with the Devil's own expression of mirth and mischief. Beside her stood another woman, older, dark-haired and light-eyed, wearing a dress of similar lines. Adriana ran a tentative fingertip along the line of the older woman's jaw.

"I love the cleft in your chin…" Her voice quavered.

Stricken by her sudden sadness, I knelt beside her and drew her into my arms. "Sweetheart, I didn't mean to upset you. I wanted something to remember you by while you're not with me. Remember, the photos don't take? I…I thought you'd like this."

She turned her head enough to kiss my ear, then whispered, "I love it. I love that you've put us together, in my time, in my home."

"Then stop those tears, you goose, and let's celebrate."

It wasn't difficult to coax her from her tears. At heart Adriana was quite happy, uncomplicated, and entirely wanton. With no hesitation she melted into my arms, her body molding with familiarity to mine. From that very first night, so many years ago, intimacy had come easily with us. Adriana's natural good humor and physical exuberance translated to a very healthy sexual appetite.

Amazingly comfortable with her own body, she was equally at ease with mine. She touched me without hesitation, without knowledge of shame or restraint, stroking me leisurely, longingly, so very lovingly. I wondered briefly, occasionally, how a woman of the repressed Victorian era had come to so naturally embrace the carnal? Then again, I never asked if I was the first she had appeared to after her earthly death. We never discussed the terms of her spirit's right to haunt the mortal world. We never spoke of other lovers, or other birthdays shared. It wasn't necessarily that I was jealous, just merely my very human tendency to want to preserve my sense of importance in a unique situation.

So I savored the generosity of her sexuality, and deepened our kiss, engaging in an intimate duel of tongue to tongue. Her breath was warm and wet, and she tasted faintly of apples and wine. Never subtle in her cravings, Adriana broke our kiss only long enough to pull my shirt over my head. She had already, expertly, swept away my bra as I still fumbled with the buttons of her blouse. Wonderfully obliging, she suddenly stood and shrugged out of the blouse, allowing it to pool on the seat of the bench behind her. At my less than gentle urging she wiggled out of the jeans.

Now I was impatient as I splayed my hand between her breasts and encouraged her to sit back on the bench. Still kneeling before her, I leaned forward to kiss the smooth insides of her thigh. Nudging her knees further apart to allow me to kiss her other thigh, I couldn't resist a taste and lapped lightly at the soft skin beside her knee. Rewarded by a breathy moan, I allowed my tongue to sample small tastes of her silken skin all the way up her thigh until I could chew playfully on a hipbone.

Not for the first time in the five years that Adriana had appeared to me, I wondered at her indeed being supernatural. Surely no ghostly apparition could possibly smell so good, taste so good, move so seductively beneath my stroking hands. As I indulged myself in her womanly charm, sliding my hands under her hips and pulling her closer to my kisses, I entertained thoughts of transparent waifs drifting like ethereal snowflakes into my enchanted garden.

Those musings melted like so much whimsical snow on a warm Southern California evening with the very real and very solid undulation of her hips, which ingenuously brushed silken curls across my questing lips. I pressed a more intimate kiss to her dampness, intoxicated by the heady scent of earth and spice and woman. Then my tongue traced the delicate folds of satin, seeking the moist intricacies of her heated essence. I felt the feather touch of her fingertips in my hair, massaging my temples and urging me closer yet to earthly pleasures.

"Rene Dumier?"

Her voice was low and velvety, and put me in mind of smoky bars and sultry redheads, with the sensual strain of a saxophone seducing heart and soul. I wasn't altogether certain at my response to her voice, but it made me wish I was a poet, or a musician, or just a lonely stranger sipping scotch whiskey in that smoky bar. I smiled to myself, thinking, *Oh, please let this be a client.*

I stopped fantasizing long enough to respond. "Yes, this is she."

"My name is Sharon Russell. You left a message at my office."

Adriana's relative. "Yes. Ms. Russell, I've been doing some research—genealogy—and I came across your name in connection with an ancestor I was curious about."

"Oh? Are we related?" A note of excitement altered the pitch of her lovely voice, making me suddenly feel unaccountably warm.

"No, no. Actually, you're related to the woman I was looking up. In truth, I've located quite a few of your shared relatives, but I was intrigued by the coincidence of you living in the same city as I."

"You're here in Long Beach?"

"Yes, on 2nd Street. You know the men's bar on Broadway, called the Mine Shaft? I live sort of behind it."

"You're not that big old red house with the overgrown front yard, are you?"

I cringed at the casual but all too accurate description of my pride and joy. "That's the one."

"I love that house! A friend and I used to ride bicycles by there. It looks positively haunted!"

If she only knew! "Well, it has its stories…"

"So." Her husky voice trailed off hesitantly, then, "Which ancestor where you interested in?"

"A Lady Adriana Wexton, of Leicester. She…"

"…died in a horse race."

"You know her...of her?"

"She's one of my favorite family stories. Her sister, Lady Eleanora, ended up marrying Adriana's betrothed...some stuffy fellow."

"Named Viscount Farnsworth."

"Exactly. Well, Lady Eleanora was my great great grandmother. My grandmother, who is 86, still tells stories about them."

I couldn't believe my good fortune. This woman not only knew of her ancestor, my beloved Adriana, but she had family stories. History for me to learn. More details of Adriana's life for me to revel in. I could barely contain my enthusiasm.

"This is so marvelous! Could you—would you—I mean, I was wondering..."

With a hint of teasing there in that sultry voice, she whispered, "And I have diaries..."

"Could we meet?"

A throaty chuckle, then, "I thought you'd never ask."

"As was so typical of the young women of quality at that time, Lady Adriana kept a diary." It took nearly every ounce of self-restraint at my disposal not to leap upon her and tear the slim ancient volume from her hand. We were sitting in my garden, on the very bench where Adriana and I had so often sat, and I caught myself wrestling with my intense desire to touch the diary and my equally intense and almost disquieting curiosity about the woman holding the diary just out of my reach. Not only was this a tangible piece of the reality of Adriana, but also a flesh and blood representative.

Unfortunately, for the peace of my reclusive existence, Sharon Russell was everything and more that her voice had conjured up in my imagination. Had I walked into a roomful of women, and been asked to pick out the woman with the voice that could melt even this jaded heart, I would have known her immediately. Because, just like my smoky barroom fantasy, Ms. Russell was indeed a redhead. And it was that thick, wavy sunset red, that made one want to take great handfuls and hold her still for…

I forced myself to focus on the leather-bound book. My link with Adriana's life. A sample of her handwriting, of her intimate thoughts, of her life in an era long past. There were two slim books, both in identical tan leather covers. One rested in Sharon's lap, while the other, belonging to my beloved, she waved casually at me as she warmed to her subject.

"Lady Eleanora kept one also, both of which my Grandma O'Connor passed on to me. But this one, Lady Adriana's… Now this one has some pretty juicy stuff." She laid it down on the bench between us, then reached across to the small wooden table where I'd set a tray with tea.

"Although she was discreet, there were several references to another woman in her social group. There were quite a few comments about this woman's pending marriage to a Marquis ruining their 'perfect friendship.' I don't know, but I have my suspicions about Aunt Adriana."

When she set down her teacup, I noticed the red lipstick on the rim. Against my better judgment I allowed my eyes to touch ever so briefly on her painted mouth, noting how it was wider then was probably attractive but quite nicely shaped. I suppose I had deliberately avoided cataloging her features, or any other personal quality about her. It was an unconscious habit of mine now. Never looking at women any way other then as clients, or models, or nameless-faceless servants in markets or restaurants. It was all part of my quest for solitude, and possibly penance for past insurrections.

Now that I'd allowed that one peek, I seemed unable to stop looking. That magnificent mane of russet hair was worn a little longer than shoulder length, and layered to allow movement and an impression of controlled wildness. I was particularly charmed by the way it curled forward over one auburn brow, giving her a rakish look. Beneath those dark red brows, which slanted roguishly up at the outside corners, were deep-set eyes of a peculiar gray-blue.

I'd never cared much for blue eyes, like my own, finding them cold and uncomfortable. Indeed, my taste ran more to warm cocoa-colored eyes, with glossy dark hair, and a clear English complexion. But Sharon's eyes were alive with warmth and vitality, hinting at some private joke to where only she held knowledge.

"Mmm, Earl Grey. This reminds me of sitting on Grandma's front porch, taking tea and listening to stories of her family in Ireland and the Langlys of South Hampton."

I couldn't help myself, as I teased, "Then I remind you of your grandmother?"

Those gray eyes twinkled. "Well. There is something very proper about you that brings to mind another era. But I suspect it's a facade. Besides, I imagine you're not much older then I am."

I ran a tentative finger along the spine of the diary lying on the bench between us. "Oh, and how old are you?"

"Thirty-eight this coming December. On the first day of winter."

I looked up. "The 21st?"

"Uh-huh. And you?"

"I was 46 on June 21st."

"Oh, we're opposites."

"Such a coincidence." I didn't believe in coincidences.

"Well, as I was saying, Lady Adriana wrote a good deal of her friend. She was greatly distressed by the marriage. According to Lady Eleanora's diary, her sister went into a profound depression following her friend's death in childbirth. She only seemed to revive and show some spirit when her father arranged her marriage."

She reached again for the teacup, and I noticed her hands were nicely shaped, with short unpolished nails. "What amazes me is that Lady Eleanora writes of being desperately in love with Roderick Langly, the Viscount Farnsworth, yet her father betrothed her sister to Langly. What an insensitive and barbaric thing to do."

From nowhere my question jumped out. "Have you ever married?"

She gave me a level look. "No. I'm surprised you had to ask." Removing the diary from my grasp she lifted it and continued with, "Anyway, it appears that Lady Adriana's untimely death was imminent, according to her sister's diary. You know, I suspect my great great aunt was in love with her friend. There's no proof, of course, except family rumor, but I'd bet Grandma's secret recipe for strawberry-rhubarb pie that Lady Adriana was also a lesbian."

How desperately I was tempted to confirm her suspicions! Yet, Adriana was my secret. Indeed, to reveal her to anyone was to invite speculation about my mental state. As an eccentric middle-aged woman living alone, I certainly did not want to attract undue attention. I liked my solitude, and my secret lover.

But I discovered that I liked Adriana's great great grandniece rather well, also. In but a very short time, Sharon Russell had managed to work her way past my carefully constructed defenses. Even the small handful of friends I'd kept in touch with had never managed such a successful infiltration. In the months that followed my initial meeting with Sharon, frequent were the unannounced visits she paid me. Most often it was to share her grandmother's latest story about our mutual interest, Lady Adriana. Although more and more often I caught her enticing me out for a walk to the beach, or simply showing up with a bag of groceries and preparing us dinner. At first I resented her intrusion, her warmth and optimism, until the day that I realized I was waiting impatiently for her and her wicked laugh to arrive.

Indeed, I had come to enjoy and even crave her spontaneous visits, and her irreverent outlook on life. She invaded first my kitchen, then my garden, until I now invited her into my studio, and my life. I'd nearly forgotten the sweet pleasure to be had from sharing a sunset, a glass of wine, a movie, and a heated debate. Was this what my relationships could have been like? Is this what could be had when lust was removed from the equation?

Hmm. An unfair question, that one. Because Adriana and I shared moments like these. Unparalleled moments of shared moonrises, wine and endless conversation, with sex. I had it all with Adriana… Once a year. But I loved Adriana. I didn't love Sharon. And I certainly did not lust for her. Well. Maybe only in those unguarded moments when she turned away from me, and I caught the glow of a setting sun in her hair. Or when she was leaning over the sauce simmering on the stove, and her shirt gaped enough for me to glimpse the swell of a breast. Or even those times when she threw back her head and laughed, and all I could think of was kissing her. Maybe just during those moments…

No. What I had with Adriana was perfect.

Summer solstice, 1997. My 47th birthday, and the first time in nine years that Adriana did not come to me. I stayed up all night, pacing my bedroom, burning incense and candles. I sat for hours in the garden, watching the moon drift across the night sky until it disappeared and the sun rose to replace it.

I couldn't believe it. I was bereft with a sense of loss that cut to the hidden depths of my heart. Where was she? What had happened? How could our birthdays have come and passed without Adriana appearing? Had I accidentally done something to disturb the delicate passageway between our two worlds? Had I forgotten some ritual? Had I moved some piece of furniture that allowed her to cross over? Had she grown weary of me and this place? Had her spirit finally chosen to travel on, to be reborn or simply go to rest in whatever place ghosts returned to?

It was 5 A.M. and without much thought of why I did it, I called Sharon. She was, after all, my only real link with the woman I had loved without condition for nine years.

"Rene? Are you all right?"

"No. Please, I must see you."

"Let me get dressed, and I'll be right over."

By the time she arrived I was more calm, more rational, more aware of the blunder I had nearly committed with Sharon. It was like that with the light of day. Ever notice how long and lonely the night is? How many problems seemed magnified by the dark, the silence, and the solitude? Ever wonder why we only have nightmares at night? Why our troubles appear insurmountable when wearing a great dark cape of night? It was perception. With the golden light of morning, and Sharon's all-too-solid presence, my great loss seemed, if not small and insignificant, at least manageable.

As I stepped out onto the porch to greet her, she ran up the steps and wrapped me up in a most possessive hug. "Are you all right? What happened?"

I didn't know where to put my hands, and I was suddenly very aware that the shirt I'd pulled on was very thin, and that I wore no bra. "Uh, I'm sorry. I just overreacted. Bad night, you know."

Smoothing a stray lock of hair behind my ear, Sharon studied my face. "It's that new account, isn't it? I knew you were stressed about that deadline."

"Uh, yeah."

She tucked her arm through mine. "C'mon, let's make some tea."

It wasn't until we walked into the kitchen that I remembered the wine—a Chardonnay, because Adriana preferred that. And the plate of sliced apples—green, like Adriana favored. Sharon's quicksilver eyes caught it all, particularly the two glasses on the tray.

While she filled the kettle with water, she commented, "Looks like you were expecting company last night."

My response was to pour the bottle of wine down the sink.

Arranging the tea cups on the counter, she asked too casually, "Birthday celebration?"

I dumped the sliced apples into the garbage and muttered, "Yes."

Her words, in that low velvety voice that conjured warm embraces and soothing kisses, nearly brought me to tears when she guessed: "She didn't show, did she?"

I could only nod my head, then leave the room. I sought the solace of my garden, needing its quiet clutter, yet fearful even that would rip my heart apart with memories. Nine years of memories.

No, not nine years. Only eight nights. In the eight months that I'd known Sharon, we'd spent collectively more time together then Adriana and I had in the past nine years. But it was different, I reminded myself. I loved Adriana.

Placing the tray of cups on the small table beside the arbor bench, Sharon sat down beside me. "Would you like to talk about it?"

My chest burned with an almost unbearable ache, and I seemed unable to speak around the lump that had formed in my throat. I shook my head and looked out into the herb garden, trying to remember if I had sown the seeds for my next crop. When I felt her arm ease around my shoulders, I blinked several times and concentrated on organizing which plants needed to be pruned and thinned, and which needed to be harvested before the heat of summer ruined their potency. Then, of course, there was my newest client, and the demanding timetable I needed to synchronize my creative impulses with. There was so much to consider...

Did I mention how Sharon finally discovered Adriana? It wasn't too long after my birthday, and Sharon was playing mother hen with what she perceived to be my wounded feelings, so she was fixing dinner for me—again. I was up in the second floor, which I had converted into my studio, since the previous owner of the house had been good enough to put in two huge skylights. While I was up there finishing the mat on an illustration that was due that week, Sharon was wandering the house—unsupervised—and had apparently walked into my bedroom. It was the one room I hadn't shown her. I considered it my sanctuary. I also felt it was wiser for all to keep Sharon away from that room. Especially if I was in it.

She says she was looking for another apron, and ended up in there. I don't know how long she was there, but I certainly learned her reaction to my private sanctuary soon enough. And, of course, with all the flavor of her expressive emotions.

"Who's the woman you have a shrine for?"

I looked up from my art table, peering over my glasses at her. "What shrine?"

"In your bedroom." Was she angry? I wasn't certain, although I noticed she appeared flushed. Probably from the heat in the kitchen.

Then her words registered. "My bedroom? What were you doing in there?"

"Admiring your shrine. My God, is that the woman you spend your birthdays with? It looks more like you worship her then love her." Yes, it did appear to be anger.

I was actually amused at her reaction. "So?"

She stalked into the room. "No wonder you're so damned interested in my ancestors. That woman looks just like Lady Adriana! I suppose you did that portrait of you and she in Victorian costumes?"

I think I liked her reaction. "How do you know what Adriana looks like?"

Crossing her arms under her breasts, she frowned. "I was told she favors the Langlys. And I remember seeing a painting of the family. How did *you* know what she looks like?"

I couldn't resist it. Her reactions were priceless. "I've met her."

Hands on hips this time. "You've met her? Lady Adriana?"

I nodded. "Every year on my birthday—which, incidentally, is hers also—for the last nine, well, eight of the last nine years."

Now Sharon was scowling. "Once a year, on your birthdays, you meet my great great grand aunt?"

I shrugged, curious to see where this was going. No doubt our relationship as friends had run its course, and it was time to be moving on. I would certainly miss her company, but she would not be the first woman I had severed my associations with. Why not go out with a bang? So I said, "Yes. Although actually its her ghost."

"A ghost?"

"Yes, a ghost."

Silence.

Then, with all the exuberance I had learned to expect and admire in her, Sharon threw up her hands and yelled, "How in the hell am I supposed to compete with a ghost?"

It was my turn to frown. "Compete?"

Walking up to me and leaning so close that I could practically count the freckles across her nose, she growled through clenched teeth, "In case you haven't noticed, you thick-headed woman, I've been courting you for the better part of a year now!"

"You have?"

She practically shook her fist in my face as she ranted, "I fell in love with you in that first phone call."

"You did?"

Turning away, she stalked angrily across the room and into my sitting area, saying, "I was being so careful, trying to make you feel comfortable and unthreatened. You're so goddamned skittish about being touched or fussed over that I assumed you'd been burned and were nursing some horrific emotional scars."

Tossing my glasses on the table and saying a silent plea of forgiveness to Adriana, I followed her. "You have part of that slightly wrong."

Sharon whirled about, and started when she realized how close I was. I stepped even closer and said very quietly, "I didn't get burned."

I slid a hand around her wrist, and so that she made no further mistakes about my physical and emotional reticence, I drew her against me, whispering, "I did the burning."

As I had long suspected, our coming together laid torch to dry kindling, igniting a brush fire that swept away all restraints. Our kisses were desperate, hungry, bruising. I had no patience, and could summon little finesse, as I tore at our clothes in an all-consuming need to be as close to her as was physically possible. And it wasn't just sex. Oh, I wanted her, and when I discovered she was hot and wet and frantically willing, I was a carnivore un-leashed. Yet it was so much more than that.

This was my companion, my confidante. This was the first woman I had bothered to become truly acquainted with. She aroused my mind, my soul, as well as my sensuality. And on the rich, thick Abusson rugs of my quaint little sitting area, I entered more than the deep mysteries of an alluring woman, and found myself drawn irrevocably into the welcome embrace of unconditional love.

Hours later, as she surfaced through the folds of the comforter I had thrown over us, Sharon asked, "How do you know she's really a ghost? Maybe she's some very clever woman who sneaks into your garden every June 21st, then slips away in the wee morning hours."

"I entertained the same thoughts." Plumping the pillow beneath my head, I added, "Until I tried to photograph her—and the pictures all came out blurred. Or like the time we tried to leave the house, to go out to dinner—and she literally vanished as we stepped out the door, and I found her back in the bedroom sitting at her writing table."

A warm hand grazed my hip. "What are the chances you're delusional?"

"Probably pretty good." I gave into her gentle urging and backed into her embrace, finding the feel of her breasts pressed to my back immeasurably comforting. "But in regard to Adriana, I don't think my imagination could give me a hickey, or leave me with achy muscles from some rather incredible bedroom gymnastics."

"Okay, I don't want to hear anymore!"

I chuckled. "Well, it seems this heroine in the Gothic romance has been rescued from spectral infatuation by the dark and brooding... Hmm, a Heathcliffe you are not."

She kissed my shoulder. "No, that's more your image. I'd say that this was a case of taming the beast with Grandma's magic recipes."

"I always suspected there was something in your cooking."

Summer solstice. Again. This time my 48th solar return. I walked out the French doors of my bedroom to stand in the garden, enjoying the night air that was warm and scented of roses and jasmine. There was a full moon tonight. Just as there had been all those years ago. I couldn't resist a glance at the arbor bench, the place where she always met me, on this, the night of our birthdays.

Would she come this year? Part of me was hopeful, but another part dreaded the choices I would be faced with. I'd always managed to avoid choices like these. But Sharon lived with me now. No longer did I view her as a visitor in my life, or as an entertaining interlude. In fact, I could barely conceive of a life without her now. So, the prospect of seeing Adriana filled me with great conflict, because I couldn't imagine not loving both of them.

It was late. Dinner had been a marvelous reenactment of one of her grandmother's recipes. After the meal we had retired to the bedroom with a bottle of Merlot—her favorite—and finished that while we burned candles and incense, and gradually found our way into bed. Our lovemaking was always a consistent blend of tender and ferocious. I discovered I enjoyed this unpredictable continuity of monogamy. As well as I'd come to know her mind and body in nearly a year of loving her, it never ceased to amaze me all over again how beautiful and generous her response to me could be.

Now, as she came up on her knees before me, gripping the headboard and pressing her bottom firmly against my thighs, I was caught up all over again in the thrill of touching her, of feeling her move. I tightened my arm around her waist, drawing her against me so our rhythms meshed. I kissed her bare back, aware of the universe of freckles there, and imagined I could taste their cinnamon and spice on her skin. Unable to resist, I gently grazed the crest of her shoulder with my teeth and was rewarded by a throaty moan.

Still holding her secure against me, I ran my free hand down her belly and over crisp auburn curls. I tunneled my fingers through those damp curls, seeking the sleek folds of satin within. She was already swollen and sensitive and bucked against my questing hand. Like soothing a skittish filly, I smoothed my hand over her hip and around to slide up the back of her thigh to finally cup her behind.

She liked that and arched her back, pressing her hips back into the cradle of my lap. I savored the tingling sensation of my own dark curls brushing the cleft of her bottom. The temptation too great, I eased my hand between us, sliding under her bottom, to stroke the wetness. Using my knee to push her thighs further apart, I took advantage of the altered position and slid two fingers into her moist warmth.

A growl escaped her as she rocked back against me, seeking just the right fit, just the right touch. I stroked deeper and withdrew, only to plunge deeper yet. She clenched around my fingers, sucking me in with defiance at my attempt to leave her again. We moved steadily, rocking, stroking, reaching for infinite bliss in a deep sea of wonderful mysteries.

It was then that I felt someone kiss my back. Before I could react and alter my rhythm with Sharon, Adriana whispered in my ear, "Let me love her."

As my mind stumbled to conjure intelligible speech, Adriana slipped between my knees, easing them more apart as she slid underneath me and suddenly lay face up beneath Sharon. Never losing the pace of my movements, and clamping Sharon tighter to me, I adjusted myself so I straddled Adriana as she reached up and grabbed Sharon's hips. I felt Adriana playfully lick my knuckles, and knew the moment her tongue found Sharon, because she shuddered and nearly choked on a religious exclamation.

If she objected to the presence of another women between her legs, she certainly seemed too overwhelmed by sensation to voice her complaint. Her only reaction was to moan more loudly and increase the undulating tempo of her movements. I quickly overcame my apprehensions, my worry and pleasure at Adriana's sudden and timely appearance, and began to revel in the feel of

Sharon's response to Adriana's mouth, the tease of Adriana's chin against my hand, and the series of exquisite contractions squeezing my fingers.

With a shout Sharon slapped the wall above the headboard, then collapsed back against me. In a sensual ballet of unrehearsed synchronicity, the three of us untangled and stretched out on the rumpled bed. As Adriana and I kissed Sharon in tandem, our lips met in a three-way kiss I could never have dreamed possible nor imagined the words to describe.

And then Sharon was taking great fistfuls of Adriana's dark unbound hair and holding her down as she feverishly kissed her jaw, her ear, her neck. One of Sharon's hands snaked out to grip mine, then guided it to the fullness of Adriana's breasts. Together we welcomed Adriana to our relationship and to a shared celebration of summer solstice magic.

The skies over my enchanted garden were paling on a morning of brilliant pink clouds. I must have dozed because when I opened my eyes to that intense morning sky, I saw Adriana sitting at the writing table, fully dressed in the silks of her floor-length dress. She smiled at me, and, glancing at Sharon, put a finger to her lips.

Quietly I eased myself out of the ravaged bedding, tucking the comforter more securely around Sharon. When I had wrapped a robe around me I followed Adriana out the French doors and into the garden. She turned and slipped an arm around my waist, walking me to the arbor bench where we had sat so many times in the past.

"Hmm, a lovely woman, this relative of mine."

I smiled. "Yes, she is."

"My love." Adriana tilted her head towards me, and her glossy hair caught the first golden ray of the morning. She looked so serene, so beautiful that it nearly hurt to look upon her. With a sad little smile she finished with, "I wish to be going home."

"England?"

She nodded, and I noticed that she appeared less vibrant, less corporeal as she said, "Will you see to it?"

I didn't want her to go. I didn't want my birthday to come and go ever again without her there. And yet mine were selfish reasons. I sighed. "How?"

"The writing table." She glanced over at the French doors, and in that movement I realized that I could see the rose vine behind her, through her. She was fading.

"No, Adriana—wait—"

"I tried last summer, but I got lost. You must send the writing table." Her soft brown eyes caressed my face. "It's time, my love. Please?"

"All right."

"I love you, Rene Dumier." She leaned forward to kiss me, and I closed my eyes. All I felt was a breath of air across my lips.

Opening my eyes on an empty garden I whispered, "And I love you, Lady Adriana Wexton."

Taking a deep breath I looked up at the French doors, and saw Sharon standing there, her hair on fire in the gold light of the morning. Her lips tipped at the corners and she lifted her hand to blow me a kiss.

Sharon came up the stairs to my studio, humming softly.

I looked around the easel at her and asked, "Who was that on the phone?"

"My cousin, William. They received the crate, safe and sound."

I wiped my brush on a rag, then after adjusting my reading glasses looked back at the canvas. "Then she's home."

Stepping up behind me, Sharon wrapped her arms around my waist and pressed herself to my back. "William is family. He promised to see that the table found a proper home." She squeezed me lightly then leaned forward to kiss the back of my ear, saying, "I recommended a finishing school."

"You're incorrigible!"

She chuckled. "And well you should know!" Looking over my

shoulder now at the oil painting I currently worked on, she said, "Hmm, I look rather stunning in that high-waisted Victorian outfit."

I snorted. "You look stunning in anything."

"True." Another light squeeze, then, "She was a beautiful girl. I'm glad I had the opportunity to meet her."

I turned in the circle of her arms, and wrapped mine around her neck. "I doubt another person of my acquaintance would have accepted such a meeting as casually as you."

Those auburn brows lifted. "Why, sweetheart, she was a relative." She gave me a quick kiss, then said, "Besides, I save my excitement for other, more appropriate moments."

Giving the Abusson rug in my sitting area a deliberate look, I said, "Could I interest you in one of those moments, now?"

In that lovely voice that still conjured images of smoky bars and sensual saxophones, she answered, "For you, always."

❧ Matches ❧

by M. Christian

The dyke couple in 6C were the first to notice the gas leak, but they were in the first rushes of move-in love and lust, and simply thought it was the general ambiance of their new neighborhood. The young one, a tiny thing name Lissa, was going to mention it to the landlord, Mr. Skila, when he came for the rent, but all he ever did was nod and say "Yes, yes, yes" in his thick (Bulgarian, Russian, Czech, Spanish, Greek?) accent and stare at her tiny tits. So she didn't.

The guy who worked at the java place around the corner was right under them, so it would have been safe to assume that he had been aware of the distinct smell of leaking natural gas—except he had lost his sense of smell in a freebasing accident (which was also why he sported his spotty and totally unattractive beard).

The apartment in front of him was probably vacant, no one could remember seeing anyone enter or leave. Rumors, at least among the tenants who spoke to each other, were that the previous occupant of 1A: (1) died, and Mr. Skila couldn't deal with getting rid of the possessions; (2) had done so much damage to the room that the lazy (Bulgarian, Russian, Czech, Spanish, Greek?) landlord couldn't be bothered fixing it up; or (3) still lived there. Fact was, most of the residents of the sad Victorian simply didn't speak to each other. The chance that yet another freak, loser, weirdo, or some such lived in the room—very quietly—was all too possible.

Above the mystery of 1A was the mystery of R. Ruge. Since R. Ruge worked late at night and slept during the day, he was rarely seen. When he was, it was on the stairs, walking up from BART, or, rarely, leaving his cave in search of greasy fast food. He didn't talk, didn't move or pause in his grinding trudge, so the other tenants saw him as a kind of clockwork; he would come slowly stomping up the stairs—bags of dripping burgers, fries, or chicken in his bloated yellow arms—filling the tiny, dark halls like a cholesterol steam roller. He was so big and unsociable that the other tenants simply stepped into the nearest doorway and let him rumble past. R. Ruge may have smelled the gas leak, but he never told anyone, let alone Mr. Skila, about it.

There were other people in the building, of course. The last number on the bashed and scarred mailbox in the lobby was 8C. But the explosion took place at 2 o'clock on a Saturday afternoon and most of them were out having lives.

The exact cause wasn't known until investigators from the San Francisco Fire Department traced the leak to Mr. Skila's workroom in the basement. No one was shocked to discover the cause of the massive explosion that killed six people, destroyed the building, and damaged several other structures in the neighborhood. Mr. Skila drank—evidenced by the bottle usually seen in the back pocket of his paint-stained jeans—and Mr. Skila smoked—evidenced by the ever-present pack of Marlboros in his shirt pocket—and Mr. Skila rarely bathed—evidenced by the garlic, stale tobacco, farts, shit, and sweat that could be smelled 200 yards away. It was easy to imagine Mr. Skila taking a break in his workroom, knocking back a good hefty swallow or two from his flask, and then lighting up a cigarette, totally unable—senses dead from the smoking and the drinking and his own reek—to tell he was taking his drink and smoke break in a room filled with gas.

R. Ruge's first name was Robert. He worked in an electronics warehouse in South City, filling little polyethylene bags with resistors, transistors, capacitors, and tiny bits of wire. He was born in Sacramento. He graduated high school, but not college. His first job was in a garage, doing lube jobs and balancing truck tires. He left home when he was 25, shortly after his first kiss: a sailor named Billy, home to visit his mother. Robert moved to the city in '69 and had a lot of fun for a few years: this bar, that bar, this guy, that guy. He avoided catching anything serious (or very serious), but he began to suffer in the looks department. Too many burgers, not enough exercise. His scores got harder and harder, and then he was having to pay, then pay more, and then pay much more. His hair was almost gone. His teeth were bad. After a point, it was easier not to try. Up until that Saturday afternoon, one of his favorite things to do was drink Budweiser, watch *American Gladiators,* and masturbate.

When the explosion roared up from Mr. Skila's workroom, Robert Ruge was going into the kitchen for another can. He wore his Saturday morning comforts: tattered old bathrobe (red with yellow stripes), old boxer shorts (once white), and the crazy-looking bunny slippers his mother had mailed to him before she died two years ago. As he stepped from the tiny living room into the even tinier kitchen, the pressure wave from the explosion smashed into the floor below, throwing him to the left, off the greasy stove and out the window. The last physical thing Robert Ruge experienced was the vibrating pain of his elbow smashing into the enamel of the stove.

R. Ruge was the second person to die that Saturday afternoon. Mr. Skila had been the first (in a flash of light). The guy who worked at the java joint was the fourth, followed by the two young dykes.

The third was the mystery in room 1A.

Death, Robert Ruge decided, wasn't half bad.

His body, at least in the last ten years or so, had been pretty much of a burden: fat, weak, smelly, *small,* and leaning towards diabetes. He had recently started to view his body as a pair of handcuffs, holding him down, humiliating him, keeping him from really enjoying himself.

He was glad to be free of it.

The transition had actually been pretty easy. The stabbing pain in his elbow, the wave of concussion, a moment of darkness, light, and then flames. But he didn't feel the fire. All Robert felt was...nothing. He was in a great ball of angry flames, watching the roof of the apartment building rush towards and then through him and all he felt was a sense of expansion.

Oh, my God, he thought—his mind blooming beyond the usual confines of his brain. *Oh, my God,* he thought, as the flames roaring up from the collapsed roof danced around and through him. No pain, no real sensation. He seemed to just be *there,* watching the fire, listening to it eat the wood and plaster. *I think I'm here,* he thought. *I think I have hands. I think I still have something like a body.*

The fire started to make him uncomfortable. He still didn't feel anything, but the sight of the flames licking away at the building scared him—because he couldn't feel it.

So he left. *Oh, my God,* Ruge thought as he hovered over the burning building and looked down at the gawkers, the arriving fire engines, his body in the street, the fireflies of embers, the thick churning clouds of smoke. Slowly, as he watched and grew strangely accustomed to it all, he became aware that he did have a body.

It was the one he always knew he had.

He was strong. Looking around, he saw himself take form. Muscles shimmered and coalesced. His hands were wide and long. His arms had become semitransparent bundles of strength. His legs were thick columns of silvery muscle. He couldn't see it, but he knew that his face was lantern-jawed, with a cleft chin, brilliant eyes, and a cascade of midnight hair hanging in a negative halo around his powerful skull (after all, he was floating). This was the Ruge that lived in the meat—the man inside.

I'm here, he thought. *I'm finally here.*

Ruge was happy. He was strong. He was well-defined. He was "Tom of Finland." He soared through the fading flames, phased through the billowing black clouds of smoke and steam, and flashed through pigeons. The weight of his ugly body was gone. His flesh lay in the street among the wreckage of the building and the frantic firemen.

No one had told the young Robert Ruge that coming to the City, coming out, and jumping in, would make him happy. No one had mislead him—but there was always a part of him that felt like a promise hadn't been kept. He had come out, moved to Sodom by the Sea, and jumped into the sparkling depths of the Polk Gulch. For a while he was part of a world that loved him and thought him sexy.

Then, gravity. Then, male pattern baldness. "Troll" used to be giggles and snickers, pointing to someone else. After a few very short years it was a sarcastic self-definition.

Some took it on as a kind of kink. Some hung up their hats and tried to find the same to grow old with.

In his cell, with masturbation and *American Gladiators,* R. Ruge seethed and hated.

Now, though, he was free. He was big and strong and huge—where it mattered. He was free and beautiful, now that he was dead.

And he wasn't alone.

The two dykes shot past him—bound for some kind of Valhalla, no doubt—fused into a churning ball of brilliant light, their lust and love consuming them and turning them into a kind of afterlife comet. Mr. Skila hovered over the steaming wreckage of his building, his own form like a kind of long-limbed gazelle or antelope: weirdly stretched arms and legs; a narrow, ribbed chest; and a streamlined head. Ruge suddenly remembered that Mr. Skila only seemed to sparkle when the Bay to Breakers poured down their street. Dead, Mr. Skila could run and run and run for all eternity.

The kid who worked in the java joint churned overhead—a great clockwork mandala spinning around and through and over itself in a dizzying display of convolutions and articulations. Too much of everything. Too many perceptions altered from high school 'til Mr. Skila's match tore his body apart. The kid who worked in the java joint was now *really* free to explore the limits of perception.

Then there was the other one.

He floated up from the remains of the now-smoldering apartment, filling Robert's vision with his perfection—a Roman statue stepping from its pedestal, a Greek god striding away from his column. Big, broad shoulders, a chest of well-defined (if spectral) muscles, legs like pillars of stone, and a face that was strong yet lit by emotion. Eyes that danced with desire and fire. Michelangelo's *David*—the man in 1A.

They were in love. It was an almost perfect match.

The attraction was magnetic, electric—sparks flew as they grew closer and touched. It was that moment—the one when attraction meets attraction. You find him hot; he finds you hot. Mutual polarity of pure lust. They touched, hands first, and felt the current flow between them. Their eyes took each other in, sized each other up, and found very little lacking.

They had a lot of the earth still about them. Their bodies, for instance, and certainly what their bodies did when they found each other attractive.

Slightly startled by this, they both looked down between them at the gauges of their attraction and laughed.

In his flesh, R. Ruge was a piggy-dicked man. When it was hard it was small and turned obviously to the left. The shaft was narrow and his circumcised head was ridiculously bulbous. Dead, his cock was spectral iron, a great jutting spear—shaft wide and strong, tapering to a perfectly proportioned head. Between them, his cock was up and ready at a 45 degree angle.

And as they danced, touching and floating above the building, Ruge rubbed against the cock of the man in 1A. *David's* wasn't maybe as pronounced and exaggerated, but it was just about perfect. It was one of those cocks that stops your breath—not huge, not monstrous, just... *beautiful.* Ruge found himself staring at it, watching it bob and weave between then, grazing his own every once and a while—sparks flying as a tense precome wave washed through him.

Ghosts, they kissed, pressing the cocks they deserved between them. It was more than their new bodies that held them together, they knew. They were just about made for each other. They kissed with lightning, feeling their tongues spark and entwine and grapple like twin magnets. They rubbed and held each other close, feeling their cocks press against their bellies (and against nipples in the case of Ruge's member). They humped and laughed and screamed with joy at their new playthings. *David* laughed, and clapped his strong, supple mouth over Ruge's bulbous cockhead and sucked and surged raw voltage through them, connecting them, negative pole to positive pole, linked and joined, mouth to cock. Free of cruel gravity, Ruge flipped himself over and completed the circuit with a spectral 69 that lit the skies of San Francisco like a lovely summer storm.

Free now to do whatever they wanted, they did just that. Ruge took the god from behind, easing himself into an asshole that was more than just a place to shit from. *David's* asshole was a portal, a door into him. As Ruge went in and out in a great cosmic butt-fuck, *David's* asshole surged and sparked and twirled around his new cock like a particle accelerator. They weren't fucking with tissues and muscle and cartilage, they were fucking with ectoplasm, electrons, protons, and quarks. When they came, and they did and did and did, they came with ghostly subatomic explosions.

David put his semitransparent hand around Ruge's new cock and seemed to lose himself. Ruge, in turn, became lost in the sensation of *David's* strong and sparking hand. Ruge became everything he ever wanted to be—the object of pure lust.

Then it was Ruge's turn to receive. While not as grandiose as Ruge's cock, *David's* was more finely conceived. While not filling him until it tapped against his back teeth, *David's* cock did fill exactly where it needed to fill. It was an almost perfect fit. It pushed every good button Ruge had. It churned his sex from the inside out. It flowed through his asshole, around his heart, and down through his own throbbing cock. It tickled around the edges of his soul and the boundaries of his Self. It was a key that Ruge knew would unlock the absolutely most beautiful orgasms of his existence.

Then Ruge was in pain, laying on the sidewalk. Someone was saying "One, two, three—*clear!*"

Course voltage slammed into him, and his teeth snapped down hard enough to chip a molar. His leg screamed in pain from where it had been sheared off at the knee. His face felt like it had been ground away. His skin felt like it was still burning. It felt like needles and soldering irons lay across him or pierced his bleeding body.

R. Ruge was alive again.

The paramedic injected something into his arm. It felt like a red hot fireplace poker being shoved through him. His scream echoed through his skull and bounced around inside the oxygen mask strapped to his face. Somewhere, someone said something about a drug, but another voice said something about the possibility of shock and a weak heart.

R. Ruge was awake. His eyes darted, seeing the fading smoke from the fire, the hurried looks from the paramedics fleeting in and out of his range of vision. Behind them, above them, he could still see the angel *David*, the man in room 1A, hovering, longing, desiring. They were so close, but there was so much between them—now.

It was too much. The pain. The taking away of all he had ever wanted—no, deserved. *David* was what he deserved above all else.

A lifetime of rage and selfishness and self-pity and destruction boiled up and through his shattered and burned body and for split second he didn't feel anything except pure hatred for everyone and everything.

The small oxygen bottle was laying against his arm. He could feel its slight coolness through his first and second degree burns. With the strength of hatred at all those who had lived so much when he had been jailed in his failing body, he lifted the bottle and smashed it across the face of the nearest paramedic.

He lost consciousness again shortly after that. When next he awoke, he was laying in a hospital bed—the beeping, dripping attendants of medical science keeping him alive and in incredible pain. Most of that day was gone, erased by whatever cruelty it is that makes us forget dreams. One thing, and one thing only remained, an image that hung over him: of the paramedic leaving his own body and traveling up and away from the street, away from R. Ruge and the fire. There the paramedic met *David*, the man in 1A, and they flew off to an absolutely perfect, perfect, match. They had been really, truly, made for each other—they weren't an *almost* perfect match.

They were a *perfect* match.

⟿ Eyes ⟿

by E.J. Galusha

"I do so love your eyes."

"Excuse me?" Such a bold approach from someone I didn't even know. But, oh, such a wondrous beauty in her own right, and such profound mystery hidden within that dark-matter gaze of hers. I couldn't help myself. And now, after three sensuously wondrous weeks, she is still so deliciously irresistible.

"They remind me of the waters around Majorca, Spain," she'd said.

"Oh?" That black-ringlet hair. The olive-gold of her skin. The boyish lines of her face. A pleasant enough diversion then. Compelling enough to have caused me to linger longer than I had intended.

"Have you ever been there?" she asked.

"No," I'd replied, mesmerized. Teeth so white behind that small, pouty smile. Lips so soft and glistening, spicy-sweet. Made more so by the merlot she'd been drinking. How I wanted to taste those lips even then!

"The waters surrounding the island are of deepest and purest

295

emerald," she'd said. "At certain times you can see a hundred feet below the surface as easily as looking through a sheet of flawless green glass. When the wind isn't blowing, you can see the sky reflected in its surface, and at night every star in the heavens. There are times when it's almost impossible to tell one from the other, when the sky and the sea are of such clarity that they bleed into one another and become a single, great sphere of bluish-green."

"Um. Sounds beautiful," I'd replied, at the same time thinking, *And you there, lying naked on the bone-white sand...a fallen goddess of dew-laden bronze.* That gaze of hers, so hypnotic, made it so easy to fall into the vision.

"It is. And such times are filled with magic."

"And you see all of this in my eyes?" I asked, while wondering, *And tell me, can you see us together, as Michelangelo would have made us if he had possessed the insight, you and I entwined so tightly as to be carved from the same stone?*

"Indeed," she'd replied, and who cared if it was clichéd? I certainly didn't. "I am drawn to those eyes as a moth to a flame."

As was I, like light around a black hole. What was the allure? What was the nature of her power? Did I even truly care? Do I care even now? "Would you like to leave this place?" I'd offered, more brazenly than I'd ever dared before, even with a man.

"As you will. I—have an apartment. Close by."

"As do I," I replied, while saying to myself, *But only yours will do.*

"But you would prefer indiscretion."

So, she could see that I was married, even though I'd placed my rings in my purse before entering the bar. So astute, and oh, so very wise to guess that my husband would not take kindly to sharing my bed with another, though the roles had been reversed often enough without even the slightest hint of censure from me. "I think—yours," I said.

"It is only a short way from here. I'll write the address on this napkin. If you should change your mind..."

"Wait for me," I replied, softly. Her hand felt so strong and hot beneath my own. Her pulse was like a hammer against the softened iron of my palm. Oh, to be consumed by the fire that was certainly raging within her. I was moist already, and I was glad the lighting was low to conceal my blush, as well as the wet spot I was sure to leave on the seat when I left.

"Please." Her petition was like a whisper of music. "Do not make we wait too long."

I wanted her to wait, to suffer, but to do so would have been more painful than even I could endure. "Give me half an hour," I said, embarrassed by the tremor of anticipation in my voice.

"Can you make it less?" Her eyes glinting with expectations of her own.

"No," I lied. "But..."

"Yes?"

Such desire in her face could not be refused. "Long enough only to make some calls," I promised. "Cancel a couple of appointments," I lied again. I had nowhere to be. Nothing really to do. My husband might be home, then again he might not. Either way, I knew I wouldn't be missed.

"I'll be waiting," she said, and I knew even then how it would be—which is how it's been ever since.

Eyes other than mine watched her go. The wanton eyes of men. The envious eyes of women. I met them all and they shied away, shamed by the realization of their own impotent longing they saw reflected in my eyes. I felt their eyes staring furtively into my back when it was my turn to leave and knew they wished their stares possessed sharper edges. I recall casting one last look back before I left and knew that even though they had averted their eyes to focus upon the drinks in front of them, they were watching me, the women wanting to *be* me, the men wanting to be *her*.

And here I am again, standing naked beneath my overcoat outside the door to her apartment. I have knocked several times and, as always, she keeps we waiting. I can hear her breath on the other side as she leans her head against the wood. She knows that I know she is there. Oh, how can she linger so? While I—I can barely keep my hands from roaming too freely beneath my coat.

"Wait a little longer, my love," she whispers from the other side.

"You know I cannot," I whisper back.

And the door opens, ever so slowly. "Then come," she says.

I already have, twice, before the door has closed behind me. I am wet and slippery. The air is filled with my own scent. She knows. She can taste it, I'm sure, as her tongue slides oh-so-luxuriously across those satiny-smooth, so very full and moist lips. And suddenly, my coat has become a mound around my feet. Her gaze lingers long on my sex, but not as long as I would like, before returning to my eyes.

"Come with me."

Her eyes, even though they have turned away, have tethered me to her will. I follow after her, unable to resist the raw power of her, to the bedroom. I catch myself leaning toward her, wanting to inhale the richness that clings to her like mist. Why? What is she? Who is she, that I, so used to capturing the souls of men, am still unable to command her? Instead, it is I who am caught, am commanded, and in so great a measure that my desire is squeezed to oozing from every pore. I am burgeoning with need, my sex so swollen that every step causes my thighs to tremble with cascading release.

The atmosphere of the next room—all blue-within-blue, a collage of azure shade and deep-ocean shadow, flickering blue-moon lamps on indigo walls, the floor a swath of eastern evening sky, the ceiling blue-black as storm, drapes like cobalt clouds over netherworld blinds—is ripe with the aura of our previous encounters.

"Lie down," she points to the bed. "There." Mussel shell quilts and satin sheets of robin's egg on the bed. The bed, so much like the lining of a coffin. A coffin, so very much like the room.

"My secret place," she says to me, as she always says to me, as she leads me to lie down.

And then she is above me. A black shadow only marginally

distinct from all the others within the room, and her eyes, pinpoint flames of antiflesh radiance; neutron stars on the verge of collapse.

"Your eyes. So full of life. So full of—magic," she says, as so often before.

Her body presses against mine. Her skin is drenched with fever. As is my own, as she moves quickly with that marvelous tongue, such a voluptuous organ that, like a bolt of wet-hot lightning, if there can be such a thing, is suddenly thrust forcefully between my legs, threatening to cleave me in two. Her probes create a series of explosive antimatter bursts that sear every nerve of my body and threaten to reduce to ashes the very fiber of my being. No man has ever shown me such pleasure, has ever before managed to stoke such a fire within me. I can barely hold my breath long enough to cry out, so great is my ecstasy!

She pauses momentarily in her ministrations. "It's said that eyes are the mirror of the soul," she says, all of which I've heard before. "Therein, a woman's every truth and lie can be found out."

Her voice so calm. So controlled. But wondering. I mean to whisper another something, another promise, another affirmation, as always to alleviate any doubt, but I find that my own voice has left me.

"There are those who believe that the last thing to be seen by a dying host will be forever imprinted on the insides of her eyes, and that, when the eyes are turned inside out, the image can be seen as clearly as if it had been photographed."

Her words are barely discernible above the sounds of my own whispers and tremulous moans as first she teases my flesh, speaks, and teases again. Before and behind each phrase, I feel her marvelous tongue pushing at the door of my womb, microseconds ahead of each ecstatic wave that leaves me adrift within an endless sea of paroxysmal catatonia.

"Carrion will always go for the eyes first. Vultures. Crows. They can't help themselves. And ants. Bury a woman to her neck in an anthill and the little boogers will always go for the eyes before anything else. In some human cultures, eyes are considered to be a delicacy. In others, they are consumed for whatever magic they might contain."

What is she saying? What is this sudden change of mood I feel that alters the very atmosphere of this room, like the hint of ozone before an impending storm? And—her squirming lance is no longer hot, but cool—and getting colder. Now chilling. Clammy. In my mind it is a blind, pink-skinned cemetery worm of gigantic proportion, trying desperately to force an entry into something freshly dead—be it man or woman or animal or thing—it is, in every instance, too terrifying and grotesque a spectacle to entertain. My sex snaps tight, a reflex to the sudden revulsion that has replaced my lust. My moan becomes a scream.

"Oh! And so, realization dawns," she announces, moving quickly to contain me within a viselike press of arms that pinions my own to my sides. There is a strange edge to her voice I've not heard before.

I feel her hands on the sides of my head. Her thumbs caressing my brows, my cheeks. Her breath is heavy on my face, a poisonous vapor I dare not breathe.

"I remember the first time, while traveling in Alaska. Fish eyes. Pickled, Eskimo style. They were sweet. The kids ate them like candy, raw."

"What are you talking about?" I gasp, twisting my head from side to side, trying futilely to dodge her flicking tongue as a dark shadow of premonition begins seeping in from around the edges of my anxiety.

"After fish eyes I tried everything else that swam or made its home in the water, which left me always wanting for more. I moved on to avians for awhile, very tasty, still lacking. After that, the usual thing, cats and dogs and farm animals, but I found them too bland. And then I went after bigger game. Predators, including men, and discovered them far more delectable, but still deficient somehow. But then came the day I took a woman. I've been hooked ever since."

Her laugh is like a jackal's. There is a new scent on her breath, like rotting meat. I cannot bear this! I must escape! But her arms press like steel clamps against my own.

"Did you know there are those who believe that to consume flesh is to partake of the victim's soul?" Her voice sounds so much like the hiss of a serpent. "Cannibals in the Amazon eat an enemy's heart to steal her courage. There are tribes in the jungles of Asia who eat the living brains of their victims in order to ingest the essence of their victims' will."

She squeezes more tightly, her elbows burrowing into my sides. I cannot breathe. Something gives. Sharp spears stab deep into my chest. My ribs—they crack!

"I tried it all," she whispers, spewing drool upon my face. "All so very yummy, but less than satisfying. For all the hype, it's nothing more than meat, really.

"But the eyes, now—especially a woman's eyes—are special, to be prized above all others. Something, I'm sure, to do in part with the powers of procreation. And *your* eyes...Your eyes are *very* special."

Her thumbs—pressing into the corners of my eyes. Pressure. Pain. *No! Please, no!*

"The stuff of magic is the stuff of souls. And eyes are the measure of it, the force of which can be gauged by many things. Color. Depth. Intensity. Size. Even shape—all indicators for measuring one's magical potential. It is a rarity to find such eyes as yours. So brightly lit. Pulsing with so much untapped reserve. A pity you never realized it, though I can't help but tell you how pleased I am to be the first to partake of it."

Oh, Jesus, please don't let this be happening!

"Careful now! Don't jump. I don't want to blind you."

Oh, my God! She's—she's—N-o-o-o!

"Ah, yes. Such beautiful eyes—hey! Don't pass out on me. You've got to pay attention—OK—there—just enough to let you get some air. Oop—you are a squirmy one—sorry, can't let you go. Now, look. Notice that I haven't severed the optic nerves. You can still see. So, when I turn them around like—so—you can see yourself."

No-no-no-no-no-no-n-o-o-o!

"I'm going to begin cutting off your wind now. I know you're confused about all of this, so I'll try to explain as quickly as I can before you go. That's not very polite of me, is it? I don't want to scare you to death. It's all got to be controlled. You see, when a person dies—like you're about to do—slowly—the soul begins to prepare for its departure from the body. As it gathers itself to make the leap from this world into the next, it concentrates all its energy in the eyes, and when the time is right it releases itself *through* the eyes. Now, I'm not sure how the process works—but when I turn the eyes so they face one another—like so—then press them together, the soul is trapped. Then at the moment of death, I simply snip off the optic nerves from just behind the eyeballs with—just a—little bit of a twist—before popping them into my mouth—l-i-i-ike—SO!"

❧ Contributors ❧

J.M. Beazer's short fiction has appeared or is scheduled to appear in the anthologies *Awakening the Virgin: True Tales of Seduction, Best Lesbian Erotica 1996,* and *Girls,* and the magazine *Pucker Up.* A MacDowell fellow with an MFA from Sarah Lawrence, she's currently revising her first novel, *The Festival of Sighs.* She's also started work on a second novel, which is based on the early life of one of Sigmund Freud's patients, a lesbian who at age 19 was sent to Freud to be "cured" of her homosexuality. Finally, she's working on a collection of stories called *Ten Little Nasties.* She lives in New York City, where she performs bimonthly readings with the queer writers' collective, Three Hots and a Cot.

Andrew Berac resides with his partner in Vancouver, British Columbia, where he works in the camera/pre-press department of a local publishing company. His work has previously appeared in the fantasy anthology *Bending the Landscape.*

Hall Owen Calwaugh is an American of Finnish and British extraction who speaks a number of languages, sadly none of them so well as English. Capricorn, Capricorn rising, Moon in Leo. As if that weren't perfectly obvious. Sigh... He has also been published on-line by www.dreams-unlimited.com.

M. Christian lives in San Francisco where he endeavors to explore most of its nooks and even occasionally its crannies. In between this he writes and sometimes gets published. If you like these stories, you can read more in such anthologies as *Hot Ticket,* (also by Alyson books), *Sex Spoken Here* (edited by Jack Davis and Carol Queen), *Demon Sex, Noirotica 2 & 3* (edited by Thomas Roche), *The Mammoth Book of Erotica III, The Mammoth Book of Historical Erotica,* as well as *Best American Erotica 1994 & 1997.* He is also the editor of the anthologies *Eros Ex Machina: Eroticizing the Mechanical* and *Midsummer Night's Dreams: Many Tales of One Story* from Rhinoceros Books.

Susan C. Coleman says, "Quite simply, I'm a native Californian living in Long Beach with my orange tabby, Maddie McGuire, a very prolific greenhouse, and a sleek motorcycle that has been referred to as 'the other woman.' My background is an eclectic blend of fine arts, martial arts, horticulture, and developmental psychology, which all seem determined to contribute their two cents' worth to my writing. Two of the guys in my foster care class recently bought a gorgeous turn-of-the-century Craftsman, complete with a secret staircase to a huge second floor that even the realtor had been unaware of. After a lengthy tour of their home, I knew it was the perfect setting for a ghostly love story. 'A Midsummer's Haunt' is my second professional sale and my first adventure with ghosts. My vampire erotica will appear in the magazine *Prisoners of the Night.*"

Ted Cornwell is a journalist who lives in New York City. His poetry has appeared in a number of journals, including *Christopher Street, modern words, The Evergreen Chronicles, Folio: A Literary Journal,* and *Spoonfed.*

Contributors

E.J. Galusha says, "Born in the Nebraska panhandle some 44 years ago, I once considered Oregon my home, until I came to the Alaska bush as a school counselor in the fall of '95. I left the counseling profession in '96 to pursue a lifelong ambition to take up writing fulltime. To date, I've written over 100 short stories and poems (not counting the rewrites), and am currently working on a novel. Some of my work has been published in such publications as *Mini Romance Magazine, Sparrowgrass Poetry Forum's Treasured Poems of America,* and the National Library of Poetry's *Days Gone By.* The story 'Eyes' is my first sale."

d. g. k. goldberg has met a vast assortment of dybbuks, demons, and ghosts. She is very grateful to the lovely gentleman of Lincoln Ghost Walks, Lincoln, U.K., for inspiring "The Course of True Love." Her work has appeared in *Tangents, EternityOL,* and the anthology *The Darkest Thirst.* When she was a little girl she wanted to be queen. She is still looking for an available country.

Carol Guess is the author of two novels, *Seeing Dell* and *Switch.* This short story is a chapter from her novel-in-progress, *Retrieval.* She teaches creative writing at Nebraska Wesleyan University.

Abbe Ireland says, "I live in Tucson, Arizona, where I work two part-time jobs to support my writing habit. I have published short stories and articles in such children's magazines as *Cobblestone, Junior Scholastic,* and *Children's Digest.* I am currently working on a short story collection of lesbian erotica. This work seems to be attracting an unprecedented number and variety of tomcats to my backyard. Go figure."

Jessica Kirkwood is the pen name of the only author in this book who recently attended a wedding reception where the guests clogged to rap music. A native Kentuckian, Jessica is still fascinated by the juxtaposition of cultures she discovers there. In school she majored in theater as well as English and believes she learned every bit as much about writing from her acting classes as she did from her literature classes. Jessica can usually be found hanging around espresso coffee bars, and her idea of a perfect evening is driving with the convertible top down, holding hands with her life partner (who also happens to be the woman of her dreams), and listening to one tape after another of old Ella Fitzgerald songs. Jessica is currently working on a novel.

Regan McClure says, "I'm a clean-cut butch who lives in Toronto. I work *w-a-a-ay* too much, but in my spare time I like to do Hapkido, javelin, hangliding, and cycling. I'm a volunteer bicycle mechanic for community-based bike clubs, and I'm working on a novel (of course)."

Marshall Moore lives and works in Washington, DC. He's a sign language interpreter by day (and most nights); the rest of the time, he writes (or tries). "Simon Says" is his first published work of fiction.

Michael Price Nelson worked at Chris Brownlie Hospice, a project of AIDS Healthcare Foundation, from 1991 to 1996. In addition to having 12 plays produced, he has written for television and is currently a freelance screenwriter in Los Angeles, where he lives with his life partner, Dale Von Seggern.

R.E. Neu's work has appeared in numerous publications including the *Los Angeles Times, Los Angeles* magazine, and the *New York Times Book Review,* as well as several humor anthologies. He was also a contributing writer for *Spy* magazine back when it was funny.

A.J. Potter lives in Vermont. He attended college to study historical prostitution. While he enjoyed it immensely, he decided not to make a career in it and has since turned to writing. His work has appeared in a number of anthologies, including *Swords of the Rainbow*, also from Alyson Publications. Another story about Evan and Brandon appears in the anthology *Bending the Landscape: Horror Volume*, from Overlook Press. A.J. likes peanut butter. A lot.

Don Sakers was launched the same month as Sputnik One. He is the author of gay young adult romance novels *Act Well Your Part* (Alyson, 1986) and *Lucky in Love* (Alyson, 1987). In addition, he is an award-winning science fiction writer. A member of the Coast-Line SF Writers Group, Sakers is Senior Editor of the gay sf/fantasy review journal *WaveLengths*. He is also the writer-producer half of sf video studio Speed-of-C Productions. Several times a year, he teaches writing for a local community college. Sakers lives at Meerkat Meade in suburban Baltimore with his husband, costumer Thomas Atkinson.

Lawrence Schimel is the author of *The Drag Queen of Elfland* (The Ultra Violet Library) and the editor of more than 20 anthologies, including *Things Invisible to See: Lesbian and Gay Tales of Magic Realism* (The Ultra Violet Library), *The Mammoth Book of Gay Erotica* (Carroll & Graf), *Bloodlines: Vampire Stories from New England* (Cumberland House), and *Two Hearts Desire: Gay Couples on Their Love* (with Michael Lassell, St. Martin's Press), among others. His stories, poems, and essays appear in over 130 anthologies, including *Swords of the Rainbow, The Random House Book of Science Fiction Stories, Best Gay Erotica 1997* and *1998, The Mammoth Book of Fairy Tales, Gay Love Poetry, The Random House Treasury of Light Verse,* and others. His work also appears in numerous periodicals, ranging from *The Saturday Evening Post* to *Drummer* to *Physics Today*. He lives in New York City.

Anne Seale is a creator of lesbian songs, stories, and plays, who has performed on many gay stages including the Lesbian National Conference, singing tunes from her tape, *Sex For Breakfast*, available for $12 from Wildwater Records, POB 56, Webster, NY 14580-0056. More examples of Seale's work can be found in the anthologies *Love Shook My Heart, Pillow Talk, Hot and Bothered, Ex-lover Weird Shit,* and in issues of *Lesbian Short Fiction.*

Simon Sheppard actually does like to tie guys up. His work has appeared in dozens of anthologies, including *Best American Erotica 1997; Best Gay Erotica 1996* and *1997; Eros Ex Machina; Bending the Landscape: Fantasy; and Brothers of the Night.* He is not afraid of the dark. Much.

Barbara J. Webb says, "I live in Columbia, Missouri, and this is my first professionally published piece. When not writing, I enjoy playing the violin and talking to my cat, Danu."

Julia Willis is the author of the novel *Reel Time* (Alyson, 1998) and the cat's baby book *Meow-Mories* (Laugh Lines Press, 1996), winner of the Cat Writers' Association's Muse Medallion for Best Cat Humor of 1997. She believes in ghosts, the magic of tinkling bells, and a host of other interesting intangibles.

alyson
books

BI ANY OTHER NAME: BISEXUAL PEOPLE SPEAK OUT, *edited by Loraine Hutchins and Lani Kaahumanu.* Women and men from all walks of life describe their lives as bisexuals. They tell their stories—personal, political, spiritual, historical—in prose, poetry, art, and essays. These are individuals who have fought prejudice from both the gay and straight segments of society and who have begun only recently to share their experiences. This groundbreaking anthology is an important step in the process of forming a new bisexual "community."

JOCKS, *by Dan Woog.* Find out what happens when the final closet door—that of men in sports—finally swings open. Is there life after coming out to your teammates? Is there life before coming out? This collection of more than 25 inspiring real-life stories digs deeply into two of America's twin obsessions: sports and sex. Journalist Dan Woog, himself an openly gay soccer coach, interviewed dozens of gay jocks and offers up these inspiring stories of men who are truly today's champions.

THE GOOD LIFE, *by Gordon Merrick.* In 1943 a high-society murder case drew international attention for its irresistible combination of violent crime, scandalous sex, and enormous wealth. Perry Langham, a dirt-poor Depression-era boy, met and married Bettina Vernon, a rich heiress, and they settled down to live happily ever after. But Perry's eternal attraction to beautiful young men got in the way of the marriage—and Bettina decided to cut him off financially. Gordon Merrick and Charles Hulse put their own fictional stamp on the story, and an entertaining romp through the lives of rich young gay men emerges.

EARLY EMBRACES, *edited by Lindsley Elder.* Tender. Sassy. Loving. Embarrassing. Thrilling. This collection of true, first-person stories by women from around the country describing their first sexual experience with another woman sparkles with laughter, awkward moments, and plenty of hot sex.

CHICKEN, *by Paula Martinac.* Forty-something Lynn is having the proverbial midlife crisis. After being dumped by her longtime lover, she is first pursued by 23-year-old Lexy, then by 25-year-old Jude. Is there any chance Lynn can keep her sanity while dealing with one ex, two demanding new lovers, and three hours of sleep a night? A lesbian tale of love, lust, and the enduringly comic search for Ms. Right in the late '90s.

These books and other Alyson titles are available at your local bookstore.
If you can't find a book listed above or would like more information,
please visit our home page on the World Wide Web at **www.alyson.com**.